Lizzy's Choice

By Clytie Koehler

Lizzy's choice

By Clytie Koehler

Copyright 2011 by Clytie Koehler

Published by Clytie Koehler

Cover photo by Clytie Koehler

All rights reserved. No part of this publication may be reproduced, stored in a retrieval system or transmitted in any form or by any means, electronic, mechanical, photocopying, recording or otherwise without the prior written permission of the publisher.

Characters and events in this book are fictitious or are used fictitiously. Any resemblance to real persons, living or dead is solely coincidental and not intended by the author.

ISBN-13:

978-1466424739

ISBN-10:

1466424737

Dedication

With greatest love to Bill and Mom, and Granddad, and Gra, and Omari – thank you for being part of my life –
I miss you all!

Table of Contents

Copyright..ii

Dedication..iii

Table of Contents...iv

Acknowledgements...viii

Chapter 1 The Carriage of Doom — 1

Chapter 2 Family Likenesses — 10

Chapter 3 First Impressions — 16

Chapter 4 Impressions Confirmed at Netherfield — 20

Chapter 5 The Cousin and the Cad Appear — 25

Chapter 6 The Magnificent Netherfield Ball — 28

Chapter 7 Pride and Mortification — 34

Chapter 8 Her Carriage Arrives at Awakening — 40

Chapter 9 A Jumble of Nightmares End the Night — 49

Chapter 10 Darcy's Dithering Thither and…Yawn — 54

Chapter 11 Darcy Attends Miss Elizabeth's Wedding — 61

Chapter 12 Nightmares Reveal Darcy's Choice — 66

Chapter 13 First, a Wild Ride — 73

Chapter 14 As Jane Sees It	80
Chapter 15 Elizabeth and Jane Adjust Their Thoughts	85
Chapter 16 Encounter on Oakham Mount	89
Chapter 17 A Knock in Exchange	101
Chapter 18 Back in the Company of Wise Jane	114
Chapter 19 Darcy Enlists the Aid of Mrs Bennet	119
Chapter 20 Incredulity Unleashed	130
Chapter 21 Darcy and Jane Become friends	137
Chapter 22 Papá Please Be Serious!	145
Chapter 23 Good Gossip and a Visit to Netherfield	156
Chapter 24 Lizzy Addresses Caroline at the Gazebo	166
Chapter 25 The Bennets' Manifold Discoveries	182
Chapter 26 Stymie and Duplicity	209
Chapter 27 Caroline's Dastardly Plot	217
Chapter 28 Ordeal of Uncertainty	233
Chapter 29 In the Face of Adversity	256
Chapter 30 A Haven for Mad Caroline	275
Chapter 31 The Delighted Conveyance	285
Chapter 32 Georgiana's Fright and Bingley's Moment	290
Chapter 33 Happy News and Obstacles	296

Chapter 34 For Caroline's Sake, Bingley Must Go	304
Chapter 35 The Bennet Sisterhood is Born	313
Chapter 36 Trepidation and Reassurance	327
Chapter 37 Advancing Toward Trust	336
Chapter 38 Life Altering Announcements	349
Chapter 39 Georgiana and Her Brother Visit Longbourn	358
Chapter 40 United by Deep Bonds of Affection	374
Chapter 41 A Shared Christmas at Longbourn	383
Chapter 42 Lady Catherine Erupts Upon the Scene	390
Chapter 43 Colonel Fitzwilliam Strides In	399
Chapter 44 Darcy Storms In	409
Chapter 45 Each Must Trust the Other's Love	412
Chapter 46 Lizzy's Choice	416
Chapter 47 Forgiveness and Blessings	424
Chapter 48 Bingley, Just In Time	429
Chapter 49 Another (Expanded) Family Meeting	435
Chapter 50 Plotting For a Much Pleasanter Theme	446
Chapter 51 A Most Accommodating Proposal	452
Chapter 52 Done and Undone	459
Chapter 53 Astonishing Disclosures and Amorous Glance	461

Chapter 54 London	**465**
Chapter 55 The Double Wedding	**468**
Chapter 56 My Lord and Lady Matlock	**473**
Chapter 57 You Are My Hearts' Desire	**478**
Chapter 58 Endnotes	**482**
Chapter 59 About the Author	**483**

Acknowledgements

I fully apprehend that the world may not *need* yet another *Pride and Prejudice* adulation, however I felt the *need* to write one – so here we are!

I like to think that mine joins the multitude of contributions, some wonderful, some not so, which together form a grand demonstration of homage to the gifts we have received from Miss Jane Austen's genius.

Miss Austen's offspring have been reincarnated in many different circumstances, times, and locales by a diverse community of Austenesque devotees in loco parentis. Yet their ultimate destiny is not to be tampered with. There are back stories, stories forward and side stories but Elizabeth and Darcy *will* be together in the end. Anne and Frederick; Elinor and Edward and the rest shall be united – but oh, the twists and turns along the way!

With heartfelt thanks to all who write and all who read Austen and her admirers I acknowledge that I have been fascinated, highly entertained, and ultimately motivated by the amazing variety of Austenesques – every one inspired by the beloved characters and classic dynamics first (or best) brought to 'modern day' life under our dearest Jane's pen.

In a more personal light I am grateful for the unflagging support of my family while I engaged in this labour of love! I especially thank Medea Yorba and Sarah Stoltman for their invaluable help in proof-reading my document. I hope they enjoyed the process and that we got it all – or *at least* almost all!

I must add a big thank you to Miranda Yorba for her help with the flower arrangements in the cover photo and another big thanks to Nikisa Valentino for putting together the cover itself.

Finally I must include my loving thanks to Alexander Yorba, Nikisa Valentino, and Miranda Yorba for their *longsuffering* patience with my obsessive work "schedule". I'll try to be more equipoised next time!

Clytie Koehler

ONE
The Carriage of Doom

Elizabeth Bennet Collins sat with her eyes cast down, waiting for her husband, the odious Mr Collins, to join her in the carriage for their trip to Hunsford and her new life there.

She did her best to repress her shudders as he heaved himself into the carriage opposite her. He hummed a tuneless self-congratulation as he settled himself, leaning back with a smile of satisfaction, for the journey to Hunsford.

Their "wedding journey" she thought wryly. Turning her face to the window, she rested her head on the firm seat-back behind her.

They travelled in a hired chaise less than half the size of her father's full coach, driven by a postilion rider. The tired old conveyance could barely seat two people comfortably. To his credit, Mr Collins *had* gallantly insisted upon her taking the single forward-facing seat. Although the leather seat was hard and cracked, Elizabeth was grateful that her gaze took in the approaching terrain and not what they were leaving behind.

She had been taken by surprise when Mr Collins proposed to her the morning after the Netherfield ball. Certainly Elizabeth had noted signs of his interest, but it was still only days since he first arrived at Longbourn – a cousin on her father's side but a stranger to the family until that day.

The significance of Mr Collins' visit was that he was to inherit Longbourn upon Mr Bennet's eventual demise, by virtue of an entail in favour of the male line – and that he was in want of a wife.

The absurdity of his manner, which was chiefly comprised of an odd combination of inflated self-importance and exaggerated obsequiousness, was exceeded only by the arrogance of his noble patroness.

Lady Catherine de Bourgh of Rosings Park attended only to her own implacable opinions and a certain self-interest in her imperious demand of her parson. She insisted that he acquaint himself with the Bennets, distant cousins hitherto unknown to himself. He was to secure a bride - preferably from among the same Bennet cousins - within a fortnight. Such was her generosity that she allowed him this time to be away from his duties at Hunsford parsonage.

Lady Catherine's direction to him, as he confided to Elizabeth in the course of his rambling and tortuous marriage proposal to her, was precise. He must acquire a modest gentlewoman as his wife. One not brought up too high to set an example of proper humility before her betters and of domestic felicity before his parish. His future wife must not be brought up too low to allow her occasional usefulness when Lady Catherine desired to make up sufficient numbers at her dining table or at an evening of cards.

Indeed, once Mr Collins' new wife was established at Hunsford parsonage, Lady Catherine intended to visit her! Such a wealth of graciousness, such a great piece of generosity, on the part of his noble and esteemed patroness nearly brought Mr Collins to tears of delight in the recital of it.

The unexampled courtesy of Lady Catherine de Bourgh's notice and condescension in the matter was to be considered of the greatest consequence; indeed it *was* so - by Mr Collins at least.

It would reflect well on him, Lady Catherine had allowed, were he to marry one of his Bennet cousins - thus relieving their anticipated distress upon Mr Bennet's eventual demise and their consequent homelessness.

Mr Collins was known to congratulate himself at every likely turn of his discourse that by choosing a bride from among his cousins he was making amends to the Bennet family for the injury he was to inflict upon them as the future heir to Longbourn.

Determined that *she* would never marry except for reasons of deepest esteem and love, Elizabeth had refused him soundly *at first.*

Mr Collins was nonsensically obsequious to all those he considered above him, yet embarrassingly full of his own consequence otherwise. Worse, he so often combined both attitudes in a single speech as to regularly render his verbosity still more garbled to the listener.

Thus in his typically heavy-handed proposal he spoke at length of all of the advantages of his situation in life, emphasizing the grand munificence of his patroness, Lady Catherine de Bourgh; ponderously laid out his practical reasons for marrying; pointedly reminded Elizabeth of those certain practical reasons for *her* marrying *him*; and finally, suggested that he might find himself run away with by his feelings for his fair cousin's many perfections! He added as a final touch of magnanimous charity that in their felicitous future together he would *overlook* the inadequacy of her dowry.

~&~

Mr Collins had so set his mind on wedding her that he could not, would not, take her repeated refusals seriously. He did have little time left in which to woo another, having wasted at least one full day thinking of Jane as his chosen intended. Their mother, who had other aspirations for her first daughter in mind, redirected his focus toward Elizabeth, her second and least favourite daughter.

His belief of his own importance and eligibility was so great that he could not imagine Elizabeth to be sincere or reasonable in refusing him. She could not be in earnest! In fact, he even went so far as to remind her, most indelicately, that it was by no means likely that she would ever receive *another* eligible offer of marriage. After all, he reminded her again, she had very little dowry and no great connections to encourage an eligible gentleman to form an attachment.

With their father's estate entailed away and their mother's portion only five thousand pounds; the five Bennet sisters had little to recommend them but their charms to secure their futures.

Mr Collins was quite certain that her excellent parents would support his suit and insist that Elizabeth marry him.

Indeed, although her dear father, upon whose support she had relied in this, had uncomfortably inferred that he would not force her to marry against her own inclinations, her mother had been merciless in her determination that her Lizzy, whose value had never before been felt so keenly by her mother, should be the next mistress of Longbourn after herself.

Mrs Bennet made her case frequently and forcefully. She insisted that by marrying Mr Collins Elizabeth should preserve herself and her mother and sisters from the most dreadful condition of want and disadvantage upon her father's fearfully anticipated demise – possibly in the very near future!

Elizabeth's best friend, Charlotte Lucas, did not scruple to join in the fray. She repeatedly urged Elizabeth to secure Mr Collins as soon as may be. She solemnly reminded Elizabeth of her own sensible views on marriage. It was, she pronounced, the only means by which a gently bred woman could secure a respectable future. One could not be sentimental in Elizabeth's circumstances; she dared not pass up a ready offer of substance to wait on a romantic dream. Marrying for love was even more unlikely than that Elizabeth would receive another eligible offer, as she had so little dowry and only questionable connections.

"There will always be trials and tribulations in marriage, Eliza. Therefore it is of little importance who one's partner might be so long as he is not vicious or of low character – *and of course so long has he had adequate means to support a wife and family.*[i]"

Charlotte had never been sentimental; she believed that if Elizabeth were not wed by the time she reached Charlotte's own age of seven and twenty, her young friend would see things much the same as she herself did. Security and an establishment of her own would go a good deal farther toward producing lasting satisfaction in life than would reliance upon the vagaries of one's emotions.

Thus they all importuned her without cessation, each in their different ways. Her father with his guilty silence and averted eyes; her younger sisters unmindful of their peril but so appealing to Elizabeth's generous nature and deep love of her family; her friend with her well-intentioned advice; and her mother in ever more heatedly shrill demands, pronouncements, and entreaties.

Mr Collins merely waited her out. He never doubted that her refusal was only a show of maidenly modesty, intended to increase his ardour.

~&~

Ultimately Elizabeth's resolve foundered in the demands and imprecations of her mother, her father's unhappy avoidance, and the reality of her family's situation, Elizabeth's confidence was shaken. It fell to *her* to assure her family's protection from *"starving in the hedgerows"* in the event of Papá's demise in advance of a better prospect for any of them.

Jane had had some hopes of Mr Bingley, but he seemed unprepared to speak. After the events at the Netherfield ball it may very well be that he never would.

In silence she bore it as long as she could. In silence she suffered her own secret heartbreak. Elizabeth told no one of the shocking revelations she encountered at the Netherfield ball. She could not burden any of her loved ones – especially Jane, her closest confidant, with what she learned that night!

At the last, worn down by days of her mother's anger and her own hopeless feelings, Elizabeth had given in to Mr Collins' repeated effusive and inelegant proposals.

Elizabeth had secured her family's serenity in exchange for her own.

~&~

Her heart ached in the knowledge that their exchange of wedding vows had been nothing but the cynical rendition of what was customary. Elizabeth believed that the most innocent and precious part of her had died with the self-betrayal of making promises against her will, against her better judgment and even against her character.

It was not so uncommon, Elizabeth knew, for people to marry for reasons of material gain and status. Many women whose marriages were without pleasurable companionship and love, apparently found a reasonable degree of comfort in their children. Somehow she would do the same – but the begetting of them!

Having lived all of her life in the countryside where farm animals reproduced as regularly as the passing seasons, Elizabeth had a fair idea of what "begetting" required of those participants.

From her mother's hints and her extensive exploration of her father's library Elizabeth understood some little of what would occur in the marriage bed – enough to know that feeling such revulsion as she did for Mr Collins she could only expect the worst indignity and discomfort imaginable in the event.

She wondered how she would bear the invasion of her private self at the end of their journey... and upon his demand thenceforward.

Elizabeth hoped Mr Collins was looking elsewhere and would not notice her shudders and furious blushing at the very idea! Already she had several times been aware of his greedy gaze sweeping over her form from his seat across from her in the chaise. In a feeble attempt at humour she privately dubbed it *"the carriage of doom"*.

Gratefully Elizabeth thought of the care she had taken to see that she was well-covered in her manner of dress and that her hands were, as always when in his presence, encased in sturdy gloves.

Ruminating thusly, Elizabeth suffered an oppression of her spirits so heavy as to leave her very nearly no will to breathe.

Indeed, as their carriage bore them nearer and nearer to their destination, so it carried her toward the rapidly approaching hour of her marital comeuppance. Elizabeth, therefore, began to experience a paucity of coherent thought about any other thing. Unsurprisingly her mind became inalterably fixed upon that which she most desired to avoid thinking about!

This would not do!

Hitherto, Elizabeth had studiously avoided any contemplation of that ultimate, and now unavoidable, truth – that Mr Collins henceforward had every right and expectation of complete access to every part of her person, to use when and as he wished, no matter how repugnant his touch might be to her – for the rest of her life!

Desperately she collected how she had been able to keep him at bay during their brief courtship, turning aside his clumsy attempts to kiss her by presenting her cheek instead of her lips and reminding him that the demands of propriety were even more stringent in the case of a clergyman than of ordinary persons. Perhaps she would discover more of those means by which, her mother had hinted; a woman could avoid some portion of her husband's marital prerogatives.

Surely her quick wit and strength of purpose would support her in those endeavours!

Thankfully Elizabeth understood that in the present moment, should Mr Collins be tempted to disregard propriety in anticipation of their wedding night, the jouncing and jarring of the carriage over the rough and rutted country lanes chosen as their shortest route made physical contact between them unlikely to be pleasant, even to him.

His effusive anticipation of Lady Catherine's magnanimous condescension in approving his choice of bride had finally suffered defeat to the clatter of hooves on hard ground and the squeaking and rattling of their poor conveyance. Indeed, the racket of their progress and constant jostling seemed to render Mr Collins attempts at conversation still less sensible than was usual for him.

Thus, though seated in the close proximity enforced by the confines of their small conveyance, Elizabeth felt momentarily safe from unwanted advances of any kind from Mr Collins. Life at Hunsford would be a different matter, she knew.

If they could both be kept busy though! She would throw herself into the life of her new community. She had always been pleased to offer assistance to her neighbours where there was illness, and support and encouragement where it was needed. At least she could still be herself in that way. Elizabeth would involve herself in the singing on Sundays, and perhaps, teach some of the younger children in the neighbourhood something useful and pleasant.

Mr Collins must have many calls to make on his parishioners, sermons to prepare, study and contemplation to engage him. Surely he could be kept busy – and tired! He must be encouraged to attend to his garden ... for the sake of his health and their economy. Elizabeth believed that Lady Catherine de Bourgh expected his regular attendance upon her at Rosings Park, necessitating his walking there and back nearly every day, and time spent there as well. Of course there would be weddings and funerals, christenings, and attentions to the sick and unruly... There would be much to keep them both occupied - and out of each other's company - in fulfilling their duties; acting as "matrimonial examples" (oh dear!); and in service to the community... and Lady Catherine, of course.

Unable to think farther ahead than this, Elizabeth curled herself against the rough seat, feigning sleep in order to assure herself an uninterrupted period of reflection on the confluence of circumstances which reduced her life to this wretched moment.

TWO
Family Likenesses

Along with her excellent constitution, lissom figure, and delicate features from her mother, Elizabeth took her intelligence and fascination with books and learning from her doting father. For this, she had always been his favourite. Her liveliness and pleasing ease of manners among others, the captivating sparkle in her expressive eyes, her delight in long walks through the countryside, and her luxuriant dark auburn curls were all uniquely her own.

Active, even tempered, and generous hearted, Elizabeth was a delightful participant and an amused observer in the ebb and flow of volition and personality amongst her family and friends.

Whether helping to tend those who were ill or infirm, or offering encouragement to those who were downcast, or simply visiting about in the course of her frequent rambles, Elizabeth's kindly attentions provided cheer to her neighbours and private entertainment to herself – and sometimes a source of shared delight with her dear father.

Only a few years after Elizabeth's birth, Mrs Bennet was brought to bed with three more girls in nearly annual succession. Their parents began to despair of ever producing a son and heir. Mrs Bennet had never been a deep thinker. Until the birth of her third daughter, her thoughts were mostly taken up with the endless delights to be found in the fluctuations of fashion and local gossip.

Increasingly, as the next few years brought forth daughters four and five, Mrs Bennet developed an over-riding obsession. The entail on Longbourn began to assume the character of a bogeyman in Mrs Bennet's fretful expectancy of the future.

~&~

Growing up, Elizabeth observed her mother's increasing anxiety about their prospects with equal parts of amused youthful confidence in the future and embarrassment at her mother's oh-so-public declarations on that subject.

From the moment Jane, the eldest and most beautiful of her five very handsome girls, showed the first sign of budding young womanhood, Mrs Bennet saw her principal business as getting each of her nearly dowerless daughters safely and promptly married.

They must marry gentlemen who could, if the need should arise, provide for her other daughters and herself when Mr Bennet should inevitably quit their company for his eternal reward. (Not that she was convinced he had earned any reward; after all, he had done nothing to correct the very unfortunate existence of that dratted entail.)

Indeed, Jane being only seven or eight years old at the time of her youngest sister Lydia's birth, left some years before any of them were old enough for betrothal. Thus Mrs Bennet's dreadful anxiety was allowed some years to reach monumental proportions.

Despite their mother's frequent lamentations and outbursts wondering what was to become of them all, Jane and Elizabeth learned to keep to their own pursuits and avoid taking up those concerns so frequently and loudly expressed by their mother.

In fact they had been so adroit in avoiding their mother's machinations toward their future wedded state that neither had formed any significant attachments prior to Mr Bingley's arrival in the neighbourhood. Thus it was that at the very ready age of twenty-two, Jane was in love for the first time. Elizabeth, at twenty, found her own heart most unruly; her thoughts often disturbed and restless – also for the first time.

~&~

Elizabeth reflected upon the recent train of events that had led to this dreadful moment in her life.

The capriciousness of the party from Netherfield was at the centre of it.

Their lives had been generally uneventful and predictable for the twenty years she had been on this earth, hardly sufficient preparation for the tumult of activity and distress which had come upon them all.

Mr Bingley's establishment at neighbouring Netherfield only two months prior to the events in progress had been the source of much interest and excitement to all of the young ladies and their mamas within the reach of Meryton, which was the principal town of any size in the neighbourhood.

Mrs Bennet, not surprisingly, was nearly beside herself with delight at the news of so fine a marital prospect locating himself only three miles from Longbourn!

For her own part, Elizabeth considered that a less ill-judged course of conduct and deduction could hardly have been undertaken than what followed. How misguided she had been! Overconfident in her conclusions and foolishly flattered to an unworthy trust, she had not hesitated to participate in gossip of the most harmful sort!

They had all erred in one way or another: the giddy propensities left unchecked; social impropriety ignored or unevenly attended; spendthrift frivolity allowed, or still worse, encouraged; education and mental discipline lax or non-existent; parental permissiveness and indolence – all contributed to the circumstances in which they found themselves.

Her two youngest sisters, Catherine (known to her family and friends as "Kitty") and Lydia, were noisy and silly of course. But at first, no more so than could be generally discounted as "just their way" – especially Lydia, the baby of the family! How could it be that in the space of only a few months everything would change so very much?

Once the militia was quartered in Meryton, Lydia and Kitty's silliness and lack of proper restraint had gone from tolerable foolishness to mortifying forwardness that brought blushes to Elizabeth's and Jane's faces whenever they were all together in public.

Four of the five Bennet girls, to be sure, had found their days enlivened by the addition of numerous dashing red-coated officers to their neighbourhood. Only eighteen-year-old Mary remained impervious to the increased availability of frivolity and flirtation. Lydia and Kitty, however, had progressed rapidly from noticing the jaunty red coats to openly flirting – and even seeking them out. At fifteen and seventeen their forward behaviour was beyond enough!

Those two began to find reasons to walk the mile from their home at Longbourn into the village of Meryton, where the young officers were to be found, nearly every day.

~&~

Lydia, at only fifteen years of age, was by far the most audacious, being her mother's favourite and therefore having received the least of all of the sisters in the way of parental regulation regarding the comportment expected of a young lady. She would not have listened in any event as she made a habit from early on to hear only that which she chose to hear when her elders spoke to her.

Lydia had managed to wheedle her mother into allowing her to be "out" even though she was so young and none of her elder sisters were yet married.

Although she was the elder of the two, Kitty followed Lydia's exuberant lead in everything. When Lydia flirted with the officers, Kitty followed suit. Whether Lydia expressed a desire for a new bonnet or a trip to Meryton, Kitty felt likewise. The pain she felt when Lydia succeeded with her doting mother, where Kitty might not, was inevitable - and petulantly expressed.

Brought up without a governess, the girls were free to educate themselves from Mr Bennet's library or Mrs Bennet's example. Thus, for the most part, their characters and habits of mind had been formed by following their own inclinations within the confines of their home and rural situation.

Mr Bennet left such matters to his lady, lacking any particular purposefulness in the upbringing of his daughters. He made certain to provide all of the necessities of life and a modest allowance for their personal uses. Beyond such general responsibilities he would not, or could not, go.

His eldest, Jane, was very dear to him for her gentle, sensible disposition. Her tall and womanly figure might first catch a gentleman's eye until he looked upon the sweet-tempered, kindly nature so evident in her countenance. Jane's shining golden tresses framed a lovely face as endearing for its perfect features and deep blue eyes as for its serene expression and pleasing smile. Thereupon a more superficial admiration was often promptly elevated to an urge to gallantry and esteem.

Mr Bennet's three youngest daughters were too silly to bear in his company for long – Lydia and Kitty with their endless twittering about fripperies and red coats – and single-mindedly studious and plodding Mary, who unconsciously echoed her father's sentiments when she responded to her sisters' lively anticipation of upcoming social events declaring: "I had much rather read a book".

Unfortunately Mary's studies of choice were unvaryingly focused upon such unenlightened works as *Fordyce's Sermons to Young Women*, from which heavy and pedantic fare she gleaned much material with which to dampen her sisters' spirits whenever the occasion offered itself. Although the least handsome of the five young women, Mary was nevertheless, or could be if she took a little trouble with her toilette, gifted with similar good looks to her two youngest sisters.

All three of the youngest daughters were blessed with pleasing figures and sweet features. Their greatest differences in appearance lay in their personal manners and toilette.

Mary's dress and coiffure tended toward modesty, even a suggestion of severity – being plainly styled and eschewing any but the simplest adornment. She was the middle daughter, middle sized and of middling appeal.

Kitty and Lydia wore the evidence of their attention to ribbons and laces, and cunning use of flounce and tuck, in every aspect of their apparel. They were nothing if not ardent students of the most becoming arrangements achievable of style and colour in every article of their clothing. They were devoted *artistes*. Their art was in the presentation of themselves to best advantage with the gentlemen. Lydia's bright countenance and buxom figure exhibited her exuberant personality. Kitty, slightly taller and more willowy, seemed always just a little discontented. Lydia, though the youngest, always was just ahead of her, and she felt it unkindly.

Mr Bennet's true enjoyment arose from the lively wit and amiable discourse of his second daughter, Elizabeth. He loved to spend time with his Lizzy in his library playing chess or discussing her current literary interests – or the follies of their family and neighbours. They shared a sardonic amusement in the study of human character in all of its various alterations. Mr Bennet and his Lizzy were often prone to raised eyebrows and twinkling glances between them when in the company of the subjects of their enterprise. Otherwise, he would rather retire to his library and lose himself in the private and fascinating world of his books.

Elizabeth, who was an avid walker in any event, convinced Jane that they both should accompany the younger girls whenever possible in order to monitor their increasingly unrestrained behaviour – and to check them when they went too far.

When word spread that Netherfield Park was let at last, Mrs Bennet's excited anticipation about the addition of a wealthy, young, *single* gentleman in the neighbourhood could not have foretold the unsettling mix of delight and pain that would follow.

THREE
First Impressions

In a tease held classic in his own estimation, Mr Bennet steadfastly refused to call upon their new neighbour, thus sending Mrs Bennet into fits of nervous agitation and resentment. In vain did she storm and rant to him of their daughters' prospects lost through his refusal to make the acquaintance of a man reputed to be both rich and single! She moaned and worried at their consequent disadvantage in the highly competitive rush to acquire that young man's attentions for the marriageable daughters in the neighbourhood.

Mr Bennet would not be moved by any of it. When at last his wife was so aggravated as to announce her defeat, saying angrily to her daughters: *"I am sick of Mr Bingley!"* Mr Bennet made it known in the mildest and most insouciant manner that he had only just called upon Mr Bingley that very morning. What joy then overcame her! With what delight did Mrs Bennet look forward to Mr Bingley's return call, and to his attendance at the upcoming assembly in Meryton!

It was only a slight cause for disappointment when Mr Bingley's call did not include introductions, or even a clear sight of him, for the ladies of the house.

They were at last introduced at the Meryton assembly, when Mr Charles Bingley attended with his two sisters, Miss Caroline Bingley and Mrs Louisa Hurst, and two gentlemen who proved to be Mr Gilbert Hurst and Mr Bingley's best friend, Mr Fitzwilliam Darcy.

Immediately upon receiving Sir William Lucas' greeting, Mr Bingley amiably began to seek introductions around the room allowing that there was nothing he liked better than a country dance, and to his mind there was no such thing as a stranger – only friends he had not met before.

Very shortly, however, he *noticed* Jane Bennet, whose shining blonde hair, lovely features and figure, and deep blue eyes were renowned throughout the county of Hertfordshire. In his eyes, she had the look of an *Angel!*

Jane's outward beauty was rendered even more enchanting by the sweetness of her character and the serenity of her expression. Mr Bingley lost no time in seeking an introduction to Mrs Bennet and her charming daughters. From that point onward his evening was spent either dancing with Jane, introducing Jane to his sisters, or affably dancing with others while glancing at Jane whenever he could find the opportunity.

Jane's modest delight in Mr Bingley's very particular attentions was easy to understand. He was such an amiable young man, with easy manners and a pleasant disposition. His natural inclination was to exude harmony and good humour in every exchange. Jane found Mr Bingley's aspect handsome and his temper in every way well matched to her own. He was everything a young man *ought to be!*

~&~

For her part, Elizabeth was confused! When Mr Bingley and his party first entered the Assembly room in Meryton, she had been dancing with a handsome young officer of the –Shire Militia which was presently quartered in Meryton. He had been pleasant and a good dancer and she enjoyed his company. However, by unspoken agreement, neither was prepared to draw undue speculation to themselves by dancing together a second time in one evening.

Looking for the first time toward the party just arrived; she barely noticed the friendly looking fair-haired young man being greeted by Sir William Lucas.

Elizabeth's attention was immediately taken by the tall gentleman standing behind the others. His striking good looks with dark wavy hair, and handsome features were well set up by his impressive figure and impeccable dress. He was looking away from the assemblage as if he felt himself to be above his company. And yet, she had a fleeting impression that he was in some sort of emotional pain or turmoil. Naturally she was intrigued. Even more, she felt moved to comfort and encourage him, as was her wont to do when her friends and neighbours were unhappy.

After only a moment's reflection Elizabeth labelled her impulse as *ridiculous!* He was obviously wealthy and accompanied by at least two very lofty-looking women who must have had all of their clothes and accoutrements from London, or even Paris! He was among his friends and might even be accompanied by his wife, or betrothed.

She experienced a fleeting sensation of regret at the thought that one of those women might be connected to him in that way – then she laughed at her own silliness. He must be accustomed to the company and attentions of the very fine ladies of the *ton*! He would never give a moment's thought to a simple country miss such as herself. It was nothing to her whether he was married or otherwise engaged, and certainly *that* man could not have any cause for the suffering she thought she had glimpsed just then.

As he turned to follow his companions farther into the room, their eyes met before he quickly glanced away. Elizabeth stifled a gasp; she very much wanted to look into those intense dark eyes again!

Alas, his subsequent aloofness and cold demeanour rapidly squelched the buzz of admiration that first accompanied his movements about the assembly room. The final destruction of her very nearly favourable first impression occurred when he audibly informed his friend Mr Bingley that he found her, Elizabeth, tolerable but not handsome enough to tempt him to dance.

Elizabeth immediately, and with little regret, dismissed Mr Darcy to the ranks of those among her acquaintance whose antics and ludicrous airs provided her with much amusement and a distinct disinclination for much time spent in their presence.

FOUR
Impressions Confirmed at Netherfield

Mr Bingley *was* a charming and friendly young man, an immediate favourite around the neighbourhood. His popularity became even more marked among the hopeful mamas in the region when word spread that his income was five thousand pounds a year - at the very least!

And he seemed to be in love with Elizabeth's eldest and favourite sister almost from the moment he was first introduced to her at the Meryton assembly. Mamá was in raptures! She could think of little else than her excitement for Jane and approval of Mr Bingley. Her fondest wish was nearly within her grasp. She was certain that an offer for Jane would soon be forthcoming and all of her worries for her girls' futures would be resolved.

Surely one good marriage among her daughters would lead to another, and another. Their Mamá could not rest (nor leave anyone else to their own peace) until she knew her daughters to be safely married and their future support no longer in question.

Easily pleased and not so easy to offend, Mr Bingley took no notice of Mrs Bennet's loud and frequent pronouncements of her gleeful expectation that he would soon propose to Jane. He and Jane simply took every opportunity to spend time together; speaking, looking, and listening only to each other, they were often oblivious to their surroundings.

Mrs Bennet was prepared to admire everything about Mr Bingley, including his two proud and disdainful London-dressed sisters, Miss Caroline Bingley and Mrs Louisa Hurst.

She surely would have been equally magnanimous toward his far wealthier friend, Mr Darcy, had that gentleman not been so far above his company as to refuse to stand up with her Lizzy at the Meryton assembly. Thenceforward, she simply could not like him.

Elizabeth seemed not *so very* deeply affected by the event as her Mamá. She laughed to herself about his affected pride and the wound to her own dignity occasioned by his slight. She shrugged it off and even made a joke of it to her friends, declaring that as *he* was of no consequence to *her*, his opinion could not bother her unduly!

~&~

Mr Bingley continued in his attentiveness to Jane (whom he very soon dubbed his *"Angel"* in his private conversations with his friend, Mr Darcy) to the exclusion of all others save for the common courtesies due one's neighbours. He worried about her excessively when she fell ill during a visit to his sisters at Netherfield. Indeed it seemed he could hardly rest until he was assured of her present comfort and imminent return to good health.

Dear sweet Jane simply smiled and *enjoyed* Mr Bingley's attentions. Her modest nature forbade her forming any expectations of him. She hoped – *of course she hoped!* Her heart was his from the start. But she could not assume that she, a country gentleman's daughter who could boast of no striking accomplishments, connections, or expectations, could inspire the same in him.

While Jane remained ill at Netherfield, Elizabeth stayed with her, nursing her tenderly until she was fit to return to their home.

During those four or five days Elizabeth delighted in Mr Bingley's amiable company but found that she spent more time than she would have wished in the company of Miss Bingley, the Hursts, and Mr Darcy.

It soon became obvious to her that the sisters' fawning friendship with Jane was in evidence only so long as they were in her, or Elizabeth's company. Jane merely provided them with some diversion from what they considered the tedium of living in the country. Otherwise they were supercilious in their superiority of fortune and fashion. Mr Bingley's sisters were particularly resentful of the Bennet intrusion into their family party.

Caroline Bingley, in particular, clearly wanted them gone. Although a source of occasional annoyance in her frequent sneering disparagement of country society, and of Elizabeth herself, the chief of Miss Bingley's contributions to each encounter (although unintended by her) was simply Elizabeth's entertainment at her antics. Her relentless pursuit of Mr Darcy was so transparently keen as to provide equal parts diversion and bemusement to Miss Elizabeth Bennet. To her, it all appeared rather nonsensical. Mr Darcy did not exhibit any particular affection for Miss Bingley, and *without that* why would she wish to connect herself to him?

Noting the differences in their comportment when they were in Jane's or their brother's company to when they thought themselves to be unobserved, Elizabeth felt herself confirmed in her misgivings about Jane's friendship with Mr Bingley's sisters.

Distrusting the sincerity of their warm and frequent professions of regard for Jane, she wondered whether they possessed the integrity of character to act honourably toward her beloved sister, who was plainly falling in love with their brother.

~&~

As for Mr Darcy, Elizabeth found him arrogant, confusing, and interesting. He tolerated or shrugged off Miss Bingley's attentions, enjoyed time with Mr Bingley and Mr Hurst (when the latter was not laid low by over-consumption of food and drink) and kept up a steady correspondence with his relations and his men of business.

Mr Darcy rarely troubled himself to speak unless he was so inclined on his own account. Yet, curiously, he sometimes seemed to deliberately initiate rather contentious verbal encounters with herself. At other times he did not deign to speak even one word to her.

Elizabeth sensed that her own inclination to quarrel with Mr Darcy might be just the least little bit heightened by her lingering pique at his original dismissal of her as "tolerable but not handsome enough to tempt" him to dance. Still, even without that her irrepressible nature had driven her to challenge him at every opportunity. She was drawn to it by his laconic wit, his arrogance and pride, and his evident selfish disdain for the feelings of others.

It satisfied something in her, pride perhaps, and a desire for justice and fair dealing when she could best him in an argument – or at least make him pause and look at her in that... way.

He did look at her in a peculiar way, and he seemed to look at her often. What could he mean by it? Elizabeth assumed that Mr Darcy was judging her, looking her over critically, cataloguing her faults in his mind, disgusted by the imperfections of an unpretentious country miss.

He often appeared stern, aloof, and almost angry. She could imagine the many ways he must find Miss Elizabeth Bennet sadly wanting in form as well as polish.

Her response, while his attention did give rise to a singular uneasiness in her, was generally to smile inwardly to herself at his self-importance. She was less intimidated than amused by his apparent censure of her - along with the ridiculous standards he affected to employ in his estimation of others.

Elizabeth's healthy self-regard rarely allowed her to resist rising to the challenge of his high-handed treatment of others.

Once or twice she had caught a look of confusion, almost chagrin in the eyes so frequently fixed in her direction. On those occasions she wondered whether he were really seeing herself, or merely gazing absentmindedly in her direction while considering something patently unrelated to her but which perplexed him.

FIVE
The Cousin and the Cad Appear

Once away from Netherfield, with Jane recovered, the two of them had barely settled in among their dear family again when Elizabeth and her sisters met Mr Wickham. That gentleman had seemed to Elizabeth like a breath of fresh air, uncomplicated and pleasant after several days in the presence of Mr Darcy's dark gaze and obscure moods.

Mr Wickham's cheerful countenance, good looks and obliging manners did much to recommend him to those of the Bennet sisters who were just then discovering the unfamiliar and generally unwelcome distraction of Mr Collins' recent arrival under their father's roof.

Handsome Mr Wickham's upright bearing and pleasing comportment were even more delightful to the youngest Bennet girls when he appeared in his red regimental uniform. The newest young officer in the militia quartered in Meryton was dashing indeed. He returned their admiration and played the gallant at every opportunity – especially to Miss Elizabeth Bennet.

Meanwhile their father enjoyed amusing himself immensely by encouraging Mr Collins' puffery and self-important nonsense at table, but that diversion swiftly paled for the young ladies. They soon found that they were not to be free of him even to indulge in such simple pursuits as walking to Meryton to browse the shop windows, purchase a length of ribbon, or visit their Aunt Phillips. He was there with them on every excursion, lumbering along, talking incessantly about nothing they cared to think about, while barely able to catch his breath.

The two youngest girls chafed under the sermonizing attentions of Mr Collins. Elizabeth and Jane tried to excuse and tolerate him, reminding each other that he would soon be on his way back to Hunsford and Rosings Park, leaving their lives to themselves again.

Mary, who spent such a *deal* of her time in studious endeavours aimed at perfecting her right to the reward of Heaven in the Hereafter (but made little effort toward perfecting the presentation of her person in the present) *should* have been a perfect friend for Mr Collins. But she could not seem to gain his interest.

Mr Collins had previously announced by letter that he was in want of a wife. Only their mother and father were privy to the fact that he had come to Longbourn expressly with the intention of choosing the companion of his future life from among his fair cousins.

Thus, he flattered himself; he could assure himself of a willing bride from among the reputed beauties in the Bennet household, while virtuously offering amends for their future injury at his hands when their family home would come to him by means of that *blessed* entail on the male line.

~&~

Bumping along in the old chaise only a few weeks later, Elizabeth Bennet Collins wished mightily that she had understood his purpose, and her own peril, in time to find some means of preventing what had now come to pass.

Making the dreadful mistake of accepting Mr Wickham's attentions, assuming him to be the honest gentleman he appeared to be, Elizabeth had foreclosed any hope of avoiding the fate that had inevitably befallen her.

Her friendship with Mr Wickham had grown uncommonly fast. Indeed, had she been less flattered by his open admiration and approval, she might have wisely distrusted such easy intimacy of conversation as they had together - after only a few encounters.

Not that her own disclosures had been indiscreet in the least. But *he* had expressed so freely to her of his own history and past dealings, his ill-usage at the hands of the rich and powerful, as to rouse in her those kindly and tender emotions that made her his gentle well-wisher and confirmed her in utter disgust with Mr Darcy. For it was Mr Darcy who had unjustly denied him his rightful place – the living intended for him by his godfather, Mr Darcy's own father.

What a fine clergyman Mr Wickham would have made with his gentlemanly demeanour and ease of address, she thought, and how pathetic his circumstances now. Elizabeth had scarcely managed to keep back her sympathetic tears when she thought of it! How *jealous and cruel* Mr Darcy had appeared to her then!

She found herself thinking of Mr Wickham with a greater degree of warmth than she had ever felt for anyone so completely unrelated to herself, before. And her opinion of Mr Darcy had correspondingly sunk to such a degree that she was certain he was the last man in the world she could ever consider a friend, or even a respectable opponent in one of their inevitable debates.

Elizabeth groaned softly to herself as she recalled how she had allowed Wickham to tweak her ridiculous prejudices against Mr Darcy into outright disgust of him. *How dramatically her opinion and understanding of the characters of both men had changed since the Netherfield ball!*

SIX
The Magnificent Netherfield Ball

Oh, how Elizabeth and her sisters had *looked forward* to the Netherfield ball! It was to be a much grander affair than the public assemblies of their experience heretofore. They all did enjoy the assemblies in Meryton very much, of course. But this was a private party, given under the orders of Mr Bingley and the careful design of his sisters, Miss Caroline Bingley and Mrs Louisa Hurst – so elegant and stylish, and ... discriminating!

Elizabeth Bennet was not much impressed with Mrs Louisa Hurst and Miss Caroline Bingley as to character or conversation, but she expected them to produce an event to remember. And they did.

Having endured several days' close confinement within doors due to an unrelenting period of rainy weather, *all* of the Bennet party was beyond eager for the anticipated delights (and relief from the agitation of his wife and daughters on the part of Mr Bennet) of the Netherfield ball.

The day dawned at last, clear and bright, full of promise and good cheer. No less than the full day was spent by the young ladies on making final choices of ribbons and coiffures - in preparations and in endless chatter about their wishes for particular dance partners – in short in excited expectation of the evening ahead.

~&~

Netherfield fairly glittered with hundreds of candles in chandeliers and in delicate crystal sconces placed along the walls, every solid surface was polished to glisten and sparkle.

A trio of professional musicians played softly in a smaller drawing room; their light melodies making a pleasant background to greetings and general conversation.

Two larger drawing rooms were opened upon each other and designated for the evening as the ballroom. A small orchestra offered the opening bars of the minuet to entice those who would join in the dance when their entertainment began in earnest.

Strategically placed mirrors reflected and multiplied the dazzling light everywhere. Great vases of colourful blooms among the seats arranged along three sides of the room for the comfort of spectators and resting dancers delighted the eye and scented the air. At one end of the dancing area light refreshments and large bowls of punch and lemonade awaited the guests' delight.

Smartly outfitted footmen were everywhere, assisting new arrivals and ready to serve wherever needed. Neatly clad maids were available to make last minute repairs or adjustments to the ladies' dress. It was quite beyond anything the neighbourhood had seen before!

The dance floor gleamed invitingly under several applications of beeswax. Two sets of French doors stood slightly ajar allowing the cool evening air from the terrace to enter the room, and for those who desired a few moments' respite from its closeness to step outside.

An adjoining room was set up with tables and comfortable seating for those who preferred card games to dancing.

In addition to the light refreshments arranged at one end of the dance floor, another adjoining room contained the more formal place settings for the midnight supper. Great tables stood laden with the finest of plate and polished silver awaiting the lavish midnight seating.

The awe-struck guests were treated to forms and varieties of hospitality hitherto unfamiliar to their simple country setting.

Caroline Bingley, with a smile that glittered as falsely as that of the mirrored candles, chatted and laughed as she moved among her guests, throwing glances of malicious triumph at Elizabeth whenever she chanced to catch her eye. *She, Miss Caroline Bingley*, had planned and prepared an event worthy of the London *ton*!

~&~

Elizabeth's happy anticipation of the evening, however, was doomed to disappointment and chagrin. In fact, before it was over and she and her family were once again returned to Longbourn, Elizabeth Bennet would know herself to be the *most foolish* of all the Bennet sisters, and the *least deserving* woman in the world of the attentions of a respectable gentleman!

Elizabeth had taken extra care with her hair and dress in preparation for the ball. She was delighted with her new gown of palest green tulle embroidered at the neckline and around the hem with delicate white flowers and dark green leaves. Loops of tiny green and white beads shone brilliantly among her auburn curls and a small cross set with seed pearls dipped discreetly toward her décolletage. The golden flecks in her fine brown eyes flashed with pleasure and anticipation. She looked forward eagerly to dancing and flirting with the charming Mr Wickham.

Arriving with her entire family, she was delighted to note Charles Bingley's joy at seeing her exquisite sister Jane.

Offering his arm to take her in to the dance, he turned with his broad smile to their parents, thanking them profusely for coming and bringing *all* of their lovely daughters! His greetings, as always, were warm indeed. But his particular pleasure in *Jane's* company especially warmed Elizabeth's heart. She liked Mr Bingley very much and her estimation of him could only benefit by his appreciation and attentiveness toward her beloved sister.

She believed that Jane would soon have her heart's desire – a marriage for love, to a man whom she could respect and admire. They were both so kind-hearted and generous they seemed perfect for one another!

Impatient to find Mr Wickham, Elizabeth endured the insincere welcomes of Miss Bingley and Mrs Hurst and stern looks of Mr Darcy until she could go in search of her new friend.

Mr Wickham was nowhere to be found! Another of the officers, Mr Denny, in speaking to Lydia disclosed that Mr Wickham was unavoidably detained in Town. He would not be able to attend the Netherfield ball. Elizabeth heard him remark that said *"business"* may have been timed conveniently to allow Mr Wickham to avoid *"a certain gentleman"*.

She was convinced that he meant Mr Darcy. Indignantly Elizabeth muttered to herself that it was *Mr Darcy* who should be practicing avoidance!

Sorely disappointed and angrier than ever with the dreadful Mr Darcy, Elizabeth sought and found her good friend, Charlotte Lucas. Within a short time Elizabeth's usual good humour reasserted itself and the two enjoyed sufficient opportunity for conversation for Elizabeth to embark upon a humorous description of her cousin, Mr Collins. That gentleman was not only present at the ball, but to Elizabeth's wry discontent, had previously secured her for the first set.

In the midst of their discourse concerning him, Mr Collins presented himself to Elizabeth for their dance. After a cordial introduction between him and her friend, she went off with him to fulfil her duty of hospitality to her visiting cousin.

~&~

Oh, dear Heaven, such agony and mortification were hers in those two dances with Mr Collins! Moving awkwardly, he solemnly disrupted every turn, either by moving wrong or pausing to apologize instead of attending to the activity at hand.

Everyone, fellow dancers and onlookers alike, stared in amazement at Mr Collins' inept and ridiculous cavorting about the floor. Elizabeth wondered in shame and resentment whether his clerical collar might be all that stood between him and outright ejection from the dance!

Finally she began to see the humour in the situation and even thought that perhaps she might giggle about the experience with Jane and Charlotte later, when it was over. But just then glimpsing Mr Darcy with what appeared to be a smirk on his face, *she wanted to slap him, or slap Mr Collins!*

Elizabeth's dismay deepened as the evening progressed. The two greatest causes of this were to be laid at the door of her dear family.

The first source of Elizabeth's pain, after dancing with Mr Collins, was embarrassment and mortification over her mother's incessant, loud, and uninhibited prognostications on the delightful expectation that Mr Bingley would soon declare himself and pay his addresses to her dear sweet beautiful Jane.

Mrs Bennet speculated in every possible way on the prospect of his five-thousand-a-year to be shared by Mr Bingley and Jane in matrimonial felicity. Always gregarious and animated in her discourse on the subject of her daughters' matrimonial prospects, Mrs Bennet's excessive volubility sounded nearly manic under the influence of *several* cups of punch! Her exuberant superlatives brought smirks and frowns Elizabeth noted, from *everyone* within at least twenty feet of her mother.

The second cause for public dismay was the *wild behaviour* of her two youngest sisters.

By the time of the Netherfield ball, Lydia's and Kitty's behaviour had become so unrestrained that others looked in wonder and derision upon her sisters as they ran about, laughing boisterously and nearly knocking the officers off their feet in their forwardness. *Elizabeth and Jane were mortified, indeed*.

Her happy distraction finally pierced by the wholesale unseemliness displayed by her youngest sisters, Jane did her best to attend upon Mr Bingley's conversation and keep his and her own attention from wandering thence. *Fortunately neither Mr Bingley nor Jane was aware of Mrs Bennet's continual onslaughts upon decorum.*

Elizabeth wondered at her father's failure to intervene, at least in her *sisters'* impropriety. She deliberated in an agony of indecision whether to speak to him about it or simply endeavour to hide herself in some neglected alcove in shame.

Pausing in indecision, Elizabeth was so unfortunate as to overhear her mother's joyful pronouncement that her *Lizzy was shortly to be betrothed to Mr Collins!* There was not a moment's doubt in Elizabeth's mind that her mother believed such a thing to be true - and that she, Elizabeth, would never consent to such an event! Glancing around to see who had heard her mother's ludicrous words, Elizabeth caught sight of Caroline Bingley's derisive smile in her direction.

At that moment she wished with all of her heart that Netherfield Park had not been let at all!

After some moments ruminating on her several sources of dismay, Elizabeth shrugged her shoulders and lifted her chin. She was not formed for ill humour! She would think on the events of the evening only as they could afford her pleasure, and leave the rest for quiet reflection – *later*.

Her mortification *was* somewhat relieved in the pleasure of dancing with one of the young militia officers who were so very plentiful and ready to dance. There was no doubt that *he* found her *quite* handsome enough to dance with!

Afterward Elizabeth went to spend a few moments chatting with her friend, Charlotte Lucas.

She was in the midst of an animated recital to Charlotte of the shameful tales she had heard about him from Mr Wickham when Mr Darcy himself appeared in front of her to solemnly request that she dance the next set with him.

SEVEN
Pride and Mortification

Weeks afterward musing to herself while ensconced within the *"carriage of doom"*, where she could find more than sufficient immediate cause to repine, Elizabeth could yet hardly bear to recollect what followed.

Already in the throes of her agitation against him, she could think of no credible excuse not to dance with Mr Darcy. Further, she knew that in refusing him she would be consigning herself to dance no more that evening. So she accepted, albeit with the greatest reluctance, and allowed him to take her hand as they walked to the floor.

Her body's instant reaction to the touch of his hand, even through the fabric of her glove, came as a *most* unsettling shock!

At first, she tried to ignore the warm flush spreading over her. The room had surely become too warm. There were too many people about. Her breathing had become rather too rapid. She felt as if she could not adequately fill her lungs; *she needed more air!*

Elizabeth could not imagine what was happening to her! Why would she react so differently to *Mr Darcy's* touch than to any of the many other gentlemen with whom she had danced since she first began to attend such entertainments?

Her discomfort was so extreme that it was several minutes before she was able to speak. Elizabeth was grateful that he too had been silent for the first few minutes of their dance together. She required a little time in which to regulate her breathing and order her thoughts.

Eventually Elizabeth began to feel that she must now establish some conversation between them. A little banal conversation must ease the nervous tension she felt every time they met in the dance.

Her first attempt at conversation was so inane; some comparison of private balls to public assemblies, that Elizabeth could not help turning it into a tease. She archly informed him that it was *his turn* to say something and gave him several equally hackneyed examples of appropriate comments, such as remarking upon the number of couples dancing or the size of the room, that he might make in order to uphold his end of the conversation.

From there they began a strained and somewhat nonsensical conversation which served not to show either in their best light.

She would assume that he would prefer not to speak, and insist that they were each of a taciturn nature, unwilling to speak unless they were to say something *so very* remarkable as to amaze the whole room and to be repeated for the benefit of posterity. *He* was engaged in mildly defending against her assumptions and assertions.

Finally Mr Darcy appeared to realize that he must contribute something of his own original direction to their discourse. He asked whether she and her sisters often walked to Meryton.

Ah! *Unfortunate* subject indeed! Elizabeth instantly recollected their recent meeting in Meryton where she and her sisters had only just made the acquaintance of Mr Wickham. She recalled the cold greeting between Mr Darcy and their new friend and was freshly reminded of the subsequent revelations that gentleman had made to her about Mr Darcy.

Agreeing that her family often took their way into Meryton she remarked that, in addition to visiting the milliners and other shops, it was equally meant for them to see their friends and form new acquaintances.

Elizabeth heard Mr Darcy's low comment that although Mr Wickham's happy manners might ensure his making new friends, it was not so certain that he would succeed in retaining them.

Whereupon Elizabeth found herself challenging Mr Darcy on the subject of Mr Wickham with *some* asperity!

All of her tender sympathy for the losses her new friend had sustained through Mr Darcy's treatment of him rose to her mind and gave impetus to her response. Elizabeth *most vehemently* accused Mr Darcy of dishonesty and cruelty toward his former friend and playmate! Indignantly she repeated Mr Wickham's stories of his ruined prospects; how he had been left in comparative poverty in *scandalous* disregard and dishonour of Mr Darcy's own father's final wishes! In short, Elizabeth assailed him in a manner entirely uncharacteristic of her generally decorous behaviour. *She felt driven by emotions she could hardly comprehend!*

At the last she found herself at the end of her shocking tirade, and of the set, with the deepest flush on her face, her bosom heaving in agitation and tears in her eyes.

To her *unqualified horror*, she became aware that the people around them were beginning to murmur and look at the two of them with open interest. Elizabeth wanted desperately to stamp her foot in fury and march back to Charlotte – and *out* of the presence of the horrid man before her! But she could not. Propriety and decorum had suffered enough under her unrestrained public confrontation of Mr Darcy!

For one long moment the two of them stood face-to-face, glaring fiercely into each other's eyes.

Elizabeth was abruptly recalled to herself when that gentleman un-gently grasped her arm and began walking her toward the nearest open balcony doors saying in a low angry voice: "You have said quite enough *here* Madam! Please indulge me with a moment of your time. You must allow me to tell you… We *must* speak further."

He stopped when they were outside the doors but still in plain view of the assemblage.

"Miss Bennet, this will *not* do! I perfectly comprehend what your opinion of me must be. I will not impose upon you unnecessarily; however I insist upon enlightening you to the true state of affairs between myself and Mr Wickham – for your own sake!" His eyes were nearly black with anger but he released her arm and faced her once again.

Elizabeth lifted her chin defiantly. "I believe that I am as informed as I ever care to be on that subject, Mr Darcy!" She trembled at his stern visage but refused to cower before him. Indeed, he should be slinking out of sight in shame instead of demanding her attention!

"Miss Bennet, I do not consider it likely that you can have known Mr Wickham for more than the short time he has been in Meryton." He held up his hand to fend off her reply. "If I am wrong in that then I beg your pardon for what I am about to tell you, but speak I must! I have known Mr Wickham for nearly all of my life. We played together as boys, and later attended University together. I know him and his habits well."

Shaken by the import already apparent in his response, and instantly alert to her own folly, Elizabeth stammered: "I do not think... that is, I think it best not to continue the impropriety I so thoughtlessly committed in raising the subject by your telling and my hearing even more of your or Mr Wickham's personal matters."

Elizabeth knew herself to be in the wrong. She was embarrassed and most unwilling to continue any discussion relating to Mr Wickham's misfortunes at the hands of Mr Darcy.

It was her urgent desire to depart from Mr Darcy's presence as speedily as possible.

Elizabeth moved toward the balcony door where the lights and music and voices of the celebrants inside offered her some respite from the sound of his stern words and the heavy tension in their private tête-à-tête.

"You are correct madam." His deep voice halted her near flight from his presence. She listened as if mesmerized while he brought her low. "Your raising such a subject on the dance floor was most assuredly improper. Even more I am astounded that you would allow him to speak of such intimate matters, as one would share only with close friends or family, upon so slight an acquaintance as yours must have been. Be that as it may, however, it is my chief purpose just now to inform you of the facts underlying Mr Wickham's wild tales. For wild tales they must have been to arouse in you such... passionate partisanship."

Thus Elizabeth learned of Wickham's treachery and lies. She wilted in shame while listening to the truth: that old Mr Darcy had generously paid for Wickham to have a gentleman's education while that young man had repaid his generosity with lies and dishonour. She heard about Wickham's vicious habits and dissolute ways so obvious to the contemporary son but unknown to the elder Mr Darcy.

Out of friendship and loyalty to his former steward, Mr Darcy provided in so many ways for young George Wickham. It was his wish, expressed in his will, that upon Wickham's taking holy orders and the living at Kympton coming available it would be bestowed as a gift upon his godson. She was stunned to learn that immediately after old Mr Darcy's death; George Wickham had announced that he had no intention of becoming a clergyman. He had asked for and was given three thousand pounds instead of the living.

As proof of his assertions Mr Darcy offered to show her the receipt signed by Mr Wickham for the exchange. He offered to give her the names of shopkeepers whose claims against Mr Wickham had been paid by Mr Darcy.

In the heat of his recitation, Mr Darcy blurted out his deepest fury and pain: Mr Wickham had attempted to seduce and elope with Mr Darcy's fifteen-year-old sister – to gain her thirty thousand pounds in dowry – and to wound Darcy in the most vicious manner he might. And there was more! Untold numbers of gambling debts, young women compromised extortions... Elizabeth could bear no more!

She put up a hand to halt the recitation of Mr Wickham's perfidy. "Stop! Please stop! I have heard far more than enough!" Stumbling blindly away from Mr Darcy, she nearly plunged down the steps leading to the garden below!

Mr Darcy's hand barely caught her before she fell, and pulled her backward to safety. The force of his rescue brought her solidly up against him and she felt for the first time the firm contact of an unrelated adult male body with her own. For one second she remained where she was, surprised and electrified by the sensation of his closeness. Then they both stepped briskly away from one another.

She stood with her head down, heart pounding, and her body trembling violently from the humiliation doubly felt from his harsh words and the shock of his touch.

"Miss Bennet, I apologize! I only wanted you to know what is necessary for you to protect yourself from such wickedness. I admit, the strong wish to clear my own name was a further inducement to speak so frankly to you, but I find that I cannot stand by and see you so vulnerable to the machinations of that scoundrel!"

"Mr Darcy, I... I cannot..."

"There is no more to be said Miss Bennet. I will send a servant with a glass of wine and to assist you as it has grown cold and you have suffered a shock."

Despite his words of apology, Mr Darcy's face appeared full of rage and offense. He shortly excused himself and walked away, leaving Elizabeth to calm herself and re-join the gathering when she felt able to do so.

EIGHT
Her Carriage Arrives at Awakening

Riding along in the "carriage of doom" Elizabeth relived for the hundredth time the devastation she felt standing there alone on the deserted balcony, knowing herself to be the greatest of fools! She chastised *him* for arrogance. And what was *her* arrogance in setting herself as arbiter of right and wrong in a situation she knew nothing of and should never have involved herself in at all?

She had lost his good opinion forever, if indeed he had ever thought the least bit favourably of her at all. His own unforgiving statement, that his good opinion once lost was lost forever, rose in her mind as the severest condemnation. Elizabeth had behaved as a country bumpkin and he knew it! She had fulfilled all of his worst expectations of her! His regular assessment of her flaws was confirmed. She had long understood that he found much to offend him when he stared at her in his dark and brooding way.

The hardest thing was the dawning realization that her vigorous disapprobation of him was founded entirely upon censorious assumptions on her part, lies from Mr Wickham, and her initial pique in response to his dismissal of her as "not handsome enough" at the Meryton Assembly.

Elizabeth now understood that she had been affected far more by his disdain than she had admitted to herself, or to her family and friends, because she had at first thought him both handsome and intriguing!

She dared not question herself on what she might think of him now. Her thoughts and reminiscences brought her to such a state of distress that she felt nearly asphyxiated with shame! Elizabeth shook herself impatiently and shifted her position on the carriage seat before she thought better of allowing any indication of her wakefulness before Mr Collins.

"Ah, Mrs Collins! You do well with all of this sleeping along the way. I shall be most pleased to have my bride fresh and well-rested when we reach Hunsford." Mr Collins thought to lean forward, had actually reached out to pat her knee, when the carriage took a particularly wide swing to the right thus requiring the use of both of his hands to remain upright upon the cushioned seat.

Not the least deterred from his message, he said: "Lady Catherine will be pleased as well, to find you ready to do her proper homage when we arrive at Rosings Park, her magnificent home. Of course we shall pause there for her most gracious and magnanimous felicitations and beneficent approval before we arrive at our own fittingly modest abode across the lane at Hunsford parsonage! I am excessively gratified and humbled at the expectancy of her unexampled kindness to myself and my bride!"

Mr Collins had been enjoying his own ponderings upon the activities to commence upon their arrival in his neighbourhood. His look clearly reflected his happy anticipation of the events to come.

Elizabeth choked and gulped and looked away, not saying a word. She could feel the blush covering her skin as well as she could feel the nauseous knot rising in her stomach.

Something of her alarm must have finally communicated itself to him. After a moment Mr Collins went on:

"Do not be *missish* my dear, you are a married woman now. You need not fear me, I am not a brute. So long as you are obedient to my wishes we shall get along splendidly. However I *shall* expect you to comport yourself as befits one who is privileged to be the wife of an esteemed clergyman in possession of an excellent living and the grateful recipient of the generous condescension of Lady Catherine de Bourgh!

"You must know yourself to be most fortunate in being chosen by a man in my position to be uplifted from the uncertain potential of penury and want, to the security and comfort I am able to provide." There was more than a hint of displeasure and warning in his tone as Mr Collins reminded Elizabeth that she no longer could claim a will of her own if it were in any way in opposition to that of her husband – or indeed, that of Lady Catherine de Bourgh!

She did not answer him. She had nothing, or too much, to say.

Elizabeth understood that her former habitual sanguinity, her self-confidence, and her customary good cheer were irrevocably defeated. Never again would she ramble as a carefree maiden along her beloved country lanes. And never again would she enjoy that inviolate privacy and peace in her slumbers without dread of intrusion of the most distressing sort. Never again, never again, the phrase clung tenaciously to her mind in the manner she imagined of the jaws of a mantrap she had seen once in the woods near Oakham Mount.

~&~

Elizabeth's heart cringed at the remembrance that hers was not the only life bewildered and destroyed by the events at the Netherfield ball.

Poor Jane! Her innocent hopes for requited love, her dreams of a happy future at the side of Charles Bingley, loving him and bearing his children, growing old together - all of those delightful prospects had been destroyed. Mr Bingley appeared to have been persuaded that his interest lay elsewhere.

The very day after the Netherfield ball Mr Bingley, Mr Darcy, Miss Bingley and Mr and Mrs Hurst departed Netherfield for London – not to return in the foreseeable future! Miss Bingley's polite note to Jane made it clear that none of them intended to return and they left nothing behind to lament except Miss Bingley's "friendship" with Jane.

It seemed that she and others in their party were quite hopeful for a connection between Mr Bingley and Miss Georgiana Darcy, Mr Darcy's young sister.

Sweet Jane was inclined to believe that Miss Bingley was aware of Jane's heart and wished to warn her away from the inevitable hurt when Mr Bingley's attachment to Miss Darcy was formalized.

Elizabeth knew the truth. Upon only a moment's reflection she recalled Mr Darcy's influence on Charles Bingley and collected his disgust with her and everything about Hertfordshire, including, most unfairly, her dearest Jane.

Mr Bingley's sisters had made no secret of their dislike of country living and their desire to return to London. Miss Bingley in particular was waspish in her derision of Hertfordshire (not as beautiful as the unmatched perfection of Derbyshire – where Mr Darcy had his estate); Meryton (tedious, uncouth, and uncivilized); and especially the Bennet family – her criticisms of *them* seemed to spring from a bottomless pit of viperous malice.

Elizabeth was certain that Miss Bingley and Mrs Hurst had joined forces with Mr Darcy to entice Mr Bingley away to London and, once there, to convince him to remain.

She suffered the deepest pain in knowing that because of her forthright but misguided words, insulting and offending Mr Darcy at the Netherfield ball, Jane's happiness was surely and irretrievably lost. Mr Bingley would not be asking that particular question of Jane; the question that had seemed to be on the tip of his tongue until that awful night.

Elizabeth felt a momentary anger at Charles Bingley. He had shown every indication of being deeply in love with Jane! How could he be so weak as to let others keep him away? Had he, after all, only been toying with her beloved sister?

Soon enough, her anger took its proper direction. It was all *her* fault and she could never lay so much blame on anyone as she deserved herself.

~&~

Elizabeth was roused from her painful thoughts by the sound of Mr Collins' voice: "You appear quite done in, my dear! I perceive most readily that the joy and excitement of the nuptials have quite taken your strength!

Indeed, you must be in the most exquisite anticipation of the awesome events to follow. Why, the knowledge that you will shortly be receiving the notice and congratulations of Lady Catherine de Bourgh herself must needs overwhelm your youthful sensibilities indeed! I myself am filled with such eager delight at the prospect of her Ladyship's most gracious condescension, her generosity and particular notice in bestowing her esteemed approval upon my marriage that I can scarcely think! Such wonderful imaginings of that exalted moment are mine that I have not the slightest interest in the passing scenery for my constant entertainment and satisfaction in the plan!"

On and on he went, indulging every affable notion in his bird-witted raptures.

What a clever stroke it is *not*, she thought to herself, to leg-shackle myself to such a comprehensive mutton head!

Elizabeth could hardly bear to look at him. She only blushed continually throughout his speech while she cringed and shuddered inwardly. "Indeed, sir" was all the response she could make to Mr Collins' verbose effusions.

I wish he may stop his mouth with a hornets' nest! Oh dear, if I do not die in childbirth, I shall be moped to death! Dismayed by the enormity of her fury she resolved to cease giving it expression: I must scotch this dangerous mood if I am to avoid a dreadful scandal!

"Yes my dear," Mr Collins puffed out his chest, "Lady Catherine will receive us as soon as we enter the neighbourhood. She has set aside time between her evening tea and a meeting with her seamstress, so you see we must be prompt!" A flicker of worry crossed his face at the thought of failing Lady Catherine's purpose.

"You will be astounded, dear Mrs Collins, at Lady Catherine's munificent condescension! She neglects not the least significant, most minute, aspect of my situation to engage her interest and kindly advice."

Elizabeth shifted a little, trying to focus only upon the lavender-scented softness of a small pillow brought from home which she had situated beneath her cheek.

"You need not suffer any undue trepidation my dear." Mr Collins' voice droned on: "Although you must always comport yourself with proper respect and gratitude for her notice, you will soon understand the natural degree of humility and appreciation with which you are to receive her recognition and gracious advice - which I do not *doubt* will come your way quite often. Of course, to be sure, Lady Catherine will not turn her attentions in your direction *every* day. However I do flatter myself that her interest in you is due to her high regard for me! I consider it a mark of her very particular acknowledgement and most gratifying appreciation of my position in the community that prompts my esteemed patroness to receive you so immediately upon your arrival within her lofty domain. Indeed I am in the most extreme transports of delight at the very notion of her unparalleled generosity being demonstrated in such a way!"

Mr Collins' steady monologue was punctuated by the jolts and vibrations of their conveyance as it continued along its way.

"Perhaps I had better rest while I may, so as to appear to your best advantage before your illustrious benefactress." So saying, Elizabeth closed her eyes and ceased listening.

~&~

She wondered what manner of imperious and unfeeling person Lady Catherine must be to quite *command* her parson to find and secure an acceptable bride within the space of a fortnight!

Elizabeth was informed by way of Mr Collins' reiterations on the subject that Lady Catherine pronounced an acceptable bride to be a gentlewoman *not* brought up too high for humble service to herself, *not* too low to possess the necessary address and accomplishments required for inclusion at table or to form a pool for quadrille when other company was lacking. All this she *must* exemplify!

Apparently Lady Catherine pointed out with less energy but equal insistence that her parson's wife must set a fine example of propriety and service for the neighbourhood as well.

In Elizabeth's mind Lady Catherine's intrusive dictum would be laughable, an oddity really, had *she not been* the anonymous object of it.

That Lady must be singularly puffed up with conceit and self-consequence to give no consideration to the wishes of those most affected in a matter so wholly personal and life-altering as marriage. *To fulfil her demand, Mr Collins was to enter an unfamiliar community and select said bride from a family hitherto entirely unknown to himself!*

What A great piece of callousness – every natural feeling must be offended by such presumption.

And what manner of poor creature *he* must be to allow Lady Catherine to lead him thus into the performance of every piece of folly she might devise!

It must be such an impetuous and imprudent design undertaken after all, to decide within so short a space of time with whom one is to spend the balance of one's life! In the most personal circumstances of all! Involving an irrevocable decision no less, conferring rights and privileges upon someone barely met with and necessarily quite imperfectly understood.

Elizabeth thought of her mother's last minute admonition regarding the wedding night, to lie back and be still whilst he took his privilege. She should think of something pleasant, her mother sagely advised, and soon Mr Collins' disgusting attentions to her person would be over.

Horrid thought! His would be the supreme right, to engage at will in such intimate activities as he chose - that it was now her lifelong duty to endure!

Surely her life could now be nothing short of insupportable!

~&~

Elizabeth stirred restlessly her body aching from the discomfort of her position leaning into the corner of the seat. How much longer could she feign sleep in this manner? Indeed, how much longer were they to travel before reaching their dreaded destination? There could be no happy outcome to her dilemma!

Almost as if her thought had conjured it up, the "carriage of doom" slowed and came to a stop. Elizabeth was nearly faint with alarm!

Mr Collins clambered out of the carriage and reached back his hand to assist her. She could not move.

"Come, my dear! We mustn't keep Lady Catherine waiting!" There was that warning tone again.

Elizabeth cautiously slid across the seat toward the door and peeked out.

There stood an exceedingly large angry personage dressed in extremely rich, if over-bedecked, finery in the style of a previous generation. Elizabeth's glance took in velvets and furs, silks and lace, brilliant hues and jewels everywhere! The woman's steel grey hair was elaborately coiffed with multiple ropes of great silver spangles woven through it. The jewelled rings on every finger flashed in the sunlight nearly blinding her with their brilliance. But when she looked more closely, Elizabeth could not make out Lady Catherine's face!

Mr Collins began to drag Elizabeth out of the carriage, urging her to pay her respects to their patroness without further delay!

Elizabeth tried again but could not bring that face into focus! She felt Mr Collins' hand push her forward just as she noticed the coiled buggy-whip in Lady Catherine's hand, raised as if to strike her!

Screaming and trying to run, Elizabeth found that her limbs were sluggish after the long cramped ride in the carriage. She could not dart away as quickly as she would typically have done. In fact, she was able to run only a short distance, feeling the whip reaching out for her, before she stumbled and fell!

Mr Collins and Lady Catherine were nearly upon her as she scrambled to get away! She felt a hand grasp her shoulder, restraining her, preventing her desperate attempt to escape!

Elizabeth rolled on the ground screaming in fright *"No! No! Oh, please, no!"*

~&~

Jane's gentle touch and concerned voice reached her through the fog of her terror "Lizzy! Lizzy! Wake up dear, you are having a nightmare!"

Elizabeth was still shaken, even after discovering that she had fallen out of her bed and had been rolling about on the floor of her room at Longbourn!

"Oh, my dearest Jane! Oh, Thank God you are here!" She cried out. "Please tell me it is all untrue!"

NINE
A Jumble of Nightmares Ends the Night

"No dear, you did not marry Mr Collins! *Heaven above*, I cann*ot* imagine our dear father allowing such a thing!"

Staring into her sister's beloved face Elizabeth struggled to separate which was reality and which could be released back into the haze of nonsense and nonesuch. There was a tangle in her mind of actual events, the Netherfield ball for instance and the conflict with Mr Darcy, but *thank all that is Holy*: she had *not* been forced to marry Mr Collins!

Gratefully she accepted Jane's reassurance that, unlike his guilty acquiescence in her nightmare, her wonderful father would *never* support such a match for her.

Still, Elizabeth understood that Jane could not say the same of their mother. And Mamá *did* sometimes get her way after she had besieged her husband loudly enough and long enough to exhaust his façade of imperviousness. There very well *could* be a limit, after all, to any person's defences, no matter how staunch they may be.

Elizabeth's trembling and tears had slowed but she still shivered at the thought of her mother's insistence on her marrying that *joke* of a man!

"Jane, Mamá does insist so! And I am fully aware that my accepting him would, once and for all, resolve her dreadful worries about all of our futures if Papá should leave us before any are married well."

"Lizzy! No such thing will happen! Mamá only allows her fears to lead her good sense astray. It will all turn out well, you will see."

"Oh, Jane, I could not bear it! I could not *live,* married to Mr Collins!"

"Dear Lizzy, I do not believe he has quite *asked* you yet – although he *has* more than hinted at it, I agree. But perhaps you will contrive to avoid him until he must return to Hunsford. He was only to be with us for a fortnight, and that is more than half gone already. That would be a great laugh would it not?"

"I confess I heard him talking to Mamá last night about having a few moments alone with me in the morning; he having something *particular* to ask me."

"Well, he is *out* there! I do believe it will be well past noon before any of us venture downstairs after such a late and eventful evening."

Dear Jane, thank you with all of my heart for being so wonderfully you! You have nearly got me laughing at myself... nearly."

"You must think of it no more. Twas only a nightmare, of course, and cannot happen in your waking state. If it helps you rest, dear Lizzy, I promise that I will not *allow* it to come true! There, does that ease your mind?"

Elizabeth smiled drowsily at the amusing notion of soft-spoken *Jane* fiercely protecting her from Mr Collins' impertinent attentions! Her elder sister always knew how best to ease her discomposure and soothe her troubled spirits.

Jane sat with Elizabeth, stroking her hair and reassuring her until she saw that she had drifted off at last.

Then she slipped into her own bed, just a few feet away from Elizabeth's, and tired again to find rest from her own uncertainties.

~&~

A very loud clap of thunder startled the horses and caused them to shy and rear violently. The carriage tilted crazily and fell on its side. Elizabeth landed with a painful thud against the wooden door.

A body fell heavily on top of her. She struggled against it. She would not be buried alive under that pathetically puffed up pompous parson!

Rain spattered forcefully against the glass window pane, somehow intact despite the jarring crash of the carriage. It sounded insistent and spiteful.

"*No*! I will *not*! *Get off of me*!" Although she was trying with all of her strength to shout, the words did not seem to be audible outside of her head!

Now an arm flung itself across her face pinning her to the ground. For a long few seconds she was unable to *breathe*!

In panic, Elizabeth's eyes flew open. *What*? She could see the morning sunshine peeking in around the drawn curtains. Jane was on top of her struggling to get up - and there *was no* rainstorm!

~&~

This would not do! Jane looked as shocked and frightened as Elizabeth felt. They stared at each other in surprise, and then they both began to giggle. The giggles turned to great gulps of laughter, and they held on to each other as if for dear life! They laughed together until they were both in tears, but calmed.

"Jane, you are feeling it as well?"

"Oh my, Lizzy is Mr Bingley in earnest, or am I only wishful thinking? I do not know, and there is a doubt piercing my heart that... that he will never declare himself. I... feel so much..."

"Dear Jane, beautiful sweet Jane! Of course he loves you! Of course he will declare himself! He only needs a little time to sort himself out; you will see."

Jane looked down at their clasped hands, "I do hope so. I suppose I am only worrying because he has gone to London today." Her voice was soft and then with more vigour she looked up and went on: "You see what we are doing? We are thinking like our mother! Oh dear! I should not have said that." But there was a twinkle in her eyes even as she clapped her hand to her mouth.

"And *that* is enough to make me determined to forsake any hope of further sleep. I can have no peaceful rest in any event. I shall go for a nice long walk. That will relieve my distress and keep Mr Collins at bay!"

"I shall help you avoid him as you make your escape! But first let us share a breakfast tray and some hot coffee as we prepare ourselves for the day. I believe that I shall be inclined after that to take some time alone in the garden. Perhaps I shall finish gathering the lavender and rosemary to dry. If by then I have not overcome my sickly thoughts; if tranquillity yet evades me I may still yet carry on to the thyme and the rosemary... parsley as well. You may help me tie them up after you return from your exercise. We shall neither of us *wilt* under the trials that beset us!"

"Tying up herbs will be just the thing after a brisk walk to clear my head and loosen my tense muscles. I confess to owning a fearfully dangerous temper at present. I shall walk and clamber about among the rocks and meadows most assiduously until I can truthfully claim to be more in charity with myself and with the world!"

"Take care not to go too far, Lizzy. It is hardly seemly for a young woman to walk far from her home alone." Jane was teasing. She knew full well that Elizabeth would walk as far and for as long as she needed to settle her disposition. Never formed for ill-humour, she would cry up the absurdity in her troubles until she could laugh them aside. She would doubtless return fresh-faced and cheery, with a bright glow in her lovely eyes.

"Yes, Jane dearest. I will go no farther than Oakham Mount."

"Lizzy! Oakham Mount is quite a distance from Longbourn!"

TEN
Darcy's Dithering Thither and...Yawn

She looked well enough, or rather *a great deal* more than well enough, with her enticing figure and exquisite features that were *vastly* appealing however much they were at variance with the current ideal set by the *ton*.

Her greatest beauty, the magnet that drew his boundless fascination, glowed in her fine eyes. He *first* admired their striking colour of lustrous dark brown flecked with gold. But it was their intelligent expression, sparkling with humour and joie de vivre that drew him most. In fact, they were quite lovely in every way.

Those were Fitzwilliam Darcy's thoughts of Miss Elizabeth Bennet upon seeing her for the *first* time.

She was seated, chatting with another young woman at the Meryton assembly, when he first noticed her. Standing nearby, he could overhear enough of their discourse to collect that she was kindly encouraging the younger girl, who seemed a little low.

He soon discovered how enticing a few dainty auburn curls resting lightly upon a shapely neck, could be. When they bounced and bobbed gently with her graceful movements he deliberately altered his stance to avoid gazing too long in her direction.

He gave no sign of his admiration however; in fact he refused to stand up with her when Bingley tried to interest him in dancing.

He would maintain his customary indifferent demeanour. His habitual reserve did not allow him to take the least notice of any of the country folk there. It was beneath his dignity and station in life to do so. He was most properly aloof and superior as the very wealthy, highly respected and sought after master of Pemberley of Derbyshire. His ancient family line had connections among the highest members of the *ton* and to numerous peers of the realm.

Besides, he was in no humour to put himself out to please anyone! His thoughts were much engaged in worrying about his sister. Georgiana's broken heart over Wickham haunted him still. He would have preferred to stay in Bingley's library, writing to her again; trying to find words of comfort and encouragement for her.

Indeed, he had been entirely put out by Bingley's insistence that they attend the country dance at all.

But *those eyes*! Those *gorgeous eyes*! The tiny golden flecks in them sparkled enticingly in the glow of candlelight – indeed, in every kind of light.

He *did* take note of her beautiful dark auburn hair, curling so sweetly around her face; and of her light and pleasing figure so petite and yet fulsome with the vitality of an active life. Everything about her drew him, fascinated him, but he was completely undone by her *wonderfully fine eyes*. They were at once full of good natured humour and something else, something that seemed to see right into him and fathom the very depths of him!

When Miss Elizabeth stayed at Netherfield to nurse her sister Jane, and whenever they met at social gatherings around Meryton, those lovely, teasing, laughing, glorious eyes seemed to look straight into his soul, take his measure, and gift him with their knowing.

Darcy delighted in her generous nature. She was amiable, and invariably kind. Even when she was teasing and arguing with him about some point of principle or philosophy, her eyes revealed her amusement at the prospect. He was mesmerized by the engaging archness displayed with one lifted brow over her lively glance; especially when she was about to deliver a clever stroke in one of their frequent debates!

Oh yes, she was intelligent! She had absorbed an extensive understanding of history, geography, literature and poetry from her father's library of treasured volumes.

Mr Bennet also shared his newspaper with her and the two frequently enjoyed uncommonly vigorous discussions related to the subjects therein.

Darcy had discovered to his surprise and pleasure that she could easily hold her own on many topics of general conversation. In fact she was knowledgeable far beyond the reach of any other woman he knew.

Yet she did not puff herself about, but delivered her contributions to their discourse in an unassuming and artless manner that simply took his heart and reduced it to a bauble for her little finger.

She was unique among her sphere and, Darcy knew, would be even more so among women of the *ton*. Miss Elizabeth Bennet was intelligent and she was kind – and she possessed a rare wit.

Her full lips would curve sweetly and her eyes would flash in happy anticipation just before she would say something very witty or challenging in response to his blunderings. And blunder he did, for he could not seem to think clearly when his eyes were joyously fixed upon her; his mind ceaselessly engaged in quarrelling between enchantment and stern disapproval of his reaction to her.

Fitzwilliam Darcy was wholly undone, enthralled! His heart was entirely lost to the daughter of a country squire before he could so much as comprehend his danger!

~&~

Her family and connections, however, were *every way* repugnant to him; his own family and associates would *despise* an alliance between them! That certainty alone must serve as an absolute barrier to *any thought* of a future with her.

Mrs Bennet's loud and incessant assertions that his friend Bingley's proposal of marriage to her daughter Jane was both certain and imminent; her vulgarly vocal and avaricious pursuit of wealthy husbands for her five daughters; her complete disregard of the two eldest daughters' discomfort at her volubility – all served to instil in him the deepest disgust toward her.

The two youngest sisters were *wild, unruly*! They clearly cared nothing for propriety, or for the comfort or opinions of others. Miss Lydia and Miss Kitty Bennet ran noisily about unchecked wherever they might find themselves, without the slightest show of modesty, decorum, or consciousness of what was proper and right. Such behaviour at whichever age would shock the sensibilities of any person of polite society. Their exhibiting so at the tender ages of fifteen and seventeen threw the *gravest* shades of disapprobation upon the wisdom and characters of their inattentive parents!

Finally there was the matter of their low connections. Mrs Bennet had a brother in trade in Cheapside, and a sister married to an attorney in Meryton. He could not congratulate himself on the hope of relations as inferior as those!

Thus the battle within him against his heart's inclination raged. Never doubting the necessary outcome, his thoughts flung his emotions back and forth. He was altogether tormented between his intensely personal and virtually constant desire for her presence, his pride of place, and his prejudice against Miss Elizabeth Bennet's condition in life.

Darcy's eventual determination that he must relinquish every thought and dream of her left him entirely grim and humourless. His customary coolly remote aspect became severely austere and stern.

He thought of nothing so much as of Miss Elizabeth Bennet; and of the impossibility of having her in his life.

~&~

The more they were thrown together at neighbourhood dinner parties and soirees the more difficult it was for Darcy to cease thinking of her, watching her, and attempting to engage her in conversation.

When the dreams began he waxed indignant; accusing himself of being featherbrained. He insisted to himself that he would not allow such unbidden and uncontrolled fantasies to afflict him. He knew himself to be Mr Fitzwilliam Darcy, master of Pemberley, not some country cork-brain, to be borne down and discomposed by a mere country miss!

The dreams continued.

Darcy endured the delectable torture of feeling *her hand rest lightly on his arm.* The next night he felt the delicate brush of *her lips upon his own.* Another time *he kissed her fully, deeply, passionately, until she trembled in his arms and he gasped for breath!*

Night after night he held her in his arms. He took long walks in the woods and countryside around Pemberley with her, holding hands and talking, and kissing. And always she looked at him with those sparkling eyes. Only now they were filled with admiration and warmth – for him.

As if they had indeed courted and married, Darcy's dreams progressed to loving Elizabeth in his bedchamber at Netherfield – and eventually elsewhere. They loved each other in his London house, on their honeymoon in the Lake District. He dreamt of her at Pemberley, in their bedchambers and even among the trees and grassy nook s in the wooded hills that rose behind Pemberley House. Always he saw his beloved's beautiful eyes, glowing with love, darkening with passionate desire – for him.

When his dreams became more real to him than the events of his days, he knew his heart to be utterly and completely lost to her.

He loved her. Oh yes, he was without question deeply in love with her. His early admiration had grown to something much deeper, more intense, and far more demanding of his soul. He loved her ardently, adored her with all of his being.

Darcy could think of little else than the conundrum of his desperately wanting Miss Elizabeth Bennet, whose family were entirely unsuitable as future connections for Fitzwilliam Darcy, as his wife.

~&~

He fought, with only a modicum of success, to put his precious much younger sister's interests above those of his insistent heart. He was devoted to Georgiana; and her marriage prospects when she came out in one or two years would be significantly reduced by her brother marrying so far beneath him.

Georgiana would be old enough to come out next year but she had begged him to postpone it for another year. He was half convinced that her wish to wait until the following Season might give her time to develop more confidence and overcome the lingering pain of the episode with Wickham. Unfortunately waiting would also postpone his freedom to follow his own heart in his choice of a bride.

His father's death five years previous, when Darcy was but twenty-two, had left him a devoted and scrupulous co-guardian of Georgiana, herself only eleven years old at the time.

Although he shared guardianship with his cousin, Colonel Richard Fitzwilliam's military duties were such that Darcy acted as her primary guardian. He felt his responsibilities toward her deeply, especially in light of his being Georgiana's closest remaining family.

Darcy was a conscientious and principled man; he would not act in any way damaging to those to whom he owed a duty of care and allegiance. He would always renounce his own happiness before he would bring shame or discredit on Georgiana; indeed his tender regard for her would never allow him to be happy if she was not.

Still, all the while, in his sleeping dreams and in his every unguarded moment while awake, his heart laboured to be heard. His attempts to command that unruly organ to cease and desist were futile. Miss Elizabeth Bennet lived within him – heart, mind, body and soul – yet he felt her absence constantly. Bereft of all hope of happiness, Darcy was desolate.

ELEVEN
Darcy Attends Miss Elizabeth's Wedding

Fitzwilliam Darcy's mind struggled to escape the horrific confusion and despair of the nightmare. It felt so real! And it brought home to him *again* the utter hopelessness of his situation.

He had slept very ill last night, tossing and turning until the bedclothes were all of a twist.

When at last he did sleep, he found himself attending a wedding. At first it was not clear to Darcy precisely who were the bride and groom. Bingley was there beside him, with his customary pleasant countenance in place, so it was certainly not Miss Jane Bennet who was the bride, nor was his friend the groom.

As the people in front of him took their seats he saw with surprise that it was the odious Mr Collins who awaited the bride at the side of the pulpit, whoever the unlucky girl might be.

As Darcy looked around him he saw Miss Charlotte Lucas sitting nearby with her family. It could not be Miss Lucas who was the bride.

Idly puzzling over the identity of one who would accept the hand of the ungainly and absurdly pompous parson; his thoughts turned naturally to his own vain wishes for a particular bride and the great felicity he imagined would accompany their wedded state. His eyes unconsciously sought the object of his yearning.

As always, Darcy could not resist the opportunity to endure that secret vice, the excruciating mix of joy and pain: looking upon Miss Elizabeth Bennet. But search as he would, he could not discover her among those gathered to witness the solemn occasion.

Where was she?

Not...not... Oh God, No! His breath caught in his throat and his blood ran cold. She was so entrancingly beautiful *coming toward the pulpit on her father's arm!*

For a fleeting moment their eyes met and he thought he saw a flash of warmth – then only anger and derision remained in her glance as her face hardened and she walked stiffly past where he sat. He knew that look, had seen it as their only dance together at the Netherfield ball came to an end. She had flung her last punishing remark about Wickham and receiving no response had walked away from him, disdaining his half-hearted attempt to lead her from the floor.

Darcy shut his eyes in mortification and bitter regret as he re-lived that moment.

His inner conflict, whether to reveal what he knew of Wickham and expose his private business to the world or continue his habitual reticence about the subject, kept him silent when he now understood he should have spoken. Or, at least, he should have asked for an opportunity to speak privately with Miss Elizabeth and her father about the predatory Wickham and the danger his immoral and nefarious ways presented to the neighbourhood.

Darcy had not spoken, however. He let her walk away believing him to have inflicted some form of cruelty on that despicable man. No doubt, Wickham being Wickham after all, the malicious lies were laid on thick. She must have heard one of Wickham's many variations on the theme of Darcy's ill usage of him by refusing to honour the bequest left to him when old Mr Darcy died.

Darcy had hoped, briefly, that Miss Elizabeth would realize the truth about Wickham – which was that he was a poseur, a charmer without substance. He was a man whose easy manners and polite bearing masked his corrupt heart and dissolute ways.

For a fleeting moment Darcy half remembered a scene in which he told her all of it – all about Wickham and his deceitful and dissolute ways – but had he actually done so? It must have been only in one of his disordered dreams.

She *might* use her uncommonly good sense to question why anyone would tell of his personal history upon so slight an acquaintance as theirs.

But of course Elizabeth had no reason to question Wickham's apparently open and good-natured disclosures. He could be very convincing in the short term.

~&~

Wide awake now and knowing he would not sleep again soon, Darcy climbed out of his bed and went to his private sitting room where he built up the fire to warm himself.

Taking up a fine crystal glass from a small table near the window, he poured himself a brandy from the elegantly god-labelled crystal decanter kept there. He swallowed half the glass in one breath-taking gulp, feeling the heat revive his heavy heart as the rich liquid spread through his tired body. Darcy refilled the glass and carried it to a side table next to his favourite chair near the fire.

He *ought* to leave Hertfordshire, lingering on at Netherfield was *folly!* Georgiana *waited* for him in London; surely she wondered why he did not come!

But he could not face her just yet, with his heart all asunder and his mind equally in disarray! In truth his head had not yet learnt to take his body away from where his heart was attached!

But this! He would *not* endure *living through her wedding* another man – especially... Oh! *God in Heaven!*

As mortifying as his dreams had been, of loving Elizabeth Bennet in every way, *this was far* more unsettling. For the first time his dream had been a dreadful nightmare!

Wrapping himself in his robe, he settled in, stretching his long legs toward the warming blaze, hoping to calm his troubled imagination.

The dark amber liquid in his glass glowed in the light of the flames as Darcy sipped slowly, letting the fine brandy roll over his tongue and down his throat in a soothing flow. Only a little calmed by the comforts thus obtained, he let his troubled thoughts return to the Netherfield ball.

No, Darcy had not spoken. He had made no effort to correct her ill-advised opinion of him. Instead he had sternly reminded himself that the vast difference in their circumstances required that he allow her to fade from his mind. Her displeasure with him would surely support the greatest distance between them should they ever meet again. He owed his sister, Georgiana, his more distant family and connections, his social peers – even the many tenants and servants on his great estate – a bride whose own status and accomplishments were at least equal to his own. They expected it of him. It was his responsibility. And Darcy never shirked his responsibilities.

Thus he reasoned with himself as he closed his mind to it. His resolution must carry him, based upon what he knew to be just and fair, he would not quail nor shrink from his duty; he would not falter before the dreary and cheerless future stretching out before him without her.

Indeed, he took it upon himself to assist Miss Bingley in guiding her brother, his friend, away from his flourishing romance with Miss Jane Bennet. He did not believe Miss Bennet's heart was engaged; with a mother like that, he assured himself – and later his friend, it was not difficult to imagine that Miss Bennet was guided more by her mother's demands than her own inclination.

A union between his good friend Charles Bingley and Jane Bennet under such circumstances would be unconscionable. Furthermore it would prolong and reignite his own agony every time he and Bingley met in the future for Miss Elizabeth was certain to be a part of Jane Bennet's closest circle at every gathering. It was well understood that the two eldest Bennet sisters were very close indeed!

Still, he was relieved that thus far they had only sought to convince, to persuade his friend away from Miss Bennet. They had not acted upon the elaborate ruse that Miss Bingley had devised. Darcy's discomfort with her ideas was extreme. Disguise of every sort was his abhorrence.

Slowly his eyelids drooped and he fell asleep in his chair.

TWELVE
Nightmares Reveal Darcy's Choice

His heart ached as he turned to watch Miss Elizabeth Bennet arrival at Mr Collins' side. *By God she was beautiful!*

She stood calmly, dressed in a simple cream-colored gown of some soft material that clung to her shape as its modest design covered her completely from shoulder to wrist - and *uncommonly* high neckline to the floor. How did she choose such an outmoded style? It was as if she were attempting to disguise her comeliness... ah, she was marrying *Collins!* She could not welcome ... *Oh, dear God!* He could not bear to think it!

She ought to be *HIS* bride! His mind shifted and he was lost to her once again.

He could not pull his eyes away as he savoured the sight of her elegant form so sweetly outlined by her flowing gown. Under a lacy suggestion of bonnet, her thick dark auburn hair was swept back into a classic chignon with a few loose curls around her face and on her slender neck. How his fingers ached to touch them, to tangle themselves into her lovely hair until his hands cupped her head and tilted her face to his! He imagined the joy he would feel when her fine eyes gazed into his, filled with delight and desire! She would smile at him, a tender intimate smile; *a smile full of love only for him.* How heavenly it would feel to have those slender arms wrapped around his neck, her body pressed to his, her mouth whispering his name against his lips!

He wanted her fiercely!

He shuddered as his entire body responded to her. *He strove desperately* to suppress the moan rising from his chest; the flush to his face; and the arousal below.

This would not, could not, do! He must not feel thusly for the bride of another; *Miss Elizabeth Bennet must not be the bride of another!*

~&~

Darcy awoke with a start. He was half reclining in his chair by the now nearly-extinguished fire in his own sitting room at Netherfield, where he had come to escape his earlier nightmare. The glass of brandy, still a quarter full, rested against his chest, held semi-upright by his rumpled robe.

Darcy drained the glass in one gulp, carefully set it down on the table, and stretched to ease his cramped muscles.

Awakening in the fullness of his passionate desire for Elizabeth and caught, if only by himself, in such a flagrant state of arousal, invariably shocked and deeply embarrassed him.

He was helpless against his need to love Miss Elizabeth Bennet, with his whole self: mind, *body*, and soul.

Wakeful awareness of the impropriety of his desires quickly cooled the ardour of his dream. He rose and walked to the window where he stood for some time, staring at nothing more than his own weary visage reflected in the glass against the darkness of the predawn hour.

Exhausted from weeks of insufficient sleep, Darcy picked up the decanter and again filled his glass. Gulping that down, he refilled it again and then carried it and the decanter back to the table near the fire.

Taking up the poker, he brought the half-burnt logs back to a steady blaze and once again settled himself in his chair.

Night after night Darcy had faced his lonely vigil, dreading sleep for its betrayal of rest, and growing more hollow-eyed and grim-faced with each succeeding day.

Bleary-eyed from drink and exhaustion, he knew only that he must find some rest! In that state it seemed reasonable to him that he should drink so much that he could not stop himself from the release of slumber. So drink he did, until he knew no more.

~&~

What a blasted fool he was!

Darcy realized that all along he had arrogantly accepted *his* power of choice. He *chose* to be resolute and dutiful and…. He *could* have chosen *her*; he could have chosen to renounce the duties and demands of station and rank. *They* did not feed and clothe him. The *ton* and its strictures on place and position did not support the roof over his and Georgiana's heads. His ridiculous fears of harming Georgiana's prospects with a marriage considered beneath him were without actual justification. The significance of her ample dowry aside, he was certain that more than one worthy gentleman was sure to find his beautiful little sister's intelligent, sweet disposition as irresistible as he found Miss Elizabeth Bennet's; *No, Mrs Collins?*

Good God! He had been free to follow his heart all along but had stubbornly refused to acknowledge the truth until it might truly be too late. He had nearly let her pass him by without the slightest effort to secure her!

And his self-centred choice had left his beloved with none but to marry Mr Collins.

She had never had the luxury of *choice* in determining her future, only the power to refuse… but for what alternative? How was she to deny her family the comfort of knowing their future secure? And what consolation would she have to look forward to if she had?

Now, unless he acted boldly, he truly had lost all! The *gift* of choice in the most important matter in his life was irrevocably and forever forfeit!

Moaning in his stupor, and only barely aware of his physical discomfort, Darcy shifted in his chair and lost himself again in the busy world of his dreams.

~&~

Try as he might, Fitzwilliam Darcy could not quite make out Charles Bingley's scrawled missive. It was not only that Bingley's hand was so atrocious. It was always writ so rapidly as to leave the letters carelessly splotched and incompletely formed. The man's letters were often nearly indecipherable.

This time, however, the letters and words appeared to shift and change, dividing and again merging to present only nonsensical shapes before his eyes. The more he strove to make it out, the more the exact words of the letter resisted his perusal and the more his distress reduced his ability to focus on it.

Yet as his eyes refused to receive the written language, his comprehension of its message improved until he was struck with the stunning clarity of it!

Darcy's breath left his body as he doubled over with a shock as great as if he had been punched in his belly!

Miss Elizabeth Bennet had married Mr Collins! *What? Oh dear God, No!*

He looked again at the pitiful scribbling.

No! They were not yet wed! They were to marry this very morning and would depart for Hunsford after a small wedding breakfast at Longbourn.

"Enough! I will not allow it! I know what I must do!" Darcy's voice came out hoarse and much more weakly than he expected when he put the words in motion. Of course the thought which drove him had its origins in the dream-state, while the actual pronouncement formed both part of, and the instigation of, his waking up.

To say that this awakening caused Fitzwilliam Darcy to be surprised, even shocked, would be to understate the condition of his mind. For his dreams still tumbled about in his scattered thoughts and feelings, confusing him mightily.

Darcy was accustomed to relying upon his own rigid self-command, even in the wake of many sleepless nights such as he had suffered of late. He was extremely discomfited, therefore, to discover the workings of his mind to be so vastly disoriented and scattered on this particular morning. Evidently the harsh after-effects of heavy drink, merciless dreams, and extreme fatigue had momentarily stopped him in his tracks.

Lifting his shoulders and straightening his spine, he was grateful that his valet had not yet come to him, although he could be heard in the dressing room making preparations for Darcy's morning ablutions.

Determined he must not be observed, even by Perkins, his most intimate servant, in his current condition, Darcy demanded of himself that he be firm in regaining his countenance and his clarity of mind forthwith!

He rose and began to pace the room.

Foggily he forced himself to review what he actually knew.

He was in his room at Charles Bingley's leasehold, Netherfield Park.

The hour must be rather late in the morning – if not early in the afternoon.

This was the morning after the ball his friend Bingley had held at the behest of the neighbourhood and, more particularly, the youngest Bennet sister, Miss Lydia Bennet.

It was unlikely that Miss Elizabeth Bennet could have married that ridiculous parson, Mr Collins – yet.

He, Fitzwilliam Darcy, could not allow such a thing to happen.

"Enough! I will not allow it! I know what I must do!" Those were the words he had spoken when he was half awake but from the insight of his dream-state. What did they mean? What must he do? He tried to remember the part in the dream where his purpose became clear. He could not.

He checked his stride when his trusted valet, knocked lightly and peeked around the door to his dressing room.

Knowing that everyone was likely to be tired after such a late night, he might indulge himself with a tray in his room rather than going down to breakfast. That would allow him a little time to think – and recover.

He greeted Perkins gruffly and asked him to send for a breakfast tray. "And be sure to request plenty of strong coffee." He thought to include: "I shall want the coffee before I bathe."

"Yes sir, I will keep your bath hot until you are ready for it, sir." Perkins left the room quietly to carry out Mr Darcy's orders.

It had taken only one swift glance to note that his master had slept very ill indeed. Rarely had he seen Mr Darcy so thoroughly out of sorts.

Mr Darcy did not drink to excess, nor did he indulge in any of the private bed-chamber entertainments that some other gentlemen did.

Perkins *had* been aware that something seemed to be troubling his master enough to disturb his sleep. It must have begun around the same time as they had arrived at Netherfield. The dreadful state of the bedclothes each morning and the increasing weariness in Mr Darcy's face had worried him of late. He was at all times intensely loyal to Darcy and would not think of speaking to anyone of his master's ragged state this morning.

It was almost as if Mr Darcy were in love, he mused to himself. He could think of no other explanation. Miss Georgiana was safely established at Darcy House in London with her excellent companion, Mrs Amesley. And there had been no urgent missives from either of them, so it could not be another problem such as the one poor Mr Darcy had discovered and unravelled earlier in the summer. There had been no express from Pemberley...

Was Mr Darcy in love? "*Dear heaven!*" he said under his breath, "Please let him *not* be in love with the scheming Miss Caroline Bingley!" He knew that *that woman* would make Darcy's life a living hell once she got her claws into all that he represented. All of her fawning attention to his master did not disguise the calculation in her eye before the servants. Her behaviour before *them*, her *treatment* of *them,* told another story - of her haughty nature and cold disposition.

Perkins could think of no other explanation for his master's recent disequilibrium. And he could think of no other young woman in the neighbourhood whose condition in life would qualify her for his romantic attentions.

Well, if that were the case, he knew that he must take steps to ensure that nothing came of such an undesirable infatuation! He did not know what he might do, but he knew he must do something. He would think on it. And he did, continuously, as he went about his duties that day and for days afterward.

THIRTEEN
First, a Wild Ride

"I know what I must do!" The words churned in Darcy's mind.

What must he do?

What did he *know*?

Nothing about his dilemma had changed except that, as a result of his awful dreams, a solution was more urgent than ever.

Perkins had brought his coffee and after downing the first scalding hot cup, he sat sipping the next while attempting to plumb his fast-fading dreams and soothe his overwrought spirits in a hot bath.

In his dream he had understood something that he could not now clearly recall.

Surely she would not agree to marry that disgustingly pompous parson!

Surely her father would not consent to such an unequal match of sense and sensibility!

Despite his repeated determinations to go about his life and forget her, he knew that he could not.

Especially he could not bear the notion of her being Mrs Collins! Why, every time he made his annual Easter visit to his Aunt, Lady Catherine de Bourgh, there she would be. There she would be with her housewife's cap covering those lovely curls, and a screaming infant on her hip... No, he could *not* bear it!

But, could he bear the thought of her marrying anyone other than himself? Some worthy gentleman – who would have husbandly rights to do everything with her that had so fired his, Fitzwilliam Darcy's imagination and inspired his dreams? Perhaps, so long as there was no *existent* "worthy gentleman" at the ready and no "worthy gentleman" of corporeal face – and hands – to *fulfil* the possibility.

His mind made a rapid retreat from that line of thought.

Despairing and at his wit's end, he wondered what it was that he *must* do!

~&~

When Perkins brought his dressing gown, he automatically climbed out of the bath. Darcy was scarcely aware of his valet seating him in the dressing room, shaving him, and dressing him in his most comfortable pair of breeches, a shirt, and slippers. When he was dressed he sat down near the window and absently picked at the food on the tray Perkins had placed there.

If only his father were alive! It would have been difficult but Darcy might have brought himself to ask for advice from the man who had his utmost admiration for excellent judgment.

Equally important to Darcy, his parents' marriage had been a very happy one, filled with love and affection. He remembered well his father's delight in teasing him to laugh aloud with his parents in the privacy of their home.

Father would have a thorough grasp of all aspects of the circumstances – and could have been relied upon for partisanship in his favour. But Howard Darcy had died more than five years past; hence the necessity of his own guardianship of young Georgiana Darcy.

And, hence the dilemma!

His father certainly had taught him much of duty and expectation, position and responsibility. Had he merely assumed that his son's heart would find its true love among the young ladies of the *ton*? Could his proud and loving father have countenanced the departure from society's expectations that was now under his consideration? How would Georgiana be affected if he chose to follow his heart? Could she marry well if he married so far beneath himself; could she love and accept Miss Elizabeth Bennet as her sister?

Dear Georgiana, he felt such a deep and abiding sense of responsibility that at times he almost forgot to simply love her in his earnest focus on her present and future well-being. How would she feel about having a woman from a lesser sphere as her sister? Would she see beyond her condition in life to the enchanting, witty, loving, kind and generous woman that was Miss Elizabeth Bennet? What *would* his sweet Georgie wish him to do?

Shy as she was, Georgiana had found her own gentle ways to hint to him that she desired very much to have a sister, for his happiness and her own. She would occasionally remark on the very quietude of their home, or the likelihood that some of the décor could use a fresh bit of lace, or colour – but that she didn't expect *him* to notice such things.

Once she came right out with her eagerness for him to marry, saying: "I hope I am not yet out and plagued with societal demands on my time and attention when you finally bring home a bride for yourself and a sister for me!" Before he could overcome his surprise, she ran blushing from the room begging to be excused as she went. Later, very embarrassed and looking at the floor, she apologized for her outburst. Darcy had not known what to say, so he simply reminded her that such behaviour was unbecoming of a young lady and that he expected better of her in the future.

Soon after that incident Georgian had carefully implied that her wishes for a sister did not include Caroline Bingley, no matter that the woman worked so very hard to ingratiate herself with her.

After a brief discussion in his study regarding her music lessons she had something more on her mind. Apologizing and looking away, she asked: "Does Miss Bingley lack acquaintance in London?" When Darcy enquired why she would think so, she replied: "It is only that she seems to be... she *spends so much time with me*, who am not yet out and who can have nothing to offer of the news of the *ton*, or discussion of balls or any of the entertainments that you and your friends are accustomed to attend. It is something of puzzlement to me, what she finds in me to draw her admiration and attention so." She faced him with a sly sparkle in her bright blue eyes as she spoke the last bit.

Darcy could barely stop the chuckle that welled up in his throat at her words. He turned his head to look out of the window as he replied: "Miss Bingley must find your musical accomplishments much to her taste I suppose."

"Perhaps, brother, but between ourselves might not she use her time more fruitfully in pursuing the good opinion of other young women of her own age – as you so often have advised me to do?"

"Georgiana, you overreach yourself!" But he did not conceal his broad smile from her this time.

Yes, she was nearly a young woman, and obviously increasing rapidly in her understanding of the world. But...she could not be expected to act as his confidante!

This was nonsense, he could not, and would not, lay his private pain and dreams open to his baby sister. She was only now about to turn sixteen years of age. It was of vital importance to him that she be pleased, that she find friendship and a loving bond with the woman he brought home as his bride. But he could not properly ask for her opinion on matters which were, and should be, beyond her experience and knowledge - as well as far too private to be discussed between them.

Another man, then; was there someone within his closest circle that he could turn to?

Obviously Bingley would be the worst choice. He was clearly smitten with Miss Jane Bennet, Miss Elizabeth's eldest sister. Bingley would probably brush off all of Darcy's concerns and suggest a double wedding!

Cousin Richard, Colonel Richard Fitzwilliam was a little older, experienced in the world, and invariably ready to be his best friend. And, he was co-guardian of Georgiana so he would certainly consider her best interests in this as thoroughly as Darcy would wish.

But Richard, at thirty, was as yet unmarried. His time between military duties was spent playing the gallant, enjoying the company of many fine ladies. Darcy wondered if he would be able to understand how significant *one particular woman* could be to a man.

Setting that avenue of speculation aside for a moment, Darcy considered his uncle.

Uncle Kedrick, the Earl of Matlock was his nearest male relative of his father's generation. He was a proud and dignified man whose expectations of lofty principles, honour, and fastidious adherence to propriety were equally applied to himself as to those whose lives were connected to his own. The Earl was also unbending in his consciousness of rank.

Darcy's specific reservations and innate reticence would make it next to impossible for him to unburden himself to any of them, and none other even entered the list.

He must get away, completely away from Hertfordshire, and sort this out on his own. He would consult no other, only his own unfettered reasoning – away from the constant distraction of *her* nearness in the neighbourhood.

Yes, Darcy knew that Bingley had left early this morning for London, expecting to return within a few days. He would follow tomorrow morning, meet with Bingley in London and excuse himself from Netherfield for an indefinite period. He would not be able to return until "important business" was resolved.

He would keep himself away until he could be certain of *what he must do."*

~&~

Having an immediate plan of action relieved Darcy's strained sensibilities to some extent.

He informed his valet of his intent and was quickly dressed for riding in a snowy white linen shirt and simply tied cravat, a waistcoat of forest green with fine pinstripes of grey under a darker green riding coat lined in the same material as the waistcoat. He wore dark grey breeches and black Hessians.

Perkins finished tugging on Darcy's tall boots, handed over his hat, gloves, and riding crop, opened the door and stood back. He knew his master well. He had served him ever since young Darcy first went up to Cambridge – quite wet behind the ears and quite determined to fulfil his father's every expectation of him. Today his urgency to be away was palpable, may it bring him some ease.

Darcy hurried down the staircase without thought of the other inhabitants of Netherfield. He was determined to work out his physical distress with a vigorous ride on his favourite mount, Zephyros – aptly named for the Greek god of the west wind.

"Why, Mr Darcy! Where are you off to in such a hurry? Can you not spare a little time to join us at tea before you dash out of sight?" Caroline Bingley, forgotten in his preoccupation with his plans, had caught him out.

She offered him a smile of calculated sweetness belied by the sharp expression in her narrowed green eyes as she stepped forward from her position near the bottom of the stairs to take his arm. She was dressed in a gown far too fine for a quiet day after a ball, and far too orange for the comfort of his eyes!

Suppressing a groan, Darcy halted in front of her, his face set in its most austere expression, while he peeled her hand off of his arm. "I apologize, Miss Bingley. I had a tray in my room earlier. I wish to enjoy a ride in the countryside while the light is good and the rain holds off. Please excuse me."

With a quick bow in her direction, he continued on his way, striding swiftly out of the room and out of the house.

Caroline Bingley stood still for some minutes looking after him. Finally she stamped her foot, turned with a huff and disappeared into the sitting room with an angry orange swirl of her skirts.

Had she looked out of the window in the sitting room; she would have observed the mad flurry of Darcy and his horse galloping at breakneck speed across the field toward Oakham Mount.

FOURTEEN
As Jane Sees It

"Lizzy! *Lizzy!* Wake up dear, you are having a nightmare!"

"*Oh, my dearest Jane! Oh, Thank God you are here!*" Lizzy cried out. "Please tell me it is all untrue!"

"What is untrue, dearest? I assure you that if you refer to the content of your bad dream, it most likely is *not* true!" Jane was ready to laugh along with her dear sister at the folly of her taking fright at a mere dream!

Seeing Lizzy's trembling and tears stopped her in surprise. Instead she suggested "Tell me about it my dear Lizzy. It will help you release your distress more quickly if you speak of it aloud."

Lizzy did calm as she described her ordeal to her beloved confidante.

"No dear, you did not marry Mr Collins! Heaven above, I can't imagine our dear father allowing such a thing!" Jane's gentle smile and reassuring words did not betray her uneasiness about their mother's part in Lizzy's plight.

Mamá *did* sometimes get her way after she had besieged her husband loudly enough and long enough to exhaust his façade of imperviousness. She pushed the thought away. She trusted their parents to allow Lizzy to decide on her own future.

"Jane, Mamá *does* insist so! And I am fully aware that my accepting him would, once and for all, resolve her dreadful worries about all of our futures if Papá should leave us before any are married well."

"Lizzy! No such thing will happen! Mamá only allows her fears to lead her good sense astray. It will all turn out well, you will see."

And heaven forbid, she thought, that anyone should have to sacrifice their own best good for the security of the family!

"Oh, Jane, I could not bear it – I could not *live*, married to Mr Collins!"

"Dear Lizzy, I do not believe he has quite *asked* you yet – although he *has* more than hinted at it I agree. But perhaps you will contrive to avoid him until he must return to Hunsford. He was only to be with us for a fortnight, and that is more than half gone already. That would be a great laugh would it not?"

"I confess I heard him talking to Mamá about having a few moments alone with me in the morning, he having something *particular* to ask me."

"Well, he is *out* there! I do believe it will be well past noon before any of us venture downstairs after such a late and eventful night."

"Dear Jane, thank you with all of my heart for being so wonderfully you! You have nearly got me laughing at myself... nearly."

"You must think of it no more. Twas only a nightmare, of course, and cannot happen in your waking state. If it helps you rest, dear Lizzy, I promise that I will *not allow* it to come true! There, does that ease your mind?"

Jane sat with Lizzy, stroking her hair and reassuring her until she saw that she had drifted off at last.

Then she slipped into her own bed, just a few feet away from Lizzy's, and tired again to find rest from her own uncertainties.

If Mr Bingley did not declare himself, if he only enjoyed her company as a diversion while he was away from Town...., it may be necessary for *one* of us to marry that prattling preacher. *Stop it Jane!*

~&~

Jane's knees were so weak that she could barely stand.

Mrs Bennet nodded with satisfaction. "Yes, I always said that you were not so beautiful for nothing! Now you have saved the family from starving in the hedgerows. Mr Collins liked you first in any event. I am so happy that Lizzy's foolishness did not deter him entirely from choosing among you for his future happiness – and our present and future benefit!"

"*Mother!*" Jane's shock at being literally thrown to the wolf – to keep the wolves from the door... What *was* that saying?

"Mother, *I cannot! Please do not* ask it of me! He is *not* to my liking, mother! You have always promised me that I would be able to pick and choose from all of the fine gentlemen; the very wealthy; the handsome gentlemen! Oh, where is my father?"

"Nonsense, my girl! You will do as you are told. Mr Collins is most amiable and his condition in life will only improve and so will yours – and ours thereby. Your father will not interfere. He knows this is the best thing for us all. *He* certainly has done nothing to protect us from that dreadful entail – although why he has not I cannot, for the life of me, comprehend."

"No mamá, I, I, I *will not!*"

"*What!*"

In her haste to rush away from her mother's awful countenance, Jane tripped over something on the floor just behind her, and fell heavily upon it. Struggling desperately to get up, to find the only person whom she could trust to be sensible (and partisan in her behalf), she heard her own dear Lizzy crying out: "*No! I will not!* Get *off* of me!"

In panic, Jane's eyes flew open. *What?* She could see the morning sunshine peeking in around the drawn curtains. She was lying on the floor - on top of Lizzy in fact!

This would not do! Lizzy looked as shocked and frightened as Jane felt. The marks of tears streaked her pale face and Jane could feel the wetness still upon her own cheeks.

"I had a fearful nightmare about..." Jane began

"I... cannot marry Mr Collins!" Lizzy said at the same time.

They stared at each other in surprise, and then they both began to giggle. The giggles turned to great gulps of laughter, and they held on to each other as if for dear life! They laughed together until they were both in tears, but calmed.

"Jane, you are feeling it as well?"

"Oh my, Lizzy, is Mr Bingley in earnest, or am I only wishful thinking? I do not know, and there is a doubt piercing my heart that - that he will never declare himself. I... feel so much..."

"Dear Jane, beautiful sweet Jane! Of course he loves you! Of course he will declare himself! He only needs a little time to sort himself out; you will see."

Jane looked down at their clasped hands, "I do hope so. I suppose I am only worrying because he has gone to London today." Her voice was soft and then with more vigour she looked up and went on: "You see what we are doing? We are thinking like our mother! Oh dear! I should not have said that." But there was a twinkle in her eyes even as she clapped her hand to her mouth.

"And *that* is enough to make me determined to forsake any hope of further sleep. I can have no peaceful rest in any event. I shall go for a nice long walk. That will relieve my distress and keep Mr Collins at bay!"

"I shall help you avoid him as you make your escape! But first let us share a breakfast tray and some hot coffee as we prepare ourselves for the day. I believe that I shall be inclined after that to take some time alone in the garden. Perhaps I shall finish gathering the lavender and rosemary to dry. You may help me tie them up after you return from your exercise. We shall neither of us *wilt* under the trials that beset us!"

"Tying up herbs will be just the thing after a brisk walk to clear my head and loosen my tense muscles"

"Take care not to go too far, Lizzy. It is hardly seemly for a young woman to walk far from her home alone." Jane teased.

It was Lizzy's way to walk until her spirits were calmed. She always returned fresh-faced and cheery, with a bright glow in her lovely eyes.

"Yes, Jane dearest. I will go no farther than Oakham Mount."

"Lizzy! Oakham Mount is quite a distance from Longbourn!" Jane worried a little, and besides, she wanted her dear confidante. They still had much to discuss!

FIFTEEN
Elizabeth and Jane Adjust Their Thoughts

A good deal of Lizzy's agitation had dissipated during her furious march along the tranquil country lanes on the way to Oakham Mount. She had not in fact, actually reached that destination at first, having turned off on a much loved path which brought her to a secluded glade crossed by a tiny but swift-moving brook.

Seating herself on a boulder warmed enough by the mid-morning sun to allow for her comfort she watched the tumbling of the brook, and enjoyed the pastoral scene around her. Lizzy took time to find some humour in her situation and finally to release her nightmares to the soft breeze that played through her curls and tempted a few more colourful leaves to drift down from the trees now clothed in their early autumn splendour.

She need not fear Mr Collins; he was of a nature that could be easily managed – and refused – or turned aside. "Hmmm... Who among my sisters might be pleased to accept his suit? Perhaps Mary..." She mused aloud.

His patroness, Lady Catherine de Bourgh, was nothing to *her* and neither could she have any interest in Miss Elizabeth Bennet. "Use your *whip* to cool your porridge and save your strength to swell your coffers, you *interfering* old woman!" Lizzy chuckled to herself.

Mamá *was* a problem though, and one Lizzy had hitherto striven regularly to solve, to no avail. This was a matter for consultation with Jane.

Surely Papá would never leave her unprotected from her mother's machinations, though! Lizzy resolved to disregard their customary mutual reticence on the subject of her prospects and speak to him directly on the subject; hopefully to receive his unqualified reassurance!

She would not think just now about her oddly tumultuous feelings regarding Mr Darcy! Of all things, she *could not* be sure whether their confrontation at the Netherfield ball had occurred in reality or simply as part of her ordeal by nightmare. A *most* disquieting state of things to be sure!

~&~

While her sister was thus engaged, Jane moved quietly about the house seeing to various matters which had fallen more and more to her lot as her mother "trained" her in the management of a household. "Your Mr Bingley will expect you to know what you are about when you become mistress of Netherfield, my dear."

Mamá, he is not *my* Mr Bingley. Indeed, he has gone to London presently and, although he has said he shall return within a few days, perhaps he will be distracted by the many entertainments to be encountered there – especially for a young single man of good fortune – and may not return for some time, if at all. We must guard ourselves against dwelling overmuch upon too high expectations *there*, and curb our *public* enthusiasm while we remain in want of a declaration by anyone." Truly Jane *did* allude to her most acutely heartfelt concerns, however mildly she spoke them.

"Nonsense, Jane; Mr Bingley is *smitten* for sure. He will return from Town quicker than you can say 'Jack Robinson'!"

Turning from Jane dismissively her mother went on: "Now, *where* is that *ungrateful Lizzy!* I *desire* her presence at once! Mr Collins cannot be expected to forever be cooling his heels while she heedlessly prances about in her wild way. How *ever* did I produce such a wilful, disobedient daughter – and one *so lacking* in feminine charms? Never mind, I insist that she present herself this minute to Mr Collins, who awaits her in the sitting room, and *do* her duty. They will do very well for each other and our home shall remain in the family."

Already having experienced far more distress in the past dozen or so hours than she could reasonably expect to endure in a month of Sundays, Jane did not incur more of the same by contradicting her mother about Lizzy, or the likelihood that Lizzy and Mr Collins would "do very well for each other".

Instead she stepped into the front hallway where she quickly donned her spencer, bonnet, and gardening gloves. Picking up an old but serviceable and capacious basket, Jane slipped away to the herb garden where she began to snip and sort among the aromatic produce there in a more than usually desultory fashion.

"'Jack Robinson' indeed!" She mumbled to herself. "Mamá! You are *too optimistic* by half! I concede that Mr Charles Bingley is a most amiable and gentlemanly - and handsome young man. And I do like him very much. I have nothing but the highest esteem for his character and good nature; and I cannot doubt the earnestness of his regard for me – *in the moment of its expression and within the confines of its rightful prospect*. I, however, cannot mislead myself as to what little I can offer him as a suitable choice for marriage. I have only very modest accomplishments and no dowry to speak of, and Miss Caroline Bingley has been so kind as to make it most apparent to me that our connections are not at all of the kind that a person of any status in society would celebrate. No, I am quite sure that he values me as his friend but must look to more fortunate Misses to share his future happiness."

It did occur to Jane in her musings that at least the awful suggestion contained within this morning's nightmare could be put aside. Mrs Bennet had made no allusion to a possible match between her eldest daughter and the *odious*, and occasionally overly perfumed and odoriferous Mr Collins. Mamá remained well satisfied that Mr Bingley would soon request an interview with Mr Bennet in order to make a particular request regarding their eldest daughter...

Still, what if things took a turn for the worse and her mother began to doubt Mr Bingley's constancy? Would she then, in light of Lizzy's recalcitrance in the matter, focus upon Jane as the more compliant one? Perhaps she, Jane, had better stop her outward protests against her mother's exasperating insistence on Mr Bingley's future intentions toward herself - however painfully untrue *she* might fear them to be.

"I will *not*, however, *ever* consent to marry that ridiculously clumsy, conceited, and condescending Mr Collins even to relieve our mother's nerves!" She spoke those words softly but more than a little vehemently. *Stop it*, Jane!

With a sigh, Jane wished Lizzy would hurry back to join her. It felt as if she had been gone for hours. Jane *needed* her sister's lively wit to help her laugh herself out the doldrums! She would be so very happy to resume her customary serene trust in the ultimate rightness of the world and its inhabitants.

SIXTEEN
Encounter on Oakham Mount

Lizzy could not bring herself to forego the short walk farther along the way to Oakham Mount; despite that she *had* been some time at the brook-side and Jane awaited her return to Longbourn and a *highly anticipated* confidential conversation.

Ignoring her remorse on Jane's behalf she hastened on, reasoning that her spirits would be just that much *more* improved by the pleasure of the additional exercise.

Before very long she began the steep ascent up the rough trail. Climbing briskly, she revelled in the physical exertion which always presaged a calming of her mind. At the summit she would be able to see nearly all of the surrounding community of farms, woods, and even much of Meryton with the old church at its centre. Longbourn was situated on the other side from her favourite resting spot and out of her view – which suited her mood perfectly on that particular day.

Soon she had come within a short distance of a rock outcropping which jutted out, causing a sharp turn in the trail near the top.

To her dismay she heard the sound of a horse making its way in her direction from above. It was a rare occurrence to meet with anyone on that little-used trail. Yet someone was certainly using it now and very nearly upon her, from the sound of it.

Lizzy looked for a safe place to step aside and let the horseman pass, or possibly to hide herself from view and thus to avoid unwanted attention if she could do so quickly. Alas, the rocks and brush at that point along the side of the trail were dense and somewhat forbidding. She stood hesitating, just a moment too long.

Just as the horse and rider appeared around the curve of the trail Lizzy made an undignified scramble far enough into some brambles to allow them to pass. Startled, the horse shied, unseating its rider who saved himself by dropping easily to the ground. Holding fast to the reins he began to soothe his mount almost before he landed, rather gracefully, just in front of the spot where Lizzy stood blushing in mortification.

"Miss *Bennet*! I hope you..."

"Mr *Darcy*! I am so..."

"Please, Miss Bennet, I must ask; are you well? You are not injured in any way?" His heart was still pounding from the abruptness of the event. No, it was because he was so close to *her*, looking upon *her* flushed face, *alone* with *her*!

"No sir, I am not injured; only a bit surprised to find anyone up here at this time of year. Indeed this trail is not much used at any time of the year." She knew she was rambling to cover her discomposure at meeting the very person whose presence served to confuse and disturb her so severely.

"But *you*, sir; I am so sorry to startle your horse! And you rather... came off... are you unhurt; and, and, your horse, as well?" *Stop it* Lizzy!

"I am so very sorry! Please accept my apology for ..." For *what* exactly? She glanced up to his face, smiling uncertainly and trembling from the fright. The shock of meeting his intense gaze nearly made her gasp aloud. No, the trembling was from her nearness to *him*. It was from finding herself *alone* with *him*!

For a long moment they simply stood looking into each other's eyes. Neither spoke nor moved while they each strove to find their voices and regain their equilibrium.

Elizabeth finally looked away. "Well, sir, I fear you may have been injured after all! Either your mind has been addled by your, er, rapid descent from your horse, or a feral cat has made off with your tongue without our noticing it!" She gave a shaky laugh: "For you have not yet answered my questions, sir."

"I beg your pardon? Oh! I am quite well, thank you, and so is Zephyros." At her questioning look he added: "Zephyros is my horse."

"Oh."

Seeing her trembling still, he moved to her side and held out his hand to her. "*You* are not well, Miss Bennet. Please allow me to rescue you from the clutches of your most inhospitable location."

"I thank you, sir. I believe I am quite able to remove myself from this position in the same way that I attained it." Lizzy felt a bit breathless at the thought of grasping his hand. She quickly disentangled her gown from the prickly brambles and stepped toward the trail, then immediately found herself swaying on a wobbly rock.

With a twinkle in his eye Darcy gently grasped her arm to steady her and guide her safely back to the trail as he offered "Let our continued discourse reassure you, the cat has gone hunting elsewhere for its satisfaction today. As for my mind being addled, I am quite sure it is true, though not from any physical injury."

As she stepped past him onto the trail he breathed deeply of her delicious scent. It was one of his forbidden pleasures – that delicate yet faintly astringent aroma of lavender. It must be a decoction of her own making as the lavender worn sometimes by his aunt, Lady Matlock, did not exude the dash of liveliness he detected in Miss Elizabeth Bennet's.

~&~

His mood had altered as his heart and body responded to her nearness. His eyes darkened, his glance was once again unreadable but the corners of his mouth lifted in a tentative smile. "There you are, safe and sound. I hope you will pardon my forwardness Miss Bennet. I only hoped to prevent any further mishap today."

His close proximity assailed her senses with the tangy scents of horse and leather mixed with his own preferred wash of sandalwood.

"Yes. Thank you again, Mr Darcy. I should have taken more care." Her voice was low and throaty with embarrassment. She looked down at his hand still clasping her arm. "I do believe I may be trusted to stand on my own now, sir!" She flashed him a bright smile as she said it, hoping desperately that he would *unhand* her and *step away*!

She was convinced her face must be as bright red as Sir Lucas' nose when that worthy gentleman had been drinking! She felt nearly bereft of self-command and utterly devoid of dignity – mortified in the extreme!

"I beg your pardon, Miss Bennet!" He released her arm immediately and all but leapt backward in his anxiety to relieve her obvious distress. What a *dolt* I am! She must think me the *worst* kind of barbarian! Where are your fine manners *now*, Mr Darcy? He berated himself. What in the world has come over you that you cannot conduct yourself properly around *her* at all? He was momentarily unable to do more than struggle mightily to conceal his discomposure.

Well, perhaps not *that* far, Mr Darcy, I find myself most unsettled by my ambivalence toward you! Despite the extreme disconcertion of my sprits when you are near, I did rather l*ike* the sensation of your hand on my arm and your eyes fixed on me *in that... way*! Oh, well...

"I bid you good day, sir." She said aloud.

Darcy saw her start to move away, up the trail toward the summit. Desperate to prolong their meeting, and hoping to redeem himself at least a little in her eyes, Darcy knew he could do nothing other than speak forthrightly to her and rely upon her good nature and common sense to accept his honest words without offense.

"Miss Bennet, if you plan to continue on to the summit, would you be willing to accept me as your escort? It is not much farther and... I would very much *like to* return there with you."

"Mr Darcy, I have visited Oakham Mount many times and do not require an escort to do so again."

He felt his heart drop when she paused, but then she continued: "However Oakham Mount is available to any person who takes the trouble to make the ascent to it, and if, perchance, we were to be traveling there at the same time, I can think of no impediment to our doing so in company with one another." Her shy smile was brightened by the flash of amusement in her fine eyes.

"Thank you, Miss Bennet." Taking his horse's reins he fell into step beside her, Zephyros following along behind them.

They continued in silence for the short time it took to reach their destination. Once there it seemed quite natural for them to take their seats side by side, but with space enough for another person to sit between them, on the flat rock of Lizzy's habitual use.

"Pardon me, sir but I was convinced that you... that the entire Netherfield company had departed for London this morning"

"No indeed, Miss Bennet, Bingley has gone there on some matter of business but I had not thought to do so."

"Oh, I am confused, sir." Lizzy blinked and shook her head slightly as if to clear her vision, or her mind.

After a short pause, during which Darcy wondered how she could have divined the subject of his own ambiguity – the notion Caroline Bingley had put forward of their entire party removing to London in order to separate Charles from Miss Bennet, he set the question aside and went straight to the point of his immediate concern.

"May we speak for a moment of the subject of our ... discourse at the Netherfield ball, Miss Bennet?"

"I fear I shall lose my present enjoyment to the great regret and humiliation that such remembrance inspires in me, Mr Darcy. May we not simply enjoy the day and think of the past only as its recollection provides our pleasure?" Several delicate curls around her face and along her neck, having escaped their pinning and the confines of her bonnet quivered deliciously in the gentle updraft perpetual at the crest of Oakham Mount.

Manfully wresting his gaze from her curls' sweet dance, Darcy forged ahead. "It is not my wish to pain you in any way, Miss Bennet. I only desired to beg your pardon for my harsh and unpleasant behaviour on that dreadful occasion! It was most ungentlemanly of me and I very much regret behaving so!"

"Sir, how can I hold *your* conduct at fault when my own was *far worse?* If you truly feel you require my pardon, it is fully yours. I can hardly expect *your* forgiveness for my rude and impertinent manners toward yourself – including forming such ill-judged opinions on the word of a despicable scoundrel!" Lizzy's confusion over which *memory* of their "discourse" at the Netherfield ball was the true one flickered briefly in her thoughts. She pushed her doubts aside and chose to credit the story she recalled his telling her of Wickham's evil.

Deep shame and contrition showed on her face and she looked down at her clenched hands as tears began to slide down her flushed cheeks. "You can hardly imagine my unqualified chagrin when I realized how foolishly I had acted throughout the evening!" Overcome, she could speak no more at that moment.

Darcy wished with all of his heart to relieve her present distress, knowing that his very presence beside her must add to it more every second he remained so. Yet, how had she come to think of Wickham with such abhorrence? He had not told her... *Had he*?

He desperately wanted a few more minutes in which to speak his piece. He could not bear to go any longer without making his feelings clear to her – whatever the consequences might be.

"Please Eliz... Miss Bennet! Please do not be alarmed. Do *not* distress yourself over misunderstandings of the past! *You* were not at fault; it was the deliberate malice of another and I would most sincerely hope that you would not *allow him* to disturb your peace any longer!" He took her hands in his and lifted them to his heart, where, ever so gently, he held them against his chest. To his infinite relief, although she did not speak or look up, she did not try to pull her hands away.

Feeling that the fragile moment could shatter at the least misstep, or even too long a time in which to reflect, he rushed on. "I am aware that you did not come up here in order to be accosted by me, Miss Bennet. Please forgive me but I must speak while I have this providential opening. I came up here this morning to clear my thoughts and try to formulate an appropriate course of action. I so wanted to find an opportunity to speak with you privately."

Elizabeth peeked up at his face. Seeing only an earnest open countenance, his dark eyes fixed on hers, she slowly straightened and lifter her head to face him fully. "It seems, Mr Darcy that discourse between ourselves may be doomed to be better held outside of the hearing of others. However I believe *some* degree of decorum must be maintained!" She flashed him a smile but this time she firmly removed her hands from his grasp and folded them in her lap.

As much as he regretted the lost pleasure of holding her hands in his own, Darcy did not miss her subtle assent to allow him his moment of privacy with her. He resolved not to let it go to waste!

"Miss Bennet, I abjectly apologize that the disclosures I must have made to you last night were made in such an unpardonably rude manner. Indeed my conduct was so abhorrent that I fear it was quite unforgivable. Indeed I began this day so shocked at my own language that my mind at first refused to allow that I had spoken to you thus." He looked down in consternation as he muttered: "I must have done, for I have an indistinct memory of it, and your words indicate an awareness that could only arise from such disclosures."

Elizabeth regarded him with some curiosity. He seemed as unsure as she as to what he had said to her during their exchange over Wickham the night before. But this was not the time to worry over their mutually confused memories of the night before. She would put that aside for another time – if indeed there was any significance to it at all. Saying nothing about it she waited for him to explain himself.

Darcy paused, then took a deep breath and squared his shoulders before he went on. "I can only assert in my defence that hearing such furious censure from your lips was unbearable to me. At the time I was quite beside myself and hardly knew what I said or how I acted. However I hope that you are able to look beyond my disgraceful manner to the truthfulness of my words. It is my most fervent hope that the information I gave you might have changed your opinion of me - at least sufficiently to acquit me of cruelty toward Mr Wickham - and perhaps to make known the reasons for my dark mood of late.

"Most important to me is that you understand Mr Wickham's true nature. He is a danger to *any* innocent young woman, for he is in want of sport as much as of funds. My precious little sister was far from being the *only* young girl who has been a target of his despicable depravity over the years. *She* was only very fortunate that with *her*, he did not succeed!"

Elizabeth gasped "Mr Darcy, please! You must know that you have my heartfelt *gratitude* for putting your trust in me in such a way! Please *do* put away your regrets about your comportment! Think no more of it, *please*! I cannot help thinking of the dreadful possibilities were I not in possession of the truth about that degenerate's appalling character."

~&~

Pausing to consider her next words, Elizabeth confided "For myself I have no fear. Although I might not always be *the excellent* judge of character that I once considered myself to be; I am not so easily persuaded to *act* upon the representations of others not well-known to me".

Wincing slightly at the thought, she added "My youngest sisters, however, could be in great peril unless protected by their family. My father is not one to concern himself overmuch with the doings of his five daughters. Indeed he likes to laugh at all of us and regularly refers to Lydia and Kitty as the 'silliest girls in the country'. However I am certain that had he knowledge of Mr Wickham's evil propensities he would take all necessary precautions to protect them – for, you see, he does love us all very much! May I speak to him of it, sir? Or might you? His discretion would be assured. He is no gossip, I assure you!"

Elizabeth hesitated and then plunged on: "I fear I cannot stop there, sir. How dare I think only of my own sisters' safety without caring for that of all of our friends and neighbours? Can *you* do so Mr Darcy?"

Darcy had not considered going so far as to warn the community at large, but looking into her worried eyes he knew he could not avoid the obvious need to do so. Mr Bennet *must* be warned – and so must the others. "You are correct, Miss Bennet. Indeed I feel it must be incumbent upon *me* to make the danger posed by Wickham known, to your father, and to all of the families in the neighbourhood. It has been *my* mistaken pride, and the urgency *I* felt to protect *my sister's* reputation, that has prevented me from doing so before now; and it is *my* responsibility to correct my error!"

He felt as if a great burden had been lifted from his shoulders – well at least a significant part of that burden. "I shall take the necessary steps to expose Wickham's menace this very day!"

She had been regarding him closely, waiting for his response to her pleading words. After this speech he saw that she had relaxed a little. Yes, he had chosen well. He was on the right course!

She seemed to be lost in reflection for a moment. "There is one small impediment to your good intentions, however!" She looked away.

"Of what do you speak, Miss Bennet?"

"Sir, I... I hardly know how to say this, but I am ... ah, not certain... that is to say there may be a few, quite a few, among the neighbourhood who would not, ah, give your information the credibility it deserves. You see, Mr Wickham and his lies have been there before you, sir!" Extremely conscious of her own ill-judgment in that regard, Elizabeth hated to remind him, again, of that most uncomfortable subject. "I am so *very* regretful of it, Mr Darcy!"

"Of course!" His face clouded for a moment before he leaned toward her and spoke softly: "Miss Bennet, I care not what others think of me so long as your opinion is... not adverse."

He lingered there; his gaze fixed on hers, watching the slow flush spreading over her countenance. Her eyes met his and held his gaze until she looked away. Finally, seeming pleased with her response, he straightened. There would be time for more personal conversation after their plan was set.

In a firm tone, but with a twinkle in his eyes he told her: "Miss Bennet, it is now my turn to insist that you cease apologizing! *Please*, let us think together of a sound approach to a disagreeable task – and not trouble ourselves any further with endless regrets but henceforth let our mutual reflections be only... *agreeable*."

"I cannot *dis*-agree with that, sir!" She laughed a little shakily. "It is not in my nature to be morose or downcast. I shall be *far better pleased* to consider solutions to problems than dwell upon them!"

"Thank you, madam! Now what do you consider an acceptable approach to correcting those good and bad opinions that are so ill-placed and erroneously shared among the local populace? Shall I post an announcement upon the assembly room door? No? Shall I march up and down the town shouting mea culpa and distributing leaflets?" Having Elizabeth so close, and in good spirits, made him so happy he was giddy with the joy of it.

"Mr Darcy! *Now* you are only being silly – not serious about our mission at all!" Elizabeth giggled as she playfully swatted at his arm, and caught her breath when he dodged the strike and captured her hand in his once more. He only gave it a gentle squeeze and let it go, with a quick smile that did not do justice to the delight in his heart.

Elizabeth's own heart was beating rapidly as she strove to keep her breathing even and her hands from trembling. This was *too* much, *by far* too much!

She cleared her throat. "If we could return to the matter at hand, sir; I think we may have a most effective ally in my mother! Unlike my beloved father, *she is* a gossip – to her fingertips!" Elizabeth was relieved to bring their attention back to the necessity of a plan.

Seeing Darcy's horrified look, and having a fairly good idea of the cause of it, she went on. "I think that if *you* could explain things fully to my father he would see the need for a very *careful* righting of wrong first impressions in the neighbourhood. He will know how to tell my mother enough, *just* enough to send her abroad to spread a cautionary tale all around Meryton. Your sister's name need *never* be mentioned – only Mr Wickham's behaviour. What do you think, sir?"

"I think you are very wise, Miss Bennet, and I... like your plan very much. I will ask your father for a private interview as soon as we return to Longbourn." Seeing her startled expression Darcy remembered to ask "I hope you *will* allow me to escort you to your home, Miss Bennet?"

Elizabeth coloured and looked down at her hands twisting in her lap. "Um, Mr Darcy, *Need* I remind you that my mother would immediately leap to the wrong conclusion and begin to spread the *wrong* tale about the neighbourhood before your interview with my father had even reached its end?" When she looked up at him again, her face was sober but her eyes sparkled with mirth.

SEVENTEEN
A Knock in Exchange

"Ah, Miss Bennet, your little joke dovetails so nicely with the direction which I hope our *agreeable* discourse might next follow!" Darcy took a deep breath and released it slowly. *He knew what he must do!* There was nothing for it but to plunge ahead!

"*Lovely* Miss Bennet! You must allow me to tell you how *ardently* I... *love*.... and *admire you.* I have felt thus almost from the first moment of our acquaintance."

Elizabeth began to speak, her voice increasing in strength as she went on: "You *are* forthright, Mr Darcy but surely you jest, sir! In these past few months of our acquaintance I have had *no* indication, *no* conception that you held me in anything but *indifference* if not a disdainful *dis*regard!"

The intensity of his look stilled her next words. "*Please* hear me out, Miss Bennet. I promise I will be brief and I will not importune you for a decision you are not prepared to make."

His face pale and breathing laboured, Darcy confessed: "At first, in the dark mood which afflicted me after my sister's terrible hurt, I was distracted and confused. Then, I am ashamed to admit, I kept myself distant out of an overblown disapprobation for the often unseemly, nay appalling, demeanour of some members of your family and a ridiculous concern over our vastly different conditions in life.

"I now... have... come to understand how little any of that matters; it is a truth, though not *universally* acknowledged, that *many* families include various eccentricities among their numbers. I have come to appreciate that it would be the *worst* kind of folly to give a *straw* for such concerns when making choice of one's closest companion in life!

"Being so fortunate a man as to be well-connected, educated and experienced, and having lived in the world, I am firmly convinced that social status, lofty connections, and wealth are *very poor* substitutes for the great happiness to be found in a loving marriage between like-minded persons."

Astonished, Elizabeth only gazed at him, utterly bemused by his unexpected words.

Having said his worst, Darcy now spoke of his love for her. "Elizabeth, Pardon me! *Miss Bennet*, I find I cannot imagine spending the rest of my life without you in it, sharing in it; enjoying all of the delights and joys – even the pains and sorrows – that will come naturally in the fullness of time. Indeed I cannot imagine *finding* joy or delight without you by my side, the two of us together discovering and living the adventures that fill the rest of our lives."

With more than a smidgen of asperity in her tone, Elizabeth said: "What *is* it that you are asking of me, Mr Darcy?"

Her surprise and unaffected humility would not allow her to believe that his was an offer of marriage; but her self-respect and innate dignity were near to inciting a furious set-down if he were suggesting anything less!

"Miss Bennet, do you... Do you find yourself with any inclination to, perhaps, agree to a courtship? I love you so very dearly and hope someday you will do me the *very great honour* of consenting to become my wife!

"I shall not press you to answer just yet. While *my* wishes and affections are *quite firmly* determined, I can see by your countenance that this line of thought is entirely new to you. I would want you to take all of the time you require to decide whether you are able to return my regard. Within the propriety of a formal courtship we could become better acquainted and... I would be *so very* pleased if you found that you felt something, some gentle kindness, for you are both gentle *and* kind – and *witty* and *lovely* and *generous*...

"You see I know much about *you* already! Your many fine qualities have long been the subject of my *utterly captivated* interest. Indeed I am enthralled, mesmerized and *fascinated!*" He finally caught himself up and stopped abruptly; collecting that Miss Bennet had as yet made no positive response even to his initial declaration of esteem for her.

Elizabeth's inclination was to avoid a direct answer, indeed any answer at all, until she could mull over her conflicting thoughts and emotions.

Perhaps she might find some humorous comment, tease him perhaps; otherwise engage his thoughts ... No, that would not do. She must think!

Her expression was very grave as she considered his disclosures with care. She stared out over the prospect from Oakham Mount, not seeing what was in front of her but rather the rapid kaleidoscope of images moving in her mind.

Her first reaction was inexpressible relief. He had not imposed upon her with any insulting offers. Indeed, he honoured her beyond all reason with his request for her hand – and his openly expressed partiality for her!

She felt flattered by his hitherto unsuspected preference for herself; and deeply offended at his frank remarks about her family's behaviour and circumstances.

Truly, despite her many reservations Elizabeth was almost inexplicably disposed toward him. She appreciated his dark good looks, intelligence, fine education and that *clever wit* displayed only occasionally - but quite *effectively* employed when he chose to allow it to appear! *Could* she, in fact, see her way clear to accepting Mr Darcy's attentions? She *ought not* to be swayed by the fright of those *awful* dreams, though!

She must proceed with utmost caution in this! She had been well aware of his general attitude toward them all. His conciliatory words about eccentricities and the unimportance of station and wealth were just that: *Words*. He might say anything to win her acquiescence and then revert to his long-held beliefs once she had given up her most treasured asset – her *choice!*

How would she be able to reconcile his derision toward her beloved family, his assumption of superiority over all of her friends and acquaintances, with allowing her early unacknowledged interest in him to develop into a warmer regard?

Impatient and frustrated with the inconclusive nature of her thoughts, Elizabeth gave herself a mental knock. *Are you naught but a green girl? All conjecture and apprehension aside, do you truly wish to rebuff him? Better to trust yourself! You do not want for sense; answer the man!*

Resolutely she turned her head to glance at him, then away. *Oh my! I must accomplish this before I lose my thoughts in contemplation of those eyes, so intently fixed on me! What is he thinking?*

To Darcy it seemed that her deliberations took an interminable amount of time. His anxiety was nearly unendurable as he waited for her to reach accord within her own mind.

When she finally turned her body to face him, ready at last to speak, his apprehension was so extreme he could barely comprehend what she was saying at first.

"Mr Darcy, your disclosures leave me cruelly bewildered. I hardly know how to answer you without more. Indeed I find there are several essential issues I must yet consider – and wonder over. You have expressed a... fondness so wholly in-evident to me before today that I can hardly credit it to be of any such depth or duration as you declare."

She held up her hand to stay his anxious response. "Yet you say it is so and I feel that I *do know enough* of you that I could never dispute your honesty or integrity in any way. At the same time your words have raised other concerns to my attention. Your contempt for my family, indeed for all of us, and our neighbours too, has not been quite *so well hid* as the partiality you profess to feel for me."

Elizabeth's light and musical voice lowered and became throatier as she continued. "I wonder how we would get on when your irritation with my silly youngest sisters; or your chagrin at my lack of the sort of sophistication expected among the *ton*; or your resentment at my father's sometimes heavy-handed teasing overshadowed any pleasure you might feel in my company.

How will you deal with my mother's overzealous encouragement of your suit? When she regales you, and everyone within hearing of her highly strung voice, with ill-advised expressions of enthusiasm on her unvarying theme of eligible marriages for her five daughters?"

She gave him a level look in which she brooked no interruption. "I am deeply honoured by your kind intentions toward me sir. And I confess that although your attitude and behaviours often puzzle me, so do they intrigue me."

Elizabeth paused to gather her unruly thoughts before she continued: "Some people might say sir that natural self-interest should lead one to waste no time in closing upon your offer - without a second thought beyond the opportunities it represents. Indeed, I am fully cognizant of the many material benefits to myself and to my family which must necessarily arise from a connection with you, Mr Darcy. However it does not follow that such concerns would ever entice me into any connection without the highest respect and regard for my prospective partner in life."

Disconcerted, she motioned to stop his impetuous movement in her direction. "Wait, sir! There is more, and it troubles me greatly to say it for I am certain that you will not like to hear it! To speak plainly, your censure of my family has filled my heart with pain, and anger. I have heard it from you before, and indeed, from others in your illustrious party numerous times when careless or unguarded speech was had amongst yourselves."

Please give me leave to finish before you reply, Mr Darcy!" Elizabeth was determined to have a full airing on the subject, and an earnest response from him, before she could believe in his sincerity. Elizabeth saw him hunch his shoulders slightly while he pressed the back of his hand against his mouth – as if to contain the words ready to burst from his lips.

Hearing her out was clearly very difficult for him.

Nevertheless, she *would* speak her mind! His spontaneous reaction to *that* would most assuredly expose his genuine feelings.

"I have no quarrel, sir, with anyone's right to be proud – of their accomplishments, their connections, or any matter that may rightly be attributed to their own contributions to the state they find themselves in, or even simply their intrinsic value as a human being – so long as they do not attempt to justify that pride by belittling the value or dignity of others."

Her beautiful eyes flashing with indignation, Elizabeth drew several steadying breaths before she blurted. "I find it reprehensible for *anyone* to condemn persons so insufficiently known to them as to render their object's *excellent qualities* - such as sweetness of temper, loving-kindness and earnest dedication to the best interest of others – *invisible to a predisposition to despise them!*"

The distress in her voice made it dreadful for Darcy to hear. "*To a stranger*, my father is only sardonic and indolent; my mother is foolish and overbearing in her anxiety to assure her daughters' futures; my youngest sisters are empty-headed, indiscreet, and boisterous; poor Mary, who tries so hard to make herself admirable and accomplished is an object of ridicule. Even my connections are not equal to your exalted state – but *they all* have loved and cherished me since long before your *very recent* arrival in our midst, sir - and *I love them dearly*, one and all!"

At the conclusion of her impassioned speech, Elizabeth arose from her seat beside him and took several steps away to stand with her back turned to Darcy. She was trembling violently. Large tears had been rolling down her cheeks since she began to speak of her beloved family.

By this time Darcy's countenance had undergone a series of changes; from the anxious thrill of relief at having opened his heart to her at last and hearing Elizabeth begin her response; to surprise at her incredulity; to shock and a flicker of anger at her censure; and at last to horror and pain as the accuracy of her complaint began to dawn upon him.

Elizabeth! "Miss Bennet would to *God* that I could return to the past and *erase* every *word or deed* of mine that has ever wounded you so callously! Your resentment and disapproval are an *agony* to me! Please believe me when I tell you that I *do* comprehend the enormous folly, the arrogance and conceit, under which I have laboured these eight and twenty years!"

Elizabeth stood still, listening. Darcy moved to face her. His voice was slightly hoarse; his words were a plea for her understanding. "I have come to a *most painful* recognition of the habitual selfish disdain for the feelings of others in which I have spent my life thus far.

"This sudden comprehension came upon me in the short space of one night. A truly devastating revelation indeed, but one which I trust will help make a better man of me in the end. I cannot disagree with your estimation of my faults. Indeed, I am sure you are too kind in that endeavour. I am determined, however, to do everything in my power to correct these egregious errors – and to make amends for them wherever possible."

Taking out his handkerchief, he gently dabbed at her tears until she took it from him and wiped her face dry, and then handed it back to him. She was startled to see him raise it to his lips for a moment and then use it at his own eyes.

"Miss Bennet," Darcy pled very softly: "May I dare ask for your patience and the employment of your generous heart to help me remedy the despicable arrogance of my past? I will trust you implicitly in this! Your judgment shall be adopted as my own – without hesitation or question. Forgiveness I *dare* not ask until I have proven myself worthy of it. And Miss Bennet, even if you should choose *not* to trouble yourself with this unworthy man, you *must know* that I shall conquer this! I *shall* become the better man who would have deserved your approbation had he shown himself sooner!"

Without doubt he was humbled as he had never been before, but his stance was upright and his purpose firm. He waited, anticipating he knew not what, prepared to assume responsibility for his fate however she should decide.

A momentary pause ensued in which the very air around them seemed to still in anticipation. Hardly breathing, the two of them looked into each other's eyes, each seeking some ineffable clue to the other's heart.

Finally, Elizabeth gifted him with a brilliant smile, full of warmth and sweetness as she arched one eyebrow and spoke. "Mr Darcy, if you are still so inclined, and with no promise at this juncture of more than friendship, I believe that I *would* enjoy the opportunity to know you better, sir."

"*Thank you*, Miss Bennet" he breathed, his eyes glittering he swayed in her direction, but checked himself an instant before he would have touched her. Darcy kept his hands clenched at his sides while he gulped several deep breaths, his face suffused with emotion.

"We shall see how much you thank me when you have endured my father's merciless quizzing and my mother's uninhibited raptures, sir!" Elizabeth chuckled uneasily, looking aside to relieve the tension of the moment.

Darcy's beatific smile nearly took her breath away when, after only a momentary pause, he gently turned her face so that he could look straight into her eyes as he replied "I believe I shall learn to enjoy the teases and bask in the praises, my dear Miss Bennet!"

"Mr Darcy, I can only admire such an ambitious beginning to your grand undertaking! Indeed, you are quite full of surprises this morning, er… afternoon!" She suddenly became aware of how long they had tarried alone – and that she had partaken of little more than coffee and a bite or two of toast from her breakfast tray before leaving Longbourn much earlier.

"Oh dear! I fear we have quite lost track of the time. I must return home immediately! My family will be worried!" So saying she headed abruptly toward the trail that would lead them down the way they had come.

"It will be my very great pleasure to escort you to your home, Miss Bennet – if you will but wait for me to retrieve my horse!" The warmth of his voice was leavened by a hint of humour.

"Certainly Mr Darcy." She waited, smiling at him, her fine eyes softened by some gentle impulse he had not seen there before.

"Although I feel we would do better to part from each other's company before we are again in view of the public!"

"Will you take my arm, Miss Bennet?" he offered as they started down the rough trail.

"Thank you, Mr Darcy. I feel as if I have had a long day already though the hour cannot be *very much* past noon." She gingerly placed her hand around his arm, her sudden weariness made her chary of his touch and the urge to draw closer to him that she knew it would invoke.

He lifted his eyebrows in a quizzical expression: "Do you mean to tell me that climbing mountains to battle wayward gudgeons and bring pompous fools up to scratch is not among your daily activities?"

"No, sir," She laughed: "At least not those occupations of substance and form! I do often climb and ramble for the pleasure and solace to be found in the activity. I delight in the constant variety of the scenes about me and find that it is most often under the peaceful influence of nature where I may settle a perturbation of my spirits or confusion of my mind."

"And for the very same sort of relief I take Zephyros out for a good run – or a trip of exploration to some place unfamiliar to me such as Oakham Mount."

"Consequently here we both are."

The pensive direction her thought had taken led her shortly to ask: "When will you speak to my father, sir?"

"What a deal I have to say to him!" He sighed. After a moment's reflection he said: "In truth I have no taste for delay on either matter, though I think it might be best to keep them separate in his mind! I fear I must speak to him today about Mr Wickham. I cannot rest until I have done what I can to diminish Wickham's ability to impose his underhanded schemes upon the community! May I call on you in the morning, Miss Bennet, and meet with your father on the subject of our courtship afterward?"

"That does seem the best course to take, sir. I agree with everything you have said. I shall look forward to the morrow – with both trepidation and pleasure!"

"Trepidation, Miss Bennet? Do you think your father would refuse me?"

"He will have his fun with us both I have no doubt, sir. And as I am his *favourite* daughter he may be inclined to resist anything that might suggest a potential division of my loyalties in the future."

Her instantaneous blush made his heart skip a beat; dearest, loveliest Elisabeth! She had *no* idea how the very suggestion she spoke of made *him* feel!

"He does have his wits about him though, and you will have given him cause to think well of you by employing your good offices today. I believe he will indeed entertain your request more favourably than he might have heretofore! However I was thinking of my mother. She will be... almost wild!"

"Ah, Miss Bennet, it appears that your mother and I will in that moment enjoy our very first instance of happy concurrence!"

"Mr Darcy!"

"Forgive me, Miss Bennet. Disguise of any sort, you might recollect, is my abhorrence! And *I shall be delighted* to be the source of any relief to your mother in her matrimonial apprehensions over you!"

"I see that you are impatient of my caveat, sir. Pray do not allow your own, *or* my mother's enthusiasm to lead you to assume that an engagement will be forthcoming as a matter of course. I am resolved to *choose* only that alliance which, taking the qualities and characteristics I hold most dear into consideration, constitutes my own best chance of happiness. I *will not* be cajoled coerced, or bullied into giving up my right to make a reasoned and volitional *choice!*"

Elizabeth's vehemence dissolved into remorse. "Please forgive my grim attitude, Mr Darcy. It is only that my mother has recently been very insistent that I should marry my father's cousin Mr Collins – and I cannot *abide* him!"

~&~

"*Good God*! Forgive me, Miss Bennet, but why in the name of all that is Holy would your mother want you wed to that blithering idiot!"

Darcy's reaction made Elizabeth laugh in spite of herself! "I see that your abhorrence does indeed include all forms of disguise, even *subtlety*, Mr Darcy!

"Unfortunately my father's estate is entailed away from the female line. Since he and my mother have produced no sons, Mr Collins will inherit upon my father's eventual demise. My mother is convinced that by marrying him, one of her daughters would preserve our home for any of us who do not marry, and ultimately keep Longbourn in the family so to speak. For reasons known only to himself, Mr Collins has elected me to be the sacrificial lamb."

She did not mention that Jane had been his first choice until their mother threw a spike in his spokes with the intelligence that Jane was very likely to become engaged to Mr Bingley.

"Has that *pork-brained mutton-head* made you an offer of marriage then?" Darcy was spluttering with indignation and mixed metaphors at the very idea – *not to mention* his lingering feeling of foreboding left over from that dratted dream!

"You forget yourself, Mr Darcy! You are speaking in *vile* terms of my father's cousin – a *relation* of mine after all!" Try as she might to feign injured feelings, Elizabeth could not contain her mirth, which was fuelled equally by Darcy's nonsense and her consciousness of relief at knowing that she was in a position to toss a much *bigger* fish into her mother's stew pot.

Darcy stopped short, causing Zephyros to bump his shoulder and Elizabeth to stumble slightly and lose her grip on his arm. Taking advantage of the scuffle, Darcy put his hand on Elizabeth's shoulder to steady her and then let it slide lightly down her arm until he grasped her hand firmly in his and placed in back on his arm, covering it with his free hand.

"My apologies, Miss Bennet, if you are *truly* affronted," He growled. "I warn you, however, that if you persist in provoking my jealousy by alluding to marriage to another man, I may well do far worse than call him a mutton-head!"

Sighing heavily Elizabeth told him: "*You*, sir, are incorrigible!"

They were nearly to the bottom of Oakham Mount when Jane appeared, trudging in their direction, and calling: "Lizzy! Lizzy! Where... Oh *there* you are at last! I was so worried..."

Looking perplexed and a little embarrassed, Jane stood still. Upon a moment's reflection she relaxed slightly and smiled her serene welcome to them both. She was relieved to find her sister whole and unharmed, and she never doubted her dear Lizzy's integrity. All would be explained when they found time for their chat.

Lizzy released Darcy's arm, first removing his hand from atop her own, and stepped a little away from him. "Please excuse me Mr Darcy. I believe I must accompany my sister to our home now. Shall I expect your visit in the morning?"

"Yes, Miss Bennet, you may depend upon it!"

"I shall look forward to it then." Curtseying quickly to him, she went to join her sister.

EIGHTEEN
Back in the Company of Wise Jane

"Why Jane, Mamá must be even more vexed with me than usual to send you scampering about the countryside to find me out! I am sorry for it, I know full well that you had much rather stroll about the garden or busy yourself with needlework or a favourite book." Lizzy called out to her sister as she neared the spot where Jane stood smiling at her.

Jane's cheerful smile faltered as she replied. "Lizzy, I am so glad to see you! Mamá is indeed vexed. She is all at sixes and sevens! Why, she even spoke sharply to *Lydia* over some bold remark she made to Mr Collins. And Mr Collins has professed himself quite *incensed* that our parents have not taken the trouble, out of respect for himself and for the *beneficence* of Lady Catherine, to curb your wild and headstrong ways.

" He begins to say that you might *not* be the proper source of his future happiness!" This last bit she pronounced with a smirk and an exaggeratedly pompous tone in a fair imitation of the man himself.

"For once that idiotic man is precisely, perfectly, and unerringly *right on the mark*!" Lizzy cried. "We must do something to celebrate the occasion!" She put her hand on Jane's arm, giggling: "Oh Jane, you are truly wonderful to bring me this news!"

"Lizzy, you may not congratulate yourself just yet. Mamá demands your immediate presence in the sitting room, alone with Mr Collins. She says you must do your duty to your family and hear him out. She has convinced herself nothing else will do but for you to marry him." At the sight of her sister's crestfallen countenance Jane took her hand and added: "I am so *very* sorry my dearest!"

Bethinking herself of her changed circumstances and wishing to relieve Jane's worries, Lizzy squeezed the hand that clasped her own and spoke quickly: "Dear Jane, I intended to wait until we could discuss this in the privacy and calm of Longbourn's gardens, but I have that to tell you which will both *agitate and ease* your mind!"

"I am all attention, dearest Lizzy, to know of anything that could put back the glow I see in your cheeks and the sparkle in your eyes after *such* a report as I have just made to you!"

"Allow me to acquaint you as we walk, with the events of my venture to Oakham Mount this day."

"At once, *please!* For you wish to tell me, and I am eager to hear it!" Looking back over her shoulder Jane noticed that Mr Darcy followed them some distance back. With a sly look she asked: "Does it pertain in any way to the *tête-à-tête* I discovered you in when we met just now?"

"Your intuition is correct, Jane. Mr Darcy and I met, quite by accident, on the upper trail on the Mount. Both of us were taking the air, each in our preferred manner – he on horseback and I on foot, in our attempt to soothe our agitated spirits after our shocking quarrel last evening."

"Perhaps you had better begin with the quarrel. I could see that you were dreadfully troubled when we returned from the ball, and I understood that it had something to do with Mr Darcy. But the cause is still largely a mystery to me."

"Oh Jane! As *enthralled as you were* with Mr Bingley's sociability, you must have observed our mother's offensive loquaciousness; our two youngest sisters' brash and unchecked forwardness; Mary's sadly ill-favoured exhibition - and even our dear father's rude chastisement of Mary before the rest of the company. Still, you missed, apparently, my own folly, which was worse even that all of theirs put together! I *warn* you, dear heart. The story will fill you with a *disgust of me* beyond anything you can yet imagine! "

"*Never*, Lizzy! I know you to be incapable of doing anything *so very* dreadful as that!" Jane's look was troubled at her sister's unusual reticence.

"Very well, but the telling of it fills me with apprehension that you shall lose your good opinion of me! However I shall not delay, as to do so must only serve to aggravate the discomfort in my anticipation of the disclosure."

"Say on, then, Lizzy. Let me hear it at once so we might put this behind us. You shall always remain my Lizzy; my own best friend and comfort – and tease!"

After a heavy sigh, Elizabeth stated flatly: "Jane, I confronted Mr Darcy with Mr Wickham's story about how he refused to honour old Mr Darcy's Will and cheated Mr Wickham out of his inheritance. And, Jane, we were on the dance floor at the time and... To my eternal shame, I accused Mr Darcy of dishonesty, of cruelly ruining Mr Wickham's prospects!"

"Lizzy! How could you do such a thing; in public, too! At Mr Bingley's ball... in his home! Oh my poor sister, you must have had *extreme* provocation to behave so!" Jane's sympathy for her sister was quick to rise. "Dearest Lizzy; I am so very sorry! You must feel wretched indeed!"

"Not so very wretched as my disclosure might lead you to expect, dearest, for I have still more to tell. And if your regard for me remains sufficient to hear it, the rest will relieve at least some of your disturbance at my contemptible beginning. I have apologized to Mr Darcy most sincerely and abjectly. And He has told me such things as to clear his own name and raise the severest indignation – nay, animosity - regarding Mr Wickham!"

"Dear Lizzy, I can easily comprehend your going along well enough once the two of you began to talk. For I have long held the suspicion that neither of you was so indifferent to the other as you would have the world believe. But, before you unravel the particulars for my edification, please tell me: whatever set you off in the first place?"

"I hardly know. Something came over me. I had been attempting to sketch his character while we danced. I simply could not make out what sort of man, so proud and upright as he appeared, would reverse himself to lie and cheat – especially to injure someone he had known all of his life, even played with as a boy! Having had no success in that more subtle endeavour, I became incensed and before I knew what I was doing I was *abusing* him on the subject!"

"Tis true that you have *always* reacted vigorously to Mr Darcy! Tell me the rest of your story *now please*, dearest Lizzy! And when you are finished, you may enlighten me as to why Mr Darcy appears to be *following us* to Longbourn!"

They were very near to their home by the time Elizabeth had disclosed all to her beloved Jane. She held nothing back of Mr Darcy's angry reaction at the ball and the furious litany of wrongs he attributed to the wicked Wickham (was that at the ball, or in her dream memories of it?). She did not leave out his censure of herself for allowing Wickham, on no more than a slight acquaintance, to speak to her of his intimate business.

Jane listened patiently without interruption while Lizzy described her meeting with Mr Darcy by accident on Oakham Mount, the awkwardness, mutual apologies, and the agreement to make all families in the neighbourhood aware of the threat posed by Wickham's presence in the locality. "And for the rest, my dear, you shall have to wait for another time, for there remains an insufficiency of *that* commodity before we arrive at our doorstep to do justice to what I have yet to tell you."

Elizabeth peeked at her sister's face and happily receiving her eldest sister's customary loving smile, brought their private discussion to an end thusly:

"As for the gentleman following at some distance after us, Mr Darcy comes to Longbourn for two reasons my sweet Jane."

Lizzy's relief at finally unburdening herself to her sister was evident in her bright smile.

"First, he intends to impart the same information he shared with me about Mr Wickham, to our father – in the form of a warning. He wishes to protect us as well as our neighbours from that man's iniquitous perfidy. The strategy to be employed I will explain to you in the privacy of our bedchamber.

"Second, we have agreed this part had better be addressed tomorrow so as to keep the two matters distinct from one another, he will ask our father for permission to court me."

"Ah Lizzy! *At last*! I knew there was romance in the air, never mind all of those vexations and misunderstandings between you! Mr Darcy has been quite obvious to me in his constant surveillance of your every activity and conversation. He is *besotted* with you I think!"

NINETEEN
Darcy Enlists the Aid of Mrs Bennet

Mr Bennet started in surprise when a firm knock sounded at his library door so soon after he took himself there. That room was his sanctuary, his escape from the everlasting prattle of his wife and daughters - and from the pompously pious pronouncements of his preposterous cousin the ponderous parson. Mr Bennet smirked to himself at his little conceit.

Having eaten sparingly of the midday meal in their company (he could not specifically identify the repast by name as it was the first meal of the day after a ball for some, and the second for more hardy, or less convivial souls) he might fairly take his ease with a book and his glass of port ready on the side table. For by making an appearance, however brief, he considered himself to have done his duty by them all - including the unexpected, last-minute, *baffling* addition to their table, Mr Fitzwilliam Darcy.

His appearance at Longbourn had been the result, he said, of a lengthy ride in the neighbourhood. Finding himself very near their home he felt it only proper to pay a call. Of course he had been promptly – if a little sourly – invited to dine with the family.

Mr Bennet jested privately to himself that Mr Darcy looked as if his small clothes were in somewhat of a twist. A situation he was likely unable to right on his own, without the services of his valet!

With a loud sigh at the imminent postponement of his peaceful solitude, Mr Bennet called out for the intruder to "Come".

Laying aside his book, he waited in gloomy resignation to see whether the opening door would reveal his wife, come to importune him yet again on the matter of Mr Collins' pig-headed pursuit of his Lizzy, or Mr Collins himself to persist in perverse predation on his privacy.

"Bah!" He groaned to himself. "I find my cousin's execrable folly insufficiently diverting to make it worth my enduring his presence any longer. How I *ever did* delight in his foolishness now *wholly* perplexes me! Ugh!"

Of course it was not Mrs Bennet, nor Mr Collins whose unlikely form advanced from behind the opening door, but Mr Darcy. Stepping firmly into Mr Bennet's retreat, he paused to allow acknowledgement and an invitation to sit.

Seen in silhouette with the light from the windows striking him faintly from the side and beyond, and the glow of Mr Bennet's reading lamp being inadequate to light his features at his present distance from it, Mr Darcy's expression was even more inscrutable than usual.

With a rare uncertainty Mr Bennet received Mr Darcy's unexpected arrival in his study. "Well, Mr Darcy, this *is* an unexpected honour! Please make yourself comfortable."

Waving his visitor to a comfortable chair situated opposite his own seat next to his book table, he added: "Would you care to join me in a glass of port, sir?"

"No, I thank you sir." Came that gentleman's cautious response.

Thomas Bennet settled back in his chair and silently fixed Mr Darcy with his expectant regard. He knew that Mr Darcy was not popular in the neighbourhood, but he was not inclined to follow the whims of public opinion – especially when said opinion was formed upon so little of substance and so much of impression. Why, he himself could be considered haughty and disdainful if he had not lived in the neighbourhood all of his life and if all that was known of him was his attendance at assemblies.

As for Mrs Bennet's disapprobation of the man, *her* hatred was based on no more than some imagined slight to her least favourite daughter. No he would not let himself be led by the opinions of others, certainly not that of his flibbertigibbet wife, or the other town gossips.

He would see for himself what the man was made of. This would be an unusual entertainment indeed!

As he took the seat offered to him, Mr Darcy's expression was remarkably uneasy. "I would wish to speak to you of a private matter which is of extraordinary delicacy and requires the utmost care in order to safeguard innocent persons from irreparable harm." Pausing for Mr Bennet's rejoinder, and hearing none, he went on "It is not my wish to burden you sir, with troubles so far outside the concerns of Longbourn and your family. However it has come to my notice that the information I hold may well be critical to the protection of the young ladies of your own home and, indeed, of the entire neighbourhood."

Mr Bennet blinked in astonishment. What could possibly incite the reserved and taciturn Mr Darcy, he who had reputedly made it abundantly clear that he felt all of Meryton and its neighbours were beneath his notice, to come to Longbourn's country squire for an apparently *sensitive* consultation?

Wishing to draw his visitor out, Mr Bennet assumed his customary pose as a disinterested audience of one to the farcical endeavours of kith and kin: "I am far from certain, sir that you have chosen wisely if you intend myself as your confidante. Whenever possible I prefer to keep my mind uncluttered by too many details of local goings on or too much female melodrama. Far from enjoying my wife's incessant illuminations of local tittle-tattle, I find such communication even more insipid than a lacklustre recitation of the History of the English Kings – and *that* is saying a great deal!"

"I assure you Mr Bennet, that the object of my errand is neither inspired by gossip nor in the nature of a farce!" Darcy was not used to so sceptical a reception.

He forced himself to shrug off the affront to his consequence with the inner acknowledgement that it was very similar to the impertinence which he found so charming in this man's favourite daughter. Ignoring the tease, he arose and began to pace slowly in a small area near Mr Bennet's table; near enough to make his low-voiced revelation heard by that gentleman.

With his hands clasped behind his back to keep them still, he carefully considered his words as he spoke: "What I have to tell you, sir, is that among the officers stationed in Meryton there is one whose manners give him the appearance of a gentleman but whose dissolute ways and dishonourable character make him an imminent menace to innocent maidens and honest shopkeepers alike.

"I do not thus describe Mr George Wickham out of hearsay or spleen but from personal knowledge gained over a lifetime of direct acquaintance. Mr Wickham's father was for many years my excellent father's steward. He served in that capacity with the greatest integrity and loyalty, and when asked, my father agreed to be godfather to the son. We were playmates growing up, and after the elder Mr Wickham's untimely death, my father took responsibility for George Wickham's education at Eton and afterward at Cambridge.

"Soon after his father's death, when Wickham was about eight or nine, he began to engage in pranks and wild behaviour. As time went on the pranks became more and more cruel and vicious, until he was the cause of hurt to many others, in the form of stolen articles, ruined reputations, undeserved punishments and wrongful dismissals.

"By the time we went to Cambridge together, we had long since ceased to be friends. Yet due to our unique connection and my father's wishes I continued to be in his company and therefore privy to Wickham's dishonesty and debauchery. Indeed, as the Darcy heir and later as Master of Pemberley it has been my unpleasant office to clear many debts left behind by Wickham, that his actions not cause harm to those who can least afford the losses, and to preserve the good name of my family – which he invokes without truth and without reserve."

Barely pausing for breath, he finished: "It will be no great wonder to find that many of Meryton's shopkeepers are already holding worthless paper on Wickham's account. Worse, I fear to discover the extent to which he has already preyed upon the innocents of the neighbourhood. Wickham does not discriminate between fortune hunting and sport in his incessant quest for dalliance. I have highly reliable intelligence of both lust and greed as his impulsion – quite independently of each other."

Relieved to have said his piece, Darcy heaved a deep sigh and returned to his seat. Leaning forward he looked earnestly into Mr Bennet's eyes "I hope you may believe that only the greatest apprehension of injury to the innocent would move me to come to you in this fashion. In light of circumstances still more grave than what I have related to you thus far, my peace would be far easier were I able to disclaim *any* historic connection with that 'gentleman' *at all!*"

Mr Bennet sat very still, staring at the hunk of amber Lizzy had given him for Christmas one year for a paperweight, as he considered Mr Darcy's words He admired Darcy's evidently sincere purposefulness in speaking them. He was very glad he had kept his mind open. *Very well done, young man!* He thought to himself.

Mr Darcy held his tongue, waiting quietly while the older man ruminated on the question of what should, or must be done.

Finally turning his eyes to Mr Darcy's he asked: "And what is your idea, young man, in coming to me with your misgivings? You puzzle me greatly. I have heard you speak more words in this quarter hour than in all of our previous encounters combined! What is your impetus? What do you expect to gain by your kindly interference?" He paused but before Mr Darcy could answer, and in happy ignorance of the truth of the matter, he chuckled with a twinkle in his eye; "I could reward you, with my wife's full approbation, with the hand of any of my fair daughters of your choice!"

Seeing Mr Darcy's deep blush, and that he was apparently struck dumb by his little joke, Mr Bennet adopted a more serious mien. "Please do not take offense; I suppose a humorous aside is not what is called for just now."

"No offense taken sir, your humour has much to recommend it. I will be happy to address that subject with you at a more opportune time."

Mr Darcy's words and his sudden smile caused Mr Bennet's eyes to widen in surprise, wondering whether it was his humour or his daughter which Mr Darcy wanted to discuss with him!

"At present I believe it is imperative that action must be taken forthwith if much suffering is to be prevented."

Electing to answer only to the issue of Mr Wickham, Mr Bennet responded: "I promise you that I will ensure the safety of my family. I have had my doubts of Mr Wickham's character before now. He is too easy in his manner - making revelations to mere acquaintances of matters not often discussed even among friends of long standing. Now it seems those same revelations were both untrue and made with ulterior intent – to disarm and win sympathy. Your information confirms me in my inclination to distrust him severely, and I thank you for it."

"I am very glad to hear that, sir. I will rest easier in the knowledge that your daughters are safeguarded from him." Darcy paused, and cleared his throat. "I am determined to alert the good people of this region to their danger as well. May I hope for your assistance in this?"

"What might *I* do, sir, as efficaciously as yourself? Your tale is most compelling, and I am convinced that you have more to tell should the need arise. I am not active in the community. Indeed I scarcely tolerate the company of my own wife and daughters for longer periods that an hour or two – and that only on particular occasions. How am I to be of service in this undertaking of yours?

"How am I, *of all people*, peculiarly equipped to warn the unsuspecting neighbourhood of their peril at the hands of Mr Wickham?" Mr Bennet could not help himself. He knew very well how "information" spread to all and sundry in a matter of hours. He was married to her! He simply could not resist the opportunity to quiz the habitually sombre and staid Mr Darcy.

"I beg you would forgive the presumption sir... um... to own the truth... well I thought perhaps you might know of someone who is in frequent contact with others in the neighbourhood and... if that person were to share such important information in the right way and in the right places..." Mr Darcy's voice trailed off into an uncomfortable silence. He dared not mention that it was Mr Bennet's daughter Elizabeth who had suggested the plan. And he was excruciatingly conscious that with every word he risked insult to her mother that her father might find hard to overlook.

"Ah! I begin to comprehend you, Mr Darcy. Your calculations are exceedingly astute! I will not tease you further as I believe you have hit upon *exactly* the right course to follow. In one fell swoop you thought to protect my family and enlist the help of Mrs Bennet in the manner most suited to her temperament and habits. I admire your perspicacity sir; by joining forces, so to speak, with your least probable ally you may achieve your object much better than if *you* were to shout your information from the rooftops of Meryton! That is a clever stroke indeed!"

Darcy's mortification was complete. Miss Elizabeth Bennet ought to be chuckling to herself if she could but overhear their conversation. *She* knew whose cleverness was responsible for his presence in Mr Bennet's library. "Thank you, sir. I cannot claim responsibility for the origin of the plan, only the willingness to carry it out. I will explain more of that at another time.

"I am most grateful that my word carries weight with you sir. I am not so confident that it will be well received by..., please excuse me sir, I am well aware that Mrs Bennet holds me in extreme disapprobation. It is most regrettable and of my own causation. But there it is. I intend to correct that ill opinion held by your wife and others by my improved conduct in future. That, I sincerely hope, will come in time; but first to the far more urgent matter at hand: *Will* she believe me now, sir?"

"Oh! You may leave that entirely to me, young man. I have not been married to Mrs Bennet these many years for nothing, I assure you!" He made it clear that he saw no obstacle to his wife's full cooperation. In fact, he envisioned an enthusiastic, even frenzied force of activity on her part once he had directed her thoughts to their most useful effect.

Mr Bennet's curiosity was piqued. There were elements of their meeting which left him with new questions and he wished very much to follow up on Mr Darcy's odd comments. However he too, appreciated the exigency of their now joint campaign so deferred his pleasure to another time.

"I believe it is time I had a little discourse with my wife, Mr Darcy. You may prefer, at this juncture, to slip out without drawing her notice to our meeting. What say you?"

"I fully trust your insight in that regard, Mr Bennet. I shall leave directly." After a slight pause he continued hesitantly: "If I may, I will return tomorrow morning to enquire of our progress, and to lend such further support as might be called for. We may have additional matters to discuss at that time – if I do not overtax your hospitality sir?"

"Certainly Mr Darcy, I look forward to it. Indeed by tomorrow morning, I venture to assure you, you will be most welcome to join the family for breakfast if you are of a mind to do so, sir."

"Thank you Mr Bennet, I shall be happy to join you."

"Until tomorrow then; if you care to use the side door just down there, I believe you may safely escape Mrs Bennet's notice as you depart."

As he stepped into the late afternoon sunshine, Darcy heard Mr Bennet saying: "Hill, kindly find Mrs Bennet and ask her to join me in my library as soon as may be."

~&~

Francine Bennet did indeed have a very busy evening after receiving her husband's summons to his library. That in itself was enough to raise her apprehension that something of decided significance was afoot.

Uncharacteristically she had much to say to her daughters about their need for caution when mixing with men in red coats! With her turn for the high dramatic, she informed them of the propensity to wickedness among some men. They could not, did not possess the maturity of mind to discern who was a true gentleman, and who might turn out to be a cad. For the very first time in their young lives she impressed upon them all that they must receive their father's approval of any man they sought to befriend – or more to the point: who sought to befriend *them*.

The girls simply looked at one another in wonder but made no comment. Lydia, and therefore Kitty, would have complained had they not been so thoroughly thunderstruck by their mother's unfamiliar behaviour.

Mrs Bennet set out in earnest the following morning, delighted to be the bearer of such news as had not yet been passed around before *and* which would astonish and alarm those fortunate enough to be at the ready for her communications. She had such extraordinary commissions to execute!

In her excitement she arose so much before her usual time that she had breakfasted and was on her way before the rest of the family, and Mr Darcy, assembled for breakfast.

Every sister looked around in bewilderment at not seeing Mamá presiding, and fussing, in her accustomed place among them at the table.

"Where is *Mamá*?" "Is she ill?" "Hill! *Hill!* Where is our mother?" "She promised to help me trim my bonnet; *why* is she not here?" "No she *did* not! Mamá has to visit our Aunt Phillips this morning. She *told me so* last night and I want to go with her!"" "But where *is* she?" "Is she having an attack of her nerves?" "Has *anyone* gone to find her vinaigrette?" "Why is she acting so *strangely* of late?"

The chorus of voices came in such rapid succession that no answer could have been made to any one of them in time to stop the next.

Mr Darcy stared raptly at his plate; a slight frown and dull red flush the only indication that he heard them.

It did not escape their father's notice that neither of his eldest daughters joined in the clamour. Unlike their youngest sisters, who were so vociferously consumed with speculations on their mother's absence, they presented a uniform presence of serene unconcern. Instead they appeared to be waiting to hear his answer with some consciousness of the matter, while quietly attending to their breakfasts. Mary's few contributions alluded to feminine modesty and decorum before their guest.

Mr Bennet lifted his hand in a signal for silence. "My dears," He said firmly: "We will have none of this cacophony of questions. Your mother is quite well, only occupied elsewhere at the moment. There is no cause for alarm. I will explain your mother's absence, as best I can, all in good time. Let us first eat our meal in peace and enjoy the novelty of the situation. Meanwhile Hill, (with a smile) you may go back to your duties as I feel certain that I am able to provide the information my daughters seek."

"Yes sir." Hill bobbed a curtsey and disappeared through the door to the sitting room where she had been overseeing the tidying up when she heard her name called out. She knew very well what was up although it was not her place to let it be known. Mrs Bennet could never keep the particulars of anything to herself for as long as overnight.

~&~

After only one more attempt on the part of Lydia to glean at least some information on the whereabouts of their mother, which was met by a stern glare from their father, the rest of the meal was finished in relative calm.

"Now my dears," their father announced, patting his mouth with his napkin and arising from the table; "I have a matter of business to attend to with Mr Darcy. We will be in my library and are not to be disturbed. You will all remain quietly at home until I am ready to see you. You are not to receive any visitors, except perhaps Mr Bingley if he should be returned from Town, (looking at Jane), nor are you to venture beyond the near garden where I can see you from my library window."

"But, Papá!" Lydia and Kitty exclaimed in unison.

Elizabeth paled; a sudden churning of anxiousness revealed in her glance at Jane who returned her look with an earnest expression of empathy.

Mary merely looked pained and asked to be excused.

"Hush now, girls. I will explain everything shortly, but first I must have some time with our guest."

TWENTY
Incredulity Unleashed

"*You what*? I believe I must have *misheard* you sir!" Mr Bennet's unfeigned shock and chagrin, entirely uncharacteristic of so cynical an observer of the follies of his fellow man, was complete. "You *are* bold indeed, Mr Darcy!"

After a brief exchange on the subject of Mrs Bennet's absence, and whether Colonel Forster ought to be informed of Mr Wickham's appalling history in order that he might decide on how best to deal with the venality of one of his officers, Mr Darcy asked to speak to Elizabeth's father on one other, very particular matter.

"Of course, sir; how may I oblige you?" Ensconced once again in his favourite chair in the library, Thomas Bennet felt himself most agreeably satisfied with their morning's work and therefore prepared to entertain any subject his new friend might wish to discuss.

"I hope we have not another unscrupulous character running around in our midst designing against the safety of our young women or the coffers of our merchants!"

His jovial remark did not lighten the mood as he intended it to do. Instead, Mr Darcy's countenance became so intensely serious that Mr Bennet sat up in alarm.

"I jest, sir. Surely we have got Mr Wickham's potential menace to our peace well in hand for the present. Whatever remains now to cause your dark looks?"

"Forgive me Mr Bennet. It is only that I must address you on a matter of the utmost importance to my future life, indeed to my dearest wishes for my future happiness, that I find it nearly beyond my power to speak of it to you."

At this Mr Bennet leaned back in his chair and waited in an easy silence for his visitor to unburden himself. He had soon discovered that the formidable and taciturn young man, who always seemed so very serious and aloof, was not as haughty and proud as he was reputed to be.

Fitzwilliam Darcy was full young to be master of a great estate- responsible for many lives and the maintenance of his station and fortune - these five years and more. Goodness, he must be the object of every financial trickster and match-making mama who could get near him! More likely he had learned to mask his uncertainties with a façade of hauteur, being unapproachable and thus less vulnerable to the schemes and whims of others.

Mr Bennet was enjoying some faintly self-satisfied rumination: recalling his own youth and recognizing the enormous challenges a young man of far greater fortune, both parents gone, responsible for a great estate and a very young sister must face. He respected the strength of character of the man who could carry so many burdens with stoic composure as Mr Darcy had apparently done since his father's death. He admired the integrity and worth of any man who would act as Mr Darcy had done in the current circumstances. Such thoughts aroused in him a new sense of affection and empathy for the young man before him.

He had been waiting patiently while Mr Darcy paced distractedly in front of him, hands clasped behind his back, frowning in concentration. What could possibly put the young man so out of countenance after all that had been spoken already?

Mr Bennet's forbearance was nearly at an end. He disliked greatly being plagued with difficulties and the events of the past four-and-twenty hours had provided more than enough of difficulties!

"Come Mr Darcy I am at your disposal! Would a bit of fortification help you along?" Reaching for his crystal decanter of port he looked to Mr Darcy with a raised eyebrow, in a gesture identical to his daughter's endearingly arch expression.

Startled out of his perplexity Darcy stopped in front of Mr Bennet and after a moment's pause he sat down in the chair he had used before. "No, I thank you sir." As the older man replaced the decanter of port on his reading table, he went on. "I will get straight to the point. Indeed I find that I cannot act in any other way. It is my sad blemish that my speech lacks the finesse I hear in that of others. That said, I can do no else than speak up, sir."

Taking a deep breath, and with a fast thudding heart, he turned his eyes directly to Miss Elizabeth's father. "I pray you will not think me puffed up or disrespectful... Mr Bennet, may I be so bold as to ask your permission to court your daughter?" Seeing his confusion, Darcy added: "I speak of Miss Elizabeth, sir."

"*You what*? I believe I must have *misheard* you sir!" For the life of him Mr Bennet could not decipher his meaning! He was incredulous; had not Elizabeth and Mr Darcy shown a marked dislike for each other before this? Hmm... there must have been *some* degree of flummery in that!

Mr Bennet felt a burst of temper coming on. He disliked feeling so very behindhand with the goings on in his world.

"You *are bold* indeed, Mr Darcy!"

"Yes sir" Darcy's sudden smile warmed his eyes and softened his countenance to a remarkable degree.

Mr Bennet stared at him from beneath his lowered brows and demanded: "Have you spoken with Elizabeth? Is she disposed to accept your suit?" If *that* be the case, he thought to himself, it had been a *great* piece of unkindness that she had not hinted to him at least that her previous aversion to Mr Darcy was no longer in effect. And what of Mr Darcy's slights and stern looks. Was that all to be cast aside in favour of this new interpretation of things?

Mr Bennet felt his customary composure begin to slip. His imperturbable manner barely managed to cover a most uncharacteristic agitation of mind. Sufficiently roused from his books to think on the goings on in his family, he felt very nearly incensed. Perhaps a glass of port might be the thing after all.

"You *cannot* have developed such a violence of affection for my Elizabeth that you could wish to *bind yourself* to her for life! You are labouring under some sort of passing infatuation, I'll be bound. When you get to know her, you will find that she is not the sort of girl to bend to your whims and then be set on the shelf! Forgive me Mr Darcy but I cannot fathom your purpose here! I do not believe that you are the sort of man who finds gratification in seducing young ladies, but otherwise I cannot comprehend what you are about!"

How could he *bear* to lose his dearest daughter? She was his *favourite*, his only companion in intellectual pursuits – and in wit. The mere suggestion of losing her sent him into a sickly dread.

"Not at all, sir; I hold Miss Elizabeth in the tenderest regard! I, I *love her very much*! If she accepts my suit it will be the greatest joy and honour of my life to ensure her happiness. My feelings are most ardent! I hold no reserve of doubt. I am not, nor have I ever been committed by honour or inclination elsewhere. I desire, with everything that I am and everything that I have, to dedicate my life to her happiness and contentment. I promise you that my intentions are everything honourable, Mr Bennet."

"So, despite the less than amiable history between you am I to understand that you and my favourite daughter are now *perfectly in charity* with one another? I confess that I am ready to *drop* at this turn!"

At this Darcy looked down, twisting his signet ring slowly and deliberately around and around on his finger. It was a long-held habit of his when he needed to calm himself and think clearly.

"I cannot presume... I dare not imagine that she yet holds as *violent* an affection for me, as I do for her. But she *has* agreed to a period of courtship. That will give me an opportunity to show her more of my character, the honourableness of my intentions, and my deep love and admiration for her. That is, if you agree, sir."

Mr Bennet's thoughts danced wildly between mirth at Darcy's discomfort, dread of losing his favourite daughter and companion, and speculative consideration about recent developments. He would *enjoy* testing the mettle of his daughter's illustrious suitor. "You are aware that my daughter will never submit to your authority, should you marry"

"I do not desire another servant, Mr Bennet. Should I be so fortunate as to win her hand, I would hope that Eliz... excuse me, Miss Elizabeth would stand by my side – not behind or below me."

"Elizabeth has very little dowry. Mr Darcy."

I am not concerned with monetary gain, sir. What I seek is a *far* greater treasure. Her heart, her companionship, would gladden my life beyond measure."

"My Elizabeth has strong opinions and does not hesitate to share them. You must not expect her to make her thoughts and beliefs subservient to your own."

"I greatly admire Miss Elizabeth's strong opinions and the honest and fair-minded way she thinks. I would never wish to interfere with anything about her, sir."

"My daughter has a fearsome temper, Mr Darcy. And she does not suffer fools gently. Are you certain that you have the determination to withstand the vicissitudes of a connection to her wit and sharp tongue?"

"I am neither a fool nor do I lack sufficient self-confidence or spine to endure her censure. Indeed sir, before she agreed to my courtship she gave me quite a trimming, all of it deserved. I have enlisted her aid in correcting those flaws in my character which she so generously pointed out to me then." Here Mr Darcy described the gist and the circumstances of his meeting with Elizabeth the day before. He glossed over just how and when he had told Elizabeth about Mr Wickham – he was still unsure of that himself.

Mr Bennet's eyebrows rose nearly to his hairline. He was truly beginning to enjoy himself. "Have you sir? She set you down thoroughly then? She took you to task over her resentments of you? And you not only accepted her reprimands with admirable grace but have asked her help in reforming your faults! My, my! I am more and more *awash* with bedazzlement! I begin to think that you show just such prodigious courage as a man must possess if he will pursue the hand of my beloved second daughter." Mr Bennet had to engross himself in the papers on his table in order to hide the mirthful enjoyment that was even then threatening to impose itself on his countenance, to the ultimate relief of his unfortunate quarry.

He could not resist one final sally "Other than her extensive reading and some ability on the pianoforte, Elizabeth has no fine accomplishment to boast of, Mr Darcy" He nearly choked on his own suppressed chuckle as he finished.

"Sir, your disposition is too generous to tease me in this manner. Might we come to the point now, sir? Will you give your permission for my formal courtship of Miss Elizabeth?"

You do speak plainly Mr Darcy! I fear you are either foolhardy or a saint to so fearlessly wish to tread that path, but I *will* give my permission if she wishes it. To that end I would like to see Elizabeth now. We will make no announcement until I have spoken with her – and Mr Darcy, it may be wise to delay an announcement until sometime after this whole Wickham affair has died down..."

"Yes sir, I take your meaning Mr Bennet. I accept your terms, and thank you for your permission for my courtship." Mr Darcy bowed to Elizabeth's father and moved toward the door. "If you will excuse me, I will leave you now."

Mr Bennet waved him out the door saying "Well, well, send Elizabeth to me in a moment if you please; I believe you will find her in the garden where I noticed her just now walking with her sister Jane."

Left alone for the moment, Mr Bennet still felt himself at a loss to understand how his daughter and Mr Darcy could be only barely conversable one day and courting the next. He could scarcely credit that his Lizzy would acquiesce in the scheme. Their dispositions were so very different! Were they not?

Waiting for his daughter to appear in his library and explain herself, his mind worked to unravel the bits and pieces of information now within his grasp. There must have been a great deal more behind those dark stares Mr Darcy had so frequently turned upon his Lizzy! And her heart, what could he comprehend of *that* mysterious organ? Ah, well, he would hear from her momentarily.

In the meantime Mr Bennet was left to his further reflections. He began to imagine how Darcy's intelligence and strong character might do quite well for Lizzy. She would always respect and esteem his strength and uprightness. As for Mr Darcy, her father could easily see how Lizzy's cheerful wit and generous nature might bring a softening and joy to the arid atmosphere that seemed to imbue much of the life he led thus far. Well, he thought to himself, they might rub along very well together. But *first*... a little fun!

TWENTY-ONE
Darcy and Jane Become friends

Darcy found Miss Elizabeth and Miss Bennet talking quietly while they gathered the last few of the summer roses, now mostly withered and dried out, to make sachets for Jane's closet.

He watched the two sisters for a moment. They were so graceful and lovely together that he was loath to interrupt their privacy.

Elizabeth was speaking in low tones to Jane. Some few of her silken auburn curls had escaped her bonnet, inviting his eyes to their sunlit dance against the creamy skin of her slender neck. He was mesmerized by the turn of her head and the delicate curve of her neck as she looked up from her labours to smile at something Jane said.

He could not see them from his position but he imagined her eyes with their golden flecks sparkling in the sunlight, glowing with love for her sister. He had seen that look when she stayed at Netherfield House to nurse her dear sister back to health. Darcy yearned to see such warmth in her eyes for *him*. He had watched in her interactions with friends and family and with acquaintances – and Caroline Bingley and Mrs Hurst. He had a fair idea of her moods, of how she responded to those she held in esteem and those for whom she felt less.

He knew she was well-read and held decided opinions on many things. Darcy had glimpsed her appreciation of the natural world out of doors. He had no doubt that he could spend his lifetime studying her, loving her, *delighting in her*!

Wrenching his thoughts away from his beloved lest he be undone by his fantasies, Darcy turned his attention to her elder sister.

Miss Bennet's taller, more willowy figure leaned toward Elizabeth in a way that bespoke the deep affection he knew the two sisters held for each other. He could see the angelic beauty that had so enthralled his friend – she with all her shining blonde tresses and deep blue eyes.

He wondered about her. *Did* she hold his friend in special regard? Was she only reserved about her feelings as he was? His mind was caught by the realization that Elizabeth would not hold such strong regard for one who was mercenary. She could never esteem passive compliance with their mother's exhortation for Jane Bennet to accept attentions from a man she did not hold in special regard. He wondered whether he might have foolishly allowed Miss Bingley's prejudice against everything Bennet to infect his perceptions. If so, he would owe his friend an apology for sowing seeds of doubt where no such blight had a place.

Just then the two young women turned in his direction. He moved forward, startled out of his reverie, hoping he had not been caught out gawking at them like a bedazzled school boy.

"Miss Bennet, Miss Elizabeth" Darcy bowed to them in greeting. "I see you are enjoying the fall sunshine. It is very pleasant here in the fresh air amid the sweet scents of your lovely garden. I do apologize for the interruption of your charming occupation; however Mr Bennet would speak with you in his library, Miss Elizabeth." Despite his amiable words, Darcy's tension was evident in the frown lines on his brow and white knuckles at his sides - and the way he twisted his signet ring incessantly.

Lizzy, who had suppressed a start at his approach, paled and bit her lip before looking up with a quick glance at Jane. Arranging her face in a cheerful smile for Darcy she curtseyed to him as she said "Well then, I suppose I had better go to him. I see that you have survived your interview with my father unscathed... er, relatively unscathed, sir?"

Darcy's frozen countenance softened at her tease. "I believe I shall survive, Miss Elizabeth." He loved to speak her name out loud. It felt luxurious to dwell on each syllable as if it held her essence in its sound. Her smile and the fresh garden air did indeed soothe him and he finally took the first deep breath he had achieved throughout the whole of that morning.

As she slipped away to meet with her father, Lizzy was relieved as well. Mr Darcy had been in with Papá for a very long time! She wished there had been an opportunity to question Mr Darcy about their meeting. She felt ill-prepared to face her father's interrogation on the subject of a courtship with Mr Darcy!

~&~

Darcy watched Elizabeth walk away from him toward the house with a sense of loss. Being in her presence for those brief moments had comforted his raw nerves, making him notice the warm sunshine on his face and the sweetness of the air with a greater appreciation than he had felt earlier.

"Mr Darcy," Jane smiled gently at him, "I hope our dear father's tease has not disconcerted you overmuch. I beg you would not take offense at his ways. Indeed I wish you will not allow his enjoyment to disturb your peace of mind. He means you no harm."

"Thank you, Miss Bennet. I believe that I begin to understand him a little. He did have his fun at my cost, however the prize I seek is worth enduring that and much more!" He knew she meant to put him at ease and he made an effort to match her lightness of tone.

"Mr Darcy, may I speak frankly?"

"Of course Miss Bennet, I hope that will always be how we speak to each other." He gave her a small smile; wondering what Charles Bingley's "Angel", who had rarely spoken to him in the whole course of their acquaintance, wanted to say to him. This Bennet family seemed full of surprises!

"As do I, sir" Jane blushed and looked down as if to collect her thoughts. "Shall we rest here on this bench for a few moments? I find that I think more clearly when I am not moving about."

"You have something awkward on your mind, Miss Bennet?" He sat beside her and turned in her direction, giving her his full attention. "Take all of the time you need, I can be a patient man and I want to hear what you have to tell me".

"Thank you, sir. It is only that... I have no doubt that our father has tested your intentions toward my dear sister in his own way; no doubt extracting every ounce of humour to be found in the situation. However I feel a need to assure myself in another way than my father's. As much as I love and respect Papá, I find no comfort in his joke that "a girl likes to be crossed in love now and then" as if heartache were a pleasant diversion. Forgive me, I do not mean to denigrate my father, he is an excellent man in every way!" Jane's blush was intense.

"Not at all, Miss Bennet; I believe your point is well taken – and with no disrespect to Mr Bennet. Please, go on."

Taking a deep breath, she plunged ahead "My younger sister is intelligent, and witty, and independent to a fault, but her heart is innocent and her nature is warm and loving. She is passionate about the things she cares about, and brave beyond anything! Indeed, there is no other like her in grace, beauty, and more innate wisdom than most people gain in thrice her years. Elizabeth is my dearest friend and by far my favourite sister. I love her very much; her good humoured wit and generous heart light my days - especially when I am dreary or downhearted." Here Jane paused to reflect on what she wanted to convey to him, but only for a moment. She knew that if she did not speak her piece promptly, she would lose her purpose in worrying that she was offending or causing pain.

Darcy's eyes were fixed on her face. He was most eager to hear more of his beloved, although a bit startled at Jane's volubility, she who spoke softly and seldom spoke to him. His curiosity, nay his concentrated interest was piqued. Where was she headed? For she clearly had a goal in mind.

"You are a good man, an excellent gentleman I know, Mr Darcy. I do not mean to accuse you of any conduct that is less than honourable, or motive less than of the noblest kind. It is only that I do not know your ways, the ways of the *ton* and what is acceptable there. What is usual in your circles might be devastating to one who knows only our simple country manners.

"You have asked to court Elizabeth. Excuse me sir, but she did say enough about your discourse both at the Netherfield ball and on Oakham Mount for me to grasp both her initial astonishment at your wholly unexpected professions of admiration, and that considerable confusion lingers in her heart and mind over your recent revelations to her.

"I shall not betray her confidences further; I simply desire you to understand that in the matter of love she is entirely naïve; her heart is untouched. I fear that her inexperience, her warm nature, will be her undoing should she bestow her sweet heart upon an undeserving, or careless man!

"Just now you said that the prize you seek is worth enduring a great deal for. I hope that you understand that the "prize" you speak of would be yours for a lifetime – with all of the joys and *responsibilities* such a magnificent gift would entail."

Jane bethought herself to mention another aspect of her sister that she felt important for him to understand. "You shall want to know something of my sister's teasing. Lizzy *does* tease a great deal. She uses it to protect her tender feelings and to give notice to the world of her love. She tries to address everyone in a way that presents the best in herself and brings out the best in them.

"In Lizzy's estimation graciousness and generosity are never wasted. One can behave kindly, practice kindness in the world, without any loss to one's self. Lizzy finds that seeing the ridiculous in herself and those around her, in addition to allowing her to regard her object with charitable feelings, brings a sparkle to her day – indeed to mine and Papá's as well if truth be told!

"Lizzy declares that wit should always arise from good nature. Whether it be giddy or dry, private or shared, it is a sign of unconditional love of oneself and one's fellow human beings.

"Cruel wit is the exception. She believes that such is only disguised aggression. Lizzy does not suffer the exercise of cruel wit against anyone!"

Suddenly conscious that she had been *lecturing* Mr Darcy *at some length*, Jane faltered. Covering her lips with her fingers she stuttered "I do, *I do apologize* sir, for my impertinence! Please forgive my interference! *Please do* forgive me!"

"No, Miss Bennet, there is nothing to forgive. Indeed I thank you for your candid words and your generosity in speaking with such courage on behalf of your sister. She is blessed by your good offices – as am I. It fully delights me to hear such as you have spoken, for I am an innocent in the affairs of the heart as well. I have spared no effort to avoid the entanglements which you might imagine have so regularly thrown themselves in my path. I did not wish for dalliance for its own sake, nor have I desired object without honour.

"I may say that it reassures me to know for certain that there is no *other* whose presence or memory might dim the brilliant future I dream of sharing with Miss Elizabeth.

"As for the ways of the *ton*, they are not *my* ways. The ladies of the *ton,* whose interests are limited to the dictates of fashion and gossip; whose demeanour is dictated by scheming and strategy; and whose integrity is only as substantial as their prospects hold no allure for me. It is only Miss Elizabeth who stirs my heart so!"

Darcy recognized that he could trust Jane Bennet. Charles Bingley had discovered what he was only just beginning to know. Miss Jane Bennet was not only angelic in her appearance; she was angelic in her loving heart. She wanted to see the good in them all, to gently encourage and nurture it to with her faith in each one. How could he ever have questioned her motives? She would never support trifling with Charles Bingley's affections any more than she would sanction carelessness with her sister's.

He opened his heart to her as he had to no other so wholly unconnected to himself – and even to some who were!

"It is through Miss Elizabeth's beautiful eyes that I have seen the man I ought to be, *must* be. Seeing my behaviour through *her* eyes I have learned to feel as if I have blundered through my life like a bull let loose in a china closet- where the blunt force of momentum inevitably smashes many a lovely item indiscriminately by the untutored and restive nature of his course.

"As a child I was given good principles, but was left to follow them in pride and conceit. I was led to think ill of those beneath my station and to discount the inherent value in others. Eliz.. Miss Elizabeth showed me in her delightful teasing way and in her furious censure as well, that I was a pretender – not a man equal to pleasing a woman worthy of being pleased. But neither does she dismiss me out of hand; I believe that she also sees that better man within me, ready to be brought to the fore. I am consumed with determination to make myself eligible for her good opinion."

Darcy took a deep breath and expelled it as a hearty sigh before going on.

"Miss Bennet, I do not often open my heart to others. Yet your dear sister, and now you, draw me out and touch my heart to a degree I would never have thought possible. I find myself easily discussing subjects I hardly acknowledged within my own thoughts in the past. I honour you for that. Seldom, if ever, have I met with such very intelligent ladies who are also admirable for their goodness of heart, strength of character, and the kind generosity of their spirits. This exchange has not been easy for me, but I thank you for making it possible."

"Mr Darcy I... I cannot explain it but I have long felt that there was a special... er, an *unusual* connection between you and my sister. Pardon me for saying so but even when she did not recognize it herself, I... I knew there was something intense... in your reactions to one another's presence..."

Jane's words held all the earnestness of her sincere heart. She had never spoken thus to anyone other than her dear Lizzy.

Utterly shocked at her own forwardness, Jane could only give a little shrug of her elegant shoulders and attempt a rueful smile in his direction. "*Oh my!* I seem to be getting myself in deeper and deeper!" Straightening herself and looking again into his eyes, she rushed out "I am most clumsily trying to tell you – to lend you my support and encouragement – for whatever that may be worth! I cannot control *or* predict my sister's heart – or her *choice*."

"I am extremely grateful for your kindness Miss Bennet, and most honoured by your confidence in me. You are indeed a remarkable lady, kind and wise, and loyal to your loved ones. I feel the honour of your confidences with all my heart and hope from this day forward we shall always be the best of friends!"

Darcy's wide smile was a revelation in itself to Jane, who had never been privy to such an expression on his face before. His dark eyes glowed and his countenance softened remarkably to one of warmth and good humour.

"Your words are too kind. I am honoured, Mr Darcy." She nearly gasped the words out in her astonishment! He was indeed a *handsome* man!

"Perhaps one day I may have the good fortune to call you 'sister'. I have always wanted another sister – especially one as admirable as you!"

"And I have always wanted a brother such as you, Mr Darcy, but I believe we are getting far ahead of events, sir! Let us amend our conversation to subjects more befitting the demands of propriety. Now that we have confided so openly in each other I believe that I shall always consider you a dear friend, at the very least!"

TWENTY-TWO
Papá Please Be Serious!

Spotting Jane and Mr Darcy sitting in easy intimacy on the old bench under the rose arbour apparently engaged in earnest conversation, Elizabeth halted abruptly in her headlong rush to reprieve after an enervating interview with her father. Their easy tete`-a-tete´ roused a quick succession of feelings in her breast, a province already overburdened by the trying emotions of the day.

She instantly cast aside the flicker of jealousy at seeing her exquisitely beautiful Jane, quite five times more lovely than any other young woman in Hertfordshire, so attentive to the man who proposed to court *her*.

Briefly her mind stumbled over an unexpectedly apprehensive reaction to his evident fascination with her stunning sister. This too, she cast aside. Surely she would not regret him if he were to prove as fickle as *that*!

Yet her feelings *were* still smarting from her father's displeasure over her spending a considerable amount of time alone with Mr Darcy the afternoon before. There had followed a lengthy diatribe on the subject of her father's real or trumped up misgivings.

He was worried that she might be too easily swayed, led by Mr Darcy's wealth and consequence, his sophistication and superior intellect, to a choice which ultimately might be her undoing. She knew too little of him, she certainly knew nothing of the sphere to which he was accustomed, what he would expect – even demand of her. She was a country miss and he a far more worldly man than the friends and neighbours of her previous association. She was inexperienced and knew not how to judge what sort of man would suit her, what sort of man he was. Her father doubted her ability to assess what truly should constitute her future happiness.

On and on he went, testing her feelings about Mr Darcy, her commitment to the requested courtship, and her judgment about her future life.

Elizabeth answered her father honestly. She apologized for her improper venture to Oakham Mount with Mr Darcy. It had been a coincidental meeting which occurred in all innocence; but it had been wrong of her to allow it to continue – especially for so long.

Elizabeth agreed that she had much to learn before she could accept a proposal from him.

She was not overly impressed by his wealth or consequence. She did esteem his education and knowledge of the world – but more so the evidence thus far of his character.

She admitted that she had agreed to a courtship only after turning down a proposal (this disclosure cost her father a flicker of shock); she had been flattered, intrigued, and taken unawares by his display of esteem for her. Lizzy confessed that she must have quite mistaken the import of his piercing stares – they were not dark looks of disapproval but rather of ardency.

She had always viewed him from a perspective predicated upon his disparaging remarks when he declined to dance, indeed even to be introduced to her - rudely pronouncing her "tolerable but not handsome enough to tempt" him. Ever since that Meryton assembly she had been most severe upon him; misinterpreting his every word and action. Her poor opinion of him, ill formed at first, should not last forever.

His desire to please her had already brought him to an increase in his awareness and concern for the feelings of others. She *was* pleased that this proud man, a man of consequence in the world, was willing to give up his privacy for no benefit to himself but solely in order to protect the innocent.

She wanted to get to know Mr Darcy better.

~&~

In the end Mr Bennet had kissed her on the cheek and said "I am satisfied that you are thinking sensibly, my dear. And I too, am impressed with Mr Darcy's character in the instant case. Indeed, I find that I like the man very much. I must say that for a man renowned for his taciturnity and reserve, he quite waxes eloquent when it comes to speaking of his feelings for you, Lizzy!" Pausing to observe her reaction, he chuckled to himself at the heightened colour in her already flushed cheeks.

"However we scarcely know him as yet. I am in no hurry to part with you my Lizzy – especially without exercising every possible caution to ensure your safety and happiness in your future life."

He paused to look keenly into her eyes. "I have already told Mr Darcy that I shall permit a courtship between you, so long as you wish for it. Do you truly desire Mr Darcy to court you Lizzy? Are you certain of your interest in him?"

Elizabeth dropped her eyes to her lap. "I, I believe so, Papá. I am *interested* in Mr Darcy." She looked up with a trace of her usual self-confident smile. "I believe that I shall enjoy his courtship very much. As to whether I can be sure what my answer shall be to a future proposal from him, should one be forthcoming, is that determination not the purpose of said activity?"

"Very well then my girl. A courtship we shall have. Unfortunately due to the exigencies of the moment, namely our mutual goal of exposing Mr Wickham as the blackguard he most assuredly must be, it will better protect your reputation, and Mr Darcy's, to keep the information between ourselves.

"As dearly as I anticipate your mother's transports of bliss on the subject of having a courtship of one of her daughters (though admittedly not her favourite and not with the man of her mother's misguided choice) actually in progress, she shall be *protected* from its knowledge *at all costs*! Else we are done for. The neighbourhood, upon receiving her shrill and instantaneous proclamations, will only believe that we wish to blacken Wickham's name in order to forward Mr Darcy's standing."

Believing her dismayed, he added "No dear, I fear you must tell no one, not a soul outside the family and... well, *Jane* of course – but no other within it. After all, if things should turn out differently than we presently expect - if Mr Darcy is the blackguard and Mr Wickham's character without blemish – why then you will find it ever so much easier to extricate yourself form his company!" This last was spoken with a twinkling eye and a smirk on his lips.

"Papá! How can you talk so?" Could her father *never* resist a tease; even when her prospective happiness was a stake?

"Thank you Papá, I shall take care to protect us *all* from folly of any sort." Kissing her father on the top of his bald spot, she hurried away, not allowing him any further opportunity to toy with her sensibilities!

Impatient of so much that was mocking in her father's treatment of her and perplexed by more than one quandary, Elizabeth chose to shake off her disquiet in favour of sanguinity. Telling herself that there was no help in refining too much upon everything at once, she immediately abandoned the house for the delights of the garden.

Thus Elizabeth hurried to join them, nonplussed only briefly at discovering Jane and Mr Darcy entertaining each other so well. Almost instantly her mind adapted to the news of their amiable relations. It was a most welcome development and highly in her favour.

Lizzy was not formed for ill humour and her dear sister could never act in such a way as to harm anyone. She need not even consider Mr Darcy. He was officially on sufferance and must earn her good opinion – or not. In either case she was prepared to choose contentment.

Jane and Mr Darcy happened to glance in her direction just then as if impelled by her arrival on the scene.

"Lizzy, here you are at last! Are *you also* in need of quizzing out of our father's unfortunate inclination to amuse himself at our expense? You look a trifle peaked my dear. Must I soothe and pet you back to tranquillity?" Jane's uneasy laugh betrayed her attempt at a joke.

All three were acutely aware that Elizabeth had yet to announce her father's consent to Mr Darcy's request.

Elizabeth's face assumed a decidedly stormy expression. "Not *you*, too, Jane! *Must* I endure yet another tease?"

Then, seeing her sister's shocked expression, she laughed light-heartedly and said "Not a bit of it Jane! There is no need to rouse your nerves, my dear; Papá and I have deliberated together and reached accord in the end. He did regale me with a great many of his *earnest* contemplations, *quite full* of punctilio. However *I do not* wilt under the trials that beset me.

I weathered the experience well enough. Indeed, I *must* have derived immense benefit from it - and in finis, knowing himself *run out* without further recourse; poor Papá could do naught but let me go!"

"Are you truly well, Miss Elizabeth? Shall you rest awhile here in the garden?" Darcy had sprung to his feet with a bow, sweeping his arm toward the bench in invitation. His gentlemanly demeanour did little to mask the agony of apprehension he endured.

"Perfectly sir, I thank you." With a quick curtsey she shook her head. "Heavens, after spending so long indoors I *much* prefer a turn about the grounds. Can I persuade you to join me in a brief stroll, Mr Darcy?"

Taking his instantly proffered arm, she turned to her sister. "And Jane, you must attend us. It would not do for a newly courting couple, secretly or no, to be left too much on their own!"

Darcy's falter midstride at hearing her words brought her attention to the expression on his face. He was looking down at her with such a warmth in his dark eyes that she blushed and looked away to hide her sudden confusion.

~&~

Soon after Jane's heartfelt congratulations and a short discussion between the three of them of how and when the couple might be in each other's company without raising suspicion, Jane retired to her bench. From there she could observe Mr Darcy and Elizabeth as they moved about the garden, while she began culling out the debris from the sweetly scented petals they had been gathering.

Mr Darcy had said nothing of his friend. Everyone's attention had been entirely taken up with the developments in *Lizzy's* situation so it did not come as any great surprise that no occasion had arisen in which to think of Charles Bingley – or for anyone *else* to think of him, at any rate. Thoughts of Mr Charles Bingley were *never* far from Jane's mind.

How she would have liked to ask her new friend whether there was any doubt that Mr Bingley would return to Netherfield as he planned. What a singular thing to ask! And how should a maiden, unconnected by any pretence of an understanding, introduce the subject without the appearance of impropriety? Hang that dratted dream! She would think on her hopes for her sister and trust that Mr Bingley was everything a young *gentleman* ought to be.

Sighing in resignation, Jane acknowledged to herself that she must be patient. She would know in due time whether Charles Bingley had intentions toward her. Fortunately for her, patience was indeed a virtue to which she could honestly lay claim – most of the time.

A moment later she heard Lydia and Kitty's voices raised in some dispute between themselves. "Probably over that *bonnet* again!" she muttered with unaccustomed annoyance.

"Lizzy!" Jane called out, taking care not to be heard by those within doors. When her sister turned to look at her she signalled toward the house, a gesture used between them many times before when they did not wish to attract unwanted attention. Lizzy waved her thanks and spoke to her companion.

Mr Darcy soon took his leave after obtaining permission to return the following morning for a conference with Mr Bennet and to spend time with Lizzy.

~&~

"I want to hear all about it, Lizzy! You were in with our father for rather a long time! Was he terribly hard on you? I imagine that Mr Darcy's errand took him quite by surprise; did it not?"

Jane was relieved to have her sister to herself again. As pleased as she was for her, it was somewhat discomfiting to be separated in such a way from her most intimate confidante – even for so fleeting a time. She did not resent the change; it was to be expected if their hopes and dreams were to be realized. Still, it *was* a change.

"Of course you must hear of it, Jane! I would not wish for you to miss one iota of our dear father's *excessively* provoking dithering. Really, it was *too bad* of him!"

"Lizzy! That is *not* respectful!"

"I am sorry, Jane, but I do think he used me with uncommon cruelty. Suffice it to say that he censured and tested me at every turn, slighted Mr Darcy and flatly told me that he doubted my judgment about my future life."

"I feel certain that Papá did not intend to insult you Lizzy. Just think how alarmed he must be at the prospect of losing you!"

"If that is true Jane, and I allow it may be something of the truth, why can he not see beyond his own selfish interests enough to think how *I* feel?

"Never mind, I cannot expect the leopard to change his spots! He is our own dear Papá after all! But tell me of what you and Mr Darcy were speaking while I was suffering Papá's benevolence"

"Mr Darcy and I have formed an alliance in your behalf! I am to trust him enough to not to interfere with his courtship of you; he is not to trifle with your affections!" Jane smiled serenely at Lizzy's indignant look. "And for the rest, of both our tales Lizzy, I fear we shall be forced to wait until we retire to our bedroom tonight. Attend! Here comes Mamá!"

"Oh! Do you know; I had completely forgotten about Mr Collins! I wonder what *he* has been about all morning."

~&~

"Papá, may I speak to you for a moment?" Lizzy slipped through the library door after her father. Supper had been noisy and chaotic, her mother endlessly repeating what she had said to neighbours and friends, and what they had said to her until everyone in the room could have recited it all back to her.

Mrs Bennet *did* bring back the information that several of the shopkeepers in Meryton were *now worried* about the extensive bills owed them by Mr Wickham. But the most shocking and disturbing piece of news involved a Miss Mary King; with whom Mr Wickham had been quite friendly since word got out that she had inherited ten thousand pounds from an uncle. She was an only child whose parents had died a year ago, leaving her in the care of an elderly spinster aunt. Miss King was only recently removed to Meryton so was not well known to the Bennets. Nevertheless, Lizzy was gratified to think that she might soon be protected from the rogue in their midst.

"Yes my child; what is it? I am a tired old man and have not much left with which to deal with any *new* matters of singular urgency." He smiled and waved to her usual chair in invitation for her to sit down.

"Papá... I do love you very much and, excuse me; I mean no disrespect with what I have to say. I simply do not like to end this very important day in our lives feeling ill-disposed toward my dear parent." Lizzy's voice, hesitant at first, was low and tremulous as she finished. Yet despite her obvious distress, her eyes never left her father's countenance.

At this Mr Bennet's gaze at his daughter sharpened and he sat up straighter in his chair. "What exactly are you trying to say to me, daughter?"

With just the slightest flinch she went on. "Sir I, I was very hurt by the way you spoke to me today. I felt that you were laughing at me – and worse. You have always encouraged me with your trust in my intelligence, my good judgment... but today...it was... it was otherwise." Lizzy stopped speaking; she was unable to speak further. The pain in her heart *would out* if she tried.

Seeing her so pained broke her father's heart. He *had* gone too far! He would amend the situation forthwith by giving her what she needed from a good father.

"Oh my dear, you well know the ways of your old Papá! Truly I wish you would not mind my little fun!

"In all seriousness, I suspect that your Mr Darcy might be just what your happiness requires. We know him to be reserved and disciplined, often appearing haughty and aloof. However I believe you shall learn that he is a deeply complex man.

"It may well be that he is, in fact, quite shy. His tautly controlled emotions and carefully guarded privacy suggest an intensely passionate nature that does not well endure the scrutiny of those who are not close to him – and I suspect that those who are close to him are a select few.

"Mr Darcy is a man who is constantly sought after for his consequence. His *condition in life* of wealth, power and as master of a great estate, make him a highly eligible matrimonial prospect. Think of your mother and comprehend that there are hundreds of match-making mamas in Town, whose campaigns are far more determinedly and efficaciously waged than any she could concoct.

"Mr Darcy is bound to be the object of financial schemers as well. He must strictly scrutinize everyone around him to discover their motives for choosing his company.

"Recall that by the age of only twenty-two he had already lost both parents and assumed tremendous responsibilities. It is to be expected that he fears any failing in his responsibilities and of losing those he esteems. The situation as regards Mr Wickham must affect him dreadfully even now, after the central events are in the past.

"I believe that Mr Darcy has learned to hide his vulnerability from everyone. Your protective, nurturing qualities will soon be engaged *there*, if they are not already so.

"Matters of the heart notwithstanding, Mr Darcy *is* a strong, confident man of great maturity and experience. He is knowledgeable, has lived in the world and endured some very harsh challenges to the benefit and confirmation of his character. He will always ensure your comfort and take good care of you.

"His intelligence and wit will always challenge you to keep your own well honed. *Your* social ease and ready wit, your own *prodigious* intellect, your self-confidence and courage, and your *warm nature* will hold him close to you. *Both of you* are loyal to those you esteem and if you do find that mutual admiration and regard from which a commitment for a lifetime must be inspired your lasting happiness will be ensured."

"Oh Papá! *Thank you for that!* And thank you for hearing me! You truly have gifted me with a father's *greatest* service to his daughter; you have taken care to think of my future in every way!"

"Well, well, off with you now; I require a vast amount of undisturbed peace in order to recover from this past four-and-twenty hours!"

As Lizzy scooted out the door Mr Bennet half chuckled and half grimaced to himself.

"Poor Mr Collins!"

TWENTY-THREE
Good Gossip and a Visit to Netherfield

Within a few days, it seemed that all of Hertfordshire was discussing Mr Wickham's disgraceful conduct. Shopkeepers and gamesters alike were equally up in arms over his numerous and substantial debts. He owed for goods and services rendered as well as pledges of honour. Worse still, several tearful daughters now admitted breaches of propriety – if not outright compromise – involving Mr Wickham.

Everyone, it seemed, was looking for Mr Wickham, including his commanding officer, Colonel Forster. Mr Wickham was understood at last to be a deserter, despoiler of young women, fraud and cheat. To the utter frustration and disgust of most, he was nowhere to be found. He had, apparently, disappeared from their midst.

Lydia and Kitty Bennet were seen to fall into fits of giggles, for no perceptible reason, at odd times – especially when they had been out walking. Lydia had recently developed an interest in the woods near their home. Kitty, of course, was *not* to be left behind on any of Lydia's exploits.

Jane and Lizzy looked at each other in wonderment each time their younger sisters set out on those walks. This was a most unusual departure from trimming their attire and squabbling over bonnets and ribbons. Indeed, until recently the two never walked anywhere except to Meryton for gossip, shopping, and the company of the officers.

Neither of the elder sisters gave much thought to the younger one's activities at first. They were entirely caught up in their own affairs.

Mr Bingley had returned promptly from London just as he had planned. Jane's giddy flutter of relief was only a little dampened by a niggling perplexity over her disquieting dreams and imaginings during his brief absence.

What had been afoot to inspire her unease? It was not in her nature to indulge in doubts of *anyone* – especially not such an enthusiastically amiable a gentleman as *Charles* Bingley! Impatient of useless conjecture, she simply delighted in their growing friendship, refusing to fret needlessly.

Lizzy was cautiously reconnoitring that common ground between herself and Mr Darcy which could be visited without inviting more intimacy than was comfortable to her. Her first ramble around the garden with him, while Jane watched over them, had been spent largely on soothing those jangled insecurities originating from Mr Bennet's helpfulness in each of their interviews with him.

~&~

Over the following days both of the gentlemen from Netherfield called upon the ladies of Longbourn nearly every day.

There was nothing to excite Mrs Bennet's attention in that, beyond the pleasure she took in anticipating an inevitable betrothal between her beautiful Jane and Mr Bingley.

As for *Lizzy*, well, Mrs Bennet could hardly see *too little* of that wild, disobedient...*rapscallion!* It was not to *her* credit that all was not yet lost. For Mrs Bennet's all-but-forgotten child, sombre, censorious Mary had been spending *considerable* time in serious discourse with Mr Collins in the small sitting room – with the door properly ajar, of course!

They spoke endlessly about matters of great doctrinal import – that were of no import at all to anyone else. No matter, if *Mary* could secure him then so be it. Longbourn would be saved and *Lizzy* would be the loser in the end.

At least her wayward daughter made a ready chaperon for Jane and Mr Bingley, and kept the ever-present Mr Darcy far enough out of the way that *Mr Bingley* would not be impeded from declaring himself – *soon*, she hoped!

There continued a steady stream of visits back and forth between neighbours and friends to keep Mrs Bennet's mind occupied, her spirits in high vigour and her self-importance mightily set up. She spent half her days at her sister Phillips' house in Meryton for the convenience of *her* ready company and to be in nearer proximity to many of her chin-wagging friends.

Mr Bennet congratulated himself on achieving a modicum of peace and quiet in which to enjoy a glass of port and a good book.

Lydia and Kitty walked out and Mary sat with Mr Collins. Jane and Lizzy spent time with one another and with their gentleman callers quietly going about the business of falling in love.

In this manner the Bennet family was dispersed – all five sisters safe from the close observation of their parents.

~&~

On the third day after his return from town, Mr Bingley invited Miss Bennet and her next sister to take tea at Netherfield. Upon receiving their note of acceptance, he sent his carriage for them.

Miss Bennet and Miss Elizabeth's prompt arrival was eagerly greeted by Mr Bingley and his friend. Each gentleman eagerly stepped forward to assist a Bennet sister to alight; immediately offering his arm to lead her inside.

Mr Darcy's *notice* of the visitors was observed with severe displeasure by Miss Caroline Bingley. She had been more than put out of countenance at his obvious fascination with *Eliza* Bennet when she stayed at Netherfield to nurse her ailing sister.

Miss Bingley disdained her brother's constant attendance at Longbourn in recent days; she *positively chafed* at Mr Darcy's accompanying him there.

Miss *Eliza's* trailing along with their *invited* guest - for Jane Bennet was her dear friend, after all – was *outside* of enough!

"How kind of you *both,* to take pity on our dullness in this way!" Her decidedly acid tone belied her polite words. "Do not you agree, Louisa, that *Miss Eliza's* condescension is our good fortune? I did not expect such a *happy t*urn, I daresay."

Everyone stared at her in surprise.

"Why Caroline, I am quite sure I informed you that I invited Miss Bennet *and* Miss Elizabeth for tea this afternoon. I spoke to you of it last evening when Mr Darcy and I returned from our ride."

"Oh Charles, surely you *meant* to do so but forgot." Miss Bingley shrugged her shoulders in dismissal. Having made her displeasure known to her nemesis, there was nothing for it but to don a veneer of politeness while she thought to discompose *"Miss Eliza"* at every opportunity.

Turning to lead them toward the sitting room she did not notice Mr Darcy's dark frown in her direction.

"Miss Elizabeth." He swept his arm in the direction Miss Bingley had taken. "I am happy to see you! I am sorry for any lack of cordiality you may encounter here" he said softly, and then more loudly "Was your carriage ride comfortable?" He was careful not to display any particular regard before the Bingley sisters or the servants. They had agreed beforehand that there would be nothing secret about their courtship if they were not careful *there*.

Lizzy merely lifted an eyebrow in amusement at him. Smiling sweetly she responded "Oh yes Mr Darcy, I am sure that must have been the finest carriage ride I have ever enjoyed – for *that* carriage was surely an equipage with the panache of Pemberley and therefore must be *vastly* superior to any other!"

"Oh, no, Miss Elizabeth! Surely that was *Charles'* carriage which brought you here." Miss Bingley struck in.

"Oh! But I *had understood* that it was Mr Bingley's purpose to set up his carriage, yes and his future estate as well, precisely in *emulation* of Mr Darcy's own Pemberley! Did I not hear *you* say so one evening when we were all together here at Netherfield, Miss Bingley? You *must* excuse me for mistaking it for Mr Darcy's, or a replica of Mr Darcy's, in *that* case." Eyes wide in innocence, Elizabeth's amiable face betrayed no hint of consciousness that she was amusing herself giving Miss Bingley a subtle knock in exchange for that ill-natured lady's absurd attempt to discomfit her.

Miss Bingley stopped abruptly and glared at Lizzy, momentarily at a loss for words.

Jane looked bemused and Mr Darcy coughed to cover a chuckle. The whole party was halted in the entry to the sitting room where they would have their tea a little later.

"Not a bit of it, Miss Elizabeth! I have been dreadfully neglectful of my sister's excellent advice in the matter of my carriage *and* my estate! However I think I should sooner buy Darcy's carriage than replicate it. It surely would not do to have our carriages just alike for *that* would be confusing indeed!" Mr Bingley's jovial rejoinder dislodged the pile-up of vitriol and humour.

Bingley and Jane were alike in their uneasiness with discord in any form. They each in their own way could always be counted on to step into the breach with soothing words or some minor diversion to bring harmony, or the appearance of it, to a tense moment.

The group continued its progress into the sitting room where Miss Bingley and Mrs Hurst promptly seated themselves side-by-side upon the settee placed most conveniently to command the whole room.

"To own the truth, I rather congratulate myself that no one could find anything wanting in my own fine equipage! As much as I admire and respect my friend, I cannot think that the world needs *two* of him, much better that I am my *own* man! Do you not agree Darcy?"

"Exactly so, Bingley. Your sister merely wishes the best for you, of course. You must count yourself fortunate indeed to have Miss Bingley's devotion to your interests in such a way. Still she must learn to trust your excellent taste for its own sake."

Believing herself complimented by Darcy's words, Caroline preened and glanced around the room exultantly as she gushed "Of *course*, Mr Darcy; I do take a deal of interest in dear Charles' every concern! However I would not wish the world to think me unappreciative of my brother's good taste – especially as regards his excellent choice of *friends*! Do you not concur Louisa?"

Miss Bingley's appeal to her sister was only pro forma – she barely stopped to listen for a reply. As good as speaking over Mrs Hurst's "Oh, yes of course my dear…" and Mr Hurst's muffled snort, Caroline turned to Jane "I am delighted you are here today as I quite yearn to show you our little gazebo which Charles has had erected in the farthest rose garden."

With a conspiratorial smile at Darcy she said "I fancy my devotion did serve a useful purpose *there*! It took only the smallest suggestion and my dear brother embarked upon the formulation of a project that must surely bring continual delight to all."

Jane's serene smile lighted her features "Oh how lovely! I'm sure I shall be thrilled to see it."

Mr Bingley's breath caught at the sight. No matter how frequently Miss Bennet rewarded her friends with that smile, her beauty never failed to take away his breath – and his composure! He resolved that he *would* speak to her; he would declare himself at the earliest opportunity. This was a matter in which *no one's* opinion held the least significance but his own – and Jane's! "It is settled then. Directly after tea we shall all go for a walk in the rose garden to admire the new addition to Netherfield's charms! Everyone?"

Everyone did indeed desire to enjoy the walk, the gazebo and, for some, each other's company.

Miss Bingley rang for tea and the group soon enjoyed every good thing the kitchen of an elegant estate could provide for what turned out to be more of a light luncheon.

While they partook of several cold meats, cheeses, fruits and small pastries, Charles was persuaded to describe how he had managed to bring about the new attraction.

'Tea' and conversation were leisurely and generally innocuous as the visit progressed.

At last, the tea things cleared away and their digestion allowed its due, six of them set out. The weather was pleasantly mild, an early December sun providing sufficient warmth to allow them a comfortable stroll out of doors.

In kindness to his friend, Mr Bingley deferred his own heart's desire - to walk with Miss Bennet - and led his two sisters, leaving Mr Darcy to escort the Misses Bennet one on each arm. Mr Hurst, as was his wont, declined the exercise – he would nap until their return to the house, he said.

Proceeding thus toward their destination, Darcy slowed his threesome a little so that Bingley and his sisters might draw far enough ahead to allow for a semi-private conversation.

"That was too bad of you, Miss Elizabeth, to mock Miss Bingley's raptures over Pemberley in such a way." The weight of Mr Darcy's murmured censure was reduced considerably by his low rumbling chuckle as he smirked at Jane before turning to gaze at Elizabeth.

"True, and not so very pleasing in *you* to come to her defence as you did, sir!" Lizzy's merry smile and light squeeze of his arm proved her tease and set his eyes ablaze.

Seeing his warm expression caused Lizzy to stumble. Her grip on Mr Darcy's arm tightened reflexively and their arms brushed slightly against each other as she regained her balance.

It took all of his concentration not to release Jane's arm and place that hand lovingly over Miss Elizabeth's captivating touch. He longed desperately to be alone with her, where he imagined he might be allowed to engage in some small liberties, a kiss to her hand, a light caress to the smooth curve of her cheek – how he would love to simply stand a little closer to her so he could inhale the faintly astringent lavender fragrance of her glossy hair and creamy skin! She could not possibly be aware of how such moments as this affected him!

"Please pardon my clumsiness Mr Darcy! I seem to be tripping over my own feet this afternoon!" She was peeking at him from under thick lashes, her face quite becomingly pink, and moving aside to put a proper distance between them. On her countenance was an expression of mock disapproval – at least he hoped it was not *genuine* vexation! His heart quaked as the question trembled in the balance. Upon a moment's reflection he let that thought go. Her ire was not so easily roused as all that!

"Not at all Miss Elizabeth," Seeing her lips curve upwards into a demure little smile, he smiled back with his whole heart in his eyes, "I feel certain there was a loose pebble just where you stepped back there. Bingley's groundsman shall be told of it on the sharp; I shall see to it myself."

Miss Bennet, who had been contentedly entertaining herself with admiring the fine set of Mr Bingley's shoulders and the athletic grace of his stride finally tore her gaze away long enough to catch Darcy and Lizzy's heightened complexions and intense preoccupation with one another.

"My *dear* friend, and *most* beloved sister, you will *never* carry off the smallest pretext of disinterested acquaintance if you do not employ greater constraint in public! The briefest glance from *anyone* will expose your secret instantly – or at the very least give away that some greater *congeniality* exists than is generally understood to be the case." She said softly, directing her attention considerately toward the shrubs and flowers bordering their way.

"You *may not* have taken note of Miss Bingley's *frequent* glances our way. I think she does not like to be so distant from us that no general conversation is to be had."

The couple instantly looked away from one another, Lizzy blushing furiously and Mr Darcy's face going pale. *Now he did* worry - that Miss Elizabeth would come to despise him for embarrassing her so! She loved to study the antics and foibles of others, he knew, but she would not enjoy being the object of *their* speculations!

Kind-hearted Miss Bennet would never intentionally make anyone uneasy. Her gentle chide was felt the more keenly for that. And it arose from *his* faulty conduct! But how was he to be in Elizabeth's company, feel the pressure of her dear hand on his arm, without thrilling to it?

He knew that *his* impertinent country miss was used to a greater degree of frankness on delicate subjects than her counterparts in *Town*. Indeed he found her self-confident air and forthright manner, united with her ready smile and sparkling eyes, *most* endearing. Still, he was insistently dogged by the thought that their courtship was *most ardent* on his side and *only tolerated* on hers. That anything at all might elicit her disgust of his suit, might spur her to cry-off their tenuous accord, simply did not bear thinking of.

"My whole dependence is upon Mr Darcy's *lofty* manner and his customary sobriety, Jane!" Elizabeth's giggle delighted and relieved him. "Certainly if *anyone* is a high stickler for propriety it must be he! If he fails me in this, then I know not what I shall do!" How he *adored* those rosy teasing lips!

"Lizzy! You are... You are quite beyond the reach of my feeble censure! Come we shall overtake the others and put a stop to your mischief directly!" Jane began hurrying them toward Mr Bingley and his sisters. Miss Bennet had *had her fill* of gazing upon *her* beloved from afar.

"No Jane, you are wrong. Indeed your chastisement has cut me to the quick! I am all propriety and obedience to my elder sister; you see? I shall accompany Mrs Hurst for the time being, and you may have Mr Bingley for it is not to be doubted that *Miss* Bingley must instantly appropriate Mr Darcy for herself!"

With another giggle Lizzy skipped toward Mr Bingley's party which was now waiting in front of the new gazebo for Mr Darcy and the Misses Bennet to catch up.

TWENTY-FOUR
Lizzy Addresses Caroline at the Gazebo

Caroline Bingley looked razor sharp daggers at Miss Elizabeth who appeared serenely unaware of the hostility directed her way. Perched on a railing and leaning back against one of the columns supporting Charles' gazebo, she had her eyes closed, the better to enjoy the mild autumn sun on her face.

Mr Bingley's gazebo was a spacious hexagon atop a small rise just at the far reaches of the formal gardens. Everyone was taken by surprise and delight with its design of delicate bentwood arches supporting a pagoda roof all softly finished in a golden oaken colour. A low wall of faded red brick encircled the perimeter, serving as comfortable seating from which to enjoy either the prospect within or the surrounding flora.

On three sides there were a great number and variety of rose bushes, now entering their winter's rest. Their dull colours soon to be pruned deeply in preparation for a glorious production of colour and scent in the following spring and summer. The fourth side lent a delightful view across a green meadow dotted with sheep to the heavily wooded bit of wilderness beyond.

Within the enclosed area were several small tables and comfortable armchairs suitable for equal pleasure in a picnic repast, a relaxing read or even a game of chess or whist in the fresh air.

Charles Bingley received their collective praises with great pleasure. He had considerable confidence in matters of business, his father had insisted he know the family enterprises backwards and forwards, for one ought always to know as much as one's men of business about one's own holdings - at the very least. However he had not often taken it upon himself to make decisions about his household or estate without having the advice and counsel of his sisters or his good friend Mr Darcy.

Once they had admired the construction and design, the beauty of the vistas it provided, and the comfortable arrangement within, the time came for the party to leave the charming gazebo and return to the house in preparation for the Misses Bennet's departure for Longbourn.

The first among them to depart was Mrs Hurst, who complained of fatigue due to the unaccustomed exercise. Jane walked along beside her to lend her support. Mr Darcy and Mr Bingley followed close on their heels, engrossed in conversation about the construction of a hunter's cabin for use during the following hunting season.

Only Elizabeth had made no move to leave. Miss Bingley chafed under the responsibility of a hostess not to abandon a guest – however heartily despised and unwelcome. Again she was to be deprived of the opportunity to claim Mr Darcy's arm on the walk between the house and the gazebo! Thus she waited resentfully for Miss *Eliza* to follow the others, allowing herself the indulgence of glaring openly at the 'imperfect' face before her. Miss Bingley had been driven, had made it her mission *several times,* to point out to Mr Darcy the lack of symmetry in Miss *Eliza's* features.

It was enough to cause Miss Bingley to start in surprise when Elizabeth spoke. "Do you suppose, Miss Bingley, that we might have some conversation together for a few moments – out of the hearing of the others?" Lizzy's eyes opened as she said these words and she gave her companion a level look, conveying a firmness of purpose which brought some little disquiet to Miss Bingley's insides.

Not to be overset by the address of that under bred little country nobody, Miss Bingley answered smoothly; "Why yes Miss *Eliza*, the others have left us behind just now, if you have something to say to me – although I cannot imagine what the two of *us* have in common sufficient to support a private conversation." Caroline Bingley's visage had already held a slight sneer. With her response she drew herself up and added a haughty glare to her countenance.

"Truly, Miss Bingley? You do not comprehend anything in our both being young gentlewomen (you do hold yourself out to be a gentlewoman do you not?); sharing a somewhat limited circle of acquaintance; and rural locality; joining together with our friends for various activities? And there *is* more. I will get to the point however, whether you are able to comprehend... or *imagine* having anything in common with me or not.

"My purpose in requesting you to join me in a brief, honest exchange is this: I hope to convince you to desist from your slights..., your attempts to show me and my sister in a bad light or discomfit us."

"My dear Miss *Eliza*, I am quite convinced that *you* are imagining things! You and I have *nothing* in common with one another; indeed you would do well to do as children are bid: to be seen and *not* heard! If you and your family make poor subjects for general observation I am sure I cannot accept the blame for *that!*"

"You imagine yourself clever, I suppose; displaying your barbed wit and discharging your hostility in one and the same breath. You fail to comprehend the fact that nearly everyone who hears you understands your heart equally as well as you do yourself.

"My dear gentle sister cannot conceive of your ugly purpose, indeed she sees only the best in everyone. She will excuse you and overlook your conduct as inadvertent, not intended to cause pain to your "friend" and thus she shall escape your unkind objective.

"I see more clearly the intentions and motivations of others. Indeed I am disposed to a charitable view of most human faults and foibles and enjoy observing them in myself as well as my neighbours with good humour until they show themselves to be malicious or otherwise unworthy. Even then, my aim is always to practice civility and kindness wherever I may.

"I *do not* succumb, however, to the animadversions of others so *lacking* in familiarity with my character or my life. You waste your breath in any endeavour to cause me distress or embarrassment. I am unmoved by your performance and it only puts *you* in a bad light with those who observe it. Your conduct has no other effect upon me than to make me wonder at such uncivil behaviour from one who styles herself as above the society hereabouts. Surely such pettiness is better calculated to exhibit the weakness of your self-regard than to diminish the natural dignity of a gentleman's daughter."

Caroline's scorn grew apace with her angry flush. Her attempt to interrupt was halted, however, by Elizabeth's raised hand in determination to say all she had on her mind.

"I have patiently borne your unbecoming attitude toward me from the very beginning of our acquaintance. It is a marvel to me how you have not observed the discomfiture others display when you persist in your attacks. Particularly I notice *Mr Darcy's* frowns following your ill conduct toward me – or toward anyone.

"No matter your manoeuvrings to sway him, Mr Darcy *will* follow his own inclinations in his *choice* of a bride. If he is not inclined toward you, nothing you do or say will alter that. *If he is* inclined toward you, then others, likewise, cannot alter his choice. I am no threat to anything you may possess, Miss Bingley.

"If you truly wish to win his regard, and it is more than evident that you do, I suggest that you attend closely to his reactions to what you do and say – and amend your comportment accordingly. You stand a far greater chance of achieving your object by pleasing him than by showing yourself to disadvantage in his eyes."

Caroline Bingley was furious; her countenance a deep red. She would not betray her reaction in words, however – at least not directly. "Why Miss *Eliza*, you are quite mistaken indeed! I would never *purposely* insult a guest as you suggest. I merely speak what is on my mind! *I* cannot be held accountable for any degradation you might feel as a natural product of your own pitiable notions of consequence and the *patent* disparity in our circumstances.

"As for Mr Darcy, your conjectures are utterly unfounded *there* as well. *I* do not pursue *him*; it is *he* who seeks *my* company. Indeed, he has not only travelled from London to see me but has extended his stay far beyond what he had promised – simply to remain near *me* – and Charles of course.

"Now, Miss *Eliza*, I believe you have had your say and I must beg to return to the house! I see the others are waiting for me, just down there by the fountain."

Miss Bingley had turned to hurry after the others when she heard Elizabeth say: "As you wish Miss Bingley, however there *is* just one more small matter..."

She half turned in her rush to put distance between herself and the impertinent chit "What *is it* Miss *Eliza*?"

"Only this: I beg you would stop calling me by that name. I do not like it and allow only Charlotte Lucas and her family to use it out of respect for our lifelong friendship. My *name* is *Elizabeth* to everyone else except my close friends and immediate family who call me Lizzy."

"I shall endeavour to remember that." *And* I shall endeavour not to address *you* at all! Caroline fumed as she all but bolted away.

Lizzy smiled to herself as she followed Caroline Bingley toward the rest of the group.   Perhaps now I shall have some civility when I visit Netherfield, she thought. If not, well, she is on notice that my tolerance for her antics is at an end!

~&~

"Are you fatigued, my dear?" Speaking softly for her ears alone, Darcy offered Lizzy his arm.

His solicitous interest arose from the sight of Caroline Bingley's indignant countenance as she dashed to his side, followed by a more composed Elizabeth whose aspect went from a look of self-satisfaction to one of slightly guilty defiance when she caught his wondering stare.

What *had* they been speaking of, lagging behind the other members of the tour for so long?

He felt utterly confounded when Caroline Bingley swooped in, eagerly grasping his arm and smiling sweetly up into his face "Oh yes, Mr Darcy, I *am* a bit foot-weary; unaccustomed as I am to walking so far!"

"Oh, certainly... Miss Bingley!" Darcy altered his movement to accommodate her at his side. "And what of *you* Miss Elizabeth; shall you condescend to take my arm as well?" So saying, he proffered his other arm to Lizzy.

"I thank you kind sir;" She chuckled lightly as she skipped ahead of them, "however I do not tire so easily as *that*, and I fear *my pace* should not suit Miss Bingley's at all!" Naughtily she smirked a little to herself, knowing that Mr Darcy would be watching her walk in front of him all of the way back to the manor. She added just the tiniest smidgen of extra bounce to her step and sway to her hips as she went along.

That great glowering goose-cap cannot frown *me* down, Lizzy mused, she bases her consequence upon artful charms lacking in sincerity; contrived connections; and a grand dowry from sources she now affects to disdain – not on the strength of her own character.

Lizzy held her head a little higher thinking of Miss Bingley's arrogance. *She* can have *no conception* of the sort of inner fortitude born and bred into a countrywoman like myself, for whom frank verbal exchanges on delicate matters are commonplace and thus not likely to shock the nervous system.

~&~

Charles Bingley and Jane Bennet walked on ahead of the others, quite unaware of the discord in their wake. They were both enjoying their first opportunity to be in each other's exclusive company, however brief that moment was destined to be.

Determined to extract the essence of the gift without delay, Bingley did not fail his purpose. Taking Jane's hand in his and speaking softly for her ears only, he discreetly kept his gaze toward the gravel walk ahead of them and said "Miss Bennet, I pray you will forgive the informality of my approach. It has been uncommonly tricky to discover the briefest moment in which to speak privately with you today, my dear! I have an urgent, er... an *important* question I wish very much to ask you. May I call upon you tomorrow morning to ask it of you, my dearest, sweetest Miss Bennet?"

Jane cast a glance at the others to ensure that they were unobserved and then looking around at the flowerbeds surrounding them she gave his hand the tiniest squeeze before she replied in an equally low tone "I shall like that very much Mr Bingley!"

~&~

Caroline Bingley kept her temper in check just long enough to farewell the Misses Bennet into *Charles'* carriage for the trip home to Longbourn. Then she signalled Louisa to follow her to the private sitting room adjoining her bedchamber. For once she did not concern herself with Mr Darcy's whereabouts, or his wishes.

"Louisa, I am in such a state of violent agitation! I am in a *fearsome* bad humour and - *oh!* My head is *throbbing!*"

Recognizing that her sister was in the fiend's own temper, Louisa succumbed at first to the temptation to give a little fillip to her perturbation. "Why Caroline, *whatever* is the matter with you?

"Bye-the-bye, Mr Darcy cannot have missed your *outright disregard* for his comfort when you hurried us away so precipitously! You will never get a husband if you *reveal* yourself so, sister." Louisa suppressed most of her smug pleasure in thus reminding them both that *she had* got a husband and never need worry over *that* again.

Caroline ignored the hint of disloyalty in her sister's comment, nothing *new* there! She spluttered angrily "It is all *her* fault! That country chit! *She* had the audacity to take *me* to task!"

"What? What in the world were you speaking of so intimately with her back there?" Louisa had not missed observing her sister and Miss Elizabeth, apparently at loggerheads before they re-joined the group upon leaving the gazebo. She had known that Caroline's nastiness to Miss Elizabeth was bound to end in a confrontation sooner or later.

Before Caroline, however, she was all innocent incredulity. "It *did* seem that you two were engaged in some sort of *heated* discourse just as we were all to walk back together. You were quarrelling over her name I expect." She said placidly."

"Her name? What do you mean, Louisa?"

"Only that I notice she does not enjoy your calling her Miss Eliza. I fancy she feels it as both overly familiar and a deliberate slight to her consequence. After all, everyone outside of her family but that insipid Miss Lucas calls her by her full name of Elizabeth."

"Oh *that!* Never mind *that!* You will not *believe* what I have to tell you, Louisa!" And she proceeded to unburden herself to her sister with many an indignant tossing of her still perfectly coiffed head and rolling of her wrathfully glaring eyes.

"My goodness," Louisa finally got a word in edgewise; "I wondered how far your vendetta would be allowed to proceed before someone spoke up. Although I *had* expected your censure to come from our brother or even Mr Darcy in defence of harmony betwixt our houses; it seems Miss Elizabeth has got there before either of them." Louisa delivered this in a calm soothing voice, her attention turned to playing with her bracelets so as to hide her smirk from her irate sister.

"Nonsense Louisa! You are such a mealy-mouthed ninny! Everyone is so drawn in by the conniving wench's arts and allurements that they cannot see *the danger* she presents to ourselves! And *you* are the worst! You *ought* to be alarmed at the prospect of losing Mr Darcy's hospitality at Pemberley and in town, and his entrée into the best society. What of all our hopes of securing those many benefits which are in his power to confer upon his wife – *and his wife's family*? Are you so content, then to confine your life to the reach of *Mr Hurst's* sorry estate? Sometimes I think you an *utter fool*, Louisa!"

A little crestfallen that she had not taken all ramifications of the matter into account, Louisa replied: "Do not be so cross, sister. What must be done now? Surely there is aught we can do to alter things as they stand amongst us all?"

"I do not know. Leave me to think on it – stay; ask Mrs Jordan to have a tisane prepared for my aching head, and then I must have quiet in which to ponder what must be done to *rid us* of that hateful wretch!"

Louisa was not usually an introspective sort of woman; she was not a deep thinker or a studier of character. However she *was* moved to give the present situation some rare moments of earnest contemplation as she left her sister's sitting room in search of Mrs Jordan.

She had been increasingly disquieted by her sister's obsessive pursuit of Mr Darcy. Caroline's single-mindedness had driven a wedge between them. Louisa had fallen into the practice of keeping her thoughts on *that* subject to herself. To attempt a reasonable position on the unlikelihood that Mr Darcy would ever offer for her sister was to bring down the wrath of the Gods upon herself!

Louisa and Caroline had never been excessively fond of one another, but they had been pleased to share the manifold private and public rewards of fashion and gossip... No, neither would have walked three miles to nurse the other's fever and sore throat as Miss Elizabeth had done for Miss Bennet – not even across the street. A servant could be sent for that duty.

All in all, though, they had always had an easy sort of friendliness between themselves. Now, Caroline's determination to be Mistress of Pemberley, her "delusions of grandeur" as Gilbert termed it; and her consuming jealousy of Miss Elizabeth ... well, even jealousy of Louisa herself it seemed, for her married state – was driving her to a *ferocity* of emotion which shocked one's sensibilities indeed!

She wondered about her brother and Mr Darcy.

What sort of men *were* they, to tolerate her sister's patently relentless flattery and fawning pursuit of Mr Darcy?

Her mind wrestled with doubts over Charles' failure to put Caroline right! How could he *stomach* her sly rudeness and condescending attitudes toward Miss Elizabeth – and displayed at times toward Miss Bennet as well?

Caroline could be so cruel – as she herself had reason to know!

What gentleman ignored the blatant disregard of common courtesy carried out by his own sister toward a guest under his very roof?

And surely Mr Darcy could not actually *prefer* the company of her shallow, self-satisfied and self-indulgent sister...

How could either of the Bennet sisters continue to feel kindly toward gentlemen who failed to protect them while in their company? She was secretly pleased that Miss Elizabeth had stood up to the conniving and heartless Caroline.

Perhaps it might be wise for the Misses Bennet to rethink their complacency. Miss Jane Bennet, in particular, was too innocent and sweet!

At last Louisa Hurst came to the realization that behind every criticism she felt toward her sister and brother, she had been *worried* about what would become of Caroline, or what she would do when she finally received the set down she so richly deserved.

Now the long-anticipated collision was upon them thanks to Miss Elizabeth Bennet!

Caroline's vengeance would not be a *pretty* thing to see, she knew.

And yet, as annoying – even frightening as Caroline could be at times, they were *sisters* after all!

Louisa, dismay over her sister's ever more dangerous mood swirling within her, went in search of her husband. She would speak to Gilbert about her sister. Mr Hurst might be indolent but he was no fool. He would know how to act.

Caroline thought her featherheaded, and perhaps she was. But her maiden sister would no doubt be astonished at the confidences shared between a husband and his wife in the privacy of their bedchambers.

~&~

"Honestly Jane! If it weren't for *your* insistence, I should not trouble myself to go to Netherfield at all! There must be several pleasanter stratagems to spend time in Mr Darcy's company than to accept Caroline Bingley's top-lofty hospitality." They were in the carriage on their way home to Longbourn.

"Oh dear, I hope you don't mean to decline her invitation to tea on Tuesday next, for I have already accepted for us both." Jane's big blue eyes fixed upon her sister in some surprise.

"When was this singular honour bestowed upon us and by whom exactly? I cannot credit it to Miss Bingley's account for that lady was quite brimming over with uncordiality when last I was in her presence!" Lizzy's sardonic tone made her sister sit up and reply in a tone of confusion.

"Why she spoke to me of it just prior to our departure. She did seem to be labouring under some sort of oppression of her spirits. I did not refine upon it overmuch, only passed it off as the effects of a sour stomach or some such thing."

Lizzy's chuckle gave her sister to understand that the matter was to be taken lightly, skimmed over on its surface. "Not at all, my dear; she was decidedly vexed. I have endured Miss Bingley's contemptuous remarks about our family and myself to the last degree. I have at last come about and caused her to stumble just a little in her high-stepping ways."

"I do notice that the two of you are not friendly – but do you truly dislike her so very much? Was this when you and Miss Bingley were behindhand returning from the gazebo?"

"*Yes* and *Yes!* I have had outside of enough of her barbs and jabs – *and* her deliberate slights and snubs."

"Oh Lizzy; *whatever* did you say to her? I do hope... Of course you are right to stand up for yourself; I would never wish you to be uncomfortable." Jane could never be anything but loyal to her dear sister.

"But I, I beg you will bear in mind that *she is* Charles' – Mr Bingley's sister!" She had no need to say that his sister's good will might be necessary to *his good opinion of herself.* And he wished to ask her an *important question* tomorrow!

"I am sorry Jane; I do not mean to upset you. I merely told her in as calm and unexceptionable manner as I could muster that I will not endure any more of her slights and attempts to discomfit me; that her behaviour does not trouble *me* but that it does reflect badly on her; that she cannot improve her chances with Mr Darcy by revealing her weak self-regard in that way; and that Mr Darcy will undoubtedly make his choice of bride in whatever direction he chooses no matter how she *manoeuvres* to sway him.

"I suppose I am in the wrong for speaking up so to our hostess; but I confess I feel a *vast* deal better for having done it!"

"Mr Bingley does have all of my attention when we are together. I know you are far too generous to make things up about anyone. Perhaps you had better tell me what I have missed while my notice was elsewhere." Jane took her sister's hands in her own and gave them a squeeze – a sure sign that she was determined to hear all that comprised her dear Lizzy's perceptions of Caroline Bingley.

This would not be the first time that Jane relied upon Lizzy's willingness to see more than the best in someone whose intentions toward either of them were not kind. There had been that poseur who had attempted to seduce Jane when she was no more than fifteen; writing poetry and disarming her mother with his pretty manners. And all the while he would grope at her budding breasts and try to force his slippery kisses upon her whenever he caught her out of the sight of her family. It was Lizzy, whose distrust of the man had come to her aid, leaping on his back and shouting for their uncle when he had cornered Jane in the pantry of the Gardiner's home in Cheapside.

Thus Lizzy recounted for her darling Jane how Caroline Bingley had tried again and again to bring her low – especially in the opinion of Mr Darcy. "From the very beginning she has disdained us and the society to which we belong. At the Meryton assembly, where first we saw her, Miss Bingley's sneers and supercilious insolence marked her out as one whose first object was to set herself above her company.

"At Sir William Lucas' party I actually overheard her snide remarks about us all in conversation with Mr Darcy. She referred to our society as insipid, noisy and self-important while in reality being *nothing* - having said first that it would be insupportable to pass many evenings in our company! It is to his credit that he did not agree with her *that* time." Lizzy paused for a moment in her diatribe, recalling that his scarcely heard response had been to speak of 'fine eyes in the face of a pretty woman'.

"I had no idea! She seemed such a refined lady! I can't think why someone with so very many advantages should need to dwell on that which is lacking in others!

"Oh, my dear Jane; when I came to you whilst you were ill at Netherfield, she was unaware that I heard her more than once criticize me for doing so. She went on and on about my muddy hem and windblown hair, and how ridiculous it was for me to walk a few miles (exclaiming over my walking '*three miles* or *five miles*') to see to you. She criticized my features, my dress, my manners, and even my *teeth* while I stayed there with you.

"She and Mrs Hurst had a good laugh over our dear Uncle Gardiner's living in Cheapside – all of our connections, you must understand, are to be denigrated and laughed at.

"All this she did while she thought me out of hearing, yet quite careless of my whereabouts.

"Then she began making verbal jabs at me in person. Why, I could not even decline to play at cards with the rest of them without her having some sly comment to make. Her accusation that time was shockingly ludicrous, Jane! She announced to the room (and I know not whence her inspiration came) that I love *only* books and *despise everything* else! All this was because I declined to play at cards where I knew they must be playing too high for my purse!"

"You ought to have told me, Lizzy!"

"And ruin your happiness with Mr Bingley? I think not my dear sister! Caroline Bingley cannot resist the briefest moment of silence which she could fill with her interminable animadversions against me. I am most emphatically ready to fall into strong hysterics with the *sheer tedium* of it!

"But do not fear that she might bear me down! No matter how diligently she may attempt it, Miss Bingley can diminish neither my self-respect, nor my self-confidence – indeed *she* is often a ready object for *my* eye for folly and the ridiculous.

"Miss Bingley's dislike and jealousy have become increasingly evident the more Mr Darcy stares at me with that dark look of his, or spends time speaking to me. It does not require a great deal of study for me to see that she is driven by desperation and anxiety.

"She has marked Mr Darcy out for her own and resents his slightest interest in any other female. Today was the last straw; why, from the very moment I stepped out of the carriage Miss Bingley's first aim was to set me apart as an 'uninvited' guest!"

"My *poor* dear Lizzy! I apologize with all my heart for my inattentiveness! You know that I would never stand idly by while you were insulted and harassed so. I promise to be more diligent in my role as elder sister and protect you from anyone's abuse in future. You should never have to endure such disgraceful treatment – for any reason!"

After a moment's reflection, she said "Poor Miss Bingley!" Jane's gentle heart could not overlook the painful feeling which must urge her erstwhile friend to such sad mischief.

She felt no hesitation, however, in choosing her sister if a choice must be made between the two.

Briefly Jane contemplated what *Charles Bingley's* choice might be if *she* were forced to choose against his sister's friendship! She could only hope that with time the sharpness betwixt Lizzy and Charles Bingley's sister would ease.

"I must tell you that I am *quite* exhausted with her incessant vituperation. I could *almost* send Mr Darcy away when he comes to call, only to have some peace, were there not a *fatal flaw* in the effort!" By this time Lizzy's wry humour had her laughing at her own vexation.

"What flaw is that?" Jane knew her part in this exchange.

"Only that I think it possible that I might *miss him*, after spending such a deal of time in his company of late!" Lizzy's bright smile signalled an end to her further earnest disclosures.

TWENTY-FIVE
The Bennets' Manifold Discoveries

Charles Bingley's 'important question' was doomed to be held in abeyance by the exigencies of inclement weather.

Heavy rain throughout the night following the tour of the gazebo succeeded by several days of unrelenting drizzle having made travel to and fro quite hazardous, the gentlemen of Netherfield and the ladies of Longbourn endured a forced interval in their comings and goings for the same period.

Everyone but Mary and Mrs Bennet rejoiced in the fact that Mr Collins had departed for Hunsford parsonage his home near Rosings in Kent on the morning before the rains began.

Mrs Bennet was frequently heard to bewail his departure without engaging himself to one of her daughters; Mary said nothing of any understanding between Mr Collins and herself.

After the downpour of the first day, conditions remained treacherous for anything but the most crucial movement about the countryside. The roads, what could be seen of them through the persistent drizzly mist, were rivers of slippery mud bounded on either side by sodden foliage and little freshets of brownish water rushing headlong to somewhere else.

Jane and Elizabeth Bennet spent much of their time in a smaller sitting room at the back of the house where they could peer out at the gardens and a pretty-ish kind of wilderness running back from the far side of the kitchen garden. This was their favourite place to be on such a day for their mother and sisters preferred the larger sitting room where visitors might be received. Their father in his library was situated more or less half-way between the two. They were working, in a desultory fashion, on their samplers; an undertaking which was never quite completed due to the young ladies' lack of industry in that endeavour.

"I cannot *like* this theme, Jane! 'To Have A Friend You Must First Be One". When I first saw the pattern I thought I understood it well enough: that a friend ought to act as a friend should *in order to be worthy*... But now I find I disagree. Are we not *all worthy* of having friends without having to do some extraordinary thing first? I would sooner have it that "To *Keep* a Friend You Must Be a True Friend' or some such!"

It was Monday, the fourth day since the rains had begun and Lizzy was restless from being indoors so long, and perhaps she did miss Darcy... a little. She tossed her sampler aside and went to look out of the window for the second time in ten minutes.

Jane set her work aside as well and went to stand beside her sister.

They were startled to see Lydia and Kitty dash out of the woods toward the barn. Lydia appeared to be carrying some sort of sack or bundle. Both girls were clearly soaked to the bone; their hair and clothing clinging wetly to their faces and forms, their bonnets drooping in lopsided disarray, water dripping everywhere. And they were laughing – *and* they seemed *anxious* to escape notice from the house!

"What on earth?" Jane whirled around, starting off at a run to gather towels and blankets for their youngest sisters. "Hurry Lizzy; they will catch their death!"

"Mamá! Papá! Make haste; something has happened to Lydia and Kitty!" Lizzy was less concerned about either of the girls catching cold than that she wanted to ensure her parents were made aware of whatever the two were up to. She had a fearful suspicion that Lydia and Kitty's peculiar behaviour had something to do with meeting an officer or officers in the woods. If that was the case, it would take more forceful authority than she or Jane could bring to bear over their sisters to put a stop to it.

Hurrying their parents to the side door, the one nearest the barn took only a few minutes.

Mamá was just asking, in her high-pitched voice of extreme distress, for the third time "But what *is it*? Where is my *Lydia*? *Oooh!*" When the door flew open and Lydia and Kitty bounced in and then checked themselves, eyes widened in shock to find their entire family to meet them inside – for Mary had followed the rest to see the cause of all the commotion.

~&~

"Oh, hello everyone! We have just been to the barn to inspect the new kittens in the loft. They are darling indeed; are they not Kitty?" Lydia gave Kitty an unsubtle nudge to agree with her. Somehow both girls had managed to don dry cloaks over their sodden dresses and arrange their wet hair into a semblance of propriety. The bonnets were not to be seen. Neither of the girls was carrying a bundle.

Taking note of all this and seeing Kitty open her mouth to speak, Elizabeth put up her hand to silence her. "No Kitty, do not make yourself a greater disgrace than you already are!" And seeing her mother drawing in her breath to dress her down for causing such a jolt to her nerves, and her father beginning to drift away -back to his books of course, she burst out: "Lydia and Kitty stay right where you are!" Both girls ceased their stealthy movements toward escape down the hallway, staring at her in shock. "Mamá, Papá! This is not as it seems. Please, hear me out, for as much as I should rather not tell tales on my sisters, this is too important to disregard!"

Both parents stood gaping at Elizabeth. Surely there was nothing so exceedingly untoward in a trip to the barn, even if it was so wet outside. Better to get the girls dry and drinking hot tea in front of the sitting room fire. "Well?" They said in unison. Both pairs of eyes were trained upon her impatiently, as both sets of eyebrows rose in inquiry.

Elizabeth quickly stowed *that* sight away for a humorous review at a more leisurely time. *Now* she must tell them "Jane and I were in the back sitting room just now working on our samplers." Ignoring her mother's dismissive roll of the eyes, she continued. "We were restless and went to look out of the window. It was still raining steadily, or *drizzling* more like, but we chanced to see Lydia and Kitty *running from the wood* toward the barn!

"They were soaking wet and laughing. Lydia was carrying something like a bundle. They *appeared* to be attempting to avoid being seen from the house.

"I feel sure that if you look in the barn you will find their wet outerwear and whatever that was that Lydia was carrying!

"Forgive me if I am wasting everyone's time with this, or raising a false alarm. I most assuredly do not *wish* to accuse my little sisters of any impropriety. However, in light of the events so recently enacted in our neighbourhood, and particular alarms raised thereby, Lydia and Kitty's occupations *ought* to be matters of concern.

"I am compelled to emphasize that this is especially the case since Lydia and Kitty, who *never walk* anywhere except to Meryton – and only *there* if no carriage can be had – have very recently taken to rambling about in the woods rather *frequently*."

Mrs Bennet had folded her arms across her breast as if in defiant protection of her *dear* Lydia. "Lydia would not do anything wrong; she is not that sort of girl! Shame on you Lizzy, for tossing up such a ruckus over a girlish prank!"

Mr Bennet, however, looked first to Jane for confirmation and, having received her sorrowful nod of corroboration, turned a decidedly wintry countenance upon his youngest daughter. "What of this, Lydia? What have you to say for yourself? No, do not turn to Kitty for support; I know very well who leads this march!"

"*Mamá!* Tell Lizzy not to tell tales on me! You *know* that I only..." Lydia tried to make one last desperate appeal to her mother.

"*Enough* of your '*Mamá*', girl! Speak to *me*! Mrs Bennet you will keep silent if you please, for I will *not brook* any interference!" Every single Longbourn lady quaked in apprehension at his forbidding look. This was indeed a new come-out for Mr Bennet, their ordinarily indolent father; and no one could doubt that he had right on his side!

Mrs Bennet's shock was so great that she, quite uncharacteristically, found herself with nothing to say. Thus she stood mouth agape, while her husband ushered his two youngest daughters, suddenly pitiful and bedraggled in their wet dresses, into his library and shut the door firmly behind them.

For the first hour or more Lizzy's and Jane's vigil outside of Papá's library door was rewarded mostly with the sounds of much crying, begging, whining and sobbing on the part of their young sisters. Their cries were interspersed with the terse and angry tones of their father.

Mary had gone quietly back to her book and Mrs Bennet sat waving her handkerchief, sipping a special soothing blend of tea and moaning to herself in her bedchamber.

Gradually the voices beyond the library door quieted and Mr Bennet's questions and comments sounded calmer.

Lydia and Kitty must have caved in and were telling him what he wanted to know. He plucked their secrets one by one until all was revealed in a sorry picture of parental neglect, foolish girls' risks taken and the stealth and cunning of a master manipulator.

~&~

Later, none could have said how much later – perhaps two hours, perhaps three – their father desired everyone to gather together in the sitting room.

They all took their seats. Jane and Lizzy together on a settee, their mother sat in her comfortable chair nearest the fire.

Mary took her seat in a corner – ready to reengage with her book at the soonest opportunity.

Lydia and Kitty, however, were directed by their father to sit on straight-backed chairs on either side of his – which was, as usual, a comfortable chair placed not too near the fire and with a reading table next to it.

Lydia and Kitty remained dressed in their now-damp dresses. Although he ensured that they were kept warm, he had not allowed them to change their clothes or eat a morsel since their appearance at the side entrance to Longbourn.

"Mrs Bennet, Jane, Lizzy, Mary...You must all have been on pins and needles to be apprised of what has been the subject under discussion in my library these past several hours, how it affects our family, and what must and shall be done regarding it." He said.

"In any other circumstance I would do all in my power to spare you all from the sordid matters of which you are assembled to learn. Indeed the subjects we shall speak of are generally considered improper for a wife to discuss with her husband. They are *highly* improper for maiden daughters to hear of. Be all of that as it may, I see no option but that we must soldier on together however we may."

Mr Bennet faced his family and summoning up all of his patriarchal dignity, waved his right hand first in the direction of one and then of the other of the two daughters who flanked him on either side.

"Here are two young, *very* young women who believed that they knew better than their parents how to answer in our behalf when accosted by a cad. Therefore I shall require their assistance in explaining it all to you; for I am heartily sick of the matter and hope they will accomplish your edification far better than their foolish old father might do."

At this pronouncement Lydia's mouth dropped open in surprise and Kitty gasped audibly.

"Lydia you shall begin by describing for your mother and sisters what the two of you have been up to – *all* of it" He said decisively.

For one brief moment Lydia looked as if she wanted to wheedle her way out of it. Then she raised her face, blotchy and swollen from crying, to them all and tearfully assented. "Yes Papá". Her gaze went to her father and remained there as he continued to speak.

"Catherine, such an *active* young woman ought not to be referred to in such a childish manner after all, you shall next advise your mother and sisters how your *activities* affect our family."

Kitty's visage was beet-red and her lips trembled as she replied softly; Yes sir" and promptly fell to studying her hands tightly clenched in her lap.

"Unless either Lydia or Catherine feels better qualified to do it, I believe I shall be the one to tell what must and shall be done regarding the situation."

"Lydia, you may begin, child." Though the words could have sounded gently; they were spoken in the tones of command.

Lydia turned her newly brave eyes toward Mrs Bennet. She regarded her mother's countenance thoughtfully for a long moment, briefly considered her serious sister Mary who returned her glance with grave scrutiny, finally Lydia let her gaze rest upon her two eldest sisters.

Jane looked back at her, alarm and compassion warring in her expression.

Lizzy merely watched; her mien steady and inscrutable, waiting for her to utter the words.

"I have made a *dreadful* mistake!" She blurted. "I have led Kitty into the worst, the very *worst* possible impropriety and... and... I am so *awfully* sorry!"

"What have you *done*, my *dear girl?* What is all this *about?*" Mrs Bennet could not contain her anxiety for her dearest child any longer.

"Please Mamá, I must have my say and you cannot help me other than by lending me your kind attention." Lydia took a harsh, almost sobbing breath and went on. "Kitty and I, at *my* instigation, well we have been helping Mr Wickham hide in Papá's old shooting cottage in the woods, the one we used to call 'Firth's Castle' after that odd young man who looked after the hunting dogs and carried himself so straight and proud."

Pausing to allow their collective gasps and murmurings of shock, Lydia glanced quickly at her father's implacable visage, then continued as if she was desperate to get it all said before she lost her courage.

"That is only the barest brush with the truth I have to tell. We have been taking him food and blankets and other things he needed. We brought his uniform home with us and just returned it to him cleaned and pressed today."

"*Mr Wickham!*" Jane gulped and Lizzy huffed the despicable name nearly in the same instant.

"*Lydia*! You must *not cover up* for Kitty! She *is* older than you after all! *She* has led *you* astray and *shall be punished directly*!" Fanning herself wildly with her handkerchief, Mamá looked around, her eyes flashing with indignation. How she *wished* to think only the best of her favourite daughter – and how *little* she concerned herself with injustice to Kitty! *Hang Kitty,* she thought, what has *she* to repine of? *Surely she* is more at fault than her *baby* sister!

At this Mr Bennet turned a scorching look upon his bride. "*Let be, Fanny!* Unless my ears deceive me, Lydia is best left to assume responsibility for her conduct and to discover for herself that she is undeservedly fortunate if she endures no *lasting effects* of the scrape she has gotten herself into. Continue if you please, Lydia."

Mrs Bennet and three of her daughters sat in hushed silence, indeed their lips were uniformly clamped shut against making any further utterance before Lydia's disclosures were finished. Kitty only stared at her lap.

"Mr Wickham is so very handsome and his manners so easy and engaging! My partiality toward him delighted in having him nearly all to myself. We spent time with him, playing at cards, joking and laughing, talking, and… kissing. Not Kitty – not the kissing part – she acted as our lookout in case we were in danger of being discovered." No one spoke; the only sound in the room was the hiss of indrawn breath.

Valiantly, Lydia announced the worst. "It was very cold in the cottage; Mr Wickham said we dared not light a fire for fear the smoke would be seen and someone come to investigate. So we huddled under blankets and kept warm by laughing and carrying on. At first Kitty and I huddled together, but somehow, over time it became Mr Wickham and I 'keeping cosy', as he put it.

"Then he would accidentally brush against me in a way that felt improper – but nice. I let him touch me more and more. It was our hilarious secret, hidden even from Kitty. We were fooling everyone – even my sister who was sitting right there!"

Finally Lydia had to look away from the stunned faces of her dear family. With her head tilted away from them, and her eyes cast inward in mortified memory she finished her confession in a rush.

"I thought we were in love and I was so happy and excited. We would wait until Kitty was busy with some momentary distraction and whisper to each other and… do other things until she came back.

"Mr Wickham took every opportunity to tell me he loved me madly and how very much he wanted to... be my husband. When I worried that Papá was not likely to agree, he said that if we spent the night together as man and wife then Papá would have to give his consent to our marriage. What a good joke it was to be that I would be married before any of my sisters – and I the youngest of them all!

"Yesterday morning I told it all to Kitty. I carried a nightdress and fresh clothes with me when we went to visit Mr Wickham. Last night I went to him."

Turning to her mother she said "I am so very sorry Mamá." And to Jane and Elizabeth; "For once I recognize that I have allowed my high spirited wilfulness and disdain of propriety to lead me into the most scandalous and sordid foolhardy conduct! I have done something utterly disastrous, so very dangerous to myself and to you all that I am nearly suffocated with shame! No matter how I wheedle or cry, I cannot avoid the likelihood of most injurious consequences for myself or for my family. My heedlessness has been unforgivable. Saying how sorry I am can have no effect upon the ruin I have courted for us all, but that is all I can do – and I *am sorry beyond anything!*"

"Mary you may wring a peal over me as much as you like. I shall not dispute your right to do so. You have so often tried to impress us all with the fragility of feminine virtue..." Here Lydia faltered, two large tears slipping down her flushed cheeks, "You were... *quite* unimpeachably correct."

Seeing his wife and three of his daughter gathering themselves to speak all at once, Mr Bennet cleared his throat. When they paused to look at him, he said "Before I am inundated with your multiple reactions to Lydia's words, let me remind you that we have not yet heard from Catherine – my *other* youngest daughter!"

Kitty raised her head reluctantly. As long as she could focus on the soft white hands clenched so desperately in her lap, she avoided the sight of her sisters' faces. Her mother's face was not *so* very difficult for her as she was quite accustomed to reading indifference or disapprobation *there*. Her elder sisters had always been kind to her though. They had tried to teach her many things – especially not to follow Lydia into her invariably hare-brained, but exciting bits of folly.

"Catherine?" Papá's gravelly voice declared him to be resolute. She had earned the task of telling what she knew, and she must do so.

"Yes father, I am prepared, sir, or as prepared as may be in such a cause."

Kitty had always sought sympathy for every hurt, every slight – real or imagined. Every wounded feeling or bruise to her person brought forth ready tears and wails of lamentation which reached not her mother's ears but Jane's, whose compassionate heart and tender ministrations had been Kitty's most reliable balm.

Today, however she did not seek Jane's eyes, but Lizzy's. The situation in which she was embroiled and her father's harsh censure had served to force a change of perspective on Kitty's self-consciousness. Today she did not seek softness and absolution; she craved the astringent weight of Lizzy's more critical mind. Lizzy loved her and would not wound her gratuitously, but neither would she scruple to speak frankly and firmly to her errant sisters.

Kitty's focus on Elizabeth's gaze held her to that determination to face this day's mortifications with inner fortitude and grace. She would model herself after the sister she so admired, dearest Lizzy.

"*Everything* that Lydia has described is true. The two of us have foolishly exposed ourselves and our whole family to shame and ridicule – even *ostracism* should word of the *least* of our improper doings get out. We shall be shunned and ignored, harassed and insulted by *anyone* we might encounter *every day* of our future lives. There shall be *five Bennet spinsters* starving in the hedgerows if *all* is known, for who would marry any of us once our family is ruined in the sight of our society?"

Standing as tall and straight as her slender young body could, Kitty glanced at her mother and around at Mary and Jane. Shifting her shoulders as if preparing to march into battle, she locked eyes with Lizzy, holding her gaze without flinching. Kitty's dark blue eyes looked almost fierce!

"*If* we are able to prevent the whispers and innuendo... Nay, the *truth* from becoming common knowledge, we may not yet be easy.

"If Lydia should have the ill fortune to come with child... the truth will have its *second* opportunity at our throats.

"Finally, should there indeed be a child as a result of last night – I *hope* it was no more than last night – then we will be five Bennet spinsters *and* our aging mother, *and* a *child,* a *bastard child,* starving in the hedgerows if our dear father should leave us prematurely."

~&~

Mr Bennet lifted his head and leaned a little forward as if about to speak.

"Oh! I have one more thing to add, if I may?"

At Papá's curt nod she told them her last small bit of devastation.

"Whilst Lydia and Mr Wickham were saying their farewells this morning, I turned a little away to afford them a measure of privacy. Casting my eyes down out of embarrassment I happened to spy a crumpled piece of paper on the floor. It looked like a note of some sort. I ought not to have done so, it was not mine to be sure, but I picked it up out of curiosity; for I could not imagine who might be sending a note to Mr Wickham in his present hideaway. I did glance at it but it made no sense to me so I put it my pocket and forgot all about it until just now while I was listening to Lydia tell you her story. I do not know whether it has any significance to you Papá, but somehow I believe that it must. Here it is." With this she pulled the creased and rather soggy paper out of the pocket of her dress and handed it to her father.

Mr Bennet unfolded the paper, straightening and smoothing it out carefully upon his reading table. "No Catherine, this was not yours to read or to take away; however I *am* grateful that you did so. For I *welcome* any clue, *any smallest thing at all,* which might serve to enlighten me as to how this situation, *this man* ought to be *dealt* with

So saying he bent his gaze to the item spread out before him. His family waited.

W

You shall have your sweet treat on Tuesday next at three of the clock.

Once you have thoroughly devoured the tart you shall have the reward we discussed.

Do not be late, for fresh sweets cannot be kept so for long.

CB

The letters were faded from the damp and somewhat difficult for Mr Bennet to make out. Their meaning continued to elude him once he had worked the words out to his satisfaction.

Shaking his head wearily he read its contents out to his family; it was too fragile to pass around.

"'W' is Wickham of course.

'You shall have your sweet treat on Tuesday next at three of the clock.

'Once you have thoroughly devoured the tart you shall have the reward we discussed.

'Do not be late, for fresh sweets cannot be kept so for long.'

It is nonsensical! And who in the world is 'CB'? This is a piece of flummery indeed!"

Kitty smiled grimly. "Well I assure you it does not stand for Catherine Bennet! Anyway *my* hand is not as elegant as that!"

"I do believe you have the right of it however, my dear Catherine. That is *not* a masculine hand!"

The others slowly moved one by one to the reading table to examine the writing on the paper. Having viewed it, they each went thoughtfully back to their seats.

"It is elegantly writ indeed." Mrs Bennet said confusedly. "But what has it to do with our girls?"

Lydia's face was a study of thunderclouds. "*Well,*" she huffed "why should Wickham be receiving notes from another woman whilst he was courting me? He surely could not have *truly* expected to be *marrying me* when he was to be off eating *pastries* with someone else!"

"*Tomorrow* is Tuesday." was Mary's solemn pronouncement.

Jane, looking bemused, said nothing. She merely listened to her family's struggle to discover either meaning or identity from the cryptic note.

"I wonder," murmured Elizabeth, "Is Caroline Bingley acquainted with Mr Wickham?"

Everyone stared at her. She shrugged her shoulders, "Who else do we know who writes so elegant a script and bears those very initials?"

"Don't be silly, girl! *What would a Miss Bingley want with a Mr Wickham, pray*? I believe *she* has her sights set on Mr Darcy, or someone of his ilk! *Caroline Bingley indeed*!"

Mrs Bennet's shrill volubility had been held in thrall for far too long. She would speak and once started she could scarcely be stopped again. "Why anyone would think Miss Bingley would write a note, especially such a silly note, to Mr Wickham - I cannot think! There must be several other people in the neighbourhood with those initials who write a fair hand... and anyway, how can we assume that we know the person?"

"Yes, *yes* Fanny. You make a very good point. We may not be acquainted with the author of the note at all. Nevertheless it *is hard* to imagine *how* such a note would *find* Mr Wickham if it did not come from someone who knows to look for him in *my* cottage!" Mr Bennet's voice had regained some of its customary sardonic inflection.

"Now I think we shall put the note aside in favour of the established agenda. Mary, please ring for tea. I imagine you are all as famished as I, and a light repast will set us all up nicely for the third act, or perhaps it is the fourth, of our family melodrama (apologies for the lack of musical accompaniment as the programme was not anticipated in time to secure the pleasure)."

In an undertone Lizzy asked Jane "Do you still have Caroline Bingley's note from when she invited you to dine? I would dearly like to see whether the hand is similar!"

"I believe I do, Lizzy. I shall look for it bye and bye."

~&~

Tea at Longbourn that afternoon was a muted affair, conversation scant and confined to the simple exchanges necessary to a meal taken in common with others.

There was much to preoccupy their minds and, although there would presently be frightening and inexorable matters upon which they must deliberate and try to reconcile, none was yet prepared to expose their doubts and fears to open discussion.

The sombre mood continued as they each took time to refresh themselves before Papá reconvened his committee of Bennets in the sitting room.

Lydia and Kitty had at long last been permitted to refresh themselves and change into fresh dry clothing and everyone was seated as before, or perhaps a little more comfortably for now that they knew the worst, as dreadful as it was, they had no other direction to go than up.

After the door had quietly closed behind Hill and the last of the tea things, Mr Bennet began to speak.

"It is now time to consider what must and shall be done to amend the matter of Lydia's situation. We may direct our thoughts to our youngest, for a resolution *there* shall in turn relieve Catherine's position.

"I believe I have reserved this task for myself unless, of course Lydia or Catherine has worked it out before me. Lydia? Catherine?"

Mrs Bennet did not wait for their shaken heads and mumbled responses before she launched her offensive, quite brief for her, but strongly felt just the same.

"Oh *Thomas*; *of course* you must *make* him *marry* her!" It was a sign of her extreme agitation that Fanny Bennet used her husband's first name as it was not her habit to do so before their offspring.

"I certainly shall *not*; I assure you Mrs Bennet!" He had had rather more time to consider the situation and had anticipated her demand. "*Folly has not a forgiving nature*, my dear, and we have allowed it *free reign* in this house *long enough!* I refuse to compound our stupidity by *shackling* one of our *precious daughters* to the *worst miscreant* this neighbourhood has *ever* had the misfortune to shelter!

"Our daughters have erred *enormously* to be sure; I cannot hold them excused from the *severest* reprimand and punishment for their *abominable conduct*. Lydia has so far *degraded* herself as can only disgust and shock the sensibilities of us all!

"The *greater shortcoming,* however, has been on the part of their parents. Had our younger daughters been brought up to behave more sensibly, to subdue their more indecorous impulses, and to impose the discipline of reflection in advance of acting upon their wayward fancies we should *very likely* have avoided this dilemma entirely.

"Instead they were provided *no bounds* to their wilfulness, they were petted and *puffed up* with conceit and consequence and taught to value nothing so much as new ribbons, trims and shoe roses – *and* young men in uniform.

"When a ruthless seducer of impressionable young ladies insinuated himself into their locale they were *utterly lacking* in either the good sense or the morality to defend themselves against a man who clearly holds no one but himself in tender regard!

"Oh yes, they *were* often treated to better guidance from *all three* of their elder *sisters*. How often has Mary been heard to remind the room that a woman's reputation is no less brittle than beautiful; that vanity is the antitheses of virtue? How frequently have Jane or Lizzy been heard warning Lydia and Catherine to check their giddy propensities, social impropriety and spendthrift frivolity?

"And all the while they were encouraged by their own Mamá, *taught* to hold those notions cheap!

"*I too, am at fault* as surely as is my *poor* Lydia who will bear the brunt of the public humiliation and censure if such comes to pass!

"I have spent my time hidden away in my library *selfishly* enjoying my own pursuits and engaging in the management of my daughters *only as it pleased* me to do so. I kept myself apart whilst my precious children were allowed to spiral down toward disaster.

"I am deeply sorry for that *and* that it is irreversibly past the time of rescue or redemption in the *rearing* of Lydia and Catherine. Without exception I have *never* before this day felt so *touched on the raw* over my *own* conduct!

"Lydia's decidedly *pungent* description of the events leading up to her downfall has dealt us *all* a wounding blow indeed! *Nevertheless,* I trust that there is yet *some hope* of a better outcome than now appears poised to overtake our family.

"I propose that we join our collective wit, wisdom and will in the pursuit of rescue *and* redemption of our family and of the Bennet family name.

"Whilst the rest of you were busy, I primed a list of the most urgent steps required of us to that end. I rely on each of you to contribute your best efforts to make my puny start as fully comprehensive as may be:

- ✓ *We shall need a detailed plan, one which all understand and agree upon if we have the least chance of preserving our good name;*

- ✓ *The authorities must be alerted immediately to Mr Wickham's whereabouts;*

- ✓ *No one who has no reason to know of it should be made aware of Mr Wickham's use of my cottage for his hideaway;*

- ✓ *No one must speak to anyone of any portion of Lydia's and Catherine's visits to Mr Wickham in the cottage or of their 'helping' him with food and clothes and such;* – and Mrs Bennet, if you find it puts too much of a strain on your garrulous temper to keep silent as the grave in this matter, I shall ensure your silence by locking you in your room!

- ✓ *Although it may very well pertain to an unrelated matter, the author of that note – and the import of its contents – ought to be found out if at all possible.*

"Now my dears let me hear your thoughts on the matter and I will add them to our list."

Jane's composed voice sounded first. "Papá, I believe we must all reserve expression of our apprehensions – even thoughts of them if we are able – to those times when we are either alone or only in each other's company."

"Yes, Jane, as unaccustomed as some among us may be to checking the transfer of thought to instant disclosure, that will be a critical exercise indeed."

"Papá, oughtn't we include the servants among those who must be excluded from hearing our confidential discussions? Lydia and I were quite stealthy in our comings and goings to the cottage. I daresay not even Hill has knowledge of it."

"I am relieved to hear it, Catherine, and your point is well taken. This family has had nothing to conceal in the past and has been in the habit of speaking freely in front of our servants. New habits among us must include waiting until the servants are out of the room and the door shut behind them before we discuss *any* family business.

"I believe that even as we improve upon our habitual conduct, it will be of equal importance that we endeavour to comport ourselves in public as nearly usual as we might. Of course that *does not* include Lydia and Kitty's prior disgraceful forwardness and immodesty."

"Yes, Mary, it certainly will *not* do to draw attention to ourselves by omission of what is expected of us than by the commission of an inadvertent slip of the tongue."

Mrs Bennet, who had been sitting quite still while glaring at her husband over his remark about locking her in her room, took the floor. "Mr Bennet I fail to see why Lydia should not simply be married to Mr Wickham and all of this folderol avoided altogether!" she said resentfully. "Anticipation of one's wedding vows is not so unusual in a country society after all. Mr Wickham is a charming and handsome man and must love our Lydia very much to have been so carried away by her charms! Surely Mr Wickham is not so very bad as everyone says – and being a married man will settle him down and make him improve his ways! Lydia's being a bride might very well set up just the right tone to bring others up to scratch and soon we should have several of our five daughter safely married!"

By the time she had finished, Mrs Bennet's active imagination and excitable temperament had conveyed her far into the land of topsy-turvy.

Mr Bennet's swift admonishment was furious and laden with sarcasm   "So then, *Madam*, I collect that the *very person* you have run about v*ilifying* to the whole county is *now* the very person who will make a most *delightful* addition to this family? You *astonish and distress* me! I have *never* known you to be capable of *such great feats* of mental gymnastics as your instant thoughts betray of you!

"Condemn any woman, let alone *my fifteen-year-old child*, to a life as that scoundrel's pitiable wife? *I think not!*

"If you *persist* in voicing such an *utter want* of either delicacy of mind or common sense, I shall indeed be forced to lock you in your room!

"Let me hear not another *word* in support of that, that *underhanded, infamous, evil,* rep..., repulsive *profligate*... being countenanced by this family let alone accepted as a husband and a son... You shock me to the *soles of my boots*! I am appalled that after all that has passed you can even *think* such a thing!"

So incensed was Mr Bennet by the foolishness of his lady that his fiercely heated shouting was finally reduced to a querulous sputtering at the end of his tirade. Rubbing his forehead wearily, in a quieter voice of resignation he said "Pray, Mrs Bennet, be so obliging as to remain steadfast in your earlier dislike and distrust of the man."

Lizzy had never seen her beloved father so dreadfully angry – or exhausted. Her mother's face was a study of confusion and pain. She looked... defeated.

A return to the making of the list would distract Papá from his fury at her mother and direct all of their thoughts toward solutions rather than that in her mother which all twenty-four years of her husband's frustration and sarcastic jibes had failed to alter.

"Papá, do you not think that Mr Darcy's assistance in dealing with Wickham could be essential? His familiarity with Mr Wickham's ways is longstanding – *lifelong,* in fact. I recall what you said in reference to that note that Kitty found in the cottage. You said that you would *welcome* any clue, any smallest thing at all, which might serve to enlighten you as to how to deal with Mr Wickham and the situation we are addressing. Indeed, he may be able to enlighten us as to the writer's identity *and* the meaning of the message."

"Lizzy, are you suggesting that Mr Darcy be taken entirely into our confidence? I do not see how we might tell him only part without leaving him to guess the rest - which I believe should be just as damaging to us in his eyes as if we tell him all."

"Yes, father. Mr Darcy is an upright and honourable gentleman. I am certain that our full confidence would not be misplaced. He will not speak of our private business to anyone, I am certain of it."

Her father waited with raised eyebrows until she mumbled softly "As to... any other considerations... *nothing* can be of greater importance than protecting my sisters – and our family name."

"Very well, then daughter, I agree that Mr Darcy may be trusted with our secrets and that his contribution to our purpose is likely to be significant indeed. I shall look for the earliest opportunity to consult with him."

Lydia arose suddenly from her seat and stood trembling before the rest of her family; "I know that I have acted rashly, and committed dreadful sins against you. I have robbed you, my good parents, of the peace of mind you deserve and the good name you have preserved for yourselves and bestowed upon all of your daughters as the gift of goodwill in the world. My sisters... apologies will never be sufficient to right the wrongs I have done you. Everything that Papá said is true. I am beyond ashamed of my wrongheadedness and unspeakable blunders. I shall not object or try to defend against it no matter how harshly or frequently you wish to vent your spleen on my head after this!

"I desire you all to know that I am fixed in my purpose - whether I am to live with the issue of my foolishness or whether I am spared any part of my just deserts – I *intend* to come about. I *shall come about*! I pray with all of my heart that I never cause such pain and injury to anyone again – especially my dear family, and if I can help it – I shall not!"

Lydia sat down abruptly. She had said her piece without any attempt to whine or win sympathy for herself. She was determined to make a fresh start and she welcomed the opportunity to practice it though the effort, and the interminable events of the day, left her entirely wrung out.

Mr Bennet looked up from his reading table when Lydia retook her seat. "My dear, it sounds as if you are laying the foundation for a mighty effort, a drastically needed effort and I am pleased and gratified to hear it."

He then picked up the page he had been writing on while Lydia was speaking.

"I have written out our list, or what I have re-entitled *Bennet Family Code of Conduct*. I want you each to read it over thoroughly. If you have questions or additions you must tell me immediately. Otherwise you should add your signature each in your turn and abide by it henceforth. Am I understood?"

Seeing their nods, he passed it around, beginning with Jane, his eldest daughter. He did not trust himself, or his wife, in that moment. She would be last.

Bennet Family Code of Conduct

- ✓ We shall need a detailed plan, one which all understand and agree upon if we have the least chance of preserving our good name;

- ✓ The authorities must be alerted immediately to Mr Wickham's whereabouts;

- ✓ No one who has no reason to know of it should be made aware of Mr Wickham's use of my cottage for his hideaway;

- ✓ No one must speak to anyone of any portion of Lydia's and Catherine's visits to Mr Wickham in the cottage or of their 'helping' him with food and clothes and such;

- ✓ The author of that note — and the import of its contents — ought to be found out if at all possible;

- ✓ We must all reserve expression of our apprehensions — even thoughts of them if we are able — to those times when we are either alone or only in each other's company.

- ✓ The servants are most emphatically included among those who must be excluded from hearing our confidential discussions;

- ✓ As we improve upon our habitual conduct, it will be of equal importance that we endeavour to comport ourselves in public as nearly usual as we might – excluding Lydia and Kitty's improper conduct;

- *Remain steadfast in dislike and distrust of Mr Wickham;*

- *Mr Darcy shall be taken entirely into our confidence in the twin expectations that his assistance in dealing with Wickham could be essential and that because he is an upright and honourable gentleman, he will not betray our private business to anyone;*

- *Should Lydia find herself suffering lasting consequences of her actions, she will be sent to stay with either the Gardiners or our more distant relatives in Hampshire until she is able to re-join her family at Longbourn;*

- *If there occurs an increase in the Bennet family, the safety and identity of any such increase shall be protected as necessary – Mr and Mrs Bennet not quite beyond the possibility of claiming it as their own.*

- *This agreement is subject to modification as future developments require.*

The undersigned agree to comply with all terms set forth above in every particular and with all of their hearts thus engaged.

Signed this day of our Lord, 8 December 1811

~&~

It was late afternoon before the Bennets of Longbourn had done with their first ever family code of conduct and the incipient causes thereof. Everyone was drained, ready for solitary meditation for some and for quiet pursuits for others.

Kitty and Lydia had little to say to one another at first. Gradually they were able to establish that both had received a monstrous shock. Papá had forced them to take a new and very hard look at themselves.

To their mutual relief each had privately decided to set a course for self-improvement. An excellent beginning could be made, in addition to strict compliance with the new *Bennet Family Code of Conduct*, by harking to the previously ignored advice and counsel of their elder sisters – the eldest two at least, for Mary may be correct but she was... still Mary.

Mary sat herself down in a corner of the back sitting room (the larger sitting room having lost its appeal for the rest of that day) to work on making extracts from several articles which appeared to support the contents, or at least the spirit of the *Bennet Family Code of Conduct*.

Mr Bennet retired, exhausted, to his library where he dared anyone, at risk of life and limb, to disturb him for the balance of the evening. His customary glass of port at his elbow, he sat staring with unseeing eyes at the newest addition to his library. What was he to do about his precious girls? What was he to do about his dear silly Fanny?

Mrs Bennet brooded in her bedchamber. In all of the years of her marriage she had not minded her husband's slights and provoking remarks. She had willingly ignored the unpleasant aspects of their life together, relying instead on his customary non-interference with her pastimes and the upbringing of their five daughters. He had been good to her in many ways, especially kind behind the closed door of her bedchamber!

But today he had shown an ill opinion of her, an insufferably overbearing attitude that set her back up considerably! Why she had half a mind to do something about it!

She considered taking her household money and giving it to Mr Wickham. She could send Lydia to him with instructions to take it and her daughter and elope to Gretna Green! She would have *one* married daughter at last!

Then the picture came into her mind's eye of her husband's fury when she only spoke of Lydia and Wickham marrying and she was afraid to do any such thing. No she dared not defy her husband. She did not fear that he would harm her, exactly, but she did not want to incite his continued interference in what had always been only her province. And she did not want to be locked in her room!

"Hill!" she called, "Hill! Bring me some of those apple pastries cook made this morning – and a pot of sweet tea to go with them!"

Her younger daughters were confined to their room until further notice. Mrs Bennet would have to entertain herself as she might in the absence of anyone with whom to share anything new of fashion or gossip.

Jane and Lizzy lay side by side across Lizzy's bed. Every known aspect of their sisters' spectacular licentiousness long since thoroughly chewed over, their desultory conversation at the present dealt mostly with matters of a romantic nature – or more accurately, with conjecture whether their romances would survive the tempest that likely could not be avoided.

Neither was sanguine about the effect that their sisters' scandal must have upon their prospects in any case.

Sadly, Jane finally told Lizzy about Charles Bingley's important question, yet unasked, and now perhaps never to be presented. Any gentleman's willingness to connect himself to such a family must wither in the face of Lydia's scandalous ruin and both of their youngest sisters' outrageous behaviour.

In subdued tones they speculated about Caroline Bingley's invitation to tea the next day. What might change between now and the next afternoon? It was possible that within the next hours their welcome at Netherfield, their welcome anywhere, might be coldly rescinded.

Eventually their painful doubts and uncertain attempts to soothe away the other's heartache - and their occasional tears - faded into silence and they each lost themselves in their own private desolation.

TWENTY-SIX
Stymie and Duplicity

No one at Longbourn had had the presence of mind to notice that the drizzly rain had finally stopped. Indeed a weak December sun cast its pale afternoon light on the muddy track where two dispirited gentlemen rode silently side by side. Mr Bingley and Mr Darcy rode slowly back to Netherfield after learning that the entire family at Longbourn was unavailable to receive visitors!

Some sort of family meeting was taking place it seemed. The gentlemen had no right to ask further questions of the servants. It would be *most* improper for them to do so; and *highly improper* for the servants to divulge any of the family's private business known to them - if they were thus importuned.

"What do you suppose is the *meaning of this?*" an anxious Charles Bingley entreated of his more worldly-wise friend.

Darcy, for once, could not give a coherent answer. He could *not fathom* why he and his friend, usually almost *too* enthusiastically welcome by some members of that family, would be treated with such incivility on this occasion. "I cannot guess, Bingley, and with no other information than that they are "unavailable" we are reduced to guessing and I do not like it at all. I can only conjure up two possibilities and neither is a happy thought!"

"Well one prospect might be that one or the other of us has said or done *something* to offend them... or, heaven forbid, *both of us* have transgressed... although I haven't the *least idea* in what manner that might *be!* Miss Bennet told me she would *welcome* my 'important question' when I asked to call on her on the morning after we saw them last. Surely she could not hold it against me that the *roads have been impassable* ever since!" Bingley said. "What is your other notion?"

"Yes I am anxious about the concern you raise; however I know of no reason for the Bennets to take offense with either of us; I am *wracking my brains* for a hint or a clue! The other question is whether someone in the Bennet household is ill or there is a family problem for which they need time - and privacy - to address…It makes me uneasy that no one saw fit to inform us of it if that were so. We might have found some means of being of assistance to them."

Darcy refrained from mentioning to his friend that ever since they had been turned away, he could not get the image of Wickham out of his mind.

"It *makes no sense* to me at all!" He did *not* trouble to disguise his exasperation, however.

Fitzwilliam Darcy was a man who was used to *promptly* obtaining all information relating to any matter that affected those who were important to him, or his estate, or other financial business. He typically reasoned methodically and resolved problems swiftly, judiciously and effectively.

In the present circumstance he was *stymied.* There clearly was a problem, a *serious* problem affecting someone *very important* to him and he *could not* repair it! This most unacceptable condition left him frustrated and inclined to worry excessively. *Neither* of his conjectures, if true, could be propitious for his hopes and dreams of Miss Elizabeth!

"I fear we have no choice this evening but to return to Netherfield and hope the Bennets will receive our call tomorrow morning – as *early* as propriety will allow! I confess, I *cannot* be easy until Miss Bennet *reassures me with her sweet smile!*" Bingley too, harboured deeply disturbing anxieties.

Whatever the meaning may be of this odd turn of events, both gentlemen were more than eager, most anxious in fact, to set about mending the matter - *at once.*

~&~

Caroline Bingley watched her brother and Mr Darcy ride dejectedly toward the stable yard. "Good! They are returned earlier than I had expected. This will allow me an opportunity to spend a long evening in Mr Darcy's company!"

"I wonder that they did not stay to visit... they have scarcely had time to ride to Longbourn and back." Her sister mused.

Mr Hurst said nothing, appearing dead to the world and laid out, on a settee some fifteen or twenty feet down the room.

"I care not for the reason Louisa! I shall be glad of the time to invent numerous ways of pleasing Mr Darcy! I *shall* gain his attentions tonight!"

Mr Hurst snorted and sat up "What? Yes... a *tedious* way to spend an evening indeed!" There was no knowing whether his words were a response to Caroline's statement or arose out of the confusion of his 'nap'.

Miss Bingley only glanced at him and turned back to observe the gentlemen's progress across the drive. She touched her hair and smoothed her dress, taking a moment to look over her attire one last time before Mr Darcy should be presented with her perfectly orchestrated arts and allurements.

Soon she and her sister and Mr Hurst could hear the sounds of Bingley and Darcy's entry into the foyer and then their progress up the stairs – presumably to make themselves presentable before entering the sitting room. No voices, no sound of laughter or easy conversation reached the listeners. Instead it was as silent as if no one had come in at all except for the thudding of their boots on the stairs and a few creaking boards under their feet.

Miss Bingley did not at first take note of the singularity of the gentlemen's demeanour; that lady was entirely focused upon her anticipated triumph – Mr Darcy would be hers! That little country bumpkin at Longbourn *obviously* could not hold his interest any longer. He must have *finally* realized that the better choice waited for him at Netherfield, thus he returned to *her!*

Forty-five minutes later neither Mr Darcy nor her brother had appeared among them. Miss Bingley had spent the time perfecting her plans and alternate schemes for a vigorous push to corner her quarry at last.

Her equanimity faltered when she had neither seen nor heard from either after that length of time. So she sent a footman to enquire when the gentlemen desired to dine, thinking her message would nudge them to appear and remind them that time was passing while they loitered about above stairs.

"*No!* He *cannot do* this to me!" Miss Bingley had just read two notes presented to her by the footman she had sent upstairs, one from her brother and the other from Mr Darcy, to the effect that they each would be unavailable to dine with the others that evening, would be grateful for a tray sent to their room and, would she please advise cook that neither would likely require more than coffee and toast for an early breakfast! They planned to visit at Longbourn first thing in the morning!

"What is it *now*, Caroline?" Louisa Hurst's tone was just this side of impatient.

"Never mind, Louisa; I shall *know* how to act!"

Feeling her sister's scorn as an insupportable injury to her dignity, she clamped her mouth shut. She would say no more to anyone about Miss *Eliza!* Instead, driven by cold fury, she meant to keep to the enterprise already set in motion by her note to Wickham.

Tea time on the morrow would be most satisfying; delightfully amusing indeed! Caroline Bingley thought of the little booklet on toxic and medicinal herbs she had received from London only three days before. That small volume, carefully perused upon its arrival, now rested in the false bottom of her traveling jewel case along with a smallish vial of oil made from several herbs – most predominantly from Pennyroyal and ginger root. The case was in turn stowed in the far corner of the wardrobe in her bedchamber above stairs. She would take it out again - immediately after her toilette on the morrow...

~&~

"Oh *good morning* Charles, Mr Darcy" Caroline Bingley curtsied elegantly in their direction. She had waited in the foyer since early the next morning to catch them as they headed out the front door to their waiting horses.

"Good morning Caroline! You are up dashedly early this morning!" Bingley barely checked his stride in his rush for the door.

Darcy murmured "Miss Bingley" bowing slightly as he also pushed on without pause toward the front door.

"You are in *such a rush* to go out this morning, brother! How is it that you have been secreted away in your bedchamber since last evening and yet already heard about the *Bennets*?"

"*What?*" Both gentlemen stopped abruptly, nearly colliding with each other in their keenness to discover the meaning of her words.

It was Charles who had spoken. Darcy stood listening intently to what was to follow.

"Of what do you speak, Caroline?" Charles' voice was strained. He made no attempt to disguise his confusion or the anxiety he felt for his beloved and her family.

"Why, I am sorry if it distresses you, brother dear, but I … I overheard the servants talking…I understood them to say that one of the Bennet sisters is *missing*. Probably run off with one of the officers, I suppose. I believe that some of the neighbours and their servants are out searching, um…, toward the far side of Meryton, I believe." Caroline quickly dabbed at her eyes with her handkerchief to hide the smirk she could not suppress at the sight of their horrified expressions. This was going very well thus far. Now if she could only *keep* them apart from the Bennet chits until *after tea* time!

~&~

The two gentlemen from Netherfield Park rode frantically in the direction of Meryton; on the lookout for any sign of a search party. Both were exceedingly eager to render any service within their power no matter how difficult, or how small or insignificant, to the family resident at Longbourn.

"They must be moving remarkably fast if they are so far ahead of us that we cannot find any sign of them whatsoever! I would expect to see a few stragglers at the least, from whom we might ask information." Darcy *would* keep his head; Elizabeth had to be safe!

"I cannot imagine that anything untoward could have happened; but is it not odd? First we were rather unceremoniously turned away from visiting Miss Bennet and Miss Elizabeth last evening and now one of the Bennet sisters is missing!" Riding at nearly breakneck speed, neither gentleman could speak clearly or long enough to form a coherent stream of conversation so they simply forged ahead, eyes straining for signs of human activity on the road in front of them.

As they came near to the town, they slowed so as not to overtake and collide with a lone rider also about to enter Meryton.

"*Mr Bennet!*" Charles called out in relief "Has your daughter been found? Is she safe? Where..." He trailed off at the sight of Mr Bennet's countenance. It showed a mixture of confusion and dread.

"Of which daughter do you speak Mr Bingley? So far as I recall my daughters are all safe at home. Have you heard of something to the contrary?" Although his tone was carefully modulated to make a neutral rejoinder, his eyes were fierce and fixed intently on the two men who had obviously been riding at a furious pace.

All three gentlemen had dismounted by tacit mutual agreement and were standing a little way off the road speaking together in lowered voices.

"Do you mean to tell us that none of your daughters has gone missing this morning; there is *no search underway* to recover..." It was Darcy who had begun to doubt the veracity of one Caroline Bingley. That woman had *no* scruples whatsoever! Nevertheless he breathed a deep sigh of relief when Mr Bennet shook his head.

"No, they are at home. I do not think even Lydia would defy my direct mandate that everyone stay indoors until I return. Where did you hear this wild tale of a missing Bennet?"

"Er... my sister told us she heard it from the servants' talk. I am mortified to think she may have deliberately misled us but she has been... Sir, she has been *quite displeased* at her failure to achieve her object with a certain gentleman and, and her behaviour has become exceedingly *peculiar* of late." Charles Bingley had guessed from the look on Darcy's face where *he* surmised the misinformation had likely come from. It *did* seem likely that Caroline had *deliberately* sent them of on a wild goose chase! He could not, for the life of him, guess why.

Mr Darcy's countenance had darkened in a sudden flash of anger. His eyes turned nearly black; his mouth was set in a grim line.

little. He looked relieved! Still, he clearly was bent on some essential purpose in his excursion to Meryton. Mr Bennet was known to be a rare visitor to the town, leaving all such activities to his wife and daughters.

As if in answer to Bingley's unspoken question and Darcy's deep distress, Mr Bennet tendered a few words of explanation. "My errand does concern my daughters' safety, however, and I think it shall be necessary to bring you, Mr Darcy, into my confidence on an extremely delicate matter. I hope you will accompany me to Colonel Forster's headquarters, sir. I shall explain on our way there.

"I apologize for excluding you Mr Bingley, it is only that the fewer people who know of this, the less chance of an inadvertent slip of the tongue – believe me, should any aspect of this matter require it; I shall *not hesitate* to take *you* into my confidence as well."

"I understand, sir. I will just make a few stops while I am in Meryton, and then await you at the Porky Pig, Darcy. It will not do for me to confront Caroline beforehand – I would wish for your thoughts on the matter first."

TWENTY-SEVEN
Caroline's Dastardly Plot

"I am heartily sorry madam, but I cannot presently accomplish the deed you require of me" Wickham's insolent smirk was quickly driven beneath an ingratiating smile by his avarice.

"What do you mean you cannot? Is she not thoroughly insensible as we agreed? Is she not placed in an attitude of easy access for you? Are you *not a man*?"

"Indeed madam, all of that is true, and in other circumstances there would be no impediment to my swift... *removal* of the obstacle to your... ambition. However, I repeat madam; I cannot accomplish it just now." Wickham *would not* allow the woman's insults to set his hackles up! What was called for in this moment was calm.

"Why ever not sir? Does your... manhood wilt at the first call to action?" Caroline Bingley's impatience was near to explosive! "Is the money all of a sudden not sufficient to entice you? In truth I cannot believe that you would *balk* so at *this* juncture for any other reason! Surely it is not a matter of your *conscience* being an impediment for I believe you have no such organ! Come man, *all is in readiness* and I have gone to great trouble to place Miss *Eliza* at your disposal and to see that she is in no condition to resist your.... advances!"

"Nevertheless madam, I cannot. In answer to your question, I am not stopped by the urge to quibble neither over my compensation nor by any reason for hesitation, or other lack of willingness as you suggest. In fact I have my own reasons for finding satisfaction in deflowering Mr Darcy's sweet little lady love! It is that I find myself unequal to the task just at present, madam. At another time I would have at her with alacrity!"

"Then Mr Wickham, what is it about the present moment that presents such an *insurmountable* obstacle to your endeavours? I cannot understand you at all!"

Miss Bingley's haughty sneer implying that he was not fit to go drove him to say in a dangerous voice: *"That dog won't hunt madam;* Miss Elizabeth Bennet is experiencing her courses. *That* is an obstacle that I cannot will my body to overcome. And even if I *were* so able under those circumstances, the young lady or her family could certainly dispute the fact of the matter."

"And how *is that* sir? I find you *too nice* in your objections!" She was desperate, frustrated, and *furious!*

Wickham heaved a mocking sigh of derision, "Madam, *proof* of our assertions would be unmaintainable in light of the presence of ... of the natural effluvia of her present situation! Miss Elizabeth or her family could simply deny that any such event had taken place and offer their own explanation for our evidence.

"I tell you madam; this plan must be abandoned for the present. It has been spoiled by natural causes beyond our control! Now, if I would discover Miss Elizabeth in the same isolation and state of availability in a week, or even two, I will be delighted to accomplish all that you require without further delay. I do not even require that she be insensible – for there is a bit of sport in the struggle for domination. And how much more delicious would be the victory if she were to find herself increasing as the natural end result of... my success!" Wickham's eyes gleamed with anticipation and greed. "You would pay an extra fee for such thorough work, would you not, my lady?" An unguardedly lascivious grin flashed briefly across his face.

"Stop! I do *not wish to hear* of your *personal predilections* or of what may gratify you in the accomplishment of the duty you have undertaken to perform. Such talk is *disgusting* to me! I wish only to concentrate upon our business dealings and the effects thereof.

"I will have to think on this. I fear I will not find Miss *Eliza* so easily available to my control another time! You must come to me again in a few days when I will have had the opportunity to consider how to proceed." Caroline did not trouble herself to tell Wickham that with what she had given Miss *Eliza* in her tea, there would have been little chance of a "natural result" such as he anticipated! In addition to the other effects listed in her hidden booklet, she had read that oil of pennyroyal was commonly used among certain circles as an abortifacient!

"Very well madam, I shall leave you now. If I may be so bold, might an instalment of the sum agreed be forthcoming now? I find myself somewhat embarrassed for funds, having expected their availability presently more so than in the indefinite future." Holding out his hand expectantly, Wickham stepped closer to Caroline Bingley.

"Certainly not! I do not pay for services before thy have been rendered!"

"Ah but Miss Bingley, I cannot maintain myself in the neighbourhood nor hold myself in *readiness* without some means of support! You would not wish for me to seek funds elsewhere... perhaps an exchange of certain valuable information...?"

~&~

What on earth is Mr Hurst speaking of? Miss Jane Bennet was indeed amazed that that gentleman had spoken to her at all!

Had he truly made such an unexpected observation as she thought to have heard? Someone here was not to be trusted! *Why ever not?*

Being the gentle and kindly young woman that she was, she turned her serene smile in his direction with only the slightest lift of her brow in enquiry.

"You ought to make haste, Miss Bennet. Look to the well-being of your sister!" With that he seemed to return to his usual state of indifferent apathy; his flaccid body draped across the full extent of the smallish settee to overflowing at either end. Why if one were to rely upon appearances, with the exception of the ever-present decanter of some form of spirits, Mr Hurst was rarely the least bit conscious of anything about his surroundings - let alone those persons who happened to occupy them along with him. (Well, of course, except at meal times – then he lost consciousness of anything other than his ragout.)

"But.... Mr Hurst, please; might you know where I must look for her?" Jane's smile was slightly uncertain by now, provoked to some disquiet by his uncharacteristic communication.

Raising himself on one elbow long enough to drain his glass and set it on the side table, Mr Hurst stared straight into Miss Jane Bennet's startled eyes. "Madam, you must *think* on it. In this house, would Miss Elizabeth willingly allow herself to be guided to any but those rooms most ordinarily open for public use? Whom would she trust, or..., what room *would* she enter with one who *ought* to be worthy of the trust of a guest?"

Having thus spoken more words in one go than she had previously heard him speak in the course of several hours, Mr Hurst closed his eyes dismissively as his mouth fell open and he commenced to snore in great gulping snorts and gasps.

This was too much! Jane's habitual serene assumption that all was well with the world and that people were guided by goodwill and good principles, did not arise from stupidity on her part – only that she saw everyone she knew through the lens of her own pure character.

Glancing around to see whether any other person had witnessed the unusual exchange between herself and Mr Hurst she saw only Louisa, apparently deep in thought, toying with her bracelets. Reassured that none had noticed, Jane stepped quietly out of the room.

Once alone in the passage, Jane thought quickly. She had no doubt that her dearest Lizzy must be threatened with something awful! Otherwise Mr Hurst of all people would not have spoken to her in such a way!

But what the danger could be, she had *no* idea. What kind of evil *could* be wrought against her good-natured and witty sister – and *who would* bear so much ill will against her to act upon it? And, most critical just now, where…?

A quick peek into the library revealed only Mr Darcy sitting alone, writing a letter. He looked up in surprise at the sight of her. "Miss Bennet! Bingley and I have just returned from Meryton. He will be down shortly and then we hoped to join you ladies at last!" He stood and bowed in greeting. "Your sister is here with you I take it?" He would not mention Wickham, or his meeting with her father, in this house. Too many ears and too much afoot!

"Yes Mr Darcy, I was just going to find her. I look forward to seeing you and Mr Bingley very soon. Please excuse me, sir, I must find Elizabeth!" Jane's mumbled reply and hasty departure left Darcy standing in the middle of the room looking after her in wonderment. What was the import of her words? Something was not quite right about her manner. Where would Elizabeth be if not with Jane?

Berating herself for failing to enlist Mr Darcy's aid in a quest which must most assuredly be close to his own concerns, Jane almost turned back for him. But feeling there might be no time for it, she considered the most likely places where Elizabeth might think herself safe to enter. Perhaps in the smaller sitting room toward the back of the house? Moving swiftly in that direction she cast her mind over the possibilities; who could wish her sister harm?

Mr Darcy's stares had long since lost their menace when he disclosed that he had vastly more *favourable* feelings toward Lizzy than not. Besides, she had just seen him in the library, apparently innocent of any wrongful activity.

Well, Lizzy *had* remarked several times that Miss Bingley was prone to make slighting and disdainful comments about the Bennet family in general, and Lizzy herself in particular. But, Jane had believed her rudeness to be only a symptom of her friend's over- exposure to the faux fastidiousness of the *ton* – not actual hostility to themselves.

Mrs Hurst was... well, she seemed to think of little and do less. How could anyone be so very fascinated with playing with her own bracelets for hours on end? Oh! She thought to herself. That was *not kind* of me at all! Still, it did seem unlikely that Mrs Hurst could be culpable of anything worse than insipidity – oh *dear*, there I go again! *Lizzy* has got hold of my temperament again!

For several reasons Mr Hurst could not be considered as a likely culprit. *He* was the one who warned her; and *he* only troubled himself to move from the sitting room to the dining room and back again throughout the day.

As her thoughts raced from one individual to the next, Jane had to allow that only *one* person had any obvious motive to so dislike poor Lizzy. Whether there was reason or not, Miss Bingley had clearly shown her jealous displeasure every time Mr Darcy paid any attention to Lizzy, even when he only tried to instigate an argument with her.

Jane wished to herself that she had attended more to the goings on around her these last many weeks instead of losing herself in Mr Bingley's smiling eyes and amiable nature whenever she was in his presence - and in thoughts and dreams of him when she was not.

Thus engaged in those self-same fascinating ruminations, she had not even noticed that her sister had left the room. Therefore when first she heard Mr Hurst's words of caution, she could not guess when or with whom Lizzy had gone.

Indeed, she might well have missed Mr Hurst's low voiced comments just now if Mr Bingley had not been elsewhere.

As she drew near the door to the second sitting room, Jane heard the sound of angry voices just beyond. It sounded like a man and a woman were arguing inside the room. Their words were muffled but Jane could not help hearing snatches of their dispute.

"What do you mean you cannot? Is she not... insensible... agreed? Is she not placed in an attitude... for you? Are you *not a man*?"

Jane was momentarily struck still by what must be the voice of Caroline Bingley!

"Indeed madam, all of that is true, and in other circumstances there would be no impediment to my swift... *removal*... ambition. ... repeat... cannot accomplish it..." Was that Mr *Wickham*?

"*Why ever not, sir*? *Does your... manhood wilt at the first call to action?*" Caroline again "money .... not sufficient to ... you? I cannot believe that you would balk ... not a matter of your conscience.... gone to great trouble to place Miss Eliza...in no condition to resist .... advances!"

What? Jane had never eavesdropped upon another's private conversation in her life! *But this seemed to involve Lizzy!*

"Nevertheless madam, I cannot. ... compensation or by any... hesitation, or ... have my own reasons for ...Darcy's sweet little lady love! ... unequal to the task.... madam. At ... have at her with alacrity!"

Oh! Dear God! What had they done to poor Lizzy?

"... what is it about the present moment... an *insurmountable* obstacle.... cannot understand you at all!"

"*That dog won't hunt* ... an obstacle that I cannot will my body to overcome. And even if I... certainly dispute the fact of the matter."

"And how *is that* sir? I find you too nice... objections!"

"Madam, *proof* of our ...her present situation! Miss ... her family could simply deny... explanation for our evidence.

Jane was no fool, and she knew her sister intimately. She suspected that the obstacle, the *proof* to be denied must be *blood!* Mr Wickham was undone by the sight of her... Lizzy was *safe*! At least for today!

"I tell you madam; this plan must be abandoned...spoiled by... beyond our control! Now, if I would discover Miss Elizabeth... in the same isolation and state of availability...will be delighted to accomplish...without further delay. I do not even...she be insensible...a bit of sport in the struggle... more delicious if she were to find herself increasing... my success... pay an extra fee for such ... work... my lady?"

The beast! Jane's shock and fright was so great that she could scarcely breathe!

"Stop! I do *not wish to hear*...disgusting to me! I wish...results... have to think... find Miss *Eliza* so easily available... come to me again in...consider how to proceed."

This was horror beyond anything she could ever have imagined of Caroline Bingley, *her friend!* Weak with alarm, Jane sagged against the wall near the door. She could not leave until she knew of Lizzy!

Jane's lovely blue eyes filled with tears as her heart pulsed with ferocity! Lizzy needed her and she would never fail her dearest sister! She straightened herself and set her shoulders, determined to confront and overcome all evil threats of any kind to her beloved sister!

Wickham's voice again; "... leave you now... instalment of the sum agreed...now? I find...embarrassed for funds... indefinite future."

"Certainly not! I do not pay for services before thy have been rendered!"

"Ah... maintain myself in the neighbourhood, nor... some means of support! You would not wish for me to... perhaps an exchange... valuable information...?"

Not desiring to be found listening to their conversation and hoping to keep her fury from their notice for the moment, Jane began to turn away. She would dissemble a bit; act as though she had only just arrived in that part of the house – until she could discover where and how her dear sister fared.

She could not mistake Caroline Bingley's derisive laugh, followed by an angry declaration in Wickham's voice: "Do not be misled by present circumstances madam! Were she not in her current condition I would be at her with alacrity were she sensible or no!"

Jane's movement was stilled by a light touch on her shoulder from behind followed by a light peck on her cheek. Her near shriek of fright was almost instantly morphed into a gasp of surprise with her realization that it was her *dear Charles* who approached her thus "*Oh Mr Bingley!*"

"Forgive me dearest Jane! I did not mean to frighten…" His contrition was only expressed to that point when the door, some few feet behind them, was flung open to reveal Mr Wickham's very red face and behind him, Caroline Bingley's disdainful presence standing over the figure of a woman lying in a posture of collapse upon the fainting couch.

Both turning in surprise, Jane rushed toward her unconscious sister as Charles stepped in front of Wickham and demanded to know "What have we here, sir? Who are you and by whose invitation are you here?" Moving closer he called, "Caroline?"

"I am George Wickham and very glad to see you here, sir! I came seeking my old friend Darcy. As he is not presently available I was looking for Miss Bingley to take my leave when I discovered Miss Elizabeth Bennet indisposed as you see. Miss Bingley arrived just as I was about to call for help."

Mr Wickham's open and honest countenance clouded with concern as he indicated the unconscious form behind him: "I fear she is very ill, sir. Perhaps her family should be informed and an apothecary summoned? I would not presume to advise you on the doings in your own household… however it appears that now both of the lovely Miss Bennets are in distress." With those words Mr Wickham stepped to the side and half turned his body to indicate Jane and Elizabeth Bennet with a flourish of his arm in their direction.

Charles Bingley's interest in Mr Wickham was immediately overcome by the sight of his dear beautiful Miss Bennet kneeling by her sister's side, holding her hand and imploring her to speak. "Lizzy! Lizzy! Oh, *what has happened* to you? Please wake up; I cannot *bear* to see you like this!" Turning her head she begged that someone call for the apothecary and for her mother and father.

Rushing toward Jane and Elizabeth, Charles Bingley barely glanced at Caroline, who stood unmoving in the middle of the room. Arriving at Jane's side he checked himself, and… checked his sister. "Caroline, what are you about? Have the apothecary called at once! As she started from the room he added: "And send a note for Miss Bennet's parents, quickly now!"

"My dear Miss Bennet, please dearest try to calm yourself. We shall take the best care of your beloved sister! Look, she breathes freely and her colour is... well she *is* pale but not so *very* bad... surely whatever ails her cannot be so very desperate. I..., I *hope!*" Wringing his hands, he wondered what else he might do to ease her distress and to aid her sister. "Shall I call for smelling salts, or a glass of wine, or cold compresses? Please tell me what I may do to help!"

Sobbing wretchedly still absorbed in stroking her sister's face and patting her hands, Jane could only say: "I don't know! Perhaps we could try all of your suggestions, beginning with smelling salts – although she *does* despise them... *oh, my poor Lizzy! What* can be the *matter* with you?"

Hearing the click of the door closing, they both realized with surprise that Caroline had only just left the room upon her *urgent* errands!

Jane's countenance when she looked up at the sound was turned away from Bingley. Had he seen her expression he would have been taken aback at its intensity. "Perhaps we should employ a footman, or a maid, to accomplish the most pressing errands, sir." She breathed softly. By the time she turned to face him, Jane's aspect was purely one of concern for her sister.

Bingley's puzzlement at Caroline's slowness to act lasted only until he bethought himself of the probable shock she had suffered coming upon their guest so very ill in their back parlour. He would heed every request from his dearest Jane, however, and thinking that with Caroline in so bemused a state, it must be better to place responsibility for all into the hands of competent staff. Thus he quickly stepped into the passageway and spoke to the nearest footman.

As the man bowed "Yes sir!" and turned to do his bidding, a great bumping and thumping accompanied by a feminine voice in full peal (surely only Caroline could set up such a screech as that) sounded from inside one of the rooms just down the hallway.

Bingley hesitated; his Jane needed him and someone was committing bloody murder in his home, under his very nose! But, *his* Jane needed him!

Quickly ducking back into the small parlour he was astounded to see his dear sweet Jane glaring at the door with an expression on her face so fierce that he nearly ran back out again! "Go get that *Beast* Charles!" She shouted. "*Get that horrid Wickham before he gets away!*"

Without a word, Charles spun around and headed in the direction of the battle going on – apparently in his scantily furnished library. Well, thank heaven for that, he thought. Not much to destroy in there, in any event. *She called me Charles!* Oh my, she called me by my *given* name! Oh my *darling Jane!* And then he was at the open library door.

Somehow his surprise was not so very great to discover Darcy and Wickham locked in a fierce struggle to knock each other down; one with the evident motive to escape and the other to subdue!

Darcy seemed to be gaining the upper hand; Wickham's cocky insolence led him to a split second of carelessness. Shifting his weight, he allowed his balance to depend briefly upon one foot. This piece of sloppiness landed him on his back on the floor when Darcy, focused and methodical as always, took the advantage Wickham offered and quick as a flash kicked his left foot out from under him.

This seemed as good a time as any for Bingley to join the fray. He rushed forward to join Darcy in wrestling Wickham to a dead stop, remembering Jane's command and grateful that he had arrived in time to play at least some part in fulfilling it.

Only then did Bingley and Darcy become aware of Caroline's ceaseless keening from the far corner of the room. They looked at her, and then at each other a silent question passed between them.

Bingley finally shook his head saying "No Darcy, I had not had a chance! I had not even encountered her as yet." To Caroline he called out "Do *stop,* Caroline! Else I shall have you locked in your room!"

The keening stopped abruptly. "Brother! This man *broke in* here and tried to assault Miss *Eliza*! I was *trying to stop him* when you came upon us!"

Instantaneously Darcy's "*What? Where is she*?" resounded through the room as he leapt to his feet, relinquishing his hold on Wickham. That gentleman began to curse Caroline Bingley every way but sideways while twisting to break Bingley's hold on him.

"*Darcy*! I can't hold him by myself! Caroline, find several footmen to tie this blackguard up! Hurry!" Bingley was straining fiercely to keep Wickham down.

Thankfully he saw Darcy halt in his headlong rush for the door, knock Wickham back down and straddle his prone body hissing "What have you *done to her*, Wickham? *I will kill you if you have harmed a hair on her head!*"

"Relax Darce, I haven't... well I haven't *harmed* her. It was that *madwoman* who hired me to... Could you get off? I can hardly breathe with you sitting on my chest!" Wickham whined and writhed against the implacable force of his subjugation. "I have information, I can help you – if you would but toss a few coins my way... I can tell you all about this detestable business... just; just allow me the means and the opportunity to... to leave this place..." Speaking in gasps Wickham tried to avoid the rage in Darcy's eyes.

"*Really* Wickham?" and at the other's frantic nod he spoke so low that none but his captive could hear him "and *what of Lydia Bennet*, Wickham?"

Just then two burly footmen arrived with rope in hand, prepared to deal with Wickham. They must have been sent by the butler Mr Salter or the housekeeper, Mrs Roberts; Caroline Bingley had gone only as far as the doorway leading to the hall.

Darcy stood, indicating that they should take over the control of Mr Wickham. "With your permission Bingley?" at his nod of acquiescence, Darcy indicated Wickham without a glance in his direction "Tie him by hands *and* feet, to a chair or a bed, and lock him in a room without windows or more than one door. Post a guard at the door and check on him, thoroughly, frequently – say every ten minutes. Do *not* allow him to talk to you – gag him if you must - but keep him from it. I don't care if it is in a closet, contain him until Mr Bingley or I come to you with further instructions."

With a fleeting look at Miss Bingley he added "Take no orders from *anyone* but myself or *Mr* Bingley!"

Receiving their bows and assurances of compliance he turned to his friend. Knowing Wickham secured, his fears for Miss Elizabeth suddenly made him quite weak in the knees "Charles, I *desperately hope* you know where to find Miss Elizabeth and Miss Bennet! I cannot delay another second before I... *please,* may we go to them?" His anxiety choked him so that he could say no more.

Of course no *more* was necessary! For at Darcy's first words to him, Charles Bingley was scrambling to his feet and guiding his friend out of the library and down the hall to the small parlour were Jane sat holding Lizzy's hand and sobbing in terror for her sister's life.

"Miss Bennet! Is she..." At the sight of Jane's anguished sobs and Lizzy's inert form, Darcy instantly crossed the room to Elizabeth's side with Bingley following close behind him.

Dropping to his knees he took Elizabeth's hand from Jane, who readily gave it up in order to seek *her* Charles' arms.

Propriety be damned, Jane Bennet would not deny herself the comfort so long awaited and very much needed! Her voice muffled by Bingley's strong and very willing shoulder, she moaned "She *lives*, Mr Darcy but she *cannot wake up*! I have tried *everything* I know – even smelling salts, which Lizzy *hates*!" With that she turned her face fully into Charles Bingley's chest and clung to him trembling and sobbing softly into his fine lawn shirt. Both of them were oblivious to his having discarded his coat and waistcoat in the fracas with Wickham.

"What has been done, has the doctor been summoned? *Elizabeth! Please*, I am here *my love*!" Elizabeth did not stir. There was not the quiver of an eyelash. *"Please my darling Lizzy, do not leave me!"* Darcy's panic rendered him nearly incoherent, indeed he knew not what he was saying, until he forced himself to do what he did best: think, analyse, plan, and then act.

Bingley stood holding his beloved, enthralled by her intimate touch and that she would trust him so completely at such a moment. He felt overcome with guilt and dread - and hope - for the life of Miss Elizabeth and at once wondering how *his* love would feel about him when she understood what he suspected about his own sister's part in the situation.

Jane turned her head to explain to Darcy that she had only a few moments before, discovered her poor dear sister. Here she choked on a sob, and added that she believed Bingley had sent for the apothecary and her parents... had he not?

"Yes" Bingley reported to his friend "I had just instructed a footman to do so when I heard the brawl occurring in the library. I confess I did not know where I ought to go first, to the aid of my dearest Miss Bennet or of my friend! Miss Bennet most emphatically sent me in the correct direction!" Daringly he placed a light kiss upon his dearest Jane's forehead and held her close for a moment before releasing her to return to her sister.

"But *what has occurred* here? What is *wrong* with her?" Information; the underpinning of effectual analysis was *information!* Darcy feared that without accurate information Elizabeth's safety might *not* be secured.

Jane touched Darcy's arm "Mr Darcy, I believe that she has been drugged to induce this unconscious state – *intentionally!*"

"*Drugged!*" Horror shot through both gentlemen's hearts at once. Bingley was beginning to guess at his sister's madness. His mind's eye saw Wickham, whining to Darcy "It was that *madwoman* who hired me to..." to *do what?*

"Drugged you say? With *what* and *for what purpose?*" Darcy's fierce demand did not frighten Jane. She understood that he was beyond politeness, beyond thought of anything but saving her sister!

"I do not *know*, Mr Darcy. I only overheard parts of a conversation between Mr Wickham and..." she looked apologetically at Bingley "and *Miss Bingley.*"

Darcy gasped and abruptly the lines in his face, already drawn with worry, deepened in a frown of anger and pain. "I think you had better tell us what you heard"

"One moment, please!" Bingley held up his hand in supplication "I must send for my sister! I am afraid we shall want... *need*, to work out what *she knows* of Miss Elizabeth's condition – and the sooner the better!" His countenance was uncharacteristically grim and determined – a sight *never before witnessed* by his friend *or* Miss Bennet. Bingley's angry steps to the door were the only sounds in the room except Darcy's low voice crooning his love and yearning for Elizabeth to awaken and relieve his agony of distress.

His errand accomplished, Bingley returned to Jane's and Darcy's position, all of them fretting over the motionless form before them.

"I apologize for..." Jane spoke tentatively, "... for eavesdropping on a private... well it sounded as if they were *quarrelling* over s... something to do with *Lizzy* and since I had already been warned to find her, I..."

"I am sure you did the right thing, Miss Bennet. Let us waste no more time on propriety when referring to..." Darcy's peek at Bingley's face instantly altered his next words "to... anything related to Mr Wickham!"

"You were *warned*, Ja... Miss Bennet?" Bingley's question burst from him, heedless of Darcy's cautious progress toward the crux of Elizabeth's ailment. He must know *who, in his own household, was implicated in this horrific turn of events.* He would soon be impelled to act and he knew Darcy would recognize the critical nature of the information he sought.

"Mr Hurst told me that I ought to make haste and look to the well-being of my sister. I was so very surprised at being addressed thusly *by Mr Hurst* that I hardly believed him at first. But when I enquired as to where I must look for her, I was provoked to some disquiet by his next uncharacteristic communication. 'Madam, you must *think* on it. In this house, would Miss Elizabeth willingly allow herself to be guided to any but those rooms most ordinarily open for public use? Whom would she trust, or..., what room *would* she enter with one who *ought* to be worthy of the trust of a guest?' So, after a few stops along the way, I found myself outside of this door. I was about to look for Elizabeth in here when I heard their voices."

Jane quickly related the scraps of muffled conversation she had overheard between Wickham and Caroline to Darcy and Bingley. "...and that is when you approached me in the hallway Mr Bingley. I cannot imagine what I should have done had you not appeared just then!"

"*Hurst! What the devil...*" Bingley began, "*Pardon me*, Miss Bennet! Where does *Gilbert Hurst come into this* I wonder?"

Both men were still darkly engaged in pondering to *comprehend the meaning* of her story when a knock sounded at the door, followed by the hurried entrance of the apothecary, a youngish man of medium height and bony construction, with a profusion of light brown curly hair so fine that it appeared to float like billowing mist from the top of his head. His grey overcoat, which he removed as he moved across the room, was neither very fine nor too shabby but plain and well- brushed. He was dressed in coat, waistcoat and trousers of the same grey as his overcoat, and a clean white shirt and simply-tied cravat. His black boots were slightly scuffed but in good repair and recently polished. He carried a commodious looking black medical bag in his left hand.

Peering at them through the spectacles perched half-way down his nose, he said, "Pardon my intrusion, sirs, madam! I am Mr Archibald Sympson, at your service, newly arrived in Meryton and currently installed at Lucas Lodge until I establish my own residence. Mr Jones sent me in his stead as I am both an apothecary and a doctor of medicine. I am told there is an emergency?" His rapid-fire explanation out of the way he was already advancing toward the supine figure on the fainting couch.

Mr Bingley cleared his throat, drew himself up to the dignity of his full height, and turned to face Mr Sympson. "Yes, sir; I thank you for your speedy arrival! I am pleased to make your acquaintance. I am Charles Bingley, the leaseholder here at Netherfield Park, and this is my good friend and guest, Mr Fitzwilliam Darcy."

Allowing for a brief bow between the gentlemen, he turned back toward Elizabeth's unmoving form. Indicating his subject with a slight gesture of the hand, he said "This is Miss Elizabeth Bennet, who, as you perceive is unconscious. We have not been able to rouse her by any means at our disposal. She does not respond to smelling salts – yet she seems in no acute distress. She is simply, terrifyingly, unresponsive. We believe her to have been drugged for some nefarious purpose but have no information as to what she was given, or precisely how long she has been in this condition.

"This is her elder sister, Miss Jane Bennet, who discovered Miss Elizabeth just before we requested your assistance. She was just relating the circumstances of her discovery to us when you arrived. It seems she overheard enough of a disagreement between the likely perpetrators to be alerted to her sister's danger. One of those two persons is my sister, Miss Caroline Bingley. I have sent for her just now."

Mr Sympson had already begun a cursory examination, holding Elizabeth's wrist to feel her pulse, testing her reflexes, lifting her eyelids and peering into her eyes as Bingley was telling him these things.

"The other culprit is one George Wickham lately of the –Shire Militia, currently billeted in Meryton. Mr Darcy and I succeeded in subduing him and have him safely under lock and key here on the premises."

Darcy stood very still, watching and listening. His countenance inscrutable except for his eyes which were fiercely intent on every step of Mr Sympson's examination of Elizabeth – darting to his face, trying to read his expression as each activity was completed.

"Is that the cup from which Miss Elizabeth had her tea? May I inspect it please?" Mr Sympson stretched his hand toward the dainty china tea cup resting on a small silver tray atop a nearby table, flanked by an armchair on its far side – which not one of them had noticed until then. There were a saucer, a few biscuits and a half eaten pear on the tray as well. Glancing around they could see a similar tray on another small table a few feet farther away near another armchair opposite and placed to be facing the setting the apothecary had indicated. The chairs and tables had clearly been arranged as if for a tête-à-tête.

Jane reached for the cup and carefully handed it to Mr Sympson who sniffed it and then dipped his finger into the half-finished cup of tea, now cold and sinister to their anxious minds.

"It is chamomile, and peppermint... and something else; something oily and pungent when separated from the other liquid. I think it is ginger mixed with oil of..."

He was interrupted by the entrance of Miss Bingley, under the strict supervision of Gilbert and Louisa Hurst!

"...Pennyroyal!" said Mr Sympson looking directly at Caroline Bingley, who gasped and fell over in a dead faint.

TWENTY-EIGHT
Ordeal of Uncertainty

"*How much* did you put in her tea, Miss Bingley?" Mr Sympson, who had appeared rather mild of manner and disinterested in the human drama taking place in the room, now spoke quite sternly. He had not asked whether it *was* Pennyroyal, nor had he questioned whether *she had* been the one who stirred it into Elizabeth's tea. He had no time for quibbling. He needed medically relevant information, immediately!

She attempted to intimidate the country practitioner at first. Putting on her most forbidding air of elegant hauteur she replied "*I*, sir? What *can* you mean by...?"

"*Stow* it Caroline! The *truth! Now!*" Bingley cut her off, his voice rough and grating, shaking in his fury. "*What sort of woman are you?* Will you not be satisfied until you have *killed* her?"

"Caroline, if *you* do not tell them the truth, *I* will!" Louisa flinched when her brother and Mr Darcy rounded on her.

"What have you two... what have *you done?*" Darcy was tongue-tied between his anxiety for Elizabeth, craving to protect her somehow – after the fact – and his lifelong habit, formed of the most rigorous training, to address a lady with respect for her dignity and his own.

"What part have *you* played in our sister's mad plotting, Louisa? Am I to bear the pain and disgrace for *both* of you?" Bingley was reduced to tearing at his hair, glaring from one to the other of his sisters.

"Easy there Bingley! Mr Darcy! Leave off of my wife. Louisa came to me last night about her fears for Caroline's... er, state of mind. It was by her confiding in me that I was alerted to warn Miss Bennet to go in search of her sister. You shall both apologize and *thank* her when this is over."

Into the stunned silence that followed Gilbert Hurst's (mostly) calm announcement, came Mr Sympson's annoyed voice "Well, Miss Bingley?"

Caroline Bingley, when all eyes were upon her once again, stood stiffly, fists clenched at her sides, shaking with rage. "I care *not at all* for that wretched little..."

Catching Mr Darcy's icy stare she faltered for a moment. Then, licking her thin lips and turning on her brother she growled in a throaty rasp "*You!* If you had *listened* to me! I *told* you and *told* you! I warned you that those *people;* those *horrid* people! They were stealing him; stealing *my* future right out from under our noses! *My life* is ruined! How *could* you allow this to happen to me! I am *your sister*! I *hate* you! I hate *Eliza* Bennet! Oooh, I *despise all of you!*" She ended in a howl. And catching sight of Jane's horrified face she cried "I hate *you* too, Jane Bennet. How could you bring that, that *conniving*...?"

Whack! The flat of Louisa's hand connected hard with Caroline's cheek. "That is enough! Stop it right now, Caroline! You will soon find yourself locked away in Bedlam – or worse, dangling on the hangman's noose! Tell them *how much you put in her tea* and save your breath for the rest! I am *sick* unto *death* of your nasty ways and evil temper!"   Louisa had finally found her own, a dawning self-awareness, a confidence born of her husband's approving support.

The sudden pallor of Caroline Bingley's visage delimited the deep red imprint of her sister's hand upon her cheek. Her eyes, wide and dark with shock stared out at them as if she were a wild animal trapped in a cave.

Everyone waited; the room was very quiet while Miss Caroline Bingley teetered on the edge of the black abyss of utter self-destruction.

Slowly her comprehension was taken over by a sheer animal instinct for survival. *Instinct for survival*: an organ whose appetite she had fed since childhood with accomplishments; and connections; and pursuit of ever more money and consequence. Caroline vaguely recognized that she had a choice. Would she fight them to the end; *Sublimely* indifferent – *magnificently - refuse* to give in to their *pitiful* importuning and *hope* for the death that *they* feared; *consign herself to all of the horrors of Bedlam; being cast off from her family and friends?* She *might* have a choice! Could she yet redeem herself? Would it be possible to somehow, eventually, return to the place in the world which she had assumed as her rightful domain and now quite *thrown* away?

Gradually her body became limp. Her shoulders slumped and she covered her face in abject terror. She *did not know how* even to contemplate her predicament; how to be humble, to search inside her heart for regret she knew not how to feel.

They were waiting. They would not wait forever. Through teeth that were chattering uncontrollably she forced out "I gave her half of this." She held out the small vial of pennyroyal oil that she had secreted in a pocket of her dress. "It is oil of pennyroyal and a little of ginger."

Mr Sympson took the vial from her hand and looked to see how much remained. "This was full?"

"Yes"

"How long ago did she take it?"

"I cannot recall."

"Where did you get it?"

"From London; I sent for it."

"What purpose did you have for obtaining it?" He was not looking at her now; he was busy measuring the contents of the vial in to a small spoon from his bag.

"I wanted to..."

"Never mind Miss Bingley; we *do not need to know why* you sent for the pennyroyal, just now. Please just... take a seat, let us all do so, until we have learned a little more from Mr Sympson." Darcy's words cut off the rest of her response. He sounded weary, quite tired of Caroline's unceasing drama.

He wished only to concentrate on Elizabeth. She was so very beautiful and so unbearably helpless lying there. A profusion of auburn curls surrounded her dear sweet face, so pale! In stark contrast her long lashes lay like dark smudges against her colourless cheeks; her delicately arched and oh-so-expressive eyebrows now unnaturally still.

Instead of sitting in an armchair he knelt on the floor beside Elizabeth, taking her limp hand and beginning to massage it lightly with both of his own.

Addressing himself to that gentleman, Darcy asked the apothecary "I have heard somewhat of the herb, indeed I believe it is used at my estate from time to time. I understood it to be a remedy for certain ailments. Why would it be dangerous to Miss Elizabeth – and what are we to expect for her recovery?"

Returning his gaze to his gentle chafing of Elizabeth's hands and arms, he felt some relief at the idea that Elizabeth had only been drugged with pennyroyal. It was a known remedy for the discomfort of gout, and certain disorders of the digestive organs and other uses he could not immediately recollect. Why, pennyroyal had been used since ancient times – it was mentioned in the Homeric Hymn of Demeter as an ingredient in a mysterious barley water drink called...'kykeon'. Strange word, that! Memorable, at least.

Jane and Bingley had relaxed a little too. They moved to sit where Jane could stroke her sister's hair.

Seated a little apart from the group gathered around Elizabeth, Mr And Mrs Hurst looked on, more than ready to know it all.

Caroline sat in the armchair she had apparently used when she sat with Elizabeth drinking tea.

"I see what you are thinking Mr Darcy. Unfortunately the pennyroyal that is safe to ingest is in the form of fresh or dried leaves, treated as one would any other herb – but in carefully limited quantities. It has been used in that form for centuries as a comestible, or ingredient in various drinks, and to relieve a number of common ailments.

"*Oil of Pennyroyal,* on the other hand, is very dangerous. Although some unscrupulous souls use a few drops of the oil in their concoctions for luckless girls in need, it *can* cause permanent damage to the liver and other organs. At the least it can induce a number of very uncomfortable symptoms and, of course, unconsciousness. The dose she was given was certainly more than a few drops, but it was less than the cases I have heard of where the result was... Fatal. I suppose the ginger was added to combat the nausea and vomiting that might be expected from taking the stuff internally. As I understand it, the oil is most often used an insect repellent!

"I regret very much that until, or unless, she awakens on her own there is little we can do for her but keep her warm and hydrated. She may be able to swallow some water every now and then, even if her unconscious state persists. In a conscious state she will be able to tell us of any other symptoms she experiences. As to full recovery, only time will give us that information. There are... there are serious complications that could arise that we cannot know for sure until she can speak to us. I am truly sorry!"

Mr Sympson's dedication to providing healing and relief from suffering in the world was sorely tired by the necessity of delivering this frightful news. He refrained from enumerating the symptoms he suspected might affect Miss Elizabeth if indeed she did awaken at all.

He could see no benefit in describing the awful possibilities of abdominal pain, nausea, vomiting, diarrhoea, lethargy, agitation, delirium, seizures, fever, increased blood pressure and pulse rate, rash, even paralysis. Worse yet some of these could be early signs of liver or kidney damage when accompanied by loss of appetite, yellow skin or eyes, itching, dark urine, clay coloured stools, or a severe reduction of urine production. In short, Miss Elizabeth Bennet's life, if she lived through the coma, could end early and miserably - an ugly prognosis indeed!

Jane Bennet's gasp at his words was followed by silent tears as she kissed her sister's face, stroking her hair lovingly, gently.

Fitzwilliam Darcy squeezed his eyes tightly shut in a vain effort to stop his tears, kissing Elizabeth's hands and then bringing them to his chest where he held them against his breaking heart. He had taken only one fleeting glance at the apothecary's countenance as he talked to them. Darcy understood at once that the worst of it was left unspoken.

Mr Sympson explained to them that it was a complicated question of the dosage she received and the strength of her constitution, neither of which he had first-hand information of. He knew that the action of oil of pennyroyal was poorly understood and therefore largely unpredictable.

Gilbert and Louisa Hurst had been murmuring quietly between themselves. Now they arose and asked to be excused. "For I fear" said Louisa, "that the best we can offer in support of our dear friends and family is the privacy and peace to care for Miss Elizabeth free of unnecessary distractions. It will be best for us to take Caroline with us to rest in our sitting room until you have the time to deal with her. That is, if you agree brother?"

Charles looked with surprise at his youngest sister. Louisa did not say things like that! She rarely said anything beyond an echo of Caroline's opinion. "What? Oh, yes of course! Thank you Louisa."

Darcy's gaze never left Elizabeth's face but he gave a slight nod of approval. Jane smiled weakly at the Hursts before lowering her head to kiss her sister's cheek once more.

"Come Caroline, you may take my other arm." Gilbert was very proud of his wife! He looked down at the lovely woman by his side with renewed appreciation. Their marriage might yet fulfil the modest hopes he had cherished at its inception some few years past. If only Caroline could be got rid of – or at least quieted! Mr Hurst led both sisters out of the room without further ado.

Louisa's mind was likewise hopefully engaged. Gilbert had risen to the occasion manfully in sending Jane to find her sister, and just now when he took over Caroline's removal from the presence of those she had injured so dreadfully - to the undoubted relief of those remaining at Miss Elizabeth's side!

Louisa allowed herself a moment of selfish delight that her indolent, much disdained and dismissed husband had come out so handsomely. Most of all, he had spoken up for her! Defended her! Twice! She held his arm a smidgen closer and leaned her head on his shoulder affectionately as the three of them strolled down the long hallway.

~&~

Very gradually Elizabeth became aware that she was lost. She wandered in a murky darkness that was uninterrupted by sound, or colour, or light. She was cold, so cold!

And she was utterly alone. She felt deeply confused; indeed she scarcely knew her own name – did she? Did she know it?

Of course! It was... it was... "Elizabeth" she sensed rather than heard the faint whisper. Yes, it was Elizabeth... Bennet! But where was she – and how did she come to be here?

Someone was holding her hands and she welcomed the exquisite sensation of warmth and comfort with a sigh of relief. She could feel the steady tattoo of drums beneath her fingers increase in speed. "Elizabeth! You are safe!" and another voice, feminine this time, "She sighed! Did you see?"

Something was brushing softly across her forehead and smoothing her hair. She willed herself toward the warmth and voices. There seemed to be a faint light beckoning to her... Alas she felt herself slipping farther into the lost place once again. She wanted to cry out but could not find her voice.

"Elizabeth! *Lizzy!* Please wake up!" Jane begged her to stay with them but she could not. The sound faded to silence and Elizabeth knew no more.

"Mr Sympson! Did you see her? She sighed and then I thought I saw her eyelids quiver just the tiniest bit."

Under the intense scrutiny of three pairs of eyes the apothecary's reply was noncommittal. "Yes, however we can know nothing for certain without her return to true consciousness. I am sorry I cannot be more optimistic without hearing from her what else she endures."

"Is there a bedchamber where Miss Elizabeth might be settled more comfortably? She will need to be protected from intrusion and perhaps a nightdress could be found for her?" At Charles' quick nod he added "Good then, let us to it. Once she is settled I shall examine her more thoroughly, with your assistance Miss Bennet? It will then be time to offer her some water a little at a time. If she chokes, then we shall desist for ten or fifteen minutes and then try again. It is important to keep her fluids high."

Everyone was glad to have something to do at last. Charles rushed to have his housekeeper make ready the guest room with the most comfortable bed, sent a footman to make a fire there, and dispatched a maid with a request to Louisa for a gown and dressing gown for Elizabeth's use. Jane stood near Elizabeth ready to assist with her removal, and Darcy wrapped his arms under his beloved's shoulders and knees in readiness to carry her wherever she was to be taken.

Bingley returned from his commissions to indicate that Darcy should follow him with Elizabeth to the guest wing.

When Darcy lifted her away, Jane saw the dark pool of blood on the cushion where Elizabeth had lain so long. She stifled her gasp and stepped quickly in front of the spot so as to shield it from observation by Mr Darcy and Mr Bingley.

Fortunately their attention was on their attempts to position Elizabeth's head against Darcy's shoulder to prevent its lolling awkwardly as he carried her. At last all was in readiness for their safe departure from the room.

Before he could follow them, Jane touched Mr Sympson's sleeve apologetically and stepped aside so that he could see behind her. "I believe my sister is indisposed in... another way, sir. Her courses arrived last evening." Her breathy voice came out so low that he could only just catch her words. Her face was fiery red.

"Thank you for pointing that out to me Miss Bennet. I can see that it is not easy for you to mention such a thing to me but it is useful information indeed! It has been theorized that the effects of certain substances may be exacerbated by the cyclical changes a woman experiences in her physical condition. Perhaps we have a slightly elevated reason to hope, after all."

~&~

Not until after carefully laying his precious burden down, did Darcy notice the blood on his sleeve. At which point he nearly fainted!

Wickham! Darcy's mind spun in a torment of supposition and rage! His jaw clenched and his hands balled into fists as he imagined beautiful, precious Elizabeth being handled, being ...; *he would kill the scurrilous dog! He would use everything he had to knock the corruption out of him! He would rid the world of that foul pestilence!*

The deepest, blackest fury he had ever known had him charging for the door before he checked at the thought of Lizzy there on the bed. Lizzy whose life and safety was all he truly cared about. He could not leave her side while she lay so helpless, in this state so near to death. So he paused, and thought again.

Had not Jane related that Wickham insisted to Caroline that there had been some impediment...

Ah! She was safe from *that* after all! Wickham would have *wilted* at the sight of blood – he always had avoided hunting and butcherings and whatnot – utterly *squeamish* of it he was!

Allowing himself a brief smirk at Wickham's weakness, Darcy knew himself to be exceedingly grateful that he had *not* followed his first impulse to find Wickham and beat him with every ounce of his strength until one or both of them were dead!

Darcy's strict adherence to propriety in every aspect of his life had not protected him from a certain awareness of matters ordinarily held to be the exclusive province of females. It was inevitable that neither he nor his young sister had known to expect the advent of *that* aspect of her budding womanhood! Another thing to be grateful for as it turned out. That and his thorough grounding in every aspect of Pemberley's operation; Darcy enjoyed hunting and knew first-hand how to butcher and to prepare meat for the table. Blood was a natural part of life and he had no discomfort with it. He merely removed his coat and returned to the side of his dearest heart without another thought for Wickham. The filthy cur would await the convenience of the house, and the outcome of Lizzy's illness.

He left the room only briefly while two maids attended to Elizabeth and Mr Sympson examined her with Jane for his assistant.

When Darcy returned to Elizabeth's room, Bingley accompanied him. Elizabeth, dressed in a silken nightshift embroidered around the yoke with dainty blue and yellow flowers, lay propped up against the pillows with her glossy curls spread out around her.

She looked so sweet and innocent – and yet so gloriously beautiful, her curves the quintessence of womanliness! Darcy gulped to swallow the groan he felt rising in his throat at the sight of her.

Jane moved to pull the coverlet higher and tuck it more closely around her. They were not to be hampered overmuch by the impropriety of the gentlemen's presence in a lady's bedchamber; however she *must* do what she could to protect poor Lizzy's privacy.

Mr Sympson had little to add to his earlier information. Miss Elizabeth appeared healthy and normal in every way, except for her persistent unconscious state. He had received an urgent message to attend a man who had fallen from the roof of his cottage while making repairs to it. He would return immediately afterwards, or if Miss Elizabeth were to awaken or any other developments occur they should send for him forthwith.

Otherwise she should not be left alone, might be disoriented in addition to her other complaints when she awoke, and they should continue to offer her water frequently. It was vitally important that everyone remain calm no matter what might happen – just send for him immediately… he would not be far and would hasten to return in any case.

Mr Sympson's instructions were delivered with an emphasis and intensity that did as much to dismay as to comfort them. Not one of them failed to note his worried countenance.

Bingley and Jane and Darcy all wanted to stay near Elizabeth. Although Wickham and Caroline's fates remained undecided, no one gave them much thought. Elizabeth, Jane's dearest sister and friend, Darcy's beloved, Bingley's guest and the victim of his own family's wickedness and so dear to his own beloved Jane was the centre of their thoughts and prayers and rapt attention. They *had* no more pressing need than to watch over her, so they each drew up a chair around her bed and waited, occasionally speaking in a desultory fashion about anything that came to their minds, mostly about Elizabeth and the events of the past hours.

Darcy could not bring himself not to touch her, so he held Elizabeth's hand tightly clasped in his own, kissing it occasionally, or pressing it to his heart.

Presently Jane's expression became puzzled, "I wonder where my parents can be! Surely they should have been here some time ago!" She went to look out of the window, "Why, it is nearly dark and will soon be too late for their safe passage along our muddy roads! Oh, I am quite amazed that I could have failed to think of them this long while!"

"I shall send a man at once to find out the cause of their delay. I am so sorry, Miss Bennet, I ought to have sent my carriage for them in the first place instead of a note. I fear it will be too late for a safe return if I send it now. I believe that a rider can get through safely enough in the dark so at least we shall be able to keep them apprised of Miss Elizabeth's condition overnight if they are not yet on their way here." Again Bingley had something useful to do and accomplished it straight away.

Another hour-and-a-half passed before they received word that after first enduring the delay of retrieving their horses from working in the fields, Mr And Mrs Bennet had not gone beyond their own drive before their progress was halted by a broken axle on Mr Bennet's carriage. Strangely it appeared as if the axle had been sawn almost in two at some time previous to that day – the break being quite clean except for the last little bit. Frantic as they were to see to their second born, they could not come until the morning.

Bingley advised his rider to rest while he might for there would likely be another trip or two to Longbourn ere the night was out. The three settled it between themselves that they would watch over Elizabeth through the night by turns, Jane would stay with her sister first, then Darcy, and Bingley would take the last four hours before daylight brought the Bennets to their daughter at long last.

Mr Sympson returned and checked his patient but could discover no change in her condition. She had not moved a muscle.

The housekeeper knocked softly at the door to announce that rooms had been prepared for the comfort of Miss Bennet and of Mr Sympson. The apothecary intended to remain at Netherfield, other than for temporary absences in the case of an emergency elsewhere, until his presence was no longer needed. No one was prepared to debate which circumstances could apply to his cryptic statement other than Elizabeth's recovery.

Bingley arranged for a maid to sit in Elizabeth's room at all times. Several would take two-hour shifts throughout the evening and the night. This would ensure that someone would always be wakeful enough to notice any change in Elizabeth's condition, and serve the interests of propriety sufficiently to protect against the worst of any servants' gossip.

The matter of Darcy's hand-holding vigil simply could not be helped. He was not to be disturbed from his post until it was time for sleep.

The kitchen had prepared a fine meal and sent word that they might dine at their convenience.

Darcy and Jane preferred to take their supper on trays in Elizabeth's room and the request was sent down accordingly.

Bingley was torn between his craving to remain by Jane's side and in the intimate vigil over her sister, and his duty to his family.

"I suppose I must deal with Caroline – and sooner better than later. I confess I have no desire to see her face, much less to sort out what must be done with her." Bingley huffed out his unhappiness at the prospect.

"Please pardon my interference Mr Bingley." Jane spoke softly but resolutely, "I thought perhaps that any difficult or weighty decisions that can be delayed for the moment ought to be left until morning or until our heads are clearer. Surely any momentous dilemma taken up while you suffer thus from great fatigue and apprehension might appear differently with the passage of a little time and rest."

"Miss Bennet makes a good point, Bingley. It would not do to trip up in our haste to get such exceedingly trying matters behind us. I expect that we shall have more to consider than we presently believe. Time and patience are bound to provide the materials we all shall require to accomplish deliberations of balance and substance." Darcy began his statement firmly, but in a voice slightly muffled, and the last few words came out in a gasping rush.

"I collect what neither of you can bring yourselves to speak. We all hope desperately for Miss Elizabeth's return to us. When she is amongst us once again, or, or, some definite outcome of her condition is, is, known to us..." Bingley's remorse for having forced this discussion by his petulance before was evident in his dejected tone. He looked uncertainly at Jane.

"Yes Bingley. You have it exactly." Darcy could not look at his friend as he answered him in a voice strangled with anguish. Still gripping Lizzy's hand in both of his own, he sat hunched over with his head down so far that his countenance was only to be guessed at by the redness of the little of it that was visible of his ears and the very edge of his face.

"Yes, dear Charles, Mr Bingley. Please do not regret your words. We cannot avoid the truth no matter how ... much we wish for it to be otherwise." After a brief but steady look into Charles Bingley's troubled gaze, Jane averted her eyes and reached out to touch Fitzwilliam Darcy's bent shoulder in a gesture of support. "I have no doubt that our Lizzy is quite determined to re-join us. We must trust that her loving heart united with her vigorous constitution shall soon prevail to *all* of our great joy and happiness!"

Darcy lifted his head to cast her grateful look. His eyes were reddened and there were traces of tears on his cheeks. He hesitated a moment and then his speech was slow but clearer than it had sounded a few moments earlier. "Thank you for that Miss Bennet. If only there were something I could *do*! I need to *do* something to help her. *Would to God that I could lend her my strength - or better yet, take her place!"*

Jane hardly knew what she meant to say before she began to speak as confidently as if she had planned it out beforehand. Indeed, a new and powerful feeling had commenced to replace the painful oppression in her breast. Her heart knew ahead of her thinking mind what they *all* needed to hear. "But you *are*, sir! I am certain that she *feels all of our caring and prayers* for her recovery. Every time we think loving thoughts of her, every time we send up a prayer, aloud or in our hearts, *she receives strength from it*. This I *know*! Let us cease abiding in fear and dread! Lizzy needs our *love to lift her*, to help her overcome this affliction – and she *shall* do so, I am *quite* convinced."

Meeting their looks of astonishment and admiration, Jane Bennet gifted them with her first real smile, her lovely blue eyes shining with love, since her arrival at Netherfield Park so many momentous hours past.

~&~

Below stairs Perkins kept his own vigil in behalf of Miss Elizabeth Bennet. Gossip was fulsome amongst the servants. There was not much of the goings on above stairs that went unknown below. He did not often listen to their chatter. But having seen neither hide nor hair of his master for so many hours, and having picked up some various clues as to the direction of his master's interest over the past week or so, he did not hesitate to gather what information he could of his master's doings this night. And once all, or most, was understood, Perkins did not hesitate to devote his own prayers and wishes to Darcy's cause with all of his heart.

Quite a few others, he had cause to note, were following his example. Miss Elizabeth was very much liked among all of them for her gracious ways and frequent little courtesies to them.

Miss Bingley, of course, received little sympathy and less mercy from the servants. She had always been haughty and dismissive, critical and often cruel in her dealings with them.

Twould be the worst shame and a disgrace to outlast every soul then present at Netherfield Park if the sweet and kind one, the one whose smiles and amiable manners had charmed them all, should be the one to die.

~&~

Bingley elected to enquire of the Hursts by way of a footman as to whether his presence was necessary downstairs. He explained that he wished to remain at the side of his friend and... dear Miss Jane Bennet in watching over Miss Elizabeth. He added the request that they hold Miss Elizabeth in their prayers and send loving strength to her in their thoughts.

Their note came back that he need not attend them for Mr and Mrs Hurst were quite content in each other's company at present. Caroline was in a deep sleep. She had been distraught earlier but would not awaken until morning as Mr Sympson had given her a calming draught. They asked to be kept informed of any changes in Miss Elizabeth's condition and promised their continued support and prayers for her recovery.

Scarcely recalling that Wickham remained locked in a closet somewhere at Netherfield, Bingley instructed his servants to provide the man with something to eat, allow him a moment to refresh himself, and then to tie him so that he could sleep before they continued to guard him as before. The morrow would be time enough to address any further thought to Mr Wickham.

Thus the three kept each other company, Darcy seldom speaking except to Elizabeth using words of love and encouragement, or lifting her in order to carefully moisten her mouth with water. Occasionally Jane or Darcy would stroke Elizabeth's cheek or smooth her hair.

At last their exhaustion forced them to acknowledge that it was time to seek their much-needed rest. It was nigh onto half past eleven o'clock after a day and evening fraught with dire events and intense emotion.

Bingley, with a gentle nudge from Jane, bethought himself to send a note to Longbourn. The family might find some little rest when they understood not to expect further communication from Netherfield for the present.

According to their previous agreement, Jane was to be first to sit with her sister while the rest of the house slept. It would be a struggle for Jane to stay awake but the gentlemen hoped that it would be easier on her than interrupting her sleep later to take her turn at Elizabeth's side.

Darcy's aching heart was engulfed with apprehension at the idea of separating from Elizabeth as that inevitable moment loomed before him. His low voice rumbled in his chest as he uttered the words: "I do not believe I know how to leave her like this."

Bingley and Jane could only watch him as he tenderly leaned his cheek to Elizabeth's, their hearts aching for their friend.

Darcy murmured softly into Elizabeth's ear, his warm breath caressing her cheek, "We *shall* conquer this! *We shall*, Elizabeth!"

~&~

Ever so slowly, laboriously, Elizabeth gathered herself toward awareness of her situation. A few bits drifted into her cognizance and she counted them off to herself.

They formed her only secure reference from which to cope with chilling loneliness in an abyss of... nothingness. She was Elizabeth Bennet. She lived with her family at Longbourn. The remembrance of Longbourn brought forth that of her parents... and four sisters. Jane! That name excited her to recall her eldest sister and dearest friend.

Jane was in love with... someone... kind and good... there was someone else who... whose nearness warmed her... But she was so very tired! Every effort to focus her mind took so much from her scant awareness. The dark silence began to seem peaceful to her... it would be so easy to simply allow it to overtake her once more... Elizabeth felt herself slipping, her thoughts fuzzy. The faint light fading... Wait! There was light glowing beyond the reach of her vision but she knew it to be real. She wanted to reach for it.

She became aware of something else. It was a feeling so tenderly comforting and yet powerful that she knew it to be a great gift of love! It was supporting her, yearning for her, urging her on. The feeling was so wonderful; she wanted more of it, to hold fast to it.

She tried. Sweetly, gently and inexorably she felt herself being lifted up out of the abyss into a comfortable bed with soft pillows and someone's gentle caresses to her hand – she could hear a fire crackling nearby. Something warm and sweet touched her cheek and she heard "We *shall* conquer this! *We shall*, Elizabeth!"

Miss Elizabeth Bennet stretched slightly and opened her eyes.

~&~

Elizabeth lay still, staring straight into Mr Darcy's dark brown eyes. She watched in wonder as their expression went form an admixture of the fiercest violence of anxiety and passionate longing to one of sheer delight, brightened by unshed tears of joy and relief.

Holding her gaze with his own, Darcy whispered "Oh Elizabeth! I love you so!" Then with more volume he said "Jane! Miss Bennet, I believe your sister has re-joined us at last!"

"*Lizzy!* Oh my *dearest Lizzy!* I *knew* you could do it! Oh my dear, never leave me like that again, *please!*" Jane's happiness spilled over in tears and smiles, stroking, and kissing her sister's hair and face. Bingley waited quietly, beaming his pleasure to see Elizabeth awake and Jane ecstatic in the event!

Mr Sympson was promptly sent for and a note to Longbourn contemplated. Upon reflection it was considered wisest to await the apothecary's conclusions before sending word to Lizzy's parents.

Bingley and Jane were excitedly babbling congratulations to Lizzy and to each other on this long, and excruciatingly anticipated development. All were overcome with elation at Elizabeth's restoration to consciousness.

Darcy's gaze had never left Lizzy's face. The confusion in her expressive eyes troubled him. She did not seem to understand... what? Where she was? Who they were?

Dear God! Was she well, or, *would she be* well?

He saw her eyes follow the motion of his hand as he reached out to stroke her cheek. Her gaze came back to his face with a faintly puzzled expression in them.

"Elizabeth, do you know who you are?" His words, spoken in a low gentle voice brought a sudden stillness to the room. Jane and Bingley peered at her in consternation. They had not stopped to question anything of her condition after seeing Elizabeth's eyes were open at long last.

After what seemed a very long pause, she gave a slight nod of her head.

"*Oh Lizzy, my dear!* Do you know who I am?" Jane leaned forward anxiously so that her face was clearly within her sister's line of sight. "Do you know me?" Blue eyes met Brown and gold ones with love and hopefulness.

Lizzy's focus became sharper and the tiniest suggestion of a smile touched her lips as she breathed "Jane". And then a barely audible whisper "Where is... Mr... Bringle, Mr Bring... Mr Bingley? He loves you, you know."

It was impossible for Jane not to smile, though her countenance turned pink – mostly with pleasure. "He is here my dear sister, right here, see?" She gestured with her eyes to indicate Charles Bingley next to her.

"Hello Miss Elizabeth! I am so pleased to see you awake that I give you leave to call me anything you like!" Taking in Jane's blushes he couldn't restrain his embarrassed chuckle.

"Thank you Mr Bingley" she responded gravely.

Immediately her gaze returned to Darcy. "Thank you, too, sir... I was... entirely lost..."

Darcy only squeezed her hand gently and returned her regard, silently pouring all of his tender love into his warm dark eyes.

Mr Sympson brought a decided shift in the atmosphere of the room when he hurried to assess his patient. The room where three souls had united in loving vigil, and which had been for so long their own little sanctuary against the trials and tribulations of the larger world, was now his province.

"Good... morning Miss Elizabeth. I am Mr Archibald Sympson, at your service. I am newly arrived in Meryton. Sir William Lucas is currently my host at Lucas Lodge. Mr Jones sent me in his stead as I am both an apothecary and a doctor of medicine." His information was the same as he had rapped out to the others upon his first arrival at Netherfield but delivered to Lizzy in far slower and somewhat simpler manner.

When she merely looked at him but made no answer he said "I am going to ask you a few questions. If you are able to answer, please do – even if it is with a shake or nod of your head. If you do not recall something you may simply close your eyes and I will understand. Oh, and with each question I shall offer you a sip of water. Please take it if you are able." Seeing her expectant look he went on "Good, are you ready Miss Elizabeth?"

She unclosed her lips to whisper "I am not... I will try, sir."

"Very well; do you recognize your name, Miss Elizabeth Bennet?"

At her nod, he asked "and is your sister Jane here in the room?" Again the nod while Lizzy's eyes sought and found her sister's face.

"Now Miss Elizabeth, do you know where you live?"

"At Longbourn, with... with my parents and... and four sisters, sir." Her voice strengthened with her increasing confidence.

"Excellent! Do you know where you are at the present time?"

Elizabeth's countenance clouded again in confusion; she sounded disappointed when she said "I do not... recognize this place. I do not think I have been here..." Seeing Bingley's good-natured face, she brightened a little and added "Oh, it must be the home of Mr Bring, Mr Bingley. He is our new... neighbour at... Never... field... *not that!*" Lizzy frowned in concentration "Netherfield Park!" she exclaimed softly in triumph.

"Very well done, Miss Elizabeth! Just a few more questions if you will bear with me please?"

"Yes sir, but... will you tell me why I am... here; in this state?" Not liking to bring it up, Lizzy knew it would not be long before she would need to release the contents of her stomach. Indeed, it was beginning to pain her dreadfully.

"Certainly I shall, may we complete our little quiz first? It will be more helpful than you can imagine at present."

Pausing only for Elizabeth's nod he asked "Do you know this man who has been holding your hand this long while?"

Her eyes widened in surprise, Lizzy looked down at her hands. She stared for a minute or two. One of hers was definitely held firmly in the clasp of the man's much larger hand! Slowly she raised her eyes to meet his but made no effort to pull her hand out of his grasp. He watched her with an expression of indescribable warmth. He loved her. She had not the slightest doubt that he loved her, and he had held onto her when she could have slipped away.

"He is my... he helped me come... out... of the dark place. He is..." Gazing into his eyes, she could read his heart, even his soul. She knew him, he held her in his heart like something precious, his treasure. He had been there when she needed him and she knew that he would always do everything in his power to care for her, to protect her. "He is Fitzwilliam Darcy!"

Everyone in the room breathed an audible sigh, a release of breath too-long held – she knew him!

Darcy's face was a study of utter delight and hopefulness.

"Are you in pain Miss Elizabeth? Do you feel any discomfort?" Mr Sympson suspected she was ill. He had noted her free hand pressing on her abdomen from time to time, and now she was beginning to turn positively green."

"Why do I feel this way? I need to..." Elizabeth's eyes were big and round with horror as she jerked her hand from Darcy's and frantically tried to get out of the bed.

Quick as a flash Mr Sympson laid hold of the wash basin and brought it under Elizabeth's violently spewing mouth, using his other hand to steady her trembling shoulders. "That's it, let it all out, my dear. There is nothing good in holding that back."

Turning his head he advised those who wished, to make themselves useful – anyone not so inclined should clear the room and allow Miss Elizabeth a modicum of privacy.

Darcy did not hesitate to take hold of Lizzy's head to stop its wobbling, using his fine lawn handkerchief to tenderly wipe her face and mouth whenever she had a moment's respite from her retching.

Jane crouched on the bed on Lizzy's other side, stroking her back, taking over Mr Sympson's task of steadying her shoulders. Although she made no sound, Jane's face was bathed in a steady stream of tears.

Bingley, to everyone's complete surprise and admiration, patiently held the basin for Lizzy to heave and drool over, only relinquishing his office when the maid took it up. He stayed in the room, however, making himself useful wherever he could. Bringing a bowl of clean water for Darcy to dip his handkerchief, a fresh basin for the continuous violent spasms that wracked Lizzy's body, he took time to encourage Jane and Darcy with gentle pats on their shoulders or a kind word in their ears.

Mr Sympson busied himself with searching in his bag for the ingredients he wanted for a special tea to calm her stomach and ease her discomfort once she had purged everything.

TWENTY-NINE
In the Face of Adversity

Lizzy was incredulous and more than a little pained to learn that Caroline Bingley had fed her poisoned tea and tried to... Well, have her ruined by Mr Wickham. Caroline's aggravation with her was no surprise, but to hate her enough to wish her ruined, or dead! She could scarcely comprehend how anyone's bosom could harbour so much hatred and wickedness as that!

She had awakened to the same disturbing thoughts this morning. She knew it must be morning because of the thin line of daylight slipping through an opening in the window coverings.

Concentrating as hard as she could, Lizzy turned over in her mind what she could recollect of the evening and, her late-night conversation with Jane.

She was most indignant when she thought how she had walked right into Caroline's trap, never suspecting a thing when Caroline asked for a few moments of privacy. She wanted to apologize, she said, for her utterly unacceptable behaviour on the day of their visit to the gazebo. Elizabeth had agreed to join her in the small sitting room at the back of the house, mentally preparing her offer of gracious absolution ... Good Lord; she had been played for a fool!

Miss Bingley had seemed so solicitous of her comfort, stirring her tea with such care... and insisting when she began to feel dizzy that she remove to the fainting couch to lie down for a few moments! If she had not already purged to the point of exhaustion, aching muscles and a sore throat, she would have been ill all over again thinking of Caroline Bingley's treachery!

She still felt queasy this morning when she thought of all she had learned from Jane in the privacy of their shared bed. Or perhaps the oil of pennyroyal's effects continued to linger.

Some of the events of last evening were still a little foggy, her mind still befuddled by the oil of pennyroyal experience and, she suspected, from the draught Mr Sympson had given her to help her rest and recuperate.

Mr Bingley and Mr Darcy had left them to their rest, Lizzy remembered, only when it was clear that their assistance was no longer desired. Mr Darcy in particular seemed to hang back until the last, reluctant to part from her. If she had not felt in *such* a muddle, and so *unspeakably*, *shockingly*, *bespattered* and *mortified* she would have regretted the loss of his company more!

Once her stomach slackened its ruckus and her mind had cleared a little more, Jane and the maid helped her bathe and change into a clean nightshift. Louisa Hurst had kindly and discreetly, by way of her personal maid, placed several necessities at their disposal.

She and Jane had talked for a long time. Lizzy had insisted on hearing the full story from her modestly gallant sister. They giggled together at Jane's confession of shouting demands at *Charles* Bingley "Go get that *Beast* Charles! *Get that horrid Wickham before he gets away!*"

This morning Lizzy thought about the attack on her life, and had it not been her life it would have been on her virtue and thus still truly on her life for what kind of future could she have had then? But no! She had forgotten in the shocks of *this* affair! What sort of future was in store for her in light of Lydia and Kitty's deplorable folly... and the possible consequences lying in wait for them all?

Lizzy's self-confidence was sorely shaken – by her naïve vulnerability to Caroline Bingley's malevolence, by her lack of control of her own reputation, of her own body! Her honour, her character, her health and vitality, perhaps even her virtue – all were or would be in doubt because of the reckless actions of others.

Beside her Jane's sleeping form had been a homey sort of comfort to her, but no more. Lizzy was overcome with a rising tide of fear and heartache. Soon she was stifling her deep, wrenching sobs in her pillow.

"Lizzy, *Lizzy* what is it dearest? Are you in pain? Shall I summon Mr Sympson?" Jane's soft voice was a caress in itself and she leaned over her and stroked Lizzy's hair.

"Oh Jane!" Lizzy turned over to face her best friend "I am so dreadfully afraid!"

"Why Lizzy! What frightens you dearest? You are safe now; you are among us who love you and will always protect you! Do not cry my sweet Lizzy; you are doubtless suffering the after-effects of your ordeal. All will be well soon, I know it will!"

"No Jane. I... she tried to kill me, or... or have me ruined by that monster! How shall I ever feel... how shall I trust...? And Lydia and Kitty; they have already ruined all of us! It simply has all happened... without our choice or... any wrong of our own doing... Jane! What is to become of us?"

"Mother!" Jane could not help it. She chuckled a little. Then at Lizzy's shocked expression she covered her mouth with her hand but her eyes would not be stopped from their mirthful twinkling at her sister who always loved absurdity.

"I did, did I not? Sound just like our Mamá when I said that! Oh my!" Lizzy's hand went to cover her own mouth in chagrin. Then the tiniest giggle escaped from her throat. Then another. Soon the two sisters were clutching their stomachs, Lizzy grimacing in discomfort, and going full tilt.

The two of them giggled and cried and giggled together until Lizzy calmed. "I know not where our paths will take us, dear sister" she said, "but together we shall always find the humour to survive it!"

~&~

They were reclining side-by-side against the pillows talking quietly with the drapes pulled back to let the morning light brighten the room when there was a tap at the door.

At Lizzy's call Mr Sympson entered to check on her and provide her with an elixir to ease the pain in her stomach, which he assured her, would probably be negligible before the day was out.

Miss Elizabeth should partake of bland foods, as much as she could consume comfortably, and as much liquid in any form except spirits that she could manage.

She was doing exceedingly well, he congratulated her. She only needed a few days' bed rest and no more shocks to be declared fully recovered – so long as no new symptoms appeared. *New symptoms?*

He did not look pleased when she asked him what *new* symptoms she might expect. He prefaced his next by saying "You must understand, Miss Elizabeth, that it is my educated opinion that you have suffered the worst of it and are on the road back to good health. If things were worse with you I believe such would have been evident by now. So saying, Mr Sympson looked away for a moment and then squared his shoulders and told her about her narrow escape.

"In addition to what you have already endured, if the poisoning is severe it can result in convulsions, excessive fatigue, agitation, delirium, seizures, fever, increased pulse rate, rash, even paralysis.

"If there is damage to the liver or other internal organs there would be yellowing of the skin and eyes, swelling and puffiness of the body and changes to urine and elimination – all of which are likely signs of impending death."

Jane's muffled cry was the only reminder that she remained in the room - for the sake of propriety and her sister's comfort, ready to make herself useful should the need arise.

Elizabeth stared at him. So the worst might not be over. "You say that these additional symptoms should appear within a few days?"

"Yes, Miss Elizabeth, I think it unlikely that you will continue to feel any ill effects beyond today, or tomorrow at the latest, unless lasting injury has occurred. The more serious symptoms would set in within three or four days at the most."

~&~

"Where are my daughters?" Their father's furious bellow from the hallway outside of the door alerted Jane and Elizabeth to the arrival of their parents. They scarcely had time to signal to each other, with a nod to include Mr Sympson in their plan, that this frightening discussion need not be shared with them when Mr and Mrs Bennet practically hurtled into the room.

"*Oh, my dearest Lizzy! Oh Jane! What you both must have suffered!*" Francine Bennet's usual complacency over her daughters' well-being had been thoroughly routed by the dreadful fright of one of them having nearly been *poisoned* to death! She hugged each of them in turn until they begged for space to breathe. Still she could not get enough of holding and kissing the daughter she had come so near to losing forever.

Mr Bennet stood just within the door, shaken to a standstill by the sight of his sweet Lizzy so weak and pale against the pillows upon which she reclined in the bed.

"*Oooh my poor, poor darling!* How *terrified* you must have been! You are so brave and strong; still I cannot imagine how you could bear it – so far from your home! *All alone!* What a *frightful* taking we have all been in! I confess I have scarcely taken one deep breath since we first heard you were so stricken down! And then, so anxious we have been to come to you – and for one reason and another- we have accomplished that only at *the devil's own* dawdling pace!"

Mrs Bennet's agitated dithering gave easy proof of the rattled state of her nerves. She had truly been beside herself with apprehension for her child.

Mr Bennet walked slowly across the room to stand beside Elizabeth's bed. There he stood, tears rolling slowly down his fatigue-slackened cheeks, helplessly watching while his wife tried to express her love and to comfort their ailing girl. "I believe I have *aged* every moment of *twenty years* in recent days." He mumbled to himself.

"Truly Mamá, Papá, Lizzy is *much improved* this morning – as you can easily see for yourselves. She needs only rest and care for a few more days to be entirely right and herself again. Is that not so Mr Sympson? *Oh, pardon me!* Have you met Mr Sympson yet?" Jane promptly took charge of her parents, ushering them to a small table and chairs, introducing the apothecary to them so that they might confer with him about Lizzy.

~&~

"Another man would have forced a marriage without delay or a moment's compunction; so long as the family name, their 'honour' was preserved. Indeed I find that I cannot bring myself to do it. I cannot contemplate solving our several immediate problems only to set my poor little Lydia in the way of every sort of lifelong misery!" Mr Bennet sighed in a despondent tone at the close of his disclosure to Bingley the facts related the day before to Darcy on their way to see Colonel Forster. Bingley and Darcy in turn had described to him the details not discussed in the presence of Mrs Bennet regarding the events at Netherfield the previous afternoon and evening. He rightly felt that there appeared to be no end to the Bennet family travail.

The three men had spent the last two hours or more closeted together in the Netherfield library engaged in a solemn interview in which the exchange of information was only the first part.

There were profound questions to be resolved; decisions to be made about Lydia's shocking predicament and potential disgrace; Miss Bingley's fate; Wickham, of course; and about courtships – acknowledged and anticipated.

None of them could assume the others' inclinations in light of the outrageous behaviour on the part of certain members of their or their close friend's immediate families.

Despite the early hour, it wanting an hour before noon, Mr Bennet had gratefully accepted the brandy Mr Bingley had thoughtfully offered around. A bit of fortification was required in order to undertake the work at hand with an ounce of equanimity. As much as he abhorred exposing his family's shame to anyone, a very little reflection had sufficed to convince him that it must be done.

Weighing on his mind to a degree still more urgent at that moment than his youngest daughter's dilemma was a roiling of anxiousness for the future wedded happiness of his dearest Jane and beloved Lizzy.

It had not escaped his notice that some sort of shift had occurred in the relationships within both couples, for they could now only be described as such, and between the four young people altogether. They must have reached an extreme level of mutual trust and regard while enduring Lizzy's frightful condition and battling Wickham and Caroline Bingley.

Three of them had surely developed the deepest intimacy of emotion during the many hours of their vigil over Lizzy – and she appeared to have responded to it, even in her unconscious state.

Mr Bennet wondered to himself whether either or both of the younger gentlemen had the intestinal fortitude to continue in his attentions to a Bennet daughter in the face of Lydia's and Kitty's fiasco. It was a very great deal to expect.

Bingley's equally agonizing doubts related to the likelihood that Mr Bennet would never allow his precious daughter to marry a man whose sister had all but murdered his other most precious daughter. And how would Jane think of him, once she had time to consider? Could she truly continue to return his regard, for he had felt so confident that she did last evening, when she recollected that his sister had tried to ruin hers? All of his hopes of happiness must be destroyed, indeed!

Darcy's dark frown arose from his certainty that no Bennet would ever forgive the man whose fault was at the centre of it all! Wickham had been reared in the heart of Pemberley, brought up amid the Darcy's like a second son.

They had nurtured and nourished the viper in their midst, never addressing his waywardness, except to cover it up or pay restitution, as he grew into the shamelessly black-hearted scoundrel who seduced innocent maidens and hired himself out to ruin... others without hesitation or qualm. He, Fitzwilliam Darcy, as the head of his family must accept the accumulated blame Wickham's behaviour brought down on their heads.

Darcy's heart cringed to encounter the depth of his inherited fault and his own folly in trying to simply rid himself of the man instead of acting to stop him once and for all. Elizabeth had known, as soon as she understood Wickham's character she had insisted that her family and their neighbours must be warned. Everyone deserved to be protected from Wickham's evil ways.

Now, because of his, Darcy's, failure to act sooner, she whom he loved beyond anything paid the price of his selfish pride. For pride, as much as anything else, had restrained him and his father before him from acknowledging Wickham's twisted soul and making the foul treachery behind his easy-going manners known to the public. It was entirely his fault!

Could she ever forgive him? Care for him despite the heavy load of guilt and despicable selfishness he dragged along with him?

If Elizabeth chose to exculpate him for Wickham's sins, what of Caroline Bingley? She was his best friend's sister; his presence at Netherfield had likely been a factor in Elizabeth's agreeing to come to tea with a woman she obviously did not esteem. It was because of him that she had placed herself in harm's way, knowingly or not.

How did Elizabeth feel about Bingley; about his friendship with Bingley? She continued to suffer from the oil of pennyroyal – might suffer a great deal more, or... Would she recoil from him or from his friend now that she had had time to reflect?

How did Mr Bennet feel about all of it? Would he rescind his consent to their courtship?

The three gentlemen had been sipping their brandies in silence for some minutes, sunk in their painful speculations.

His last words left unanswered, Mr Bennet broke the silence at last. The slightest quiver vibrated in his voice when he spoke. "I assure you Mr Darcy, that neither I nor Lizzy shall hold you bound to continue in your recent courtship, in light of her youngest sister's disgrace – and my refusal to demand Lydia's honour be retrieved by way of marriage to Wickham." He had been reluctant to raise the issue of Darcy's intentions, dreading the worst. But he had to know.

Darcy looked up in shock to encounter Mr Bennet's grave countenance. "Sir! *That* was not a thought that had ever entered my mind! I have spent this time worrying over whether *you* would decide against *me*, or whether Miss Elizabeth could ever find it in her heart to forgive me... "He looked away to hide his anguish at the thought of Elizabeth's disapprobation returning in even greater force than before.

"Why, pray tell me, would you be apprehensive that I would change my mind about you? Have you done some dastardly deed of which I am unaware?" Mr Bennet was not, any more than his favourite daughter, made for ill humour. Thus, as was his wont when he met with intense emotions in another and caught a spark of the absurd, he was tempted to tease a little.

"As you know, sir, Wickham's conduct has long been the bane of my family. It is also true that I, and my father before me, have failed to check him in his life of profligacy as we ought to have done long since. Every time we looked the other way, every time we paid off a debt of honour or an angry merchant, or covered up his dissolute ways we made the man we find in him today. I am heartily sickened with guilt and shame. I can have no illusions about the rejection and scorn I deserve from your family." Darcy's confession was hard wrung from his grief-stricken soul.

"But if you are not inclined to turn me away, then I must know how I stand in Miss Elizabeth's opinion." He continued fervently.

Such open and frank distress brought Mr Bennet to respond with like seriousness.

"No Mr Darcy, I am not so inclined. I believe you take far too much upon yourself in Wickham's dishonourable conduct sir. He is what and who he is by choice. If an easy passage were all it took to make a man a villain, then how is it that you, who have had everything in your favour from your birth, have been formed as a man of honour and excellent character?"

The older man shook his head and continued "No, I make no doubt that neither you, nor your father, could ever have altered Wickham's course by much. While it is true that exposure of his true nature might have protected those wise enough to listen, your swift action, once you saw the need, in utter disregard of your own pride and comfort speaks powerfully in your favour."

"I thank you sir, for your kind words although I know in my heart that I do not deserve them. Had I been more forthcoming when I first discovered Wickham's presence in the neighbourhood, neither Miss Lydia's tragic circumstances, nor Miss Elizabeth's plight might have arisen. For that I cannot forgive myself.

"As it is not possible to undo the original injury to either or should I say any of your daughters, I beg you will allow me to do everything in my power to be of service to your family."

"I am quite certain that whether I allow it or not, the opportunity will arise, for our family is in a fine mess! I count on your assistance, Mr Darcy. I rely on your excellent judgment to help me sort us all out." Mr Bennet said ruefully.

"I am exceedingly grateful to continue in your good graces, Mr Bennet, and if I am so fortunate as to survive equally unscathed by the rigors of Miss Elizabeth's contemplation of these matters I shall never cease thanking God!"

"Yes sir, which brings me to a difficult point. I must ask you not to importune Lizzy about her feelings for the time being. I know that my request seems harsh, and I am sorry for it, but she has suffered grievous injury, not only to her physical well-being but from the great shock of knowing it to be deliberately plotted against her.

"I believe she needs peace and rest in which to heal and come to a reasonable degree of comfort with what has occurred. There must be no taxing of her sensibilities until her health is truly secured."

Darcy dropped his head for a moment and then looked up at Mr Bennet. "You are correct sir and I shall honour your wishes. My concerns will wait. I hope you do not bar me from seeing her, however, for up until now she has seemed to respond to my presence as if it might soothe her a little. I would be honoured to be allowed to be near her, if she accepts it, from time to time. Perhaps I might read to her or simply sit quietly in the room – with someone... a maid at least present as well, of course!"

"I sincerely hope that she does accept it Mr Darcy, but I make no promises. Lizzy shall choose for herself. I trust you understand?"

"Of course, sir."

~&~

While the other two gentlemen were thus engaged, Mr Bingley remained silent, staring at his empty glass, his face slowly going from pale to ashen.

Bingley's look had not escaped Mr Bennet's notice. Unwilling to draw any premature conclusions this time, he thought to draw him out. He was cognizant of Bingley's likely preoccupation with his sister; and his responsibilities as the master of the estate where she and Wickham awaited their destinies; and where a dreadful injury to a guest had occurred - a guest who had just been confirmed as all but betrothed to his dearest friend. And he, whose very presence in the room demanded justice for all, was her father. It was no wonder, he mused to himself, the poor young fellow looked so ill!

There was yet another matter between them which, if settled to his satisfaction, might bring ease to sore hearts and therefore became the most urgent in the hierarchy of the numerous candidates for immediate discussion.

"My eldest daughter, Jane, seems to have played the role of heroine in Lizzy's rescue last evening. She has stayed by her side; devoted herself to Lizzy's care ever since. I know that she will be delighted to know of your steadfastness toward her sister, Mr Darcy."

Darcy and Mr Bennet both turned at the sound of Charles Bingley's agonized groan. "Would that I dared ask my poor neglected 'important question' when my unfortunate sister has made me forever ineligible for consideration..." His hand over his face muffled the halting words so that the others had to strain to get his meaning.

Ah, yes! It was as he had expected. This could be put right forthwith. After a short silence for Bingley to compose himself, Jane's father spoke kindly to Bingley's despair. "Mr Bingley, I do not wish to put words into your mouth. Are you saying that you had something you wished to discuss with Jane but now feel you cannot suppose her good opinion, or mine, to be yours?"

"Sir, I ... my sister has... How can Jane, Miss Bennet love me now?" And with an apprehensive glance at Darcy, "How can you, how can either of you accept or... consent to my suit when I am brother to a, a madwoman?"

"Well Mr Bingley, I cannot speak for Jane, of course. However I see nothing in her that does not speak of her... fond regard for you, and I am prepared to overlook a great deal in behalf of any of my daughters' happiness – as you well know!"

Mr Bennet paused for his reaction and seeing only rapt attention, he continued. "You are an honourable gentleman sir; I intend to support Jane's decision, when it is made. All I ask is that both of you gentlemen be absolutely certain of your intentions before things go any further. I confess myself astonished that neither of you seems to have taken Lydia's and Kitty's situation into account. They may well be your future sisters. No Bennet will tolerate a rupture in their family relations, you must think on that before you speak your piece."

"Miss Lydia and Miss Kitty are high spirited, to be sure. There is nothing so very dreadful in that. Surely they will learn to be more circumspect and mindful of the matters we adults value as they mature, sir; they are full young to be blamed for their youthful pranks and consequent victimization by a practiced seducer of young women!" Bingley had thought things through and his conclusions came out in a rush of feeling. "I believe I should be proud to gain a close connection to all of Miss Bennet's sisters and to act in every instance as a loving brother to them all – specifically to Miss Lydia and Miss Kitty in their present difficulties."

"Bingley, you astonish me! Your assurances express my own sentiments precisely. Mr Bennet, there is not one family of my acquaintance which has not its share of eccentrics and miss-steps in its history if not in the present generation.

"My allegiance to Miss Elizabeth and your family has been established, in my mind at least, for some little while now. I offer myself and my resources in behalf of Miss Lydia and Miss Kitty without reserve. And Bingley, if it is our great good fortune that each of us wins our future happiness with a Bennet sister, I shall be most pleased and proud to call you brother!"

"Then, may I be so bold, Mr Bennet, as to ask for a few minutes in private with Miss Bennet after discussion of the other matters awaiting our attention is concluded?"

"You may, sir, so long as she is not otherwise distressed and is willing to hear you; of which I have not the smallest doubt."

"Now gentlemen, with the first matters of the heart sufficiently resolved that we may set them aside for the present, might we turn our collective attention to the *other* urgent problems confronting us?"

~&~

Mr Bennet, Mr Darcy and Mr Bingley deliberated for some time upon the best course to take in the matter of Bingley's sister Caroline; and whether Colonel Forster might deal with Wickham's future without requiring certain private facts to become fodder for public speculation; and When they could consider Lizzy's complete recovery to be assured; and when they would meet again to revisit the morning's conclusions and to decide together where Lydia and her family could best be situated to await her accouchement should such prove necessary.

Mrs Bennet, of course, was to be told as little as possible. In fact, only Jane and the Hursts were to know of some parts of their conclusions, and Jane and Elizabeth were to know of those matters pertaining to their younger sisters. Elizabeth would learn the whole of it when her strength returned to normal.

Not once during their lengthy meeting did anyone acknowledge the possibility that Elizabeth might never be wholly herself again – or survive to see their plans come to fruition.

~&~

Below stairs the mood was one of cautious relief. Combined with their pleasure at knowing that Miss Elizabeth Bennet had regained consciousness and seemed on the mend, were uncertainty of their positions and a hearty distrust of Mr Bingley's temperamental sister.

Perkins awaited his master in his private quarters, sipping a scant tot of Mr Darcy's brandy, celebrating Miss Elizabeth's survival and Miss Bingley's downfall. He knew from his master's absence most of the night and the rumours among the servants that it had been a most trying time for Mr Darcy and his friends.

Attending to his bath and beard and helping him dress in fresh clothing early that morning, Perkins took the opportunity to observe Darcy's demeanour. Long experience in service to his master told him that although some matters had improved greatly, Mr Darcy's heart remained extremely troubled.

Surprisingly this did not alarm Perkins overmuch. With Caroline Bingley out of the way, so to speak, and Miss Elizabeth close by it was only a matter of time until all would be resolved favourably. He allowed himself a chuckle as he carefully cleaned and put away the glass he had used; his worries had been for naught. Mr Darcy had met his match! He would *soon* be bringing home a bride. He would have a *fine* mistress for Pemberley and a delightful companion for his future life!

~&~

Miss Jane Bennet was exceedingly relieved to see her father return to Lizzy's room. She had been hard pressed to restrain her mother's constant fussing and chattering over her two eldest daughters and the ordeal they had endured. Now they were fending off another sort of ordeal – their mother's fond attentions.

Taking in the situation at a glance, and satisfied that Mr Bingley and Mr Darcy knew his wishes with regard to the numerous points of their discussion, he said firmly "Come Fanny, Lizzy needs her rest. We are invited to partake of a luncheon with Mr And Mrs Hurst and then we must be on our way. Let us not dawdle for we must see to our three daughters at Longbourn. I trust Jane and Mr Bingley to watch over Lizzy's care."

"Mr Bennet, I do not like to leave our Lizzy in this house! What if she needs me? How shall Jane protect her from those…?"

"Mrs Bennet!" He cut her off before she could say more; there was a footman at the door and a maid tidying the room. "Have no fear for Lizzy my dear, she will have our Jane, and everyone at Netherfield to keep her safe. We shall return on the morrow to sit with her again. Perhaps she may be so improved that we might bring her and Jane home with us by then."

"Why Mr Bennet! I cannot imagine that poor Lizzy could be so much herself again so soon as tomorrow! Surely she must stay right here and recuperate for several more days at least!"

"Mrs Bennet, do please make up your mind. I compose myself to see things your way until I believe that I quite agree with you, only to find that you no longer agree with me! Well, well, never mind my dear. Come along; we shall discuss the pros and cons of it further as we take our way home."

Lizzy laughed weakly to Jane as soon as their parents had at last taken their leave and departed. "I wondered whether they realized that I am right here!" She muttered, "But I did not want to alert them if they did not!"

~&~

Darcy's application to enter Miss Elizabeth's room had followed swiftly upon the heels of her parents' quitting it and Bingley's permissive wave of the hand. His friend was off to meet with the Hursts on the subject of their sister Caroline.

Colonel Forster had come whilst the gentlemen were still engaged in private discourse in the library and retrieved Mr Wickham to place in military confinement as a deserter. He left a message that he would delay any further action until he could meet with all three gentlemen to learn what other charges, if any, should be brought against the man.

Darcy was most anxious to see for himself how Elizabeth fared after being separated from her by the hours-long conference in the library and her mother's presence at her side.

Jane had admitted him saying that her sister had been tired by the earlier visit with her mother. If he would limit his stay to only a few minutes, Lizzy might be sufficiently improved after a rest to be dressed and, perhaps transfer to the sitting room next door to receive him properly.

Somewhat reluctantly, Darcy agreed, he certainly would not wish to impede the progress of Miss Elizabeth's recovery by his selfish desire to remain in her presence overlong. He did beg the privilege of carrying her to the sitting room in his arms when she was ready, to avoid the reoccurrence of her fatigue too soon.

To this Jane's face was overspread with a slight blush but she only responded with a demure smile that they must await her sister's wishes. It must be her choice.

Returning her smile with one of fondness and gratitude, Darcy took up the same position he had occupied the night before. He seated himself next to Elizabeth, where he could gaze at her beloved face and take her hand if the opportunity arose.

She lay with her eyes closed, a slight frown on her brow. He could not immediately ascertain whether she slept or merely shut them in an effort to suspend what must have been an onslaught of iniquitous information and her mother's well-intentioned but excessive fluttering and fretting.

He marvelled at the changes this woman had wrought in him. He had just now softened his reflections upon Mrs Bennet's ubiquitous nervous, and often inappropriate, chatter.

Before Elizabeth he would never have unbent sufficiently to form a friendship with Jane Bennet, nor shared his feelings so openly with her, and her father. Nor would he have lent himself to the service of an inconsequential country squire, or spent hours in an unrelated lady's bedchamber! How insignificant and even ludicrous all of his previous preoccupations with rank and propriety seemed to him now!

Unable to resist, he brushed his hand over hers ever so slightly hoping that it would not disturb her if she were indeed asleep. Darcy's heart lifted to see her eyes open and look directly into his own. Elizabeth smiled the sweetest smile! His breath caught in delight when she turned her hand over and joined it with his in a clasp redolent of trust and tenderness.

"How are you feeling today my dearest one?"

His low rumble was a caress, smoothing the frown from her brow and deepening her lovely smile. "Tolerably well, sir. I believe you are aware that my parents were here just now. I fear that my mother's anxieties have quite worn me out. I shall soon rally, I am sure, once I have recovered from her visit!" Elizabeth's rueful expression, gave way to a yawn and a flickering of her eyelids. "Forgive me sir; as much as it pleases me to see you here, I fear I must ask you to excuse me to my sleep." She did indeed appear to be drifting off.

"Of course, sweet Elizabeth," he crooned softly "If I may come again later, and if you wish, I would convey you to the sitting room if you feel equal to leaving your bed."

"That sounds quite lovely sir." As she closed her eyes again, Jane stepped to Darcy's side with a speaking look. Darcy nodded and rose to leave the room.

"Either this ailment has adversely affected her independent spirit or she did not take my meaning just now!" He grinned sheepishly at Jane "I did not expect her to agree to being 'conveyed' quite so readily!"

"I believe my sister has developed an unusual degree of trust in you sir. That is hardly surprising given your recent demonstrations of respect and admiration for her and your steadfast devotion since her affliction."

Jane could not resist giving him a quizzing glance: "Or, perhaps she *was* merely overcome with exhaustion!" She giggled at his glare of feigned disappointment.

"It is too bad of you, my dear friend, to trifle with my sensibilities so!" He chuckled, "I shall leave you now Miss Bennet, before you destroy my ferment of sanguinity entirely!"

THIRTY
A Haven for Mad Caroline

While Mr Darcy kept himself company in the library, Mr Bingley conferred with Mr and Mrs Hurst. Louisa did not scruple to express her disgust with their sister, a reaction, it was to be understood, which had been a long time in its formation.

His brother, much to his wonderment, was not only quite sober but sat upright in his armchair prepared to participate fully in their discourse.

They summoned Caroline herself after they had exhausted an exchange of information among themselves regarding her recent activities and, of course, the progress and prognosis of Miss Elizabeth's recovery.

None of them had seen Caroline since the evening before when she had been escorted out of the room where Elizabeth lay unconscious.

Once she had slept off the draught from Mr Sympson, their sister had remained confined to her room. Her breakfast, sent in on a tray, was returned untouched. No other attentions had been paid to her throughout the morning save those of her personal maid whom she had sent away the moment she appeared, declaring that she did not desire her services at all that day.

No one knew quite what to do with her, some were fearful of her, so they all put off seeing her until ... someone could decide what was to become of her.

In point of fact, no one had actually seen Miss Bingley; every communication had been made through the closed door – her tray, left on a table in the hallway, had never entered the room.

"Begging your pardon ma'am, Mr Bingley asks that you join him and Mr And Mrs Hurst in their sitting room." It was the voice of one of the maids. Caroline had never bothered to learn any of their names.

"Tell him I shall not leave this room. If he wishes to see me he must come to me here." She absolutely could not bear to be seen by anyone! She hoped that Charles would not force the issue. He might decide to put things off for another day.

Perhaps tomorrow she could put together those eloquent words of persuasion and excuse best calculated to disarm them all, words whose very meaning eluded her at present. *Where have your wits gone a-begging? Caroline?*

She had nothing to say for herself, no lofty display of hauteur, no piteous forms of ingratiation. She could neither divert them with her witty social solecisms nor any pungent on-dit of the ton. She had drawn everyone's wrath down upon herself and she could see no remedy while they were arrayed in a censorious mood against her.

From habit she strolled to sit at her dressing table, to check her appearance. She stared into the enormous oval mirror with deeply bevelled edges, which inhabited an area six-foot across against the wall above it.

Stunned at her reflection she vaguely recalled that sometime last evening, before she fell asleep, she had taken her embroidery scissors to her hair. It stuck out in angry tufts two or three inches long all over her head! Looking around in bewilderment she notice locks of her hair strewn everywhere on her dressing room floor. One or two seemed to have wrapped themselves around her left foot as she walked through the discarded locks of hair on her way to the dressing table. Worse yet, her face was haggard and bruised. She must have fallen or... collided with something – like the floor for instance or mayhap someone had beaten her, she might convince them of that!

Did any one of them hate her enough to do attack her? No, *she* was the one suffocating in hate and spite. They showed only scorn, disdain, and shame for her; she could not escape the image of Mr Darcy's curled lip when she passed by him on her way out of the small sitting room.

She sat with her head bowed, no longer desirous of seeing her image in that great hulking mirror. She could not recall where or how she had come by those bruises on her cheeks and forehead – or her swollen nose. She blinked away the tears threatening to cascade from her eyes. Then she saw the blood.

Her gown was soiled with blood. It was not fresh but formed several rusty smears across the skirt of her gown. Where had it come from? Was she... no, not now... Then she remembered the embroidery scissors. She had used the scissors to... "Oh God!" she breathed, "I have cut up my legs!" Lifting her skirts she saw them; three deep red cuts across her right thigh. She knew she had done it herself. For the first time in a very long time Caroline had indulged an old secret urge, she had cut on herself!

Well, that's that! Caroline Bingley had *run mad* and she could never think how to hide the evidence of it for more than a few hours. Powder... and a frilly bonnet, perhaps? She ought to change out of her bloody gown.

Once they saw her hair and the bruises on her face it would be all over. Charles and Louisa would insist on summoning a doctor and the rest would soon be known.

A tentative rap on the door to her bedchamber door brought her hurtling dizzily to the present. "Miss Bingley, pardon me again ma'am, Mr Bingley sent you this note, um... I shall just slide it to you under the door, shall I? Here 'tis ma.am."

The note, when Caroline finally picked it up after some ten minutes of hesitation, was unambiguous.

Caroline, it pains me to say this but if you do not come to me immediately I shall be forced to send someone to bring you here by force. The time for shilly-shallying is over! Come at once!

CB

Another ten minutes or so drifted by while Caroline deliberated upon which way she was to make herself presentable.

Then another ten minutes elapsed while she wondered whether she ought to bother putting on a fresh gown if she could do nothing for her face and hair.

~ & ~

Charles Bingley, Gilbert and Louisa Hurst, and Mr Sympson all stared open-mouthed when Caroline finally stood in the doorway in response to her brother's command. It had been the better half of an hour since Charles' note to his sister.

She had made no push to alter her appearance from what it had been when she first received it.

Miss Caroline Bingley frankly could not gather her wits about her enough to think of and then act upon a necessary action. She simply went to her brother and sister, without disguise or artifice, just as she was.

Carline knew herself to be in grave trouble.

"Oh Caroline!" Louisa's gasp seemed to echo around the room gathering force from each shocked face as it reverberated over and over in her head.

"Yes" she said flatly, stepping forward into the sitting room so that the door could be closed behind her. "I have come to you Charles. What will you do with me?" The lack of inflection in her tone brought the question out sounding more like a statement. She could just as easily have said 'Do what you will with me' and the meaning would have been the same.

A quick glance at each other confirmed her brother and sister of which option under consideration they must choose. Charles paused only for a scant breath before taking the lead. "Please join us, Caroline; we must discuss your future."

She wandered in a desultory fashion into the room to take a seat on a small settee placed near but not quite within the grouping where her family was ensconced.

Caroline did not speak. Indeed, she was oddly disoriented in a room where she had spent many hours since coming to Netherfield Park. But *then* she had been confident, her own mistress – acting mistress of the estate. Now what was she?

She studied the blood smears on her skirt and waited for her brother to tell her.

Not knowing what his sister was thinking, how she perceived her role in Elizabeth's near demise, he began with the matter of potential charges against her. "I am very happy to report to you, Caroline, that you are not yet a murderess. Miss Elizabeth appears to be recovering this morning. There is some lingering fear of complications however; which, if they occur, could nonetheless end her life."

In the brief silence that followed her brother's words, Caroline considered whether she cared for Miss *Eliza's* life. She could not decide.

"Do you understand what I am saying, Caroline?"

She looked up and met his eyes. There she recognized that he was deeply angry, but there was hurt and… sympathy as well. Caroline Bingley could not abide sympathy! She looked away and shrugged her shoulders.

"Very well, Caroline; you shall be kept somewhere safe, on a small island called Lundy actually, in the Bristol Channel about 12 miles off the coast of Devon. You will be safe there, with a family I know from Ireland.

"The island is no more than three miles across but it is quite beautiful, and quiet. It belongs to an Irish acquaintance of our father's, Sir Aubrey Vere Hunt[ii]. I believe they may have had some business connection for a time. Father always spoke of Sir Aubrey with respect for his honest dealing and for his visionary ideas for the future of society.

"With Mr Bennet's very generous agreement not to insist upon handing you over to the authorities, I have written Sir Aubrey with a request for permission to sequester you on his island for a time and to ask whether he knows of a family particularly suited to keep you while you rest and reflect upon the course of your life thus far."

Caroline held herself rigidly upright. She would not allow herself to cry or grovel.

She was lucky, she supposed, that no one seemed disposed to hand her over to the constable, or sheriff or whoever was charged with the incarceration of miscreants in this Godforsaken place! She *would* not care.

Her life was useless to her now. It mattered not where she existed.

"In the interval while we await Sir Aubrey Vere Hunt's response, you shall remain here, under close… supervision. I wish for you to have everything needed for your safety and comfort but, in light of the peculiar delicacy of our situation, you may not venture from your room or speak with anyone but myself and Louisa – beyond the common civilities of course.

Louisa had patiently waited for her brother to pronounce her sister's sentence before she spoke. "Now, Caroline, What have you done to yourself? I see bruises on your face, and that you have nearly shorn your head, but no source for the blood on your dress. I do not know how you contrived the damage to your aspect, but I suspect that you have been cutting your legs again! Is that true?"

Caroline stared at her sister. She was not accustomed to hear Louisa speak so firmly or, or almost indifferently to her closest friend. Ah, even Louisa could discard her relative without indecision. This was a pretty pass, indeed!

Her momentary indignation subsided as swiftly as it had appeared. She had always known that she and her sister had enjoyed each other's company through an accident of kinship, rather than any true affinity of interest or personality. Indeed, she was used to dominating and deprecating her elder sister more than not. Louisa's defection was no cause for surprise or disconcertion after all. Only her forthright manner of addressing her thus in front of her brother and husband was a bit of a stunner.

"Well Caroline?" Charles leaned toward her intently, his very posture demanding her answer to Louisa's question.

Caroline heaved an impatient sigh "Yes, Louisa, yes Charles, I am quite unspeakably ruffled. Beyond the pale of reason, I imagine. If you would be so kind as to excuse me now, I shall go and make myself presentable and begin my packing." Rising abruptly from her seat on the settee, Caroline Bingley walked quickly head held high, back stiffly straight. She was raw and edgy in her confusion; she had at once too little and too great a notion of her own consequence.

"Very well Caroline, we shall speak again before your departure for the north." Her brother's unhappiness, palpable in the heavy discouragement of his tone, was equally evident in the slump of his shoulders. Charles Bingley, usually cheerful and optimistic when confronted with any new challenge, did not relish the weight of his responsibilities in this troubling dilemma!

No one made a move to stop Caroline's progress across the room to the door. Charles only stepped forward to open it for her, and to indicate to the footman outside that she was to be accompanied to her dressing room. At least one maid was to enter with her and remain present until relieved by another. A footman was to be stationed in the hallway nearby to Caroline's suite of rooms.

He had given the same instructions to the housekeeper earlier but wished to take no chances of Caroline slipping out of his care. He could not trust that in her current condition she would not again make an attempt to harm another, *or* that she could take care of herself!

~ & ~

Darcy was not, as expected, in Miss Elizabeth's company. She was sleeping, Jane said, but still recovering without any new symptoms. Thus after a few precious moments' conversation with his rather preoccupied lady love, Bingley sought his friend in the library.

When he had finished telling Darcy about his plans for Caroline, he waited expectantly for his opinion. His friend could be counted upon to give it in most instances and he felt certain that his would be no exception.

Bingley thought surely he had done well in choosing how best to deal with his sister so he was taken aback when Darcy said calmly "No Bingley, forgive my interference but you must not send your sister to the island of Lundy."

Is there some worse fate you would have me subject her to? Would you have her face criminal charges? You know that I cannot...:

"Bingley! Hold off your sputtering for a beat or two. The objection is not to your very wise plan, only to the destination you have chosen for its unfolding.

"The place has a nasty reputation for lawlessness.[iii] Lundy has been used for everything from hosting of pirates in olden times, to the recent housing of convicts supposed to be transported to Virginia, and to being the locale of a shipping insurance swindle.

"Sir Aubrey Vere Hunt has indeed established a small, self-contained colony of tenants from his Irish estate. I am told that they are experiencing severe agricultural difficulties on the island.

"The place has its own constitution and laws; you could not expect the protection of English law to govern your sister's circumstances or care.

"Word is out that Sir Vere Hunt has not found the yield from his investment in the island to his satisfaction. He has not prospered on Lundy and neither have his tenants.

"The likely temptation to profit from Miss Bingley's presence there could prove stronger than honesty and kindness to an Englishwoman in their midst – especially one so haughty and unstable as, as is her current conduct."

"Good lord, Darcy! I certainly shall not send her there!" Bingley wondered aloud "But where? There must be some out of the way place, preferably beyond easy reach - or escape, where Caroline may live safely and privately until she is ready to return... I cannot think she will not recover her reason, Darcy!"

"My uncle, the Earl of Matlock, has some holdings, a well-appointed hunting lodge as I recall, in Scotland. I was there once with my father and Uncle when I was a mere pup of a lad. It is situated near an isolated village called Achachork[iv], which lies some miles distant to the north of Portree - which is the largest town on the Isle of Skye. The scenery is spectacular, and, of course, the wildlife is abundant I am told.

"Portree is a harbour town where I believe shipping of agricultural and other products occurs. It is also where my uncle's local man of business, a Mr Harold Potter resides. A very accommodating fellow, he is one of many among the populace who speak English as well as their local Scottish Gaelic.

" If you wish I would be happy to enquire of Uncle Matlock whether an appropriate situation might be set up for your sister at or near his lodge."

Bingley's demeanour had brightened considerably while Darcy was speaking. "That sounds splendid, Darcy! Please do make enquiry of your uncle about it!" For a moment his expression darkened "But will your uncle be willing to shelter a, a …"

"We shall simply tell him the truth - that your sister has been ill and requires complete rest and quiet for her recuperation. He would not probe further; he is quite the stickler for privacy."

THIRTY-ONE
The Delighted Conveyance

Carefully sanding and sealing the letter to his Uncle Matlock, Darcy rose from the writing desk in the library, taking it with him to find a footman to send it by express. He was hopeful that his uncle would agree, and that a solution to one problem, at least, was at hand.

Moments later he again presented himself for admission to Elizabeth's room. Darcy hoped that she would be awake, refreshed, and dressed for her visitor. He could hardly suppress his excited yearning to carry her delightfully alluring body in his arms to the sitting room where they would spend a little time, peaceful time, together.

Jane's smiling face when she swung the door open in answer to his knock, invited him to enter.

Returning her smile with a grin, he stepped eagerly into the room, expecting to find Elizabeth on the bed. Not there! His eyes anxiously swept the room in search of her.

Ah! She sat smiling up at him from her seat near the window where she had obviously been enjoying the sights and sounds in the garden below. She was so lovely, so utterly beguiling in her innocent pleasure at achieving this much; he wanted to take her in his arms and hold her close, and after that to pour his tremendous love into devastating heart-stopping kisses that he...that he had better *not* imagine just now!

"Well sir? Will you not greet me; congratulate me on my escape from that confounded bed?" Lizzy's eyes danced with merriment at his sudden apparent inability to move or speak.

He wondered how long he had been standing there with his heart in his eyes and his throat closed up as tight as a rain-swollen door in winter – and just as useful for speech!

Still rooted to the spot he replied "Er, ah, of course, Miss Elizabeth! I do congratulate you on your escape, and upon your entrancing beauty and wit which never fail in combination to destroy my equanimity whilst I am rewarded with the happiness of seeing you again."

"Such a pretty speech, sir, deserves a greater reward than merely 'seeing' someone. Perhaps you will join me for a light meal. I am under orders to eat frequent small meals and drink a quantity of fluids. Perhaps you might assist me to the sitting room, Mr Darcy? I believe a lovely repast is laid out awaiting us there."

So saying, and seeing his expression of delight, Lizzy began to rise from her seat, steadying herself with a hand on the arm of her chair. "I am so very much improved over this morning, but I will appreciate your lending me your arm, sir." She faltered and bit her lip as she used both hands on the chair arm to regain her balance.

"Lizzy do not...!" He was vaguely aware that Jane had cried out.

Darcy's single-minded purpose was to reach Elizabeth before she fell. In a flash he was beside her, taking her arm to guide her to him.

Saying firmly "No Miss Elizabeth, with the permission you granted me this morning, I shall *convey* you to the sitting room!" he swept her up with alacrity into his arms, hoping her sharp gasp was not one of real alarm, and carried her to the sitting room.

"Now my lovely lady, where would you like to sit? Next to the window as you were before, or over here on the settee where there is room enough for us to sit together, or in that very large armchair that looks as if it might swallow you up in its comfort?"

Darcy worked valiantly to hide the way her nearness made him feel: so befuddled and full of longing for more of her – he could never have enough of her warmth, her scent – everything, just... *HER!*

Not for the first time Lizzy employed her smiles and teasing to cover her discomposure. In her innocence she did not realize that her arch looks held significantly more invitation in them than she meant to express.

"I believe the settee will do nicely, Mr Darcy, if we may have the small table a little closer so that we can serve ourselves without the necessity of a servant, do not you think so?" Lizzy felt the flush on her cheeks; she could do nothing to prevent or disguise it. But she hoped that Darcy would not realize her trembling was the effect of having been held in his arms, so close to his body that she could feel his heart beating in his chest. Or was that *her* heart beating so wildly?

She turned her head to ask the question just as he bent his to answer and suddenly their faces were only inches apart. They stared into one another's eyes, both forgetting to breathe, mesmerized by proximity and desire.

"Mr Darcy, I believe the settee is available sir!" Jane's not-so-gentle reminder startled them into action.

"Of course Miss Bennet... Miss Elizabeth! Please pardon my... er, my distraction!" He said carefully settling Lizzy on the settee. "I nearly forgot, Miss Bennet, Mr Bingley begs the honour of a few minutes of your company in the front sitting room if you will? He wished to come and ask you himself, and would have done, had I not intimated to him that too many visitors at one time might not agree with Miss Elizabeth's progress."

He busied himself with the rearrangement of the table in front of Elizabeth while both young women laughed merrily at his blatant attempt at manoeuvring to be alone with Elizabeth.

Soon Jane had gone, leaving the door discreetly open to the hallway and the ubiquitous maid on duty in the bedchamber.

Elizabeth and Darcy were nibbling on fruit and cheese when Mr Sympson appeared to check on his patient. Darcy obligingly stepped out into the hallway while Elizabeth was thus engaged.

Miss Elizabeth's strength had improved although she still experienced weakness and fatigue, and occasional nausea. No new symptoms developing allowed Mr Sympson to expect that she was likely out of danger – but he *would have* one, or better *two* more full days of uninterrupted progress, and a cessation of the nausea and weakness before he could pronounce her safe without caveat.

Darcy had just resumed his much-prized seat on the settee beside Elizabeth when a footman appeared at the open sitting room door and tapped lightly on its frame.

"Pardon me sir," the man said "there is a young lady downstairs who says she is your sister."

~ & ~

"My *sister*? My sister is here?"

"Yes sir, Miss Georgiana Darcy, as she says she is sir."

Darcy's shock could hardly have been greater. "Good God! How in the…"

Turning to Lizzy he said "Miss Elizabeth, I pray you will forgive me! I cannot imagine what would cause my sister to leave her establishment in London and come all the way to Hertfordshire unannounced… why, she never travels without first applying to me for permission! I must go to her at once!"

Turning around full circle he asked "Shall I help you back to your bedchamber Miss Elizabeth? I dislike leaving you here like this!"

"I pray you do not distress yourself over me, Mr Darcy. Please do go and see to your sister. I shall enjoy this change of scene a while longer. I am not yet as bored with this room as I am with the other. Go, go, there are more than sufficient able and willing helpers available to me should I require any such thing."

With a gesture toward the door she added "I do hope there is not some difficulty troubling your sister. Perhaps she simply missed you and decided to take matters into her own hands."

THIRTY-TWO
Georgiana's Fright and Bingley's Moment

"Oh, brother!" Georgian threw herself into his arms in the way she had done as a child. Her perfect golden coiffure and finely dressed womanly figure were not proof against the frightened child she felt in that moment of reunion with her brother.

Here was her tall, strong, wise, and loving brother who had guided and protected her from her earliest recollection – even before their father's untimely death had left him as her guardian. Fitzwilliam had watched over her and played with her and taught her all manner of things about life, about Pemberley, and about being a Darcy. He was well; she could see he was well!

Burying her face in his welcoming shoulder, she cried in relief. "I thought you were *dying*!" she sobbed. Miss Bingley's note said you were *gravely ill*! I hastened to be at your side and, and somehow *make* you be well and, and here you are... You *are* well, are you not?"

Darcy had been certain that his immense fury at Caroline Bingley was at its peak, until he understood how his *terrified little sister* had been tortured by that woman's malicious interference in their lives! To be told that her brother was gravely ill and then to travel frantically all the way from Town in dread of finding him at death's door! To what purpose; what could Caroline Bingley have hoped to gain by doing such a cruel thing to a mere girl? Georgiana was hardly more than a child! He could *not* see the back of Miss Bingley *soon enough!*

Clamping down hard to curb his anger he began to soothe her, stroking and patting Georgiana's back, he held her gently to his chest while she cried into his handkerchief. "I am quite well indeed my dearest! I am not, nor have I been ill. I know not what could have been Miss Bingley's purpose in frightening you so; perhaps she hoped to use you against Miss Elizabeth in some way. I fear you are simply the latest victim to fall prey to Miss Bingley's venomous deceits."

"What do you mean brother? What has she done?" Georgiana looked at him, wonder in her puffy reddened eyes, sniffles competing with a sudden onset of hiccups.

"Come, my sweetest, would you like to refresh yourself first? I shall request tea for us when you re-join me in the library. There I shall explain it all to you. Indeed I do have much to tell – and not *all* of it bad!"

He took his tear-dampened handkerchief from her and used it to wipe her tears and blow her nose, just as he had all of the years of her growing up. Then he took his young sister by the hand and led her out in search of Mrs Roberts, the housekeeper. He knew that good woman would have made a room ready for Georgiana immediately upon hearing of her arrival.

~ & ~

Charles Bingley could scarcely believe his good fortune! Not only was he alone with Jane, but they had managed to wander all the way to his gazebo, the very place where he had originally planned to declare himself and ask for her hand in marriage!

They had noted the arrival of an unknown carriage some few minutes earlier but had agreed to ignore it until or unless someone came to fetch them. Ordinarily a gregarious, amiable sort of man, who liked nothing more than seeing old friends or meeting new ones, Charles was determined to take his time to do this thing properly.

Once the admirable gazebo had been given its due, he helped Jane to a seat and took one close by her side. His heart was pounding furiously and his hand shook slightly when he reached for hers. "My dearest, most beautiful and amiable, kindest and sweetest Miss Bennet... I have waited as patiently as I could manage for this moment!

This gazebo was *built* with *this precise moment in view as its finest hour!*

If you do not know it already, or even if you do know it, I *must tell you that I love you with everything that I am and everything I ever shall be, I love you! Please tell me, my angel on earth; please do tell me that you will be so kind as to honour me with your hand in marriage! Will you marry me my dearest Jane?"*

He had been holding her hand so tightly between his own that he feared he might have hurt her, so he kissed her hand fervently, again and again while he watched her face, his eyes shining with love and hopefulness.

His effusions so overwhelmed Jane that she could not speak at first, for the lump in her throat. Swallowing hard to make room for speech she gave dear Charles a look so full of love that he barely needed to hear her say the words she finally got out *"Yes Charles, yes, yes, and yes. I will be honoured to be your wife!? I do love you so!"*

There followed a lovely interlude of kisses and caresses, even a daring tongue - at first startling and then quite pleasing in its effect!

When their mutual delight generated more heat than they knew they *ought* to radiate whilst yet unwed, they talked. A little of this and a little of that and ultimately they spoke of wedding plans. They had just agreed that they would be the happiest couple alive when Charles remembered Caroline. And Jane remembered about Lydia.

Abruptly they turned to each other, both having the same apprehensive turn of mind. "My sister..." they said at the same time, and then they laughed together. They needed neither questions nor reassurances. They would be together, after all.

~ & ~

Darcy held Georgiana comfortably against his side with an arm around her slim shoulders. They were sitting together on a wide sofa near the fire in the library.

He had held nothing back from her in telling of his time at Netherfield Park. He described for Georgiana the tumble of Caroline Bingley's jealousy into apparent madness, her plot and poisoning of Elizabeth with the expectation that Wickham would violate her while she lay unconscious and helpless. He spoke of the lethal oil of pennyroyal and its worst potential and how they were hopeful that Elizabeth would recover fully but could not be confident of it just yet. Holding her hand tenderly in his, he told Georgiana of Wickham's vile manipulation and ruin of Elizabeth's young sister.

Georgiana had cried throughout his recital but upon hearing about Lydia she gave way entirely, sobbing until she had worn herself out. Then Darcy told her the rest. She learned of his love for Miss Elizabeth Bennet, and of Bingley who was, no doubt, at that very moment finally paying his addresses to Miss Bennet. "And the Hursts, for goodness sake!" he chuckled "You will be amazed to set eyes on that newly reunited couple! They can't see anything but each other!"

"Yes, but... I knew you must love her very much, Miss Elizabeth I mean!"

"And how is that my poppet?" He stroked he hair affectionately.

"While you were telling me all this you kept forgetting and calling her 'Elizabeth'. I cannot think of any other young lady whom you would even think of without the Miss before her name!"

"Quite right, my girl! Quite right! I have long since thought of her *without* the Miss, as you say!"

"Will you marry her Fitzwilliam?" Georgiana's tone was suddenly grave. She turned her head so he could not see her expression.

"I hope so my dearest, does that trouble you?" Darcy cupped her chin with his hand and brought her gaze back to his.

"I do not know... I am not used to sharing you with another... What if she does not like me and wants to send me away?" Georgiana's clear grey eyes went wide with apprehension.

"Oh little sister! Of course you are used to sharing me! When Bingley stays with us or Cousin Richard comes to visit we certainly spend considerable time engaged in pursuits where you would not wish to follow! I am unaware that you have ever resented sharing me on those occasions. And, although I cannot imagine Eli... Miss Elizabeth would think of doing such a thing, I assure you that *no one* could *ever* persuade me to send you away!" He gave her a loving smile, his eyes kindling with the warmth of his brotherly regard. She delighted in that smile - especially reserved only for her, his sister, in their private moments.

"What is it that makes you so uneasy at the idea of having Miss Elizabeth as your sister? You have not yet made her acquaintance, my dear!"

"I don't know. This is very sudden for me Fitzwilliam. I have just hastened to your 'deathbed', only to find you hale as ever – and in a state completely unfamiliar to me: *in love!*"

"Am I to understand, Georgiana, that you would not wish me the joy of a loving marriage?" Darcy did not believe for a moment that his dear sister would wish him anything but happiness so he raised his eyebrows in mock surprise and asked his question in such a way that she would know it to be a quiz.

"No brother, of *course* not!" She gave him a faint smile to acknowledge his humour. "It is just that... are you *certain* she is the one? I mean, will she be content to live at Pemberley and, and not demand to live in Town?

"I confess that I have long dreaded your engagement to Miss *Bingley*! Forgive me, brother, but she has made me most uncomfortable with her insistence on praising me to the skies – and her prying into your privacy. My most sincere apologies to Mr Bingley but I cannot abide his sister! As she is the only young lady I have known you to spend any amount of time with…I thought you might not… you might not *recognize* her, her true motives… well, I am *exceedingly* grateful to know that there is no question that you would wed *her* now!" Georgiana half covered her mouth with her hand as if she had not meant to be so frank.

"My dear Georgiana; there *never was* any question in *my* mind as to whether I would take *Miss Bingley* to wife!" Darcy gently pulled her hand away from her face saying "and your opinion matters very much to me in this. Therefore I prefer that you not censor yourself. I am confident that you will adore Miss Elizabeth, once you get to know her. I hope to introduce her to you very soon."

Recalling to herself the graciousness and strength of character Darcy had instilled in her from the very beginning, along with her implicit trust in *his* goodness and wisdom, Georgiana straightened her shoulders and replied. "If *you* love her, and I can easily collect that you do, then I must love her as well."

"Well then, all that remains is Miss Elizabeth's *choice* in the matter!"

THIRTY-THREE
Happy News and Obstacles

Darcy's and Georgiana's visit to Miss Elizabeth was delayed for several more hours. Indeed it was well past supper time when he brought the parade of distractions to an end.

The first of them was a fairly brief but amiable welcoming of Georgiana by the Hursts.

They shared tea and a light meal. Louisa and Gilbert Hurst sat close together and Darcy saw their hands brush each other occasionally as they chatted with his sister, asking for news from Town and about her progress on the pianoforte.

Darcy realized with a jolt of surprise that they were essentially trying to act in Caroline's stead, to fulfil Bingley's role as host while he was unavailable – presumably somewhere in the park with Jane Bennet. Allowing himself the slightest smirk at the thought of his friend, he sat back to enjoy the show.

Darcy doubted that the Hursts truly listened to Georgiana's answers; they were far too interested in each other! His smirk deepened when he noticed the way they were leaning in to each other, Gilbert's leg just happening to bump against Louisa's! Still, they took care to attend to his sister, smiling and nodding at her shyly offered on-dits and her descriptions of several musical performances she had seen recently.

Amazing! He had never, in all of the years of his friendship with Charles Bingley, seen either Mr or Mrs Hurst bestir themselves in anyone's behalf – well, until the previous day!

"Miss Darcy! How good it is to see you again! What has got you grinning like that, Darcy? Tis a rare sight indeed to see you with such a smile plastered all over your face!" Bingley swooshed into the room with such exuberance that everyone simply stared at him for a moment.

He held a blushing Jane Bennet by the hand and brought her forward with a flourish. "Miss Darcy, everyone, it is my great honour and pleasure to introduce to you my future bride, Miss Jane Elinor Bennet!"

So began the second distraction from Darcy and Georgiana visiting Elizabeth that afternoon. Charles and Jane could scarcely take a seat for the immediate outburst of excited congratulations, hugs, and slapping of backs.

Louisa Hurst, who only days prior had listened in acquiescence to Caroline Bingley's bilious diatribe against the whole Bennet clan, enjoyed very much taking her turn to welcome Miss Jane Bennet to the family! Her husband kissed Jane's hand with a wink and a muttered "Good girl!"

Darcy eventually escaped the happy hubbub to learn whether now might be a good time to... Mr Sympson had just entered Elizabeth's room to assure himself of her continued recuperation. Not now, then. Three distractions down, perhaps soon he could introduce the two most precious women in his life to each other.

Next Colonel Forster arrived seeking a brief interview with Miss Elizabeth regarding Wickham's avowed 'friendship' with her, and to go over some last details of the story of his presence and conduct at Netherfield with Mr Bingley and Mr Darcy. Four! Blast and Damnation!

"This will not do!" He growled in frustration, "I must have my share in the pleasure of *her* company!"

Mr Bennet had ridden over to check on his favourite daughter. He was with her now, unaware that he was *number five* in Darcy's litany of ill-timed distractions!

Fearing that by the time he could find her alone, she would be too exhausted to see him, Darcy took Georgiana's hand. "Come Georgiana, we shall take this opportunity for you to meet *Mr* Bennet *and* Miss Elizabeth Bennet!"

"Oh Fitzwilliam! Do you think we ought to impose on their privacy?"

"Yes, my dear, I do think so. Mr Bennet is a kindly gentleman, with a bent for sardonic humour I admit, he is well aware of my feelings for Miss Elizabeth. I did explain to you that we have his sanction for a, an unannounced courtship, did I not? Besides, I believe Bingley has something to ask him!"

Turning back into the sitting room they had just left, he called out "Bingley! Mr Bennet is above stairs if you should want him for any reason!"

Thus it was that all four of them, Bingley and Miss Bennet, Darcy and Georgiana excused themselves from the Hursts, who seemed quite content to be left alone, and made their way to Elizabeth's sitting room.

~ & ~

Mr Bennet was agreeably interested to meet Miss Darcy, whose story he had heard from her brother when first that gentleman sought to warn him of Wickham's menace to his own family of daughters and to the neighbourhood. Her open countenance and wide-eyed innocence reminded him of his Jane and stirred his fatherly urge to protect this fledgling sister of Mr Darcy's.

He took care to speak kindly to her; she was so young, and understandably had not yet fully regained her confidence in company. "I am so very pleased to meet you, Miss Darcy; I feel we are already acquainted through the loving accounts of you we have had from your brother." He said with a gentle smile.

"I thank you sir; I am very pleased to meet you – *and* your two daughters." She blushed faintly and returned his smile with a timid one of her own. "Fitzwilliam's last letter contained much to charm and to draw my curiosity in his descriptions of his experiences in Hertfordshire and in company with your family."

"Well my dear, I hope we shall have the pleasure of your visit to our home at Longbourn whilst you remain in Hertfordshire. For Mrs Bennet and my other three daughters will be anxious to make your acquaintance as well. But I must warn you, my youngest daughters are not at all like Jane and Lizzy!"

"I confess that I am somewhat nonplussed by the idea of *five* sisters. I have only Fitzwilliam and cannot imagine what it must be like to have so many siblings! They must have great fun together, do they not?"

"I believe they do, Miss Darcy, despite their very different personalities. Ours is a household of constant female chatter and giggling! You must come and spend some time with us when Lizzy comes home, to experience them for yourself."

His rueful face made her giggle "I shall like that very much sir! I thank you for inviting me!"

"You are very welcome, my dear!" he said with a twinkle in his eye. "Now, I apprehend that Mr Bingley's patience has worn quite thin! Do you suppose that he has something particular he wishes to speak with me about?"

Georgiana studied Mr Bingley's eager look for a moment and answered "I should not like to make him wait any longer for your attention, sir. Please excuse me; my brother beckons to me!"

Although general introduction had been made when the four of them first entered the room, Mr Bennet had engaged Georgiana's attention almost immediately. She had not yet truly spoken with Miss Elizabeth. At first Fitzwilliam, Mr Bingley and Miss Bennet had gathered close to Miss Elizabeth. There had been a stifled exclamation when, Georgiana felt certain, Miss Bennet had shared the news of Mr Bingley's proposal with her sister.

She did not notice until then that Mr Bingley had left the group around Miss Elizabeth to approach Mr Bennet. Indeed, after a short time Miss Bennet stepped forward and rested her hand lightly on Mr Bingley's arm.

Beyond Mr Bingley and Miss Bennet were Fitzwilliam and Miss Elizabeth. He was holding her hand and smiling down at her with an expression so intense that Georgiana felt reluctant to intrude on their momentary tête-à-tête.

Hesitating, she vaguely heard Mr Bennet teasing Mr Bingley as they left for the privacy of Netherfield's library. Abstractedly she heard Mr Bennet say from the doorway "Come along Jane, there can be nothing in this that you should not be privy to in one way or another. You may as well hear it all first-hand!"

Georgiana's attention was on Miss Elizabeth's expression. There was warmth in her regard of Fitzwilliam, but something else, too. She seemed vulnerable, even fearful. What could it mean?

Miss Elizabeth seems very uncertain, Georgiana thought. She must suffer a dreadful apprehension about possible lasting effects of that poison, did she continue to endure symptoms from it – surely she was weak and tired at the least! And what a frightening thing it would be to know that someone had made an attempt on one's future in such a way! Georgiana realized in a flash of insight that her brother was showing too much insistence on his own wishes and hopes.

Poor Miss Elizabeth! As courageous and independent as he had described her to be, *anyone's* sensibilities would surely be overwrought with *all she* had endured of late! She must be suffering the most *frightful heartache* and anxiety over her *sister* Lydia as well! She, Georgiana *knew* something of *heartache associated with Wickham!*

Joining them, she seated herself so that they formed a close group around the table where Miss Elizabeth had been reading before her father arrived.

Miss Elizabeth smiled kindly at her and asked her about her travel from London that morning. "I am *so sorry* to hear what a shocking piece of nonsense you received from Miss Bingley, and for the *terrible alarm* you must have endured for those *long hours alone* in the carriage!

"However I confess, Miss Darcy that I *am* very pleased that *you are here!* I have so looked forward to meeting you; I have heard such *wonderful things* about you, you see! I am so eager to hear you play the pianoforte; you *will* do me the honour of playing for me, will you not? Mr Darcy has told me so much about your tastes in music, and books that I feel we shall have *much in common* with one another! And now we are to become acquainted - *friends,* I hope, at last!"

Georgiana's heart melted for the woman who, with all that she had to occupy her mind, still put on a cheerful face to make her welcome. She was not being insincere, Georgiana perceived. Miss Elizabeth was actually *appreciating* her being there in the midst of so much of trouble and worry!

With unusual boldness she reached out for Miss Elizabeth's hand and with Fitzwilliam looking on, beaming delightedly at them both, she answered "I thank you for your kind words, Miss Elizabeth. I believe I shall very much enjoy being your friend!"

Georgiana Darcy was utterly relieved. She would love this woman because her brother loved her – *and* because she was the friend, the sister, she herself had yearned to have.

"Then we must make a start by your calling me Lizzy, as my family and friends do!" The merry sparkle in Lizzy's eyes captivated both Darcys with her charm.

"I shall be delighted Lizzy, and you must call me Georgie – my brother's and Cousin Richard's name for me!"

~ & ~

I do not like to think so, but I fear you must be correct Georgiana. It is only that I am so deep in love with her, and she shows only friendship in return…"

"But, Fitzwilliam!" Georgiana cut in impatiently "How can you expect her to know her own heart when it is so comprehensively occupied with other concerns? She has a sister, or perhaps two, whose future is in direst jeopardy; she has not got over being shocked beyond words by the attempt on her own future! *Think* of the myriad confused and complicated feelings she *must have* about Wickham and Miss Bingley! She still suffers the effects of that horrid poison; *and* she cannot yet trust that she *has* a future to share with you – or with anyone!"

Darcy and Georgiana had been about to retire after a pleasant supper in the company of Mr Bingley and the Hursts, Mr Bennet having returned to Longbourn with Jane and Bingley's joyful tidings to gladden Mrs Bennet's fretting heart.

Elizabeth had earlier given in to fatigue and excused herself to a quiet supper in her room with Jane, and then to bed, Miss Bennet and their father supporting her out of the room. Darcy's assistance had been politely but firmly declined.

As they trudged up the staircase to their rooms, Georgiana had decided to talk with her heart-smitten brother about his nearly overwhelming attentions to Lizzy.

Motioning him into the sitting room of her suite, she had confidently told him what she believed he ought to do. "I tell you brother; Miss Elizabeth appeared quite exhausted when she left us to her repose. And how could she be otherwise with all of us clamouring for her attention?

"She had to be utterly worn to a frazzle with so much to do simply being ill! Be kind and thoughtful, but do not hover over her." She continued "Allow her the time she requires to rest and recover. If I am not mistaken, Lizzy's greatest need is uninterrupted time in which to consider everything that presses upon her mind and heart - including your wishes - without the distraction of your... yearning looks."

Darcy chafed at Georgiana's advice to spend less time with Miss Elizabeth. It would be difficult, though he knew she had the right of it, to do as his sister urged.

How he wished *he* might use Elizabeth's given name alone, he mused, the syllables gentle as a whispered endearment in his thoughts of her - or call her by her sobriquet, *Lizzy*, as he did sometimes while dreaming of her in his arms! Best not think of those dreams in the presence of his sister if he wished to maintain his dignity! He forced his thoughts away from the precipice of his undoing and firmly toward Miss Elizabeth's fragile state.

According to Georgiana he must put away his wishes until *Miss* Elizabeth was free to entertain them wholeheartedly.

"I believe... no, I *know* you are correct – very wise, in fact! How did my little sister come to such wisdom? You have taken me by surprise, my dearest, with your astute assessment of the situation in so short a time!"

"I have lived through my own heartaches, as you very well know brother, and with your care and support I have learned some very valuable lessons from them."

THIRTY-THREE
For Caroline's Sake, Bingley Must Go

The next morning Darcy received an express from his Uncle Matlock granting permission for Bingley to use his hunting lodge near Achachork, or the overseer's cottage which was currently not in use, for as long as he needed it. He had not been to Scotland in over five years and surely would not go for another five at the least. That ought to allow plenty of opportunity for the young lady's rest and recuperation.

Darcy stuck to Georgiana's strategy. Elizabeth had made her way downstairs for the morning repast, so he had no need to haunt her door for the morning greeting and short visit he allowed himself with her.

Soon he and Bingley were in the library, studying maps and planning how Miss Bingley should be conveyed to her destination. They spent many hours on the project.

In addition to the physical removal of Miss Bingley to Scotland, they could not assume that many items she would require for a long sojourn would be readily available in the vicinity of the very small village of Achachork. Nor could they assume that there would be sufficient numbers of locals available to take on her care.

Therefore the next task was that of choosing at least three trusted individuals in addition to her personal maid to guard and care for her on the trip and possibly to remain with her in Scotland.

When two footmen and a matron of good character, willing to go to Scotland for an indefinite period, were selected, everyone including her maid must be carefully interviewed.

All were to be sworn to absolute faithfulness to their charge which was, in fact, to *follow Mr Bingley's orders* in every particular for the care of his sister. It was most essential that each of them, especially the maid, give a solemn oath to carry out only *Mr* Bingley's orders no matter whether Miss Bingley attempted to persuade them differently.

Everything would be done to protect Miss Bingley, *and* her privacy from any source of danger – including her own lapses of reason.

The two men worked steadily until late afternoon, stopping only to partake of a cold collation and tea provided by Mrs Roberts, or to refresh themselves.

Satisfied at last that everything had been put in train for Miss Bingley's departure within the week, Darcy and Bingley were of one mind – to see Elizabeth and Jane, without further delay!

Pausing only to change into fresh clothes, Darcy chose to skip the brandy Perkins offered, in his eagerness to know how Miss Elizabeth's recovery went on.

He found her next to the southwest-facing window in her sitting room enjoying the last rays of the setting sun. Georgiana was beside her. They were chatting quietly. He waited in the open doorway, savouring the sight of his precious sister and his...*Elizabeth,* sharing the peaceful moment together, until they looked up.

"Hello brother!" Georgiana's smile showed her pleasure in the situation.

"Mr Darcy, come join us. We have been enjoying the lovely sunset." Elizabeth stretched out her hand and patted the seat next to hers in invitation.

He strove to conceal the kick of elation he felt at her invitation. Taking the seat she indicated he realized to his joy that it placed him so that Georgiana and Elizabeth, on opposite sides, framed the window before him.

"Thank you Miss Elizabeth, I accept with pleasure! Bingley and I have spent the entire day hard at work on business matters. I believe I am due for a glimpse of something lovely." His smile and the direction of his gaze made it clear that he was not referring to the sunset.

Remembering himself he tore his gaze from his beloved and smiled at Georgiana before he glanced out of the window. "Yes indeed, I find much loveliness to appreciate from this vantage point!"

Georgiana giggled and Lizzy smiled and looked away, blushing quite charmingly.

"Might I enquire whether Mr Sympson has been to see you today, Miss Elizabeth?" Darcy was desperate to get his mind off of her beauty and her blushes so he asked the first thing that popped into his mind. He thought better of it immediately for it might destroy Elizabeth's tranquillity to focus on the state of her health.

He was disabused of that notion instantly when she answered him with her devastating smile, brown eyes dancing with golden sparks of joy and a single eyebrow lifted in delight: "Mr Sympson has indeed been to see me, and he has pronounced me *fit* to go home after another day of good progress! I feel wonderful and can hardly bear to stay indoors even *one* more day!" She chuckled happily "Perhaps I might persuade Mr Sympson to allow me a few minutes in Netherfield's lovely gardens tomorrow if the weather is fine!"

"I would be honoured to escort you out of doors tomorrow Miss Elizabeth, with Mr Sympson's approval of course. If the weather permits, you might sit on one of the benches for a time with Georgiana to watch over you, and I could return to assist you inside when you are ready." Darcy was careful not to ask too much of her, mindful of Georgiana's admonitions in her behalf.

"That sounds perfect Mr Darcy, thank you!"

The three of them chatted for a while longer, enjoying the reds and oranges and purples the setting sun cast across the scattered clouds in the evening sky.

Darcy and Georgiana wished Elizabeth a good night when the supper bell rang. Elizabeth would have hers on a tray in her room and by unspoken agreement between the siblings; they would be satisfied to leave her to herself after their very agreeable visit. Jane would be with her soon. Darcy had no doubt, his sweetest, loveliest Elizabeth would not feel herself neglected.

~ & ~

Lizzy's final day as resident invalid at Netherfield Park began smoothly enough, nothing new to tremble at and her troubles moving toward resolution as much as might be. Now that her head was clear and she was no longer preoccupied by weakness or worry about her condition, she could sort out her feelings about Caroline Bingley.

There was not so much to sort out regarding Mr Wickham, she was content to leave his fate to others. Anyway, he was only a hired mercenary. His capacity for evil, disturbing as it was in other ways, was only frightening when it was directed at her. Without a purse in front of his nose, like a carrot on the end of a stick, he had no reason to think of her at all.

Caroline Bingley was another matter entirely! She had been driven by hatred, a malicious intent that *was* directed specifically at *her*, at Elizabeth Rowena Bennet! *That* made her actions and intentions much harder to set aside. Only *thinking* of Caroline Bingley's vendetta against her made her heart pound, while tendrils of cold chill wound their way through her stomach and turned her hands and feet to ice.

How could such venom toward oneself be dismissed, or reconciled with familiar human interactions so that it lost its terrifying aspect and became innocuous, non-threatening and ultimately forgettable? Lizzy could not fathom what prompted such feeling toward herself and thus could not form any notion of how to alter her behaviour so as to prevent it happening again.

Without knowing what to look for, *where the danger lurked*, she could not feel safe. If she could not feel safe, then how was she to resume her life, *walk alone* through the countryside, or *trust* anyone?

The single time she had responded in opposition to Miss Bingley's barrage of snide and disagreeable attacks on her had been at the gazebo; Caroline's anger toward her was well-established before that day. It had been in exasperation with Miss Bingley's nastiness that Lizzy's had allowed herself to give the woman a set-down at last.

Ought she now to fear speaking her mind when it was called for? The very idea sounded ridiculous! But how was she to understand it? How could she ever feel free to be herself again?

Lizzy mulled it over and over without coming to any useful conclusions. When Mr Sympson came to see her in the late afternoon, she spoke to him of her confusion – and the icy fear she had not been able to release.

Lizzy liked and respected the apothecary very much. He was so direct and honest. He did not talk down to her once he saw that she could hear what he had to say without flinching, and he had saved her life. Being both an apothecary and a medical doctor he was knowledgeable about so many things – and a good thing for her that he was!

Lizzy had no doubt that few people would have recognized the cause of her illness or known what to do if they had. Giving her liquids had helped dilute and later release the oil of pennyroyal enough to allow her recovery.

So she had waited for his visit to ask him about Caroline Bingley. She knew that he had assessed Miss Bingley's condition for her family and treated her with sedatives. Lizzy hoped very much that he could ease her mind in this highly unsettling situation. She counted on him to provide her with some wisdom that would make it all clear to her.

Mr Sympson listened attentively while she talked. When she stopped and looked at him expectantly she was unnerved to hear him say "No one really knows much about the workings of the human brain, Miss Elizabeth. The why or when, or even who, are rarely clear or foreseeable. I have no answer for you as to how you, or anyone, might prevent the onset of an illness such as Miss Bingley suffers from. There is a great deal of disagreement among practitioners in the medical fields as to both cause and cure – or treatment of an illness like hers.

"I can tell you that based upon my studies and experience on the subject, I believe that it *is* an illness, possibly inherent in her makeup, or brought on by overexcitement of her brain. The only humane thing to be done with her is just as Mr Bingley proposes to do. He will place her in a pleasant, safe, but isolated spot with caretakers to see to her comfort and safety – and to see that she is not again let loose on an unsuspecting victim.

Lizzy shuddered, thinking of the invisible nature of Miss Bingley's illness, and feeling the helplessness of all the best minds in the world to identify it before it struck, or to cure it once it had laid hold of its host. "I might almost feel sorry for her if she had not dealt with me so harshly!"

"Miss Bingley does deserve your pity Miss Elizabeth, when you feel able to give it. Who would willingly choose to make of herself an outcast, give up an enviable position in society, abundant wealth, family and friends if they did not suffer from an aberration of the mind? As helpless as you feel to protect yourself from her sort of aberrant behaviour, she is helpless to return to her senses, to make herself sane.

"When you feel fearful that such a one might do you some ill again, ask yourself this question: do you walk in continual fear of influenza, or broken bones, or the small pox? They are all afflictions, Miss Elizabeth. We simply do everything in our power to avoid having them in our lives – but they are no respecters of persons and if they want us they will find us."

Taking a deep breath and giving her shoulders a shake, Elizabeth looked calmly into Mr Sympson's serious eyes and said "Thank you sir! I believe that you have just answered the question I did not know to ask!"

~ & ~

"This will be next to the last time Mr Sympson will see Lizzy before we go home tomorrow. Except for her time in the garden this morning with Georgiana, she has been very quiet all day. I do hope she is truly feeling as well as she says."

"Do you have any reason to suspect otherwise Jane? Aside from her quietness, I mean."

"Only that she seems deeply preoccupied. I know she is troubled; that she cannot grasp why she was made a target... I am sorry Charles! I know that it must be very painful for you to be reminded of what Caroline has done!"

"Yes, but I think I will feel more *pain for her* when I have gotten over being quite so *angry at her!* I cannot tell you how much I regret that I did not take her peculiarities more seriously! Now all I am left to do is send her away, far away, and hope that someday my mad sister will come to her senses!"

"Are you not going with her? Taking her there Charles? Please tell me you do not intend to send her with only servants to see her settled!"

"Well, I..."

"Oh Charles! No!"

"I did not like to leave you for so long, my love! There are several other matters as yet unresolved here in Hertfordshire. I would wish to face them by your side!"

"I could not ever be gratified by your kind attention to my family's concerns while poor Caroline would be neglected so! You must accompany her, Charles. I promise that I and all of the complexities of our lives will still be here when you return!"

"I may be gone several weeks, my darling Jane, how *ever* shall I bear missing you all of that time?"

"You shall be very busy, Caroline is not the most docile of companions, remember to ask Mr Sympson for something to calm her when it is needed, and a recommendation for someone to assume her care once she is established. And, my dear love, please do take the opportunity to have an adventure. I imagine there will be many new sights to see on your journey!"

When he opened his lips to offer another objection, Jane touched her fingers to them to stop his words. "No more, Charles. Do it for *me*, please!"

It was her delicate touch on his lips that set them off. There followed an interlude so sweet, so full of caresses and nibbles and kisses that they were lost to their surroundings for quite some time. Before they parted at last, their increasingly drawn out kisses had progressed to the dancing of tongues and moans so deep that they would not have recognized their own voices - if they had been listening.

Jane's countenance was serene as ever, although her lips were suspiciously puffy and red, when she and Charles explained to everyone about the decision that 'they' had made.

Charles was to accompany Miss Bingley to Scotland; Mr and Mrs Hurst or Darcy were to act in Bingley's stead in matters of the household and hospitality; Darcy would hold Bingley's power of attorney in the management of any estate matters at Netherfield, and Jane would busy herself at Longbourn in behalf of everyone. Georgiana should enjoy her unexpected break from her studies to become better acquainted with the Netherfield and Longbourn families. Lizzy was to continue to regain her strength and keep everyone, especially his Jane, in good spirits.

In a private interview with Darcy later that evening, Bingley informed his friend that he planned to make a very short trip to London to meet with his solicitor. He would have the power of attorney drawn up - and a codicil to his will "in case anything should happen to me on my travels, I want Jane to be provided for. I would not leave her without the comforts I plan to provide for her when we are wed."

After another very pleasant evening spent in the company of the Darcys, the Hursts, Jane and Mr Bingley, Elizabeth retired for the night, eager to go home in the morning. Although she had been able to forget for some of the time that Caroline Bingley remained within Netherfield House, confined to her room Elizabeth understood, it would be a relief to be away from the place where that brooding, unstable mind, still lived.

CHAPTER THIRTY-FIVE
The Bennet Sisterhood is Born

Lizzy was not to walk any farther than the edge of their modest park - Mamá's orders. For once Papá agreed with her. They were taking no chances with any of their daughters, especially the one who, only a few days since, might have died without ever a last farewell. The enforced idleness was not at all to her liking; she wanted to wander off by herself to think about the only remaining question that depended on her for its answer – Mr Darcy.

So much had occurred during their 'courtship' to confuse and divert, even stop her mind from its customary rational approach to important decisions. Then there were her feelings when he was near, when he looked at her with *that* look which she now understood to be... *very warm*, or when he touched her – when he insisted upon *carrying* her from her bedchamber to her sitting room that first day she was out of bed!

Her feelings were not rational at all! She was going to require time, alone, uninterrupted or distracted, to sort out the matter of Mr Darcy – and his very engaging little sister! No, *not* now, Lizzy!

Instead she chose to reward her beloved Jane's loving care during her illness with the thing she desired most: to talk about Mr Bingley, his amiable nature, his handsome good looks, his kindness and generosity, his absence overnight to London, the planned trip to Scotland and their forthcoming wedding.

When at last that delightful set of subjects seemed thoroughly explored, temporarily at least, she struck in with another that had been niggling at her since arriving at Longbourn the previous afternoon.

"Have you noticed anything odd since our return home? About the family I mean?"

"Do you refer to something other than our mother's continual fussing over you Lizzy? I must say *that* is a new come-out for her! I suppose the shock of nearly losing you has given us all cause to give over taking each other for granted!"

"No Jane, something far more desirable and pleasant than my being the object of Mamá's flutterings and vapours!"

"Then what is it?" Jane wrinkled her brow in puzzlement. The two were sitting on the wide plank seat of their old rope swing under the tree nearest Longbourn House. They were huddled together, sharing a thick shawl to ward off the crisp chill in the air. Every now and then Lizzy would give a push with her foot to set them swaying gently in the too cool shade.

The enormous old elm was bare of leaves for the winter just begun. But its numerous branches, which cast a deep welcoming shade in the heat of summer, filtered the weak afternoon sunshine of December; little warmth penetrated to the two sisters where they lingered under its skeletal canopy.

"Why Jane! Surely you cannot have failed to notice that Lydia's conduct has altered so!" With a happy chuckle Lizzy added "She is positively demure! And she seeks father's approval in everything she does. Had you truly not noticed? I have not heard a squeal, or whine, or witnessed the least bit of boisterous or unruly behaviour from her since we have been at home! What on earth can it mean?"

"No Lizzy, I have been so filled with happy thoughts of my Charles that I have scarcely been aware of anything in my surroundings. But I believe you are correct; there is something... almost... *peculiar* about Lydia. She certainly bears little resemblance to *our* Lydia!"

"Well, I would not call her *peculiar* exactly, but certainly changed!" Elizabeth did not want to mention that her most recent association with the word 'peculiar' had been in reference to the mad behaviour of Caroline Bingley.

"I suppose she has been forced into some degree of heightened maturity or awareness and reflection on her conduct in light of her present circumstances. Do not you think so, Lizzy?"

"Perhaps, shall we ask her? She might be encouraged by our noticing the change."

Spurred to action by the novelty of the topic under discussion, Jane and Lizzy left their swing and entered the house in search of their youngest sister.

They came upon Kitty first, in the parlour, disconsolately looking through a basket of ribbon scraps with a view to refreshing an old bonnet with new trim.

Scarcely bothering to lift her head she muttered "I do not see why Lydia gets all of the attention! I helped Mr Wickham just as much as she did! More too, for I acted as lookout for them when they..."

"Kitty! How can you say such a cork-brained thing? You display an *astonishing* want of common sense when you cavil against your sister's *calamity* as if it were her good fortune! It would behoove you far better to spend your time thanking every source of good luck on earth and in the heavens that you are *not* the one who is ruined, than becoming moped simply because Lydia receives a little attention! . *You* are not; thank the good lord, living your life of ease and goodwill in the neighbourhood on borrowed time! How can you make such a mutton-head of yourself?"

Jane reached to remove the basket of ribbons from Kitty's lap; already some fine pieces bore the smudgy marks of Kitty's slow tears. "Pray do not be so harsh on her, Lizzy; mayhap Kitty misses Lydia's laughter and hijinks. Life must be dull as ditch water for Kitty without Lydia to entertain her." Jane understood both Kitty's unacknowledged loneliness and Lizzy's impatience with her childish notions. Therefore, as much as she disliked doing so, she felt impelled to speak repressively to dear Lizzy in compassion for poor forlorn Kitty.

While Lizzy stared in mortification at her elder sister, Kitty let out a wail. "I cannot help it! Lydia has always been Mamá's favourite and now, next to Lizzy, she is Papá's!"

"Kitty, dearest Kitty, do you not see that our father is only trying to guide poor Lydia safely through the *most* terrifying and hazardous of times? She is in a terribly precarious position! *One word* from Wickham, one slip of a tongue from one of us and she will have *no hope* of ever gaining the attentions of an honourable man. And if she increases, *all* of our caution and care will not be enough to protect her from the censure of the world.

"Why my dearest Catherine, you said it yourself at our family meeting – I was so very proud of you as you stood so tall and spoke so forthrightly! You said that the two of you had foolishly exposed our whole family to shame and ridicule – even *ostracism* should word get out. We would be shunned and ignored, harassed and insulted by *anyone* we might encounter *every day* of our future lives. You were so *fierce* and *eloquent* when you said: "*If* we are able to prevent the whispers and innuendo... Nay, the *truth* from becoming common knowledge, we may not yet be easy for if Lydia should have the ill fortune to come with child... the truth will have its *second* opportunity at our throats."

"Whence comes this bitterness now? Clearly you do understand that if *any* of her or *your* conduct ever becomes known outside of our circle of discretion, *we all* shall suffer the disgrace together? I believe Lydia must feel an almost intolerable weight of responsibility and regret upon her young shoulders." Lizzy was speaking gently this time, alive to the ill humour she had shown at first.

Kitty was not at fault for her ignorance and thoughtlessness. She was the product of neglect and selfish, frivolous example. "Lydia is but fifteen years old, dearest, a child still; full young to take on herself the sort of troubles that have been the destruction of many a grown woman. Can you truly wish to be in her shoes?"

By this time both Jane and Lizzy had taken seats on either side of Kitty on the settee, and were stroking her hair and patting her shoulders gently.

"No, when you explain it that way I am sure I ought not to envy Lydia. I suppose that you are correct, Jane; I am simply sad because I miss the fun and high spirits we were used to enjoy. She is not the same Lydia anymore and I am quite lost without her liveliness to lead me along."

Kitty sniffled dejectedly and blew her nose into her handkerchief. Peeking at Elizabeth, she added "I am sorry; I forgot myself. I have no right to let myself fall into the blue devils. I promise to try harder to remember what Papá told me: that it is time I grow up and think responsibly. I am Lydia's *elder* sister after all" Kitty lifted her face to her sisters doing her best to reproduce the confidence she had shown on the day Elizabeth recalled being so proud of her.

"Yes Kitty, that is true, but I want to ask you something. Kitty... Catherine, what is it about Lydia do you think, that you admire the most? What is it that draws you and others to her? Or... what do you miss most just now when you are feeling bereft of her companionship?"

To Kitty, Jane's query was easily answered. "She used to laugh, and make me laugh. She was always happy and looking for the fun in everything. She could entertain herself no matter where she might be, for if there was no entertainment to be had, she would make some up!"

"Tell me dearest, do you not admire Lizzy's ability to please and brighten the countenance of most everyone she meets?"

"Yes! Of course I do but what..."

"Catherine, does not Lydia share the same wonderful qualities as Lizzy only uses them with too little care for propriety or the feelings of others? *Neither* is formed for ill humour, *both* love to laugh and cheer others to smiles or laughter, *both* look for the humour in every instance and delight in finding the smallest cause for entertainment wherever they are.

"Only Lizzy *thinks* to treat her friends and the objects of her humour with *kindness and respect, and includes them* in the fun. Lizzy looks first to the comfort of others and thus assures her own. Lydia has yet to learn generosity of spirit and graciousness of conduct but I believe she may be beginning that maturation process now.

"As you have reminded yourself, you are the elder sister. If you use your greater maturity over Lydia, and emulate the behaviour of those you admire and respect, you shall reap the dual benefits of your own improvement in temperament (with all of its attendant pleasures) and the good example you set for your youngest sister."

"I do see... I had never thought of it that way before! But I believe that I see my way more clearly now! Thank you both for caring about me enough to talk with me when I must have presented a most disagreeable picture!"

"Of Course we care for you! How could we not? You are our own dear Kitty!" The several warm sisterly embraces which followed went a long way toward soothing aching hearts.

"Jane is right Kitty, you are our own family and as precious as any one of us is to the other! We were on our way to find Lydia; in fact we wanted to quiz her a little about her newfound decorum. Would you like to come with us?"

"I would indeed! I seem to have lost my taste for trimming bonnets for the present."

The three of them strolled along the hallway, peeking into the parlour, the front sitting room, the back sitting room; they even checked the kitchen but did not find Lydia. They had all along heard and ignored the sound of Mary's ponderous efforts at the pianoforte in the music room; the only place left below stairs not yet visited in their hunt.

Three sets of twinkling eyes under three sets of lifted eyebrows met in the briefest inquiry; then, smiling and nodding, Lizzy reached out and opened the door.

Mary ceased her practicing instantly when she heard them come into the room. She was chary of criticism and did not like to be observed until she was confident of her proficiency with a piece. "What is it?" she asked with no little pique. "What do you want?"

"Actually we were looking for Lydia. We apologize for interrupting your work." Lizzy soothed her solitary sister. "I don't suppose you would know where we might find her? Well, we shall just be on our way then. Sorry again for..."

"I do. I believe I do know where Lydia is." Mary's flat statement interrupted their departure and turned all three of her sisters around to stare at her in surprise.

"You do? Why that is wonderful, Mary! We shall be out of your way as soon as you tell us where to find her!" Jane always tried to be kind to Mary, who often seemed implacably set against any sort of sisterly amity.

"I saw her earlier entering the stillroom with a basketful of some herb or other. I did not stop to see what it was but I believe she intended to do something with it in there; hang it for drying or some such." Mary did not involve herself in the homely pursuits of kitchen or garden; she had much rather read a book, of course.

"Oh! Famous! I shall love to see Lydia doing something..." Catching Lizzy's eye, Kitty stopped abruptly and hung her head. "I mean to say, good for Lydia; she must be congratulated on choosing to do something beneficial for the house."

Under Lizzy's delighted smile, Kitty beamed with pleasure.

"Intrigued by this unusual exchange between Lizzy and Kitty, Mary could not stop herself from asking "What do you all want with Lydia?"

"Oh," Lizzy replied airily "we are planning to discover from her what has brought about the splendid change we have all noticed in her demeanour. You should come with us, Mary! It will be great fun; all of us together without our parents for once! I don't believe we have all been in the same room together on our own, for more than a minute or two, in a long, long time! Come with us, Mary, do!"

"I should think that would be obvious, Elizabeth." Mary grumbled primly, but she had turned and was poised to leave her bench as she spoke.

"You are right of course, Mary. But I wonder if there might be more than her wretched circumstances that has effected this apparent transformation. Come along! We shall do her the kindness of distinguishing and appreciating her exertions!"

Lydia was outside of surprised to see all four of her sister come trooping into the stillroom to find her. She had been learning from Mrs Hill's young helper Dolly, how to hang chamomile, lavender and other herbs to dry. It being early winter she had not much to work with. The gardens were mostly brown and dead. But she wanted to learn and used the few straggling plants which had survived thus far for her practice.

Dusting off her hands, which were dry and grimy from handling the aging leaves and stems of the herbs, she turned to query them. "What in the world is this? How do you all find yourselves here in the stillroom of all places?" She was pleased to see them and made it known with her cheery voice and pleasant smile.

"We have come for *you*, Lydia!" Lizzy chuckled "We mean to quiz you! Have you had enough of your domestic activities? Good! Come let us closet ourselves in the back sitting room where we may indulge our sisterly curiosity and confidences undisturbed!"

~ & ~

"I shall be happy to tell you if you will answer some questions of mine." Lydia bargained, smiling back at three of her sisters and casting a glance at Mary's unrevealing countenance. "It is not a great puzzle, only a great shift in my perspective."

Receiving cheery assurances from the other three, Lydia turned to her middle sister to ask earnestly "Mary, do you agree to be one with us, no holding back?"

This brought all of their attention to Mary's unhappy face. "I, I am very uncomfortable about... about something I have done. I fear when you hear of it none of you will want me to be among your company!"

Pushing away the feeling of dread that washed over her at Mary's words, Lizzy said "Why Mary! In truth you *are* one with us. We could not escape it should we wish to. No dear, we shall not turn against one of our own; we five sisters shall always stand strong together!"

Mary's tremulous smile touched them all, for she rarely permitted any sentiment but indignation to show itself in her countenance. "Very well, I shall say it quickly before my composure fails me! I wrote to our cousin, Mr Collins of..."

She paused at their collective gasp of alarm "of Lizzy's conduct which, forgive me Lizzy, has lately seemed to me to violate the dictates of propriety with regard to Mr Darcy, the nephew of his esteemed patroness, Lady Catherine de Bourgh. I only desired his counsel as a clergyman."

Directing her gaze to Lizzy, "I have noticed how much time you have spent in Mr Darcy's company and then I heard that you actually allowed him to carry you to the sitting room at Netherfield and that he has spent considerable time in your room while you were ill...I feared for your reputation – and for your heart. You are always so self-assured and free; you might have been heedless of your danger! I do apologize for my interference, Lizzy! I ought to have had more trust in your good sense!"

Mary expected to see derision on the faces around her so it confounded her greatly to see smiles of amusement and relief instead. After a moment's reflection she burst out "Oh! Did you think I told him about..." with a quick glance at Lydia "Oh, never! I promised I would speak of that to no one and I have *not* broken my promise!"

"Dearest Mary! I never thought you would break faith with the *Bennet Family Code of Conduct!* Let me hasten to put your mind at rest on the cause for your application for Mr Collins' advice. I can see that it was wrong of me to leave you in the dark about this; moreover it is this intelligence which is to be *my* piece of news so I shall announce it now.

"Mr Darcy and I had spoken and I had agreed to a courtship on the day following the Netherfield ball. That was when we also discussed Mr Wickham and decided that the community as well as our family ought to be warned of the threat posed by his very presence in the area.

"Mr Darcy informed Papá, with my encouragement, that very evening of all he knew of Mr Wickham's perfidy in hopes that he would tell Mamá, who would... be herself. Mamá *did* do an excellent job of spreading the word – to all but our Lydia, unfortunately!

"Mr Darcy waited to ask our father for permission to court me until the next day so as not to confuse the two matters.

"Papá was not best pleased by Mr Darcy's application for a courtship between us; I expect he was not at all prepared for it and not anxious to contemplate the usual consequence of a courtship, that of parting with one of his daughters.

"I must tell you, however, that that outcome is not at all assured in the present case and I made Mr Darcy well aware of that caveat before I consented to the arrangement.

"The courtship has been kept secret until now by our father's command. He taught us to believe that an announcement at that time would lessen the impact of Mamá's diligent efforts to safeguard our friends and neighbours from Wickham's predations upon them.

"As for Mr Darcy carrying me to the sitting room, it was done in the presence of our dear Jane, only to allow me the much needed relief from lying in bed hour upon miserable hour. Perhaps that office might have been filled by one of the footmen; however I should still have been *carried* by some unrelated adult male. I confess that I *greatly* preferred that it be done, if it must be done, by a gentleman!

"So you see, Mary, your worry over me was for naught! I am engaged in a very respectable, and respectful, courtship with Mr Darcy!"

Her three youngest sisters declared their surprise and congratulations in their various ways.

Jane, who had been privy to it all as the events unfolded, beamed lovingly upon all of her dear sisters. She would wait until Lydia and Kitty had their turns before she would announce her news.

She did have one more question for Mary before they moved on. "Mary, I *did* wonder whether you might have *other* news for us on the subject of *Mr Collins?*"

A conscious expression belied Mary's charge "I can't imagine what you are speaking of, Jane."

Lizzy struck in with good-humoured impatience "Let us *not* play at cat and mouse, dear! *Did he or did he not* make you an offer of marriage – or have you formed an understanding with him? You *did* spend *considerable time* in one another's company before he left for Hunsford! Come Mary; out with it!"

Somewhat indignantly Mary implored "I *beg* you would not think so *poorly* of me! Our cousin, whose learned discourse I had enjoyed *innocently* for several days, did indeed make me such an offer. I informed him without delay the same as I shall say to you – and I *do hope* I shall *never* hear another word on that subject!

"I certainly admire and respect Mr Collins for his piety and his education; I hope we shall always be friends. I should like to trust his spiritual advisement in matters of doctrinal importance.

"However I have no more inclination to *wed* him than *any* of my sisters possess. I find it absurd and offensive to hear professions of devotion and hopes of marital felicity from a man who has scarcely risen and dusted off his knees from similarly importuning another – *even if she is my sister!*"

Cries of "*Bravo!*" and "*Well said!*" and "*Good for you Mary!*" resounded among the sisters. At first Mary looked startled upon hearing their congratulations; she soon began to smile and then to chortle, ending in a fit of giggles among them all!

Drying her eyes with a dainty handkerchief as their laughter faded away, Jane's thoughts returned to her youngest sister.

"Lydia, my dear, please tell us now about your 'shift in perspective'. I am quite intrigued and anxious to hear of it."

"Yes Lydia, we began this quest because all of our interest was piqued by your altered demeanour. Keep us in suspense no longer if you please!" Lizzy felt quite delighted with the confidences shared thus far; their sisterly rendezvous was unfolding in the most satisfying manner!

"My disclosures shall, no doubt, fall rather flat in the wake of Mary's and Lizzy's marvellous contributions. Of course I am dreadfully set down by the bad judgment and foolhardy actions I thoughtlessly blundered into – especially endangering the good name and future connections of all my dear family. As you must recollect, I made a vow to change, and I meant it with all of my heart. But there is something which has made my exertions *much* easier and strengthened my resolve *tenfold*.

"It is simply that for the first time in my life Papá has shown me that I matter to him. He actually *cares* for me! I never knew that! He has laughed at me and teased me, and *dismissed* me all the years within my memory. The parent who loved me was our mother so I followed her ways and thought Papá's love belonged only to… others.

"It is odd to think that it took my very worst, most disgraceful and disgusting disregard for every canon of propriety and any concern for my family to teach me that my father loves me! He cares for my safety and happiness and his censure of my conduct was because it hurt him – *no*t because he disdained *me*! That revelation brought home to me quite forcibly how much I *needed* his love, and how very much I wanted to please him! I want to make him proud of me. More than anything I wish *never* to do anything to cause him pain again!"

The pathos of Lydia's confidence, and the thrill of hope it inspired in them left her sisters without words to express how deeply they felt for her.

It was Kitty who finally broke the quiet of astonished admiration that held them in its thrall.

"Lydia, Papá *is* proud of you; he *must* be so! I see the changes in you and love you so much for your courage; I have also striven to come about but I have been jumbled in my feelings. For I have been as misguided as you in believing that our father had no interest in me.

"But you have shown me how wrongheaded that belief must be. I suspect that Papá has always been our anchor of wisdom and right thinking if we had but known it. I thank you; truly I do, for opening my eyes to the *most* compelling inspiration for mending my ways – Papá's approbation!"

Mary, flushed with uncommonly amiable feelings toward her younger sisters, responded with all of the solemnity the occasion required of her. "To own the truth such a notion had never entered my head; nevertheless, Lydia's and Kitty's professions have touched upon my tenderest sensibilities. Furthermore, viewed in the pure light of dispassion, I am convinced of their truth. I shall consider my own past conduct in the hope that I too may derive benefit from their wisdom."

Relief from the intense direction the five-sister session had taken was due, and Jane was quite ready to introduce a lighter subject. "I have something of import to share..."

What a hubbub of felicitations and joyful speculations there was following the news of Jane's engagement, made official by their father's consent!

THIRTY-SIX
Trepidation and Reassurance

Mr and Miss Bingley departed a few mornings later on their long trip to Scotland. She was apathetic; he was anxious to see her comfortably ensconced in her haven of safety, and to return to Jane's side.

Bingley was sharply aware that his dear love and her family continued to face the worries of Wickham's loose lips and Lydia's predicament -as well as uncertainties of Miss Elizabeth's narrow escape from the harshest effects on poisoning by oil of pennyroyal.

He regretted immensely that he must away at such a delicate time. But Jane had commanded him to accompany Caroline and he could not give *her* opinion anything but the highest deference. Go he would, and hasten back, *please God!*

Jane echoed his wish, *vehemently*, watching his carriages leave early that morning. She had walked with Lizzy to the edge of a wooded area near Netherfield's long sweep of lawn which bordered the drive near the main road. From their vantage point they could witness the departure without risk of encountering Caroline or delaying Bingley's purpose by drawing his attention to themselves.

Charles and Jane had said their farewells the evening before after he took his leave of her family. Jane refused to allow him to see anything but a serene and loving countenance in their last time together. She meant to ease his heart with that memory whilst he was parted from her warm and loving presence.

Letters would be unreliable because of the remote regions he must pass through and the uncertainty of the time it would take between one stopping place and another. But they would each write and hope for the best, secure in the knowledge that the other was doing the same.

"Your Mr Bingley is an excellent man, Jane! He is everything amiable and kind!"

"I confess that I am quite proud of him that he willingly undertakes this journey – that he looks out for his sister with so much care despite all of the shame and trouble her actions have brought upon his head. But then, I never expected less of him. He would not be *my* Mr Bingley if he did not do all in his power to see her safe and comfortably looked after at the least."

As the last carriage moved out of sight she breathed "There! He is *gone*. Now I must only think of a *successful return* for his efforts and our sacrifice!"

Fighting her unruly heart to keep her calm demeanour in place, Jane desperately desired a change of subject.

"Does Mr Darcy plan to call upon you this morning, Lizzy?"

"I expect so, Jane. If not I shall beard Papá in his den! I so want to hear what they all decided when he and Mr Darcy and Mr Bingley met with Colonel Forster yesterday! I don't suppose Mr Bingley wasted any of his precious time with you on speaking of Mr Wickham's fate, did he?"

"No dearest, I fear neither of us gave a *fig* for Mr Wickham during our *little time* together! Howbeit I shall be *very pleased* to distract myself with every possible speculation on that head now!"

~ & ~

Lizzy had been relieved that Mr Darcy was not able to call on her for the past several days. He had been occupied for much of the time assisting Mr Bingley with last-minute preparations for his travels so that his friend could spend time with Jane. In addition there were letters of business to attend to and at least one conference with Mr Bingley, her father and Colonel Forster.

All of that had been to the good. Lizzy had a choice to make. Should she withdraw from Mr Darcy's courtship, or announce it to the world and give it her wholehearted acceptance? Her natural ebullience *disliked* equivocation! She had important matters to consider and must take time in which to do them justice.

First, settling in at Longbourn had revived her apprehensions over Lydia's and Kitty's debacle. She wondered whether her family would be forced to leave their home to shield Lydia from public knowledge of an ill-begotten child.

Second, she wanted time, *abundant* time to settle her mind and know her feelings on the subject of Mr Darcy. She did not want to make any irrevocable choices affecting her future happiness until she was entirely free of the influences of recent events – and his frequent *exceedingly* close proximity and *intimate* endearments!

Finally, regardless of her feelings or inclinations she wondered whether it was fair to saddle a man of such consequence in the world and pride in his heritage with a family as ramshackle as her own.

By the time of Mr and Miss Bingley's going away to Scotland, Lizzy felt much better about her family – as much better as one could feel with a very young unmarried sister who might be increasing, and a mother whose good sense so often went a-begging!

Lizzy thought with the utmost pleasure of the impromptu rendezvous of sisters. They had revealed so much of themselves to each other! She felt that, more than ever before, they had fashioned deep bonds of honesty and mutual appreciation to last a lifetime.

She was filled with admiration and delight when she recalled the courage and goodness each had displayed that day. There could be *no more doubt* that the Bennet's would survive and overcome the opprobrium of their neighbours if need be.

But what of Wickham, she wondered. Would that blackguard find some self-interest or relief from his difficulties by telling of her sisters' folly? She did not fail to recognize that his silence was purely dependent upon what he saw as his best advantage.

How could he be worked upon, she wondered, to make him want to keep the story to himself?

Once she had exhausted all other avenues of thought, Lizzy could no longer avoid thinking about Mr Darcy, her *feelings* about Mr Darcy! Oh *hang* it all! She needed to *decide* whether she desired to entrust her future happiness to Mr Darcy!

"I am afraid you have caught me out, Jane!" With a rueful smile to her sister, Lizzy took her hand and turned them toward home.

"Whatever do you mean, Lizzy? I only said that I wanted to distract myself with the question of Mr Wickham's fate. How does that catch you out?"

"I wished to be distracted also, else I would again return to the subject of my ambivalence! I tell you my dear, when it comes to Mr Darcy I can find no tranquillity no matter how I mull things over in my mind. Indeed I find myself *locked* in a solitary battle of indecision. I have entered the fray so often that I believe I am far too much addicted to the sport!"

"Lizzy, do not make yourself uneasy! You must disabuse your mind of such stuff!"

But Lizzy had opened the floodgates of her heart and indeed it *was* a flood that came rushing out!

"You may laugh, I see the amusement in your eyes, but truly Jane I am ruffled this way and that until there is no bearing it! In one moment I am ready to scotch the whole thing and send him on his way; the next I am ready to fall into his arms! Where once I was sublimely indifferent to the gentleman, I now find myself susceptible to his slightest hint or look in my direction! My heart pounds when he is near and it sinks when I ponder our family disgrace!

"If Lydia is to bear Wickham's child I cannot imagine that Mr Darcy should do aught but rush away to Derbyshire, never to be heard from again! How shall my poor heart withstand his defection if once I give it?

"I detest this dreadful uncertainty! I dither about undecided, yearning for I scarcely know what!

"As for whether we make a good fit, that question is no more settled in my mind than the wisdom of the match. It seems that we are often perfectly in charity with one another, yet at other times my every feeling is offended by his pride and conceit!

"How can I trust myself to a man who regularly takes too much upon himself in making decisions for me and others? I fear my own self-assurance and fiercely independent spirit should either clash with him dreadfully or wilt entirely away under his autocratic ways!

"Oh, I confess that I do not see him attempt to dominate everyone so much as in the past, but still I often feel that he assumes too much! He *will* have his way, you know. He did not request my permission when he carried me to the sitting room, which unthinking arrogance has caused me prodigious embarrassment with my family!"

"Oh but he did ask, Lizzy; and *you agreed* that he might convey you to the sitting room!"

"I *did?* I do not recall that at all! Are you certain, Jane?"

"Absolutely certain; he asked earlier that morning if he might do so later if you were up to leaving your bedchamber and you said 'that sounds lovely Mr Darcy' – those were your very words!"

"Oh *dear;* then I have been harbouring resentment against him for doing something I had *allowed* him to do! I feel such a *gudgeon!*"

"You were quite done in at the time; perhaps you were half asleep and not attending dear."

"Each time I endeavour to marshal my thoughts on the matter of Mr Darcy's intentions I am presented with a quandary I cannot resolve - and it unsettles me severely! My recent affliction notwithstanding, I would almost rather be doing anything else in the world than entertaining such a vexatious muddle!"

Seeing that her sister's rant had at last come to a close, Jane gathered herself to speak. "My dear, you are *not* thinking of crying off from your barely established courtship already, are you? All things considered, Mr Darcy has offered you a most singular honour, if you do indeed consider it as such.

"'Tis curious indeed, that you of all people should be stymied at the prospect of an occasional spirited exchange of opinions! *You* may argue it as you will, *I* perceive that the two of you get on quite famously; it is only in your contentions against his suit that you use him with such dreadful harshness, Lizzy!"

Jane's tone quivered on the edge of laughter at her usually clear-sighted Elizabeth, but she subdued the impulse and rallied her instead. "It is a great deal too bad little sister that you do not credit him with the patience and humility he has shown of late!"

"How can you say so? You must know that I could not endure his highhanded ways without either becoming moped to death or responding with some decidedly pungent piece of incivility. As his wife I would be utterly at his mercy and I cannot assume that his recent transformation would not succumb to the habits of a lifetime!"

"Dearest Lizzy," Jane trusted her instinct to comfort her sister. "I know not why you have fallen into a manner of thinking that dwells upon every unpleasant possibility between yourself and Mr Darcy. I assure you that *I* do not find him unkind or harsh in the least; and certainly my *Charles* would not tolerate a friend as irrational and oppressive as you describe.

"Come dearest, you have a disposition too generous to think so ill of Mr Darcy! Is there some other reason for your worries? Has he been overly forward with you? Do you fear his… enthusiasm for you?"

"No Jane, he has been everything proper and respectful outside of his hovering over me and insisting on carrying me at Netherfield, which you tell me now I had agreed to.

"He *does* persist in using such *terms of endearment* when he speaks to me! At Netherfield I was too ill to protest; since I allowed it *then,* I find it difficult to tell him to cease speaking to me in that manner *now*. And, and in a way, I am not displeased by it – only *unsettled and embarrassed!*

"I believe… I *think* it is his *effect* on me that frightens me. Yes I *do* feel a *powerful* reluctance to put myself in his charge! Even Papá knows not to exert more control of me than I can abide. Moreover, when I am in *Mr Darcy's* company, especially when he holds my hand or sits too near, or looks at me in a certain way – which he does all of the time - I find I care less and less about my *right* to *choose*; I begin to be more driven by a desire to please *him* than myself! Jane, his presence causes me to *tremble*!"

Lizzy relapsed into a blushful silence waiting for Jane's rejoinder.

"Well, Lizzy, your relationship with Mr Darcy or any man is your own affair. Nevertheless, as you appear to be seeking my opinion, I shall give it. You *may prefer* to continue you as you are, frustrating yourself with the continuous mulling and dithering as you describe. If that be the case I shall not be offended; I shall be by your side in a spirit of love and harmony in *whatever* vexation you *choose* to entertain.

"Now then, it *does* appear to *me* that you could simply take every opportunity of enjoying yourself with your suitor whilst you become better acquainted with his deeper nature; without wasting your time attempting to decide your future until you feel prepared to do so. Was that not your original intention when you agreed to the courtship?"

"You have the right of it Jane. Only, *so much* has happened in the short time since then! Lydia's *calamitous* errors would be enough to cause me second thoughts, because of the harm a connection with our family could bring to Mr Darcy *and* because of *horrid* Wickham's part in it.

"My sojourn at Netherfield and the circumstances of it complicated my feelings exceedingly. I was quite *afraid* because of Caroline Bingley and at the same time I could hardly open my eyes without being confronted with Mr Darcy and all of *his* eager wishes.

"I was torn between the comfort he offered me and feeling oppressed by the intensity of his wishes for my good opinion. It was *far* too much too *soon* and it left me wanting to draw back form him, actually from everybody at first, but him most of all. He sought more of me; *demanded* more than I could even comprehend... Mr Darcy's *wishes* always seem to assume the nature of *demands* in my reaction to them!"

Jane grinned at her embarrassed sister "Yes, I notice that Mr Darcy regularly has that effect upon everyone he meets! None can resist doing his will, even when he has not expressed it in that way."

Putting her arm around Lizzy's shoulder in a quick hug Jane made her final contribution to the debate raging in Lizzy's breast. "I think that when you examine the strength of your reactions to him, you may realize that you are already in love with Mr Darcy; else why so much dithering and worry? It is because of the vigour of your regard for him, and perhaps apprehension at those unfamiliar feelings that you struggle so!

"You are aware, are you not my Lizzy, that it is your very *independence*, your *impertinence* as Mamá calls it, that *enchants* him so? I believe that it is the self-confidence you consider an obstacle to your felicity with Mr Darcy which has been his *undoing*!"

"I had not... Thank you for your patience with me dearest Jane; you have afforded me both the relief of unburdening myself to you and much to think of in our talk. I shall take your advice as best I am able, to take more of enjoyment and less of fretfulness from Mr Darcy's visits!"

With a peek to assure herself that Jane did not appear troubled by any of her nonsense, Lizzy changed the subject. "I suppose that we might have moved on to speculations about Mr Wickham next had we not just now arrived home! Perhaps a respite from serious subjects is due, in any event."

THIRTY-SEVEN
Advancing Toward Trust

Jane and Lizzy walked in the front door at Longbourn just in time to see Mr Darcy following their father into his book room.

Lizzy was to learn after that gentleman's meeting with her father that one of the reasons for his request for a private conversation with Mr, Bennet was to seek his approval of making their courtship public at last. Open acknowledgment of Wickham's incarceration obviating their original purpose in keeping it secret, Mr Bennet approved so long as it was Elizabeth's wish as well.

In the brief interview with Elizabeth that followed, only the matter of the courtship was discussed. After proper greetings had been given, the question was asked. Elizabeth hesitated only for a fraction of a second before she agreed to reveal their courtship to the public. The second subject of the gentlemen's meeting was not mentioned.

Mr Darcy did not wish Elizabeth to know just yet of his offered sanctuary for Lydia and her family in Nottinghamshire. He owned a small, somewhat isolated property there which his ancestors had acquired sometime before 1568, while the county was still loosely united with Derbyshire under a single Sheriff[v].

It was situated not half a day's ride distant from Pemberley, in Derbyshire – a fact which conferred much satisfaction on Mr Darcy's anxious heart, and likely to be most pleasing to his friend Bingley as well.

The portion he offered consisted only of a house and gardens, the balance of the land attached to it being worked by tenants who looked to Darcy's under-steward for their instructions. Mr Claxton Doyle lived in Bakewell for convenient oversight of several of Darcy's scattered holdings in the region.

The house, which was called The Squyres Club for reasons lost in antiquity, was currently occupied by a young man by the name of Alfred Collier who was Mr Doyle's nephew. The young man had been in apprenticeship to his uncle for several years, preparing against the day when his training was complete and a position became available to him.

It was Darcy's proposition that Mr Collier should be sent to manage Longbourn while The Bennets were away in Nottinghamshire. There would be no cost to Mr Bennet for Mr Collier's service as the assignment would afford the fellow an excellent opportunity to gain experience on his own, in a modest setting where there was little chance of error, while increasing his worth to a future employer.

Once Elizabeth left the room, the gentlemen continued to converse on the subjects closest to their hearts.

"You have relieved my mind of a great burden, Mr Darcy, I accept your offer with pleasure and, if it is acceptable to you, I would wish to make the change forthwith, to avoid any suspicion among my neighbours. If it becomes evident that we might not be required to remain away for so long, I shall happily return my family quite promptly to Longbourn!

"We shall put it about that I seek the cool air of the north for my health. For the time being I shall inform my family that we go at the invitation of a distant cousin of mine. They are aware that we do have a few relatives in the north, although I hardly know whether they still live - or where to find them!"

Rising to shake the hand of his young friend in thanks for his well thought-out generosity, he added, "I fully comprehend your reasons for leaving Elizabeth in the dark about this for the present. I share your wish that her choice of a husband not be influenced by gratitude or anything except the expectation of her future happiness."

"Thank you for understanding sir. I hope to win Miss Elizabeth's good opinion without recourse to the material benefits in my power to bestow *or* to gratitude, which can be too closely akin to a sense of obligation. I hope I do not expect too much for myself when I wish for a bride who returns my tender regard without the motivation of either greed or gratitude – such a woman would be the only inducement for me to marry!

"Miss Elizabeth could never be called greedy, but I do fear her gratitude when her sense of honour is engaged."

"You are wise, young man!" Mr Bennet wished he *could* count this admirable young fellow as his future son, but Lizzy had been through so much! "I wish I had assurances for you, but my daughter does not seem to know her own heart, as yet." He said with a shrug of regret. "From what I know of her, Mr Darcy, I trust that she is not indifferent to you, however."

"I know not of the wisdom you ascribe to me sir, but when it comes to matters close to my heart I can be a very patient man. At Netherfield my sister admonished me that Miss Elizabeth needed less of my... hovering, as Georgiana put it. I have taken her advice and made a point of giving Miss Elizabeth relief in that quarter.

"I agree with you that Miss Elizabeth does not seem indifferent to me. At first the very *sharpness* of her rebukes, uncharacteristically harsh for your compassionate daughter, may have been an indication of an unusually strong reaction to me. And more recently there have been... other signs that she does not... *entirely* disdain my company."

"*Signs*, sir?" Mr Bennet's eyebrows did such a perfect imitation of Elizabeth's beguiling expression that Darcy almost laughed, until he tried to formulate an acceptable answer to her father.

"Well, yes, she *smiles* at me on occasion, and, er, sometimes there are blushes that are not, that do not arise from the topic of conversation...She *did* agree to a courtship, albeit with some misgivings I suspect."

Darcy thought it too much to mention that he had felt Lizzy trembling in his arms when he conveyed her to the sitting room on the occasion of her first venture out of her bedchamber at Netherfield. But he treasured the memory of it all the same.

Thinking that enough had been said on the state of Lizzy's heart; Mr Bennet cleared his throat and said "Yes well, perhaps you could summon Mr Collier so that I may spend some time with him before we depart for Nottinghamshire. It ought to require no more than a few days to acquaint him with the running of Longbourn. I shall be glad to know that my estate shall be looked after and not left to rack and ruin in my absence! Again sir, I cannot thank you enough!"

"You are very welcome Mr Bennet; no further thanks are wanted or necessary."

Turning to the subject of their meeting with Colonel Forster and Bingley the day before, he asked "Are you quite satisfied with Colonel Forster's proposition for Wickham, sir? He will *escape* the most severe consequences of his depravity, the hangman's noose, by forced transportation to the eastern coast of Australia to work as an indentured servant for life."

"Mr Darcy, there *is* no punishment severe enough to answer for what he has done to my Lydia, and to God knows how many others in his miserable life. Nevertheless I *must* be satisfied with Wickham's banishment from the land of his birth, and consignment to a life of servitude in a harsh new locale, as the alternative is to expose Lydia and her sisters to the worst humiliation possible for gently bred young women.

"He shall suffer as much punishment for his lifetime of debauchery and wickedness as the good Colonel can meet out to him without *my daughters* suffering *worse* for a few hours of youthful folly. Yes, I *must* be satisfied with Colonel Forster's disposition of the matter, Mr Darcy."

"I am sorry sir, I, too would *almost* have preferred to see him dead! I *would* have preferred it had I not grown up with him and known him when he was yet a charming young boy! But Wickham has grown up to be a man without morals or feeling for others. He would not hesitate to smear Miss Lydia with his filthy lies if he thought it would help save his life. The same is true of Miss Elizabeth if he was to be charged in connection with her poisoning and his attempted... his attempt on her virtue.

"This way the good names of all of your daughters as well as Bingley's sister are spared destruction forever under the lascivious titillation of those who report and consume that sort of information.

"But sir," he finished with the faintest tremor in his deep voice, "there is nothing to stop us from hoping that he will *not survive* the voyage, *or* the vicious society awaiting his arrival in that distant colony of crooks and convicts!"

~&~

Lizzy and Jane were alone in the breakfast parlour, nibbling at a late breakfast, when Mr Darcy and their father emerged at last from Mr Bennet's sanctuary.

"Won't you join us, Mr Darcy? I feel sure that you have either missed your breakfast entirely or partaken of it so early that you are quite prepared to fill your stomach again!"

"I thank you sir, I shall be delighted to enjoy your and your family's company for a while before I return to Netherfield. Georgiana will likely be at her practice on the pianoforte for another hour or two at least." With a bow and a greeting for Jane, Darcy took a cup of coffee and a plate of ham slices and buttered toast and, following Mr Bennet's lead, seated himself across from the two young women.

"I can see that *you* are well, Mr Darcy. Might I enquire about Miss Darcy, sir? Is she well and is she enjoying her stay at Netherfield?" Jane felt that she should ensure that all of the proper cordialities were fulfilled.

"Yes, Miss Bennet, Georgiana is very well. I believe she is grateful for the change of scene and respite from her accustomed routine of studies and practice – excepting her pianoforte of course! She could hardly avoid using the very fine instrument at Netherfield.

"Most of all, she has confided to me how very much she has enjoyed making your and Miss Elizabeth's acquaintance – and your parents' of course!" Darcy spoke to Jane but his eyes were on Lizzy who sat very still and kept her eyes on her plate where rested her half-finished toast and an apple with a single bite out of it.

"She is a delightful young lady; which is hardly a surprise considering that she is your sister, sir." Jane paused with a smile. "I noticed that she and Lizzy had much to say to one another, did not you, Lizzy?"

Jane hoped that Lizzy or their father would join in the conversation soon. She liked Mr Darcy very much and wished for Lizzy to allow herself to show more than mere civility to him. If Papá engaged him then Lizzy would be reminded of Mr Darcy's intelligence, knowledge and an occasional flash of dry wit - not too unlike Mr Bennet's.

But Lizzy would not be drawn, and the gentlemen had spent a good deal of time together already.

Lizzy simply answered "What? Oh yes, Georgiana is a dear girl" in an abstracted way and subsided into silence once more.

They finished their meal and Mr Bennet excused himself to his library. Mr Darcy invited Miss Elizabeth to take a turn in the garden with him before he left for Netherfield. As Mr and Miss Darcy were invited to dine at Longbourn that evening he felt it was best if he did not try Lizzy's patience overmuch in advance of what he hoped would be a pleasant visit for Georgiana later in the day.

Elizabeth agreed to walk out with him and at once asked Jane if she would like to join them.

Darcy did not allow the slightest flicker of surprise to cross his face; always a gentleman, he immediately seconded the invitation, encouraging Jane to take the fresh air with them while the day was mild. Propriety *did* require a chaperon but Elizabeth seemed remarkably determined to avoid any possibility of a momentary lapse in that regard.

He was puzzled, by Lizzy's abstraction and apparent unwillingness to be alone with him. Grimly he wondered whether she was unhappy at the decision to announce their courtship to the world. Dear God, he hoped not!

Jane's acquiescence in the plan was more the consequence of her desire for harmony among them than a belief that her presence in the garden truly was wanted, or even wise. When they went for their wraps, she took Lizzy by the arm and whispered "What are you doing, Lizzy? Are you upset with Mr Darcy? Why are you avoiding talking with him?"

"Jane, have you thought of how Mamá will behave when she learns of this courtship? I shall be utterly mortified! And, what will she do when she knows you are actually betrothed! How shall we bear it? I wish Mr Darcy may be a thousand miles away when Mamá learns our news!"

They continued to whisper as they climbed the stairs to their rooms.

"No, I had not thought of Mamá's reaction at all! I am ashamed; I ought to have told her right away but... with Charles leaving, I suppose that I had other things on my mind!"

"I don't think I can bear her poking and prodding at Mr Darcy's business as she is wont to do, Jane!"

"What if we ask Papá to call another family meeting after Mr Darcy leaves? We could tell her our news and he could explain to us all what is to become of Wickham and any other new information he has for us. What do you think? If we do it early enough Mamá should be somewhat sensible by the time Mr and Miss Darcy join us in the afternoon."

"Excellent Jane; I am quite impressed with your brilliant strategy! In fact, that gives me the idea to inform our mother and sisters that Mr Darcy is a very private man and I hope they will not drive him away with impertinent questions!" Lizzy smiled widely for the first time that day.

By the time she and Jane returned to Mr Darcy in the entry hall, he had worked himself up a degree of agitation too great to allow him to take note at first of the sparkling eyes and ready smile directed at him form the very quarter he had just been supposing to be set against him! Hearing the trill of delight in her cheerful words brought him up short in surprise.

"May I take your arm, Mr Darcy? Jane will attend us shortly; she had something she needed to do…" The enchanting arch of her eyebrow and delighted smile on those oh-so-tempting lips of her pretty mouth were his complete undoing. He swayed toward her, caught himself and promptly offered his arm. Darcy did not understand what had happened to make her upset earlier, but he was vastly relieved to comprehend that it was nothing to do with him!

~&~

Lizzy relaxed into the pleasure of walking in the garden with Mr Darcy. For the first time ever, she wholly let her apprehensions and reservations go while she was with him. She chose to listen to her elder sister's sound counsel; trusting Jane as implicitly as only a younger *can* trust an older beloved sister. Their early morning conversation had altered her perspective about Mr Darcy and about her reactions to him. Jane's opinion of him allowed her to trust her situation and her own capacity to choose wisely – and firmly.

The plan to ask for a family meeting in order to keep Mamá's first and worst effusions from Mr Darcy's hearing persuaded her to a renewed courage vis-à-vis announcing her courtship.

Mr Darcy could be a fascinating and charming companion when he was not engaged in self-censure or excessive worrying – well, even at those times, Lizzy recalled, she found him rather more appealing than not!

They ambled slowly toward the far end of the garden where the remains of an ancient cedar which had been felled around the time Lizzy was born, lay partially obscured from view by the unfettered growth of a bed of lavender pasqueflowers and blue delphiniums in front of it.

Her fascination with climbing on it when Lizzy was quite small caused Mr Bennet to have it cleared of its smaller branches and a wide seat smoothed into its main trunk. The huge column, which divided in two directions about a dozen feet from its beginning, ended in a number of branches big enough around to allow a small child to play among them endlessly, using them for handholds.

It had been Lizzy's favourite place to amuse herself when she was too young to walk alone in the countryside. Later it became her special haven for many hours of reading or daydreaming.

Occasionally Jane would sit with her in the comfortable seat where they would share their girlish dreams and giggle over some antic of their own or of their neighbours.

"What an enchanting spot this is!" Darcy looked around him appreciatively, noting the graceful lines of the downed tree against the wooded copse beyond it. The dense growth in the flower beds on the other side of a narrow footpath in front enhanced the intimate mood, enclosing the small area almost like a woodland glen. He understood instinctively that in bringing him to this place, Elizabeth signalled her acknowledgement of his new position in the sphere of her connections.

His happiness increased as she took his hand and led him to her favourite seat, saying light-heartedly "Come Mr Darcy, you are invited to enjoy my special refuge with me. It has been my own since I first learnt to walk. Later it was the scene of many imaginary adventures there among those bare branches, then shared confidences and daydreams with Jane – and books, of course! To this day none of my family cares to use it without my invitation!"

"I thank you, Miss Elizabeth" he rumbled with a solemnity which belied the surge of excitement her words caused him to feel "I am deeply honoured that you have chosen to allow me to be here!"

Still holding her hand after they were seated, Darcy regarded Lizzy's countenance which was overspread with a delicate blush. His mien was serious, and warm. He had felt her hesitant attempt to withdraw it *and* her faint squeeze of acquiescence when he did not relinquish it easily. "Miss Elizabeth may I, or might I be so bold as to ask you a personal question? Actually *three* personal questions, more like!"

She returned his look with her own, slightly startled but steady gaze. "You may ask, sir, and I shall choose whether to answer." She added with an apologetic smile "I hope I have no deep dark secrets... of which you are *as yet* unaware!"

"Miss Elizabeth! Well perhaps I shall begin with this one! Might we be allowed to call each other by our given names now that our courtship is to be known? May I call you Elizabeth and you call me Fitzwilliam?"

"I... shall be pleased to have you use my given name and to call you by your given name Mr D... *Fitzwilliam* in private until my mother has been made aware of how things stand between us. Once she has recovered from the shock I shall like to hear my name on your lips and to use your given name among our family and intimate friends." Her blush deepened as she said this but her eyes sparkled at him and her smile never faltered.

"Thank you Elizabeth! You have made me very happy! He sealed the exchange with a daring kiss to her hand. In fact he lingered over it so long that both of their hearts were pounding and Lizzy's face was pink with pleasure before he lifted his head to show her the rare sight of his broadest smile, complete with twin dimples on either side of his handsome cheeks!

Lizzy forced herself to retain, or at least *project* a semblance of her composure, remarking somewhat breathlessly "*Oh my*, sir! I tremble to learn what your *next* question might be!" She immediately regretted her unfortunate choice of words, for she was indeed *trembling* and the cause was nothing to do with his *questions*!

"Nothing so very frightening, my dear," He laughed softly, "I simply wished to know when you plan to inform Mrs Bennet that you and your father have consented to my request to court you!" He was unable to quell the exultant gleam in his eyes; he was aware of her trembling and could guess its cause.

He immediately regretted his question, however, when her aspect became uneasy and the flush on her face faded to a queasy pale colour. "Oh dear; I assume my father has told you of our *Bennet Family Code of Conduct* and the family meeting which preceded its inception?"

At his serious expression and nod of agreement, she went on: "I have been... rather apprehensive of my mother's excessive... agitation when she... hears of our... Well Jane suggested and I agree, that we hold another family meeting early this afternoon to share our news with her, along with some things our father might have to tell us . We hope to give her time to indulge in the more ah, effusive reactions we expect of her prior to ah, well, hoping to relieve you and Georgiana of the exposure to the worst of it. I intend to remind her that you are a very proud man, and that she must take care not to drive you away in her excitement."

Elizabeth dropped her eyes to her lap; she seemed surprised to see their hands entwined there, and glanced up involuntarily at his face.

Darcy studied her face for a moment, thinking over what she had said – and not said. "My dearest, loveliest, most foolish Elizabeth;" He could not stop himself from taking her other hand and, after kissing them, holding both of them against his heart. "Do you have so little faith in my constancy that you believe I would be put off by a little extravagant language or eccentric behaviour on the part of your mother?"

To his utter joy, Lizzy leaned toward him and rested her head on his chest, nodding slightly as a few tears ran down her cheeks. Holding her hands with one of his he slid his other arm around her shoulders and gently held her there while she composed herself.

"My dearest, *dearest* Elizabeth," His voice rumbled in her ear along with the strong, steady beat of his heart, "After all that has happened, all that I have said to you and tried to show you by my care and, and efforts to please you, how can you imagine that anything or anyone could tear me away from you – save your own command? I *love* you Elizabeth! I am *not* some callow youth who utters words of love carelessly and runs away at the first bump in the road, or speaks of love without comprehending the depth of devotion and commitment implicit in his declaration! I am a *man!* I am a man who *knows* what he *wants*, what it *means*, who will *do everything* honourable to secure it, and who wants and loves *you* – desperately, honestly and without reservation!"

"I am s, sorry sir, *Fitzwilliam!* Please accept my apologies for... for my *foolishness!*" Her voice was low, and muffled by her efforts to wipe away her tears with a delicate embroidered handkerchief.

She kept her head bowed, near but no longer against him, unwilling for him to see her face which was flushed with embarrassment and... another emotion she was not prepared to acknowledge or define. His eloquent declaration had rocked that little of her equanimity yet remaining to its foundation! Would she never again spend more than ten minutes alone in conversation with this man without finding herself unsettled – *alarmingly* unsettled?

Darcy took her scrap of a handkerchief away and replaced it with his own, tenderly wiping the tears from her face as he told her "Let it go, my dear, I am very grateful to know what has been troubling you this morning – in truth since we agreed to make our courtship known to everyone. I believe I collect the cause of your distress, do I not, Elizabeth? Have you been fretting over the scene of your mother's uninhibited joy at our news?"

Hearing her soft "Yes, yes I have..." He patted her shoulder gently and said "I no longer have need to ask a third question for you have answered it already. I am very sorry that this has been... a bit painful for us both Elizabeth, but I believe it has led us to a better understanding of one another, has it not, my dear?"

Elizabeth looked up at him with a tentative smile. Her face appeared calmer, although in want of restoration to its normal colour. "I believe you are correct, Fitzwilliam."

"Shall we return to the house then? I trust you have something to speak to your father about, and the time is passing."

Standing and helping her to her feet he offered his arm, which she took without hesitation. "By the by, have I told you how I adore saying your name? It has both soothing sweetness in its syllables and a little zing – like that of your sharp wit – in its sound! You are most aptly named, sweetest, loveliest Elizabeth!"

THIRTY-EIGHT
Life Altering Announcements

"Well Lizzy, are you ready to hear your mother's enthusiastic approval of your situation?" Mr Bennet addressed his wry question to her hard upon the heels of Mr Darcy's departure for Netherfield.

"Jane informed me of your plan whilst you and your young man wandered in the garden. I shall have news for you all as well. I confess I like the idea of another family meeting for the purpose; I have some hope that hearing all of our notable pieces of intelligence at one and the same time, will take the force out of her *reception* of each."

"I feel the same, father. Although Mr Darcy said much to dispel my qualms over the possibility of *his* being exposed to a display of her *delight* in our courtship, *I continue* to hold a strong preference for avoiding such a scene!"

"Your sister has expressed as much, my dear, along with her own similar feelings on the subject of her betrothal to Mr Bingley." He smiled lovingly at his daughter whose mood seemed quite unexpectedly cheerful after her dullness at breakfast!

Then, anticipating the meeting he was called upon to orchestrate, he heaved a heavy sigh and remarked "Ah well, I suppose I must resign myself to a veritable avalanche of female perturbation and alarums after all is said and done!"

Lizzy gave her father a look of inquiry at his pronouncement but did not voice her surprise as she let herself be shooed into the breakfast parlour where a cold collation was laid out for their convenience before the momentous family meeting began in earnest.

Mr Bennet waited without comment while first Jane revealed her engagement to Mr Bingley, then as soon as his wife could be quieted sufficiently to hear it; Lizzy announced that Mr Darcy had received permission to court her.

Mrs Bennet's raptures could not be expressed loudly or long enough to satisfy her exuberant feelings at the news. Mr Bennet winced occasionally but sat silently with his eyes closed until he could reasonably expect to interrupt her without raising her ire overmuch.

Not one of the three younger sisters seemed the least bit surprised, he noted; each one of them beaming their pleasure at Jane and Elizabeth without any urgent need to speak. He had noticed that his daughters appeared to be in uncommon charity with one another. The changes in Lydia's comportment... Kitty's as well... why even Mary was smiling and nodding her pleasure and support for her sisters! My goodness! Would wonders never cease! He would be very interested to learn whence this new sisterly affection came!

Never mind that now. It was time to change the subject to another source of excitement – this time not so happy if he understood his family aright.

But first he would speak of Wickham. Reluctantly holding up his hand for their attention he made his preliminary announcement, that he had two more items for the agenda and he should be grateful for the opportunity to address them forthwith.

"The first matter," he began once he had their attention, "is the decision taken by myself, Colonel Forster, Mr Bingley and Mr Darcy regarding what must be done with Mr Wickham."

"Incidentally, you should know that I have it from Colonel Forster that it was Wickham who sawed the axle on our carriage. Apparently he hoped to slow my movements should I discover what he was up to."

He saw indignation, anger, disdain, and disgust on their faces but no wistful longing or warmth on the assembled faces before him. He was exceedingly relieved and grateful for that.

Mr Bennet told his family straightforwardly and without any attempt to soften the facts, about the whys and wherefores of the only reasonable decision the four men could have made under all of the circumstances.

There were a few tears of shame, perhaps of regret that anyone should have to suffer the fate that Wickham faced, and some amount of relief to know that the decision had been made. Wickham would soon be to them almost as if he had never existed – almost.

Lydia swallowed hard as she wondered whether she carried his child, but Lizzy was looking at her with such consciousness and sympathy that she steeled her resolve *never* to think of any child she might bear as having any connection to such a one as him! Smiling confidently back at Lizzy she lifted her eyebrows and gave a slight shrug, as if to say "This has nothing to do with me!"

They all agreed to rejoice in Wickham's life being spared, they could not in Christian charity wish for his death, and that it was to be spent at such an extreme and impassable distance that he would never trouble any of them again.

Lizzy knew there must be more to tell, her father had a dogged look in his eyes and she recalled his words ahead of the meeting about 'perturbations and alarums'.

She did not believe that anything quite as dire as he appeared to expect had come about as yet, so "Papá," her voice sounded unnaturally loud amid the softer tones of the others who were still lingering over the subjects discussed previously. "Papá did you not say that you had *two* items to discuss? You have spoken only of what is in store for Wickham. Pray what is it that remains for you to tell us?"

As soon as everyone had quieted once more, Mr Bennet laid a paper on the table beside him and commenced to recite its contents to them. It read:

Bennet Family Code of Conduct

- ✓ We shall need a detailed plan, one which all understand and agree upon if we have the least chance of preserving our good name;

- ✓ The authorities must be alerted immediately to Mr Wickham's whereabouts;

- ✓ No one who has no reason to know of it should be made aware of Mr Wickham's use of my cottage for his hideaway;

- ✓ No one must speak to anyone of any portion of Lydia's and Catherine's visits to Mr Wickham in the cottage or of their 'helping' him with food and clothes and such;

- ✓ The author of that note — and the import of its contents — ought to be found out if at all possible;

- ✓ We must all reserve expression of our apprehensions — even thoughts of them if we are able — to those times when we are either alone or only in each other's company.

- ✓ The servants are most emphatically included among those who must be excluded from hearing our confidential discussions;

- ✓ As we improve upon our habitual conduct, it will be of equal importance that we endeavour to comport ourselves in public as nearly usual as we might - excluding Lydia and Kitty's improper conduct;

- ✓ Remain steadfast in dislike and distrust of Mr Wickham;

- ✓ Mr Darcy shall be taken entirely into our confidence in the twin expectations that his assistance in dealing with Wickham could be essential and that because he is an upright and honourable gentleman, he will not betray our private business to anyone;

- ✓ Should Lydia find herself suffering lasting consequences of her actions, she will be sent to stay with either the Gardiners or our more distant relatives in Hampshire until she is able to re-join her family at Longbourn;

✓ *If there occurs an increase in the Bennet family, the safety and identity of any such increase shall be protected as necessary — Mr and Mrs Bennet not quite beyond the possibility of claiming it as their own.*

✓ *This agreement is subject to modification as future developments require.*

The undersigned agree to comply with all terms set forth above in every particular and with all of their hearts thus engaged.

Signed this day of our Lord, 8 December 1811

"- And there follow all of our signatures in agreement to those terms. I am very pleased and proud of all of you for your compliance with everything we have done here, I have not been aware of one whisper thus far, of what has transpired either here at Longbourn or at Netherfield except from the gentlemen with whom I met yesterday regarding Wickham.

"All of those gentlemen, Mr Darcy, Mr Bingley, and Colonel Forster have seen this document and understand its purpose. They also have been sworn to absolute confidentiality in every damaging particular. I tell you this only so that you are fully informed of who does or does not have knowledge of our concerns – and to ease your minds should certain awkward issues arise with respect to Mr Bingley and Mr Darcy.

"Both of those gentlemen have been unequivocal in their commitment to aid and support us in any manner which might be suitable, and in their constancy toward their particular favourites among my daughters.

"Several of the listed items here are resolved or no longer relevant. We know who wrote that note and what it meant. Conduct has been altered to the vast improvement among you and I must express again my pride and gratitude for the excellence of my dear my family." He paused to smile, somewhat sadly, at his wife and daughters.

Mrs Bennet was desperately fighting to control her agitation. She suspected that they would soon hear something dreadful and wanted it over quickly. But she knew that her husband was not to be rushed. Indeed, urging him to hurry on was more likely to produce the opposite effect than to speed up his delivery so she chewed her lip and held on.

"What I have to tell you, the reason why I direct your attention again to our agreement, has to do with the final three items before our consent to be bound by the document and signatures:

- ✓ *Should Lydia find herself suffering lasting consequences of her actions, she will be sent to stay with either the Gardiners or our more distant relatives in Hampshire until she is able to re-join her family at Longbourn;*

- ✓ *If there occurs an increase in the Bennet family, the safety and identity of any such increase shall be protected as necessary — Mr and Mrs Bennet not quite beyond the possibility of claiming it as their own.*

- ✓ *This agreement is subject to modification as future developments require.*

As we agreed, the particular plans for protecting both Lydia's and the Bennet names are subject to modification as required.

I have fashioned a plan that will answer our needs more definitely and safely than the other two items could have contemplated. Therefore, Lydia shall not be sent away to the Gardiners or any other relatives on her own. The entire Bennet family shall go away – together."

"Oh, Mr *Bennet!*" cried his wife "*How shall we manage? Where are we to go? What is to become of our home? What is to become of us?*" All at once a rather odd look came over her face and she wondered aloud "We might go to *Brighton*, or even London...!"

"No my dear, I am sorry to disappoint you but we shall not be going to any place as exotic as that! We shall not be going to any place where Lydia might be exposed to public attention. Now, if you will allow me to finish?"

Their daughters simply sat and gaped at him, unable to take into their minds a proposed change of such magnitude as leaving their home and all of their familiar haunts, friends and neighbours – even Aunt and Uncle Phillips!

"Our removal shall be for a period of a year or so, from Longbourn. We are invited to stay in a very private but pleasantly situated home in Nottinghamshire belonging to one of my very distant cousins. It consists only of a house and gardens; the balance of the land which is attached to it is being worked by tenants who look elsewhere for their instructions.

"I shall have no burden of estate management to distract me from my family and books. We shall stay until either we are certain that no consequences are expected in Lydia's situation, or until said consequences have made an appearance. We shall then decide how best to welcome my first grandchild into the family.

"I have engaged the services of a young man by the name of Alfred Collier, who has been in apprenticeship to his uncle for several years. Mr Collier's uncle is a steward on a large estate in another part of the country. He comes to us with excellent references and should arrive at Longbourn within the week   I will familiarize him with the running of Longbourn before we depart so that he is prepared to manage Longbourn whilst we are away."

~&~

Everyone had questions and comments about the new plan – the whole family to remove en masse to some isolated little home they had never heard of before, in a place they had never seen before!

Lizzy brought out her father's atlas to ascertain the actual *location* of Nottinghamshire.

Mr Bennet had few answers. He trusted the person who thought the situation would do well for them; he did not know when, exactly, they would depart; yes, they should take their most favoured belongings for they might be away for as long as a year.

When queried as to what their neighbours would make of their removal, he *was* prepared with answers which he hoped would not require too much application.

They should put it about that he had been wheezing for some time, which was true enough as he suffered from allergies brought on by the fall harvest in the fields near Longbourn every year since his early twenties. His condition had come on gradually but had worsened of late (this had enough relationship to truth that no one need feel dishonest in saying so). He had seen a doctor while visiting the Gardiners in London (he *had* done so at some time or other) who advised him to spend some time in a cooler climate, perhaps somewhere toward the north or on the coast. Certainly any medical man worth his salt *ought to* have given him such advice if he had been consulted in the matter!

Mr Bennet deeply regretted asking them to dissemble or distort the truth, but there it was. There was no other way and they must all do what they must do. The best thing would be to keep their information vague and brief. That would help them all avoid being discredited by any unforeseen inconsistencies among their various accounts of the matter.

Jane delayed her *most pressing* question until her mother and three youngest sisters had wandered off to chat and plan what they would choose to carry with them into the unknown environment of a temporary home in a county far from their own.

"Papá," she ventured at last, "I am worried that we shall have left Longbourn before Mr Bingley returns to Netherfield. I should be quite miserable if I thought he would hasten to return to Hertfordshire only to... discover we had departed! And if he wishes to find me, how shall he...? Oh Papá, do you think he will come after me? He will only have just returned from travelling all the way to Scotland and back in service to his sister and then to expect him to... how I *wish I* had not insisted that he escort her! But then if I had not, or if he had not done so, I would have been very unhappy about *that!*"

Quite uncharacteristically, Jane leaned on her father's shoulder and wept as he patted and soothed her back to her customary calm faith that everything would turn out for the best. Perhaps that faith had been too severely tested of late, he thought to himself, for her to shun the contemplation of potential disaster as easily as she might have done before.

"Jane, Jane my *dear* girl, do not trouble yourself so, child. I make no doubt that given the chance Mr Bingley would travel to Scotland and back many times over just to prove himself to you. A short jaunt to Nottinghamshire will be as nothing to a young man as besotted as he is with you."

Mr Bennet kept his tones to the calm, slightly dry-humoured delivery he was accustomed to use. Familiarity would comfort her as much as his words.

"Trust me Jane; I know a thing or two about this that I cannot reveal to anyone at present. But all shall be well, you may count upon it, my dear.

"And now," Mr Bennet added, patting his eldest daughter's hand, "I should like to spend some time in peace and quiet. I shall be in my library, not to be disturbed for an hour at least!"

THIRTY-NINE
Georgiana and Her Brother Visit Longbourn

Georgiana Darcy looked around her in awe at the half-dozen Bennet women at their various activities.

When Fitzwilliam was away, her life in London consisted of her studies; reading; practice on her pianoforte; or shopping now and again. Occasionally she walked in Hyde Park with her companion, Mrs Annesley, attended always by a robust footman. Virtually all of her time was spent with her tutors or masters, or in the company of Mrs Annesley, whose calm and compassionate manner had been well-suited to soothe Georgiana's agitated feelings after Wickham's attempt to seduce her – but did not offer much in the way of stimulating social intercourse!

Summers at Pemberley were everything wonderful. She enjoyed walking or riding along the many footpaths that meandered through the gardens and nearby countryside, carrying a canteen and some bread and cheese or an apple to enjoy in some delightfully shady glen or flower-strewn field. At Pemberley it was safe for her to be permitted to walk alone, or ride with a footman following at a discreet distance behind her. She relished the freedom and solitude found only at her beloved Derbyshire home!

Away from her music master and French tutor she continued her other studies and indulged in reading for the pure pleasure of it, not to fulfil anyone's expectation of her. Of course her *pianoforte* never stood neglected for the whole of one day. But life *was easier*, more relaxed at Pemberley, she savoured the long sunny days of peace and comfort in her dear home.

Fitzwilliam worked hard throughout their time at Pemberley, yet he seemed to have more time for her, and to simply enjoy his favourite pastimes – like riding and fencing, visiting with his oldest and dearest friends, and reading for his own pleasure while they summered at Pemberley. They often spent their evenings discussing the books each of them had been enjoying.

During the long months in London, she was happiest when her brother's busy round of estate management and social obligations left him free to spend an afternoon or evening with her. He might take her to a concert, or a play, or simply spend an evening listening to her play the pianoforte. They might peruse and discuss the London papers or a book one of them had been reading.

Occasionally, one or both of Fitzwilliam's two closest friends, Mr Charles Bingley and Cousin Richard, would join them and they would be almost... jolly; although the gentlemen sometimes discussed subjects she did not understand. She made a point of questioning her brother afterwards so that she could learn from him of the interests of educated gentlemen of good moral character.

But they both had grown too inured to loneliness, she admitted too herself. Neither of them was at ease among large gatherings, or cared for table games other than chess – or checkers when she was younger. Both were deeply attached to their few dear friends, and to those of their family to whom they felt close ties of love and kinship. It was time, she was sure, that Fitzwilliam expanded their circle of family and acquaintance; he must marry Miss Elizabeth and banish the habit of aloneness from their lives.

Thinking thusly, Georgiana was utterly enthralled with the idea of so much feminine camaraderie in one home! If Miss Elizabeth were to join their small family...my how their world should expand!

Someone was playing the pianoforte. Mary, she believed. She would refrain from comment about *that* sister's accomplishments, poor dear; she suppressed a chortle to herself – it was enough that she felt free to *endeavour* to play a complicated piece without apprehension of criticism or complaint from her family!

Two young women – girls really – were busily trimming bonnets in a corner of the parlour. They were Miss Lydia, the youngest, and Miss Kitty, her next older sister. Georgiana was glad to use the rather childish nickname for that one! How very peculiar she would feel to address that sweet young flibbertigibbet by the same name as her imposing Aunt Catherine! Whatever made them giggle so?

Miss Jane Bennet's serene smile and gentle ways caused Georgiana to wonder how such diverse personalities could come from the same family! Jane, for so she had been invited to call her, had been most gracious and welcoming. She was attentive to the comfort of the guests and contributed quietly to the general conversation about her, showing a sincere interest in everyone's comments and opinions. Georgiana decided that she admired Miss Bennet very much!

Her opinion of Miss Elizabeth could not be contained in mere words. Georgiana's face lit up at the thought of *Lizzy* as her future sister! She delighted in fantasizing about their life together as a family. Fitzwilliam would be so happy! There would be love and laughter to dispel the pervasive solemnity of their stately home in London and in the vast halls and rooms of Pemberley. Georgiana imagined her new friend, enchanted by the lake, and the streams, and... Lizzy would *adore* the beautiful gardens, and wooded hills, and vast meadows of Pemberley. If only he would *ask* her, and *she* would give the answer to all of the Darcys' prayers!

"Miss Darcy? Are you well?" Georgiana came back to her surroundings with a start at the sound of her name!

"Oh, please forgive me! I was lost in thought I am afraid. What were you saying, Mrs Bennet?"

"Tis nothing my dear, I was only asking if you might like to join Kitty and Lydia for a turn in the garden. I see your brother and my Lizzy are about to embark on a stroll out of doors, ah, and Jane too! Perhaps a little walk in the fresh air will be welcome after sitting so long in one attitude?"

"Please, do join us Miss Darcy. We are eager to hear all about your life in London; it must be so exciting!" Lydia's invitation came promptly upon the heels of her mother's. She was learning to think of the wishes and comfort of others, and was pleased to employ her newfound cordiality to her sister's friend.

"You must have so much to tell us, of fashions, *and* shopping, and all manner of entertainments. We shall dearly love to hear about your life in Town." Kitty added her encouragement to that of the others. "I hope you will enjoy our gardens, howbeit they are presently not so green or full of blooms as they will be in a few short months."

"Thank you, I believe I should like to walk in the fresh air with you all, I shall use my imagination to brighten the colours of your garden, if need there be, your company will surely provide all of the pleasure I could desire."

Georgiana felt no little gratification in her emergent ability to engage in polite conversation with her new acquaintances.

"However I feel myself obliged to confess that my life in Town is not so *very* interesting as you surmise. I live quietly for the most part, as I am not yet out."

~&~

Darcy and Miss Elizabeth had found their way again to her private bower; *he* relishing the opportunity to be in her sole company again and savouring the feel of her hand resting lightly on his arm; *she* experiencing the *not* unpleasant sensation of warmth spreading from her hand where it rested on his sleeve – to her entire arm, which appendage she could not stop from brushing against him from time to time, making it the tingly focus of an interesting commotion in her breast.

"Will you sit with me, sir?" Indicating the seat carved into the cedar log with a gesture of her free hand, while almost surreptitiously removing her other from his arm. Elizabeth's increasing pleasure in the sensation of Darcy's touch warred with her trepidation about surrendering her heart. She simply could not fully overcome her fear that she would *lose* herself, her independence, her *right to make choices* about her manner of living – about anything or everything – if she were to make the *wrong* choice now.

"Sir? Am I not to have the pleasure of your calling me by my given name this afternoon, *Elizabeth?*" Darcy gave her a quizzical smile, waiting for her to take her cue.

"*Oh!* Will you not sit down, *Fitzwilliam?*" The greater equanimity, which she had assumed the break in physical contact with his arm should afford, eluded her still.

My goodness! Merely *thinking* of her dilemma caused her to feel her heart flutter in her breast, and her breath to come in short puffs! She forced herself to speak calmly when she went on with a hint of archness in her smile. "Of what shall we speak today my... dear? I have not been reading quite so often of late. However I daresay we must have many literary interests in common, recent impediments to the activity notwithstanding."

Books ought to be a safe topic, steering their conversation toward *books* should be just the thing to calm that too warm look in his dark eyes and banish the blushes she could feel creeping up her neck and over her face!

Why could she not *simply be easy* in his presence? Why should *his* company affect her thus and not that of any other man of her acquaintance? She bit her lip in frustration. It seemed that every time she allowed herself to feel comfortable around him, she sensed, and feared, her susceptibility to the magnetic effect of his bold dark eyes - eyes nearly as black and vivid as sable - captivating her, persuading her, enthralling her!

She felt herself drawn, inexorably, in by his stunningly handsome smile – his even, white teeth and those delightful dimples - and dark brown waves of hair reaching below his collar in a most alluring and disturbing way! She did not dare to consider of his tall muscular person! Her body's response to his masculine vigour frightened her, made her *exceedingly* ill-at-ease *again!*

"I am always delighted to discuss books, or any subject of interest to you, Elizabeth. I agree that our mutual delight in reading and in lively discourse holds promise of endless satisfaction between us two.

"I *had* thought that perhaps... Do you not wish to speak to me of more... of matters related to your family's future plans? I understand from your father that he proposes to take you all for a visit, an extended visit I should say at some distance from Longbourn, from Hertfordshire in fact."

He had been watching her closely; the shifting expressions in her countenance puzzled him. Darcy thought he understood her warm blushes and confusion and was delighted at these reassurances that her feelings toward him were not apathetic. But the suggestion of something akin to fear, or dread which settled over her face set his own insecurities to screaming in his head. He must stay calm! He must keep his wits about him if he hoped to lead her to accept his company with tranquillity.

Thus, well aware of the maidenly tumult she was feeling, Darcy wisely chose to turn her focus to a subject less fraught with tension between themselves and yet of vital importance to them both, the Bennets' forthcoming removal to Nottinghamshire.

Just as Darcy had hoped, Elizabeth's colour began to subside to its normal hue and the tension in her expression eased. Apparently she was more at ease with the difficult subject of leaving her lifelong home, friends and neighbours, than in contemplating whatever it was that took the pleasure out of spending time alone with him!

"Tis a daunting prospect, truly outside of my reach, to comprehend how we are to accomplish a removal of such proportions as that!" Elizabeth had not the least reticence about disclosing her thoughts about this matter. She did *not* appear overly fearful of the abrupt and rather extreme change of abode and environs in the offing. "Indeed, were it not for the circumstances of our removal, I would quite appreciate the challenge! I have always longed to travel; this will unquestionably afford me the opportunity to see and experience new places!"

It was fascinating, touching in fact, to see that Elizabeth had returned to her light-hearted tone, eyes bright with anticipation and her smile as wide and guileless as a child's.

If theirs was to be the honest and open relationship he desired, Darcy reasoned, he must simply ask her directly for the cause of her fear. Leaning closer without touching her he locked his gaze on hers and, refusing to be put off by that flash of wariness in her answering look, he asked. "Elizabeth, have I done something to make you... are you *frightened* of me? I cannot help noticing that you appear to draw back from me at certain times, and something in your expression causes me to wonder whether I have said or done something to disturb you so."

Startled by the plain straightforwardness of his address and obvious hurt on this particular theme, she instinctively rested her hand on his arm in kindliness, looked down at her hand in surprise, jerked it away and blurted: "No! Yes! I mean... Fitzwilliam, I *am* frightened but you have done nothing to cause me to fear you. Indeed, I do not believe that it is you that I fear, rather it is..." She hesitated and then took a deep breath, ready to clear the air between them, and plunged on "I fear *losing myself*, my own autonomous capability to reason and to make choices about my life. I fear that my self-assurance will be overwhelmed by the strength of your influence over me – even your authority over me should I choose to be your wife!"

"You believe that I would want to rule over you?"

"Whether that is your intention or not, sir, if I allow you to rule in my heart, you shall surely rule over my life!"

"I believe that I comprehend your meaning, Elizabeth, for *you* have ruled *my* life from your sovereignty in *my* heart for quite some time now. But you see, yours is not a power which you choose to have, nor do you now choose to wield it against my best interests. And though *I would give up my life for yours without hesitation*, I would *not* go against what I believe is morally right if I could not agree with your reason for asking it of me.

"It is simply in the nature of love to admire and wish to please the other, to care for their opinions, interests and values - not to be subsumed under differences of opinion or principle - *or* personal choices which might be adverse to one's own.

"And Elizabeth," he said stroking her cheek lightly with the back of his knuckles and then taking both of her hands in his, "I shall never, ever, ask anything of you, my dearest, that you do not willingly give to me." He kissed the inside of each of her wrists, held her hands to his heart for a moment and then rereleased them to her lap.

Lizzy had been listening intently; watching the way a gentle smile lurked at the corners of his mouth, how would those lips feel on hers when he finally kissed her? She took in his reassuring words while his eyes drew hers with a gaze full of earnestness and warmth. She *so* longed to reach up her hand to smooth back the ruffled curls from his noble brow... and to press her cheek to his... that it took a moment for the meaning of his last to reach her. Instantly she dropped her eyes, and turned her crimson face in an instinctive flinch away from him.

"But sir; it is when I feel the suggestion of *willingness* steal over me that I am most afraid!"

"Elizabeth! My love! I would never..." Forcing himself to speak more calmly, Darcy gave up all pretence of adhering to the bounds of what was considered proper fodder for discussion between a gentleman and a lady.

"Forgive me, Elizabeth, for what I am about to say. I know of no proper way to speak of this other than thusly. I know that you must have heard many expressions which suggest that in certain... that within a marriage – indeed between unmarried persons in private encounters – it is the man who... dominates, or who makes demands upon his partner. Common expressions which refer to 'having his way with her' or 'her marital duty to please him', or to 'submit to his demands' infer an unequal relationship between a man and his wife."

He paused to see how she was bearing up under his frankness. Lizzy was trembling but turned her face to him and met the question in his eyes with a nod. Perhaps she, too, was relieved to address her darkest fears candidly.

She pre-empted his next words, saying indignantly "Yes, and such is codified in the law by virtue of the right of property ownership being solely vested in the husband and in the common law 'rule of thumb' which allows a man to beat his wife with impunity so long as the instrument he employs is no greater than the thickness of his own thumb!" Her eyes flashed dangerously as she declared vehemently, "I shall never *submit* to being beaten, or... or, abused in other ways!"

"Elizabeth, May I please hold your hand while I say this?" Receiving her still-trembling hand in his, Darcy very kindly told her "Thank you my dear one! Pease understand, my heart, I am master of a great estate, several lesser estates, and have many other matters of business under my control - investments and the like.

"I employ hundreds of people to do the work of producing crops and other means of income, and to keep my home and properties well run and well-tended. I like to think that I treat them all honestly, dispense justice with an even hand, and ensure that their compensation is suited to their needs and rewards their contributions fairly.

"They are my servants, Elizabeth, servants and tenants, and their numbers are so great that I cannot call to mind exactly how many there are without recourse to an accounting book! If I have need of another servant, I *hire* someone suitable and treat that person equally as well as any other.

"In courting you I do *not* seek another servant!

"Please forgive my immodesty, dearest. It is only meant to convince you that I am a man who deals with others fairly, honestly, and justly. If I can do that much for my servants and tenants, how much more gently and kindly would I deal with the woman I *love,* my *wife!*"

"Your *words* are very pretty sir, I almost could have fallen into your arms in relief had I not recalled your *assumption of the right* to "dispense justice", even-handedly of course! But subject to your estimation only!"

In her agitation she pulled her hand from his and stood abruptly. Turning away as if to walk off on her own, she tossed a final piece of impertinence over her shoulder "I believe you ought to go and commiserate with Jane, Mr Darcy, for she is more inclined to overlook your arrogance than I!"

In a flash Darcy was before her, blocking her way but not touching her. His face flushed with anger and his eyes black as two polished stones, he kept his voice low though the intensity of his feeling was unmistakable. "You *must have done* with this, Elizabeth! I do not know what it *is* that *continually* sets your heart against me when it is plain to see that you would... that you *do* care for me when you allow yourself! As it is you are trifling with my heart most unkindly! Oh yes, and with regard to my 'arrogance', I *meant* for you to understand that in courting you I was not seeking... I am *not* in need of another servant! What I have in mind is a far *different* relationship!"

Suddenly Darcy's furious defences dissipated. "Miss Elizabeth I did not expect you to 'fall into my arms', only to accept my company after the fashion of an ordinary courtship wherein the concerned parties take time to explore their friendship, their attraction to one another, with the hope and expectation that it will lead to a desire to form a deeper bond in the future."

Elizabeth had been standing with her arms folded tightly across her chest, her head held high in defiance of his anger. Slowly she allowed her arms to drop to her sides; her expression lost its tautness to register her shock when she understood that she had been wrong to accuse him of arrogance – at least this time!

Elizabeth had not failed to note his return to calling her 'Miss Elizabeth'. She had wounded him – again! She felt ashamed of her petulance toward him. He was correct; there was plenty of time yet to come to a better understanding of him.

"I apologize most sincerely, for I have failed miserably at restraining my eagerness to win your heart. Clearly the ardency of my feelings has only driven you farther from me."

Darcy was no longer watching her face. Intent as he was on his own inner grief and turmoil. He did not see that her countenance had softened, and her stance lost its verve.

"I believe it will be best for me to leave you to consult your own heart, undisturbed by my presence, for a while. After our supper with your family this evening I believe I shall take my leave of the neighbourhood for a time".

"Please do *not*, Fitzwilliam. I have something I must say to you." She spoke softly, almost tentatively. She was embarrassed and unsure whether she could convince him to stay.

Darcy looked up sharply, studying her face for a hint of her intention.

She had gone shockingly white in her dismay over his pain and her own thoughtlessness – and the improper confession that would leave her more vulnerable and open than she had ever been to anyone in her life.

"Elizabeth! Are you well?"

"I am as well as I deserve to be, Fitzwilliam. I was wrong to accuse you. I am very sorry to have caused you pain with my thoughtlessness. And if you must leave me after I tell you this then I shall understand. I shall never make any claims against you or allow this to sully your name in any way."

Now Darcy's pallor matched her own. He had no improper pride to stop his gasp when he heard her words, kindly meant but dismissing him just the same. He listened in dread to her painful confession.

"I know that you think me witty and strong – well my wit has *been* my strength; I employ it to deflect attention when I am uncomfortable or unhappy.

"I do not know why this is the case, but I have not *always* had the use of my wit as a defence since I was so ill at Netherfield. I especially feel its lack when it comes to you, Fitzwilliam. For it is in your company that I have need of it the most!

"The *truth* is that I have... *feelings* that are... improper, *un-maidenly*, when you... touch me or... when you are near and... you look at me in that... way."

She did not understand that her feelings were normal; they were just what he would wish for her to have for him!

He was halted, however, in his impulse to reach for her, to hold her and comfort her - by her violently hurling herself away from him. She came to a stumbling rest against the trunk of the old cedar, where she braced herself with both hands, pale and trembling, tears flowing down her delicate cheeks.

"*Please!* Do *not* comfort me for I fear that if you touch me I shall... I do not know *what* I might do! I am utterly *wanton!* Just like *Lydia!*" Ending in a wail of despair Lizzy collapsed to her knees in the drift of dead leaves which had accumulated along the footpath, blown from the wooded copse on the far side of her glen beyond the old cedar trunk.

She could do nothing to hide her pain or to protect herself from his scorn – not even if he should choose to use the intelligence she had just given him to... to seduce her – but he would not, she felt sure, he was not that kind of man! But *she was* that kind of woman!

Crumpled in a small heap of tears, and leaves and wrinkled gown, she gave in to her great sorrow and regret at all that had befallen herself and her sisters in their ignorance and fault. There was no sound but her sobs to stir the air, and no movement to make her wary. He was gone; she thought sadly, the great Darcy's persistence had worn out at last.

She cried over his defection when she had used up her tears for her sisters and herself. Who could expect Mr Darcy of Pemberley to wait around in a puddle of tears to lift her up and kiss her sloppy-wet face back into peace and serenity? Well of course not! She would be everything *but* serene if he were to kiss her on her face – sloppy-wet or not!

But that is just what he did. She felt herself scooped up in his arms and carried like a child to their seat on the cedar log. Instead of setting her down, he sat down and situated her on his lap, took out his handkerchief and drying her tears, began to kiss her tenderly. He stroked her hair with one hand and held her close to him with the other, speaking gentle words of comfort while his lips left sweet caresses all down the side of her face, along her jawline, across her forehead and one last tiny brush against the tender skin below her ear. Every sensation was exquisite! She had no more will to fight her improper desire to be held in his arms; she relaxed against him and gave herself up to this new *deliciously* tingly warmth!

Elizabeth was giddy with pleasure and shock. She delighted in Fitzwilliam's ministrations to her, wished for *more*, wished he would kiss her lips, *yearned* for him to kiss her lips, but she knew that before things went much further she would stop him. She *would* stop him!

But first, she must have that kiss!

She angled her head so that her lips were only inches from his. "Are you taking advantage of my weakness for you Mr Darcy?"

"Not at all Miss Elizabeth, I am only expressing *my* weakness for *you!*" The love and delight in his eyes assured her that he was very far from displeased with her. "Shall I unhand you now my dearest, are you easier with, er, how things *are* between us? I hope you have learned to trust us *both* to curb our *natural* responses to each other sufficiently to keep within the bounds of propriety?" His breath warmed her face and made her lips burn in anticipation.

His reluctant move to release her and help her to rise from his lap was stilled when she answered without moving.

"I believe so, *Fitzwilliam*; however there is still one matter which troubles me greatly!" She could not help licking her lips. "I do pray you will not object to assisting me in just this one small matter?"

"What may I do for you my lady? I am at your service, as always!" Darcy had no idea what she might wish from him, but his eyes were riveted on those full rosy lips, so temptingly near his own, that she had so tantalizingly moistened just then!

"Fitzwilliam," his eyes flicked to hers and what he saw made him gulp! They were beautiful as always, with a glint of humour and something else... Was that... did she want him to...?

"*Oh God! Elizabeth!* May I...?"

Their first kiss was a revelation to them both. Elizabeth had never imagined how soft and warm his mouth would feel moving tenderly over hers. At first she revelled in the sensations of warmth and intimacy being held in his strong arms and inhaling an enticing mix of lime, and something dark and spicy, and his own manly scent – and the sweet torture of his kiss.

Darcy could scarcely believe he was finally kissing her! The feeling of jubilation and sheer bliss was far more than his poor imagination could have encompassed! Her lovely body in his arms, her lips moving under his, Elizabeth was everything his joyful heart could desire! He inhaled deeply of her familiar tangy lavender potion. How he loved this beautiful, innocent, honourable woman!

He almost laughed out loud when he realized that she was holding her breath! Lifting his mouth from hers momentarily he said "Breathe through your nose, my darling!" and immediately returned his lips to their entrancing pursuits.

Cautiously, careful not to frighten her, he deepened their kiss. Caressing her lips with the tip of his tongue until they parted to allow him in, he proceeded to thoroughly plunder her luscious mouth. Instinctively Lizzy raised her hands to his powerful shoulders, turning her body to him, marvelling at the intense sensations in her body upon coming into contact with his manly figure. From thence she allowed her fingers to slide upward into his hair, tangling in his curls and drawing him, urging him closer, as if she could never get enough of his soft, warm lips.

Darcy was lost in her embraces, pouring all of his love and desire into this magical moment. He had her permission, her encouragement to show her the tenderness, the desire, and the ardency of his passion and he was utterly undone!

Breathing in shallow puffs, trembling and tentative at first; she returned his passionate kisses glorying in the ecstasy of his lips on hers and the feel of his muscular arms wrapped about her.

Both of them startled when the sound of voices came to them from beyond the bed of pasqueflowers and blue delphiniums, headed in their direction!

Lizzy jumped up from Fitzwilliam's lap with a soft giggle and a whispered "I believe that shall have to do for us for quite some time!" She shook out her skirts, rubbed her face and seized his hand to urge him to his feet.

Breathing heavily, they each took a moment to compose themselves; he turned away from her to adjust his clothing and hide the evidence of his arousal from her maidenly sight.

Then Elizabeth took Fitzwilliam's proffered arm and they proceeded to stroll in the opposite direction from the sound of the voices, Darcy moving somewhat awkwardly in his tight breeches.

FORTY
United by Deep Bonds of Affection

"Come in Mr Collier! You are most welcome!"

The whole party had been assembled in the sitting room, Mrs Bennet and all five of her daughters, Mr Bennet and Mr Darcy, when Mrs Hill announced Mr Alfred Collier at the door.

Darcy looked up to see the neatly dressed young man of twenty-two years enter the room, bowing at each introduction and obviously taken aback, if not bedazzled by finding himself confronted with a bevy of lovely young ladies, smiling young ladies.

This was the nephew of Mr Claxton Doyle, Darcy's under-steward in Bakewell. He had met this young man but a few times, leaving his supervision to Mr Doyle.

Collier seemed a pleasant fellow, a respectable young man whose duties were promptly completed with an admirable thoroughness and attention to detail. Darcy had found him respectful, without obsequiousness, a man free of bad habits and who always took care to keep himself presentable before his betters. No arduous task as he was blessed with a tall slightly angular stature topped with the shade of blonde which was often compared to that of ripe wheat. Other than the slight narrowness of his nose, his features were otherwise unremarkable: regular, somewhat tanned, and set off by light grey eyes under thick brows of the same hue as his hair.

Mr Collier had previously been carefully instructed to show no recognition of his employer when they met at Longbourn. Dutifully he bowed politely and said all that was required but showed no sign of recognition when he was introduced to Mr Darcy of Pemberley.

Darcy did not engage Collier in conversation. He abhorred deceit and would find it most uncomfortable to speak with him as if they had only just met. Instead he sat back to enjoy the tableau unfolding before him.

Mrs Bennet played her part to perfection. She could not have been more effusive in her welcome, or more interested to learn Mr Collier's situation - in every particular.

That gentleman, accustomed to a quiet life away from the opportunity to socialize with many young ladies, was understandably shocked to nervousness by the array of lovely faces and forms - and smiles - before him! He had little to say at first, but the Bennet ladies would have no great extent of that! They set themselves to draw him out, and so they did indeed.

That they were well disposed toward him was evident in their attentive looks and sparkling eyes. Everyone was interested to make the acquaintance of the man who would preside over their home for the many months of their absence.

To Darcy's surprise neither Lydia nor Kitty exhibited their former brash and forward ways. They were friendly and engaging to be sure but demure in their glances and courteous in their speech.

He was just congratulating himself on the excellence of his plan when he chanced to turn his eye on Elizabeth. His Elizabeth was beaming in the direction of Mr Collier, her breath-taking smile in full force and a speculative look in her sparkling eye!

Instantly he began to berate himself! Damn and Blast! How could he have been so stupid? How *could* he have missed the obvious truth that Mr Collier would be perceived by the young ladies as *handsome*? *She* thought him handsome; *she* was attracted to him!

In a mad panic he thought of sending Collier back to The Squyres Club and finding another of his men to act as steward at Longbourn; or mayhap he should call him out! Helplessly he watched *his* Elizabeth *admiring* the wretched man! For certain he was that *his* ladylove, the beautiful and desirable woman he had so recently begun to initiate into the delights of shared passion, was even now considering whether *Mr Collier* might afford her a similar pleasure!

Fitzwilliam Darcy's haughty glare was not often displayed of late, but he now sent it with every ounce of his being toward the younger man whom he had viewed in so beneficent a light, only moments ago. If his glowering look could cast real daggers there would be instant expiry in the Bennets' sitting room!

His Elizabeth was *speaking* to the bounder! He must have his share in *that* conversation! Leaning forward to catch her words he nearly fell out of his chair when he heard her say "I believe we ought to have a small dinner party sir, You shall enjoy meeting our closest neighbours, Sir William Lucas and his lady have sons close to your age and two lovely daughters. The Longs as well, have several nieces who are out – and then there are the Hubbards, who live at a little greater distance... We have very enjoyable public assemblies nearly every fourth week..."

Darcy had heard enough! More embarrassed than he had ever been in his life before, he looked around hoping that no one had divined the ridiculous fright he had entertained upon seeing his beloved looking... kindly... upon another man!

Apparently they had not. Mr Collier had everyone's attention, a fact which pleased Darcy more fervently than a moment ago would have seemed possible!

At his audible sigh of relief, Lizzy gave him a quizzical glance, captivating him with the sweet arch of her raised brow, the faintest quirk of amusement in her smile. She held his gaze momentarily; mesmerizing him, taking away his breath. Her beautiful sparkling eyes held him, a willing hostage to the intimate glimpse she allowed him of her secret delight at his discomfiture.

~&~

Lizzy and Darcy scotched their original plan the following morning to walk to Oakham Mount together in favour of an extended ramble through the garden and small wilderness nearby. Lizzy could not be so unkind as to require their faithful chaperon to walk so far.

Jane would be content to attend them from the seat in the cedar log, her yet unfinished sampler to hand for employment should her constant thoughts of Charles Bingley call for it. Lizzy had wished for one last visit to the Mount before the rapidly approaching time came for her family to absent themselves from the neighbourhood. Such was not to be, however, so she philosophically turned her attention to enjoying her morning with Mr Darcy.

They had been wandering among the winter-darkened flower beds for only a short while when she thought she might embark upon a tease.

"Fitzwilliam," said his companion with a mirthful expression upon her lovely countenance, "Whatever were you thinking of last evening, when we were all in company together with Mr Collier, to produce such a scowl upon your face? I pray you will enlighten me for I should *dearly* wish to avoid *that* look ever being turned upon *myself!*"

He coloured at her question; he should have known she would want to have her fun with him. The recollection of his preposterous, his *unspeakably* ill-considered apprehension at the time mentioned embarrassed him acutely. The worry that she might, she *ought* to be insulted by it afflicted his mind and a roiling of anxiousness gnawed at his insides.

Pausing to clear his throat, and for time to form his answer, he said "Dearest, loveliest Elizabeth, it was my fervent hope that you had not observed my ill-founded fit of temper!"

"In truth I did not *observe* it, so much as *experience* it. It seems that there is a... some sort of connection between us – similar to that which I share with Jane. We often know each other's feelings even when we are apart. I did not see your expression until I glanced at you while speaking with Mr Collier. Then the relief upon your face was palpable! But I had no doubt that you had been scowling a moment prior."

"That is remarkable indeed, Elizabeth! Now that I think on it I believe that *I* have felt a heightened receptivity to *your* feelings as well – a condition quite a lot more perceptive than I have ever known with anyone before. How does such a thing come about, I wonder?"

Lizzy looked away, flushing with embarrassment. "I had always *believed* that Jane and I were united in that way by the bonds of our deep affection for one another." She said softly.

Darcy did not miss the implication in her words, of a 'deep bond of affection' being the catalyst for their sensitivity to one another's moods, but he could not so easily believe himself forgiven.

He stopped abruptly and turning to her he spoke with abject shame on his countenance and in his voice. "My Dear; then you must be *aware* of my *asinine* jealousy when I saw you looking upon Mr Collier in such a way that I feared your approbation of him for yourself!"

Placing his hand over hers as if to stop her removing it from its position on his arm, he begged her "*Please* forgive me for my stupidity Elizabeth. My sickly thoughts were not a reflection on your integrity! They were inspired by my own *lack of confidence* in my ability to inspire strength in your regard for me. I know that I am not worthy; I carry my pride too high and am only a novice at learning compassion for the feelings of others. Indeed I have *many* faults, I do not deny it.

"But you must know that my greatest wish is to ensure your happiness in every way open to me. You might *think* it impossible but I love you more each day! My heart fills with new joy each time you are near and when I am not with you I am bereft. I pray you will not turn from me over a moment of exceedingly unfortunate weakness last evening."

Darcy's eloquent mea culpa produced an astonished response from his ladylove. "Your apology perplexes me greatly, Fitzwilliam! Should I be displeased that you care for me so much that you occasionally engage in foolish bouts of jealousy? I do not mean to say that I *like* the idea that you suffer, but what lady could be offended by the strong feelings which drove your distress?"

Gifting him with her devastating smile, she encouraged him to resume their ramble. "Come sir, let us leave that sorry subject; it has had more than it deserves of our time this morning! I have a mind to discuss another matter with you which arises from the same cause but which has been on my mind to question you about for some time."

At his enquiring look she continued. "It concerns our encounter at the Netherfield ball. I have *two* memories of the... scene between us after I reproached you so improperly about what I then understood to be your injustice to Mr Wickham."

"You have two memories? I will be glad to hear of them as I have some confusion of mind on the same subject. Did I, or did I not disclose what I knew of Wickham to you on that occasion?"

What he said aroused no little excitement in her breast, for *he* laboured under the very same confusion as had befuddled *her* mind since the morning following the ball. "Precisely, Fitzwilliam; You have spared me the necessity of introducing the nature of my muddle! I *recall your anger* at my impertinence in abusing you roundly about him during our dance together. What occurred afterwards diverges in *two* directions neither of which is compatible with the other!

"In one instance you refused to continue the subject, only suggesting coldly before we parted that I should *not attempt* to sketch your character as you feared the performance would reflect poorly on us both.

"*In the other memory* you took me out to the terrace, furiously insisting upon explaining to me the true state of affairs between yourself and Mr Wickham. You first censured me on my impropriety in listening to the personal business of one so slightly known to me - and then proceeded to tell me how you had known Mr Wickham for nearly all of your life, played together as boys, and later attended University together.

"I learned from you then of Wickham's treachery and lies!

"I was *horribly ashamed* while listening to your story - of how your father had paid for Wickham to have a gentleman's education and provided for him in his will while Wickham repaid his generosity with lies and dishonour; vicious habits and dissolute ways - all so obvious to you but unknown to your father.

"You told of Wickham's seductions and compromises of innocent young women; of gambling debts, and shopkeepers' claims paid by you - and how immediately after your father's death, Wickham announced that he had no intention of becoming a clergyman and was given three thousand pounds instead of the living your father had intended for him.

"The most horrendous, reprehensible, *shocking* piece was Wickham's very recent attempt to seduce and elope with your young sister! Georgiana was but fifteen years old!

That man, who had professed to me his *undying gratitude and loyalty to your father*, who had been reared *almost as a brother to you and your sister* could...!"

Lizzy stood still, fighting to control her breathing and the tears welling up in her eyes, horrified all over again at the scene and the information she had just described. "It is true, is not it? I know that it is all true but I do not know *which memory* is of something which actually occurred in the ballroom at Netherfield!

"No one has spoken to me of my outburst as *I* recall it, and I *did* have an *exceedingly vivid* dream that same night after the ball, in which I was..." She stopped, uncomfortable with telling him about her nightmare of being wed to Mr Collins!

Darcy listened in amazement! "I have been of two minds as when or if I had spoken to you of Wickham; and I too, had *vivid* dreams –*nightmares more like!* At least three separate times I endured the sheer torture of knowing that you were..." It would be unthinkably abhorrent to suggest such a thing as *Elizabeth in all of her elegant beauty and charm*, wedding the revolting Mr Collins!

"*Marrying Mr Collins?* It was precisely *that* nightmare scenario which *sent me scrambling up Oakham Mount that next day!*"

"*And me to ride feverishly to the same place!*"

"Where we met..."

"Where, to my everlasting joy, *we met*, Miss Elizabeth Bennet!"

Spotting them on her quest for a warmer wrap, Lizzy's sister was struck by the sight. Jane wondered what they could have been speaking of; they stood so long without moving. They appeared to be simply staring into one another's eyes.

Smiling her serene smile, Jane reflected with pleasure on the evidence of a flourishing attachment between her dearest sister and *her Charles'* dearest friend.

FORTY-ONE
A Shared Christmas at Longbourn

With the passage of a few more days, the preparations for the Bennets' departure had moved forward apace. Mr Collier and Mr Bennet had conscientiously ridden out to inspect the land or visit the tenants every day and spent several long evenings in the study, poring over Longbourn's accounts. The younger man was as well prepared to assume Mr Bennet's role as ever he could be. The family had made most of their adieus in the neighbourhood and the belongings they believed necessary to their plan were readied for transport.

Bingley was in Scotland still, not likely to return within the week.

Darcy had offered his carriage to carry some of the Bennets on their journey. He would escort them to their destination. He did not say so but it was plain to some that he would be easier when he knew that he and his own trusted men accompanied them on their travels.

Georgiana, who had been well occupied forming bonds of friendship with Miss Elizabeth and all of her sisters, must be returned to Town beforehand as no one but the servants would remain at Netherfield until Bingley's return. The Hursts had quietly slipped away to their family seat near Peterborough in Cambridgeshire two days after their brother and sister departed for Scotland.

Christmas almost slipped past before the busy occupants of Longbourn and Netherfield took note of the date, so preoccupied were they all in plans and worries and forming new alliances.

~&~

The Bennet household was in so much confusion that all agreed that a simple observance of the Holy Day would suffice for this Yuletide season.

On Christmas Eve, Georgiana happily joined Lydia and Kitty and Mary at decorating the main rooms of the house with holly and small branches from a giant fir which grew near Longbourn's stable yard. They found and hung the old "kissing bough", which had not been out of the attic within their memory! Indeed there was a deal of delighted surprise in finding it, buried as it was under some of the other decorations of bright ribbon and coloured glass ornaments stored away up there.

The Darcys arrived promptly in their carriage from Netherfield to share an early breakfast of steaming hot coffee, ham slices and buttered toast with the Bennet family.

The whole party walked through a cold, wet, and foggy morning to celebrate the Holy Day in the small chapel at Longbourn. Some in the party were especially amused to hear ancient Mr Rowland's pleasant, if slightly disconcerting, message of "Goodwill toward men and the Glory of the Resurrection"!

Chuckling together over the old clergyman's combining the messages of Christmas and Easter; they hurried back to the house through the damp and chilly day to find the cheery warmth of the Yule log blazing on the hearth and the wassail bowl already brimming with hot, spiced wine.

Dinner, which was served punctually at midday, was superb. Mrs Bennet had managed to arrange a delicious repast of roasted goose with currants, potatoes, and bread, Brussels sprouts, carrots in a thin buttery sauce, and plum pudding topped with a sprig of holly.

There were mince pies, and a Christmas cake for them to enjoy later in the afternoon with tea or coffee.

After the midday meal, Darcy and Lizzy kept company with Jane; talking of Bingley and of the future amid the bustle and swirl of the younger girls' Christmas diversions. The young ladies were happily entertained by performing carols and telling stories handed down from generations past.

With a gleam in his eye, Darcy fought to keep his lips from forming into a grin when he asked Elizabeth if she might kindly fetch him one more cup of wassail from the next room.

"I will be most pleased to do so, sir!" She replied merrily as she twirled around to go in the direction he had indicated.

As she approached the doorway through which she was to pass, Darcy darted stealthily after her so as to catch her as she stepped under the Kissing Bough the younger girls had surreptitiously hung whilst Elizabeth was distracted.

Just as he reached her she whirled around and reaching up to grasp his shoulders, rose up on her tiptoes and kissed him soundly while their sisters giggled appreciatively!

"Did you truly believe that I would not be prepared to avail myself of the opportunity to behave badly sir?"

"My dear Elizabeth!" breathed a startled Darcy, "If that was your idea of behaving badly, I believe that my opinion of misbehaviour has recently undergone a most profound transformation!"

Late in the afternoon, after their Christmas cake and other delectables had delighted them all long enough, came the time set aside for the exchange of gifts.

There were embroidered handkerchiefs and books, and colourful new ribbons. Each of the six young ladies was delighted to receive a simple golden locket engraved with her initials in an elegant script on the front and the date on the back.

For Mamá there was a lovely new shawl of the softest lamb's wool in a delicate pale blue with a border of darker blue binding. When Papá remarked that he could hardly expect her to go travelling around the countryside in winter without something to keep her warm, she coloured like a maiden and tears formed in her eyes!

Georgiana had received gifts of sheet music and a book of poetry from her brother earlier at Netherfield.

Darcy waited until everyone was occupied and then reached into a pocket in his waistcoat to withdraw something from it. He handed Lizzy a flat jeweller's box which was wrapped in gold foil, and waited eagerly for her to open it.

Lizzy hesitated, trying to read his expression but he only flashed his entrancingly dimpled smile and motioned for her to look.

Inside she found a delicate strand of seed pearls interspersed with tiny golden stars at two inch intervals. At either end was a cunning miniature hair comb of gold, crowned with miniscule pearls, meant to secure the ends of the piece when it was woven through an elegant coiffure.

Elizabeth's delight was tempered by her doubt that she ought to accept such an expensive gift from Mr Darcy when she had not yet accepted his offer of marriage. "It is lovely!" She murmured, her eyes glowing with pleasure at the sight. "But Fitzwilliam it must be far too fine a gift for propriety to condone!"

"Georgiana helped me choose it for you. It is from both of us but she said you would likely hesitate to accept it."

"Then she must agree that I ought not!"

"Not at all dear one, but she understands you well enough to realize that *you* might raise the question and require reassurance on the matter. Hence it is to be understood that it is a gift from us both."

"*That* smacks of *circumlocution* sir!"

"Elizabeth *please* allow me this *small* indulgence! Indeed it is *my selfish* desire to shower you with all manner of lovely adornments. Though I could search the world over and never find any article of metal and stone to match your exquisite beauty!"

"Very pretty words sir, but we are only courting; this is a gift appropriate for an engaged couple!"

Darcy's speaking look made her yearn to end the suspense between them and give him the answer he wished for at once. But she still held herself back; she would not allow herself to rush into this!

Darcy sensed her turmoil and comprehending that she was inclined to give him something, if not his heart's true desire, he entreated her to "Wear it for *my* pleasure dear heart, and you shall delight my very soul!"

Elizabeth was humbled, understanding that Darcy received as much pleasure from giving to her as she could ever have in the receiving.

She soon recovered herself sufficiently to say with a mischievous sparkle in her eyes, "I suppose I *ought* to have something to give you, my dear, but I have had little opportunity for shopping!"

"My dearest; I did not mean for you to feel...!" she stopped him with two fingers placed gently against his lips.

"Hush, Fitzwilliam, tis nothing so very grand, but I do have something for you!" and so speaking she reached into the pocket of her dress and brought out a small round box of some kind of dark, exotic wood. On the lid was a delicate carving of two figures in flowing robes, standing side by side, holding hands. "The box I had from my Uncle Gardiner, it came in one of his shipments from India. The contents are... a small token from me to you."

Handing the box to him, she bade him open it.

"I am... I have not the words to express how touched I am that you would think to give me a gift when...When you have had so much else to think of!" Darcy was a man who was well acquainted with the joy of giving. So seldom did he receive a gift from anyone other than his little sister, that he hardly knew how to do it.

"I promise you it is nothing very wonderful, Fitzwilliam, though I would have had it so if it were within my reach! Please open it my dear, and relieve me of my dread of your disappointment!"

"I could never be disappointed by a gift from you, Elizabeth, merely knowing you thought to give it to me would make any smallest thing a treasure!"

So saying Darcy removed the lid from the little box and stared in surprise at the contents. There lay a dainty lock of Elizabeth's hair, plaited in a miniature braid, elegantly tied with a petite yellow ribbon and gracefully coiled to fit in the box. At one end it was secured with the ribbon, at the other a few tiny curls were allowed their freedom to lend a hint of impertinence to the scene.

"Elizabeth; dearest loveliest Elizabeth; this is wonderful! I shall carry it with me always, this symbol of your beauty; this part of *you* to bear me company and keep me steady wherever I am! *Thank you my love, I shall treasure this gift always!*"

~&~

Darcy and Georgiana stayed in Hertfordshire one more day, ostensibly to recuperate from the Christmas revels. In truth they did not want to be parted from Lizzy and her family. On the twenty-seventh of December they finally tore themselves away.

Darcy would be away for three days, allowing him time to escort his sister to their home in London, meet with his solicitor and catch up with the most pressing of his extensive correspondence before his return on the 30th of December.

The entire party would set out for Nottinghamshire on the First day of the New Year of 1812 - the second day following Darcy's reappearance in Hertfordshire.

Elizabeth and her whole family stood on the front steps to watch Darcy's carriage bear him and Georgiana on their way at last to London after many fond farewells and a tender kiss on her hand from Fitzwilliam.

The parting was a reluctant one on all sides for there had grown a great fondness for Georgiana in the hearts of all, which she returned in kind. Although his popularity with her family had increased with better intelligence of him, Elizabeth and her father felt the loss of Darcy's company *most* acutely for their different reasons.

Mr Collier had gone away to collect his belongings and secretly to ensure that The Squyres Club was made ready for the Bennet family's occupancy. He would return on the same day as Mr Darcy.

Longbourn was a ferment of perturbation, ladies reconsidering which items they might need and which to do without, bustling about, checking to see for the fifth and sixth time that all was in readiness and their nightclothes, and the dresses and toiletry articles they would need for the next few days were the only items left out. Everyone except Mr Bennet had lists, and checked them against their progress every time an item left their hands. Their father, not uncharacteristically, remained closeted in his library for much of the day, emerging only occasionally for meals or to stand on the front steps, or walk 'round the perimeter of the house, surveying his ancestral estate one last time.

Elizabeth anticipated that upon Darcy's absenting himself for a few days, there would be some relief from the distraction of his and Georgiana's daily visits. She would be glad of the chance to put her mind wholeheartedly to the same round of tasks as her mother and sisters in preparation for the shift to Nottinghamshire. That respite which she had looked forward to with a confidence born of inexperience in the ways of love did not, in fact, come into being.

Instead of swiftly and rationally organizing her belongings, she found herself wasting much of her time simply handling them, moving them about while her mind was engaged in thinking of Darcy. She imagined him on the road to London, reading a book or chatting with Georgiana. Was he thinking of her? She wondered about his London home, was he there yet? Who would he visit, or dine with, or... Would he miss her? Was he well? There had been rain the day they left; did he and Georgiana arrive safely? How horrible if he were lying someplace along the road to London, or in his Town home, ill, perhaps gravely so – and she knew nothing of it! Would Georgiana write to inform her of it?

Such thoughts and others of their ilk passed through her head over and over until she stamped her foot in irritation and insisted to herself that all was well and Darcy would be with her in another day or two. She would see him and know that all of her anxieties had been the foolish imaginings of an utter corkbrain!

Lizzy forced her thoughts to the future. She wondered whether she would enjoy life at The Squyres Club. It might be diverting to live in an unfamiliar house in a neighbourhood unknown to her. There would be much to learn of the place, and new people to become acquainted with.

Feeling a little more settled; she began in earnest to sort and pack her things. She was *asserting* her common sense at last, behaving *rationally* again, until the question of Darcy's visits struck her forcibly. How was he to call upon her with any regularity? He could not live with them; Pemberley must be far away indeed – not even in the same county. What was the distance between Pemberley in Derbyshire and The Squyres Club in Nottinghamshire? She would ask her father the next time he showed his face.

She worried that even though the two counties were next to one another the distance between Pemberley itself and The Squyres Club might be as much as a day or more of travel. Once again her hands lost their purpose as Lizzy moped, fallen into her black boots over that *most important* constituent of her future life.

FORTY-TWO
Lady Catherine Erupts Upon the Scene

In the early afternoon of the second day of Darcy's trip to Town, a grand carriage swept up the drive and came to a halt before the main entryway at Longbourn.

Thankfully, Mrs Bennet and her two youngest daughters had gone to Meryton to visit the millinery for a few extra ribbons, for who knew what might be available in so remote a site as their destination!

Lizzy and Jane had been somewhat disconsolately working on their still unfinished samplers and exchanging commiserations now and then on the absence of Mr Bingley and Mr Darcy.

Mary was putting the opportunity to practice upon the pianoforte to good use.

Mr Bennet was in his library, ensconced in his favourite chair, sipping a glass of his best port. After all, there was no sense in saving it. He would not assume that he would be so fortunate as to survive being transplanted from his home and accustomed pursuits. His books he must leave behind, Mr Darcy assured him of the loan of anything he desired from the fabled library at Pemberley, but he *could* enjoy some of the excellent port he had laid by for special occasions.

Lizzy and Jane, therefore, were quite alone in the small parlour at the back of the house, as unaware of the visitor's arrival as everyone else.

Mrs Hill's agitation was extreme when she opened the door to announce "Lady Catherine de Bourgh to see Miss Elizabeth Bennet!"

Rudely brushing Mrs Hill aside, an august personage of middling height and iron grey curls, dressed in an overabundance of grandiosity, swept the room with an unfriendly eye and demanded imperiously "Which of you is Miss Elizabeth Bennet?"

Both young ladies had arisen upon her entrance, Jane's eyes widened in shock, Lizzy distractedly thinking what a peculiar notion of propriety that Lady had to arrive unannounced, demand admittance without the courtesy of invitation, and to behave so rudely in general in the home of a gentleman.

Ruminating thus, she stepped forward calmly to curtsy and reply. "I am she, Lady Catherine. This is my elder sister, Miss Jane Bennet."

Jane's smile was unwontedly timid as she curtsied and said "We are honoured to welcome you to our home, Lady Catherine."

Throwing a dismissive glance at Jane, Lady Catherine declared in trenchant accents that she wished to speak privately with Elizabeth; preferably far away from that dreadful pounding on a pianoforte!

Spotting the very woods of Lydia's infamy, she demanded more than requested Elizabeth to bear her company there.

By the harshness of her manner Elizabeth suspected the nature of Lady Catherine's 'visit', and preferring to spare Jane from any further discomfiture on her behalf, she readily agreed.

Stopping only to don her bonnet and pelisse, she picked up her gloves and accompanied Lady Catherine from the house.

With little in the nature of preamble that formidable Lady gave her to understand that the purpose for her visit was to scotch the rumour which she, Elizabeth, had put about that she was to marry Lady Catherine's own illustrious nephew, Mr Fitzwilliam Darcy. Elizabeth must give up any thought of such a scandalous thing, for she, Lady Catherine de Bourgh, would certainly put a stop to it!

"Are you engaged to him?" She demanded to know.

"You may ask questions of me, Lady Catherine, which I may *choose not* to answer, coming as they do from someone so wholly unconnected to me."

"I am almost Darcy's nearest relative and I have a *right* to know his concerns!"

"In that case you might apply *to him* for he has not given me leave to discuss his concerns with anyone. Respectfully I must dispute your right to know mine!"

"Answer me, Miss Elizabeth Bennet! Are you engaged to my nephew?"

"I am not, Lady Catherine."

"Do you promise then, not to enter into any such connection with him?"

"I certainly shall not."

"Do not dare to trifle with me young woman! Do you know who I am?" she snapped "I will not be put off!"

Seeing Elizabeth's half- humorous, half-sceptical look, she brought the main force of her arguments forward without delay or scruple of civility.

"I did not at first credit the story overmuch, but seeing your impertinent expression teaches me that I must disabuse your mind of illusion! You must cease indulging your fancy with girlish dreams at once for you are wholly ineligible to fill the position of Mistress of Pemberley! The very great disparity of your circumstances, the dictates of polished society, family expectations, and your own conscience must impress you with the impossibility of such a scandalously imprudent match!

"Darcy has every advantage of birth, rank and future. Weighed against his consequence in the world, your paltry existence cannot be too much disdained! An attachment between the family of a country gentleman of no consequence who married the daughter of a tradesman, and the Darcys an ancient and distinguished family with peers of the realm in their history and close connections, does not bear thinking of!"

"You cannot expect to wed a man who has been promised since their infancy to *my* daughter!" Lizzy showed no surprise at this pronouncement for Darcy had long since told her of his Aunt's insistence on a hopeful prediction made between herself and his own mother, which commitment neither he nor his father had ever looked upon with favour. She knew from him of Miss de Bourgh's ill-health and disinterest in being wed - to anyone.

Further incensed by Lizzy's failure to be impressed with the news of Darcy's betrothal to her daughter, Lady Catherine continued to expostulate with her.

Attending as well as she might to the repetitious tirade, Lizzy attempted to sketch that Lady's character. She wanted, in charity to Darcy's relative, to credit her with motives of affection and a true interest in his future happiness. But listening to the nature of her exclamations, she heard only an exhibition of Lady Catherine's obsession with family status and her daughter's rightful place at Pemberley.

She admitted to herself that Darcy's Aunt appeared to be every bit as full of unthinking arrogance and pomposity as she had been painted. How any of her family endured her highhanded ways, was a mystery to one not at all inclined to do so! Lizzy could almost pity the woman's lack of intelligence in the matter if she were not utterly and completely annoyed with her!

Lady Catherine must have read the expression in Elizabeth's eyes for she had approached very close to Elizabeth, apparently in an attempt to intimidate her. "Are you listening to me? I am not accustomed to such insolence! I am moved to dispense with any presence at civility! You *will* accept an accommodation of ten thousand pounds and renounce any connection between yourself and Darcy forever!"

Her stance, almost as if she held a *whip* in her hand, roused Elizabeth to speak.

"You may have no such recollection Lady Catherine, but I feel that I have met you before. I confess I am no more desirous of submitting to your will now than I have ever been!"

"Impertinent, provoking girl!" shouted Lady Catherine, who then, bent on annihilating the country nobody before her, became still more abusive, addressing her in the curtest terms. "You, Miss Elizabeth Bennet, are an incorrigible trollop driven by shameless avarice to use your arts and allurements to snare susceptible gentlemen! You have maneuvered and insinuated yourself into an infamous attachment with my nephew! I know all about you from my clergyman, Mr Collins!" throwing a scorching glance of disapprobation at her, she accused Elizabeth. "You, an accomplished flirt, little better than a *Corinth* have schemed to excite Darcy's admiration, to lure him in!"

"Unlike you, I am always actuated by a sincere interest in the strictures of propriety espoused by polished society! I am aghast at your appalling greed" announced Lady Catherine contemptuously, "You may think me without recourse in this detestable affair but I assure you that I shall know how to deal!"

Lizzy was far from unaffected by Lady Catherine's tirade. Her accusations against her, though absurd, affronted her far beyond anything she had felt before. Nevertheless she did her best to subdue her impulse to make a sharp retort. Her pride always rallied to govern her demeanour in any situation. She had a duty to herself, her family and to Darcy to behave with reserve. Elizabeth *would* be her own mistress despite the incredulity and gall swirling within her at the antics of Darcy's abominable relation.

Gathering herself to speak, Lizzy resolved to steer a course better calculated to promote a truce, in the future, between herself and the top-lofty Lady Catherine de Bourgh, than further enmity in the present.

"Your animated language notwithstanding, Lady Catherine, I believe we must both accord Mr Darcy the dignity of consulting his own wishes - and graciously accede to *his* determination in the matter. You may argue it as you will madam, however until his wishes may be consulted by either of us, the issue is outside of our reach. May I suggest that we converse in language befitting ladies of refinement?"

"Nonsense! I will *not be hushed* by your *presuming* to know how our family's wealth and consequence shall work on Darcy's considerations! You are to be pitied after all, for your thoughts and wishes are not of the least consequence! I shall take the necessary steps to amend the matter myself." Lady Catherine's rigid pride would not admit any acknowledgment of Lizzy's heroic attempt at civility.

"In that case Lady Catherine I beg you would excuse me for I have a strong disinclination to hear more of your spleen this afternoon. The accusations you make against me are so far from the truth as to be too ludicrous to truly offend except in your evident desire to injure and discompose me."

Directing a thoughtful gaze at the Lady's angry visage, Elizabeth could see no remedy to their contretemps but to be frank and allow the future to take care of itself.

"You have spoken your vile allegations, I suppose, with the design of leaving me disconsolate and cast down. I will only allow myself to bring some small measure of equipoise in closure to our *conversation,* if so civil a work may be applied to it, by telling you *this*: In most cases I do not like to disappoint anyone, Lady Catherine, but I find I cannot gratify your uncordiality in this one.

" I cannot contrive to suffer a diminution of my confidence or to be borne down by your ill-advised words of censure. I have weathered the experience to this moment and now choose to put an end to our fruitless discourse. You will excuse me, I am certain, to return to the house."

Elizabeth ignored lady Catherine's spluttering imprecations as she walked swiftly back to the house. She checked her stride only once, when she realized that there was a young woman sitting in Lady Catherine's carriage.

Noting Miss Anne de Bourgh's embarrassed expression; she nodded and smiled, meeting her eyes in an implicit acknowledgment of mutual understanding. She did not stop to speak, fearing that Lady Catherine's unflagging wrath might find its next object in her daughter if any cordiality appeared to exist between them. Lizzy contented herself with a quick curtsy as she passed Lady Catherine's imposing carriage, and entered her home, closing the door firmly behind her.

Once inside she went straight to Jane, who was privy to the same intelligence as she regarding Darcy's Aunt Catherine, from Mr Collins and from Mr Darcy, and knew of her appearance in Lizzy's nightmare after the Netherfield ball.

"Lizzy! Are you well dearest? You are quite flushed!" Although her curiosity pled for it, Jane would not ask about Lady Catherine's unexpected visit in case Lizzy wished to keep the story of their meeting private. The courtesy of her restraint, she soon found, was not at all required.

"You shall be amazed, Jane, *shocked*, at the arrogant effrontery of Lady Catherine de Bourgh! Why after an hour in her company I feel myself equal to anything!" Thereafter Lizzy shared with her sister as much detail of her bracing interview with Lady Catherine as her excited memory could provide.

"Had she addressed me in the manner I should expect of a Lady of her consequence, or in any civil manner at all, I believe that our encounter should have gone much differently, Jane! But as it was, I was hard-pressed to forbear giving as good as I got; I was so extremely disgusted with her charges against me! I had thought to laugh them aside at the beginning; it might have been more prudent and worlds more refined in me to do so, but she went on and on and by the end had set up my hackles so far that I could not oblige propriety so well."

"Well Lizzy," Jane responded when her sister had finished, "I am quite proud of you! I know your temper must have been sorely tried and I congratulate you that the set-down you gave her was done calmly and with as much self-possession as you could muster. I doubt that anyone would have been able to support such unconscionable, such *egregious* claims without saying more than did you! I am so very sorry that I did not insist on accompanying you. I did fear that she had only unkindness to offer but I hoped that you would not allow her to abuse you in such a dreadful fashion!"

"What *could you have done* Jane, more than suffer her insults and arrows alongside of me? I admit that I was deeply pained by her ugly opinions, but I was *glad* that you were spared the first-hand experience of them!"

"I should have been by your side; you ought not to have borne such an attack alone!"

"Perhaps it is for the best in an odd sort of way," said Lizzy musingly "that I know precisely how Fitzwilliam's family views our connection – *if* we should go so far as to form one."

"I hope that you do 'form a connection' for I should despise to see such an evil, ill-natured person win her point!" Her retort was surprisingly sharp and unforgiving for Jane!

Another moment's reflection brought forth "What excuse might she offer her nephew, if he should hear of this, I wonder?"

"I do not know. For my part I shall try to pass it off as a trivial matter, to avoid his and my own mortification! Indeed I refuse to grant her the power to unsettle things between Fitzwilliam and me – now they have come to admit of some tranquillity at last!"

"I apprehend that Lady Catherine is no match for you in a battle of wits, *or* the wisdom of love!"

Jane's little chuckle lifted the corners of Lizzy's mouth into a grin of satisfaction.

"I do believe that I ought to *thank* Lady Catherine for her visit today! Perhaps I shall write her a note of gratitude for *banishing all* of the insecurities and worries that have plagued me in Fitzwilliam's absence. Despite the hurt of her accusations I find myself *quite complacently* awaiting his return with nothing else to worry me but this infernally interminable preparation for our removal!"

After a moment of thoughtful silence, Jane replied in mock solemnity, "Might we next invite Lady Catherine to visit *me*?"

Mrs Bennet and the two youngest Bennets heard Lizzy's and Jane's merry laughter as they entered the house upon their return from Meryton.

"Whatever can they have to laugh at?" Their mother wondered aloud.

CHAPTER FORTY-THREE
Colonel Fitzwilliam Strides In

Lizzy awoke before dawn from pleasant dreams of Fitzwilliam on the morning of the day he was to return from London. She yawned and stretched like a cat, luxuriating in the cosy warmth of her bed, and smiled sleepily.

He would arrive today! Likely it would be toward late afternoon before she saw him. He would stop at Netherfield to refresh himself and make himself presentable before coming to call on her.

She thought of walking to Oakham Mount. This might be the last morning she would have time and cooperative weather enough to ramble through the countryside for many months to come.

She did not attempt to stifle her gasp as her toes curled in protest against the icy floor. Jane was sleeping soundly and was not disturbed by Lizzy's moving about early in the morning.

Rushing through her morning ablutions, she dressed quickly and brushed her hair into a simple coil at the nape of her neck. She was quite unconscious of the dainty tendrils of curl which began almost immediately to work themselves loose, framing her face most charmingly - to the delight of those who observed her.

Mayhap she would ask Hill or her daughter Annie to arrange it more fashionably for her later but it would do well enough for a brisk walk in the crisp morning air before breakfast. It would be very cold this morning so she donned her stout walking boots, a warm bonnet and a heavy woollen cape she had long ago cadged from her father for just such mornings as this.

The eastern sky was beginning to brighten as Lizzy stepped out through the door leading to the garden. She loved to take a few moments each day to observe the changes there as the seasons progressed. There would not be much to see at this time of year, most of the flowers and herbs being dormant from the frost, or the shrubs and trees cut back in anticipation of new growth in the spring.

She would not be at home to see it this year, when the new buds opened in all shades of yellow and white, and blue and lavender, and pink, orange and red - and the bright green leaves appeared overnight on branches and twigs. Bees would busy themselves among the flowers, gathering nectar for honey and ensuring a good production of fruits and berries and more flowers. And she would miss it all.

It felt odd to think of Longbourn without the Bennets, the seasons passing in all of their different forms of loveliness but no Bennets at Longbourn to be a part of it all. Never before had Lizzy imagined Longbourn without Bennets to live in it and love it.

Of course they had all heard their mother fret about the day, in a future so distant that it could not be taken seriously, when her dear Papá would be no more with them and Mr Collins would take their home for his own. It was a dreadful prophecy they had heard so often from their mother that it held little more reality than a child's tale of the bogeyman.

But this, this life-altering trek to an unknown, as yet unloved destination was real. And it was only a day or two away. And it was about to change Lizzy's perspective on her life, her home, her family – on everything, forever!

Instead of walking to Oakham Mount as she had planned, Lizzy chose to wander the grounds of Longbourn's park. She preferred to save the walk to Oakham Mount for a romantic walk with Fitzwilliam.

Rather she felt drawn to all of the nooks and crannies, the planting beds, the wooded copse with its walks so delightfully shady in summer, and her great cedar trunk festooned with upright branches just right for a child's handholds. All of her favourite haunts tugged at her to visit, to pay her respects, as it were, to her lifelong friends and companions. She had romped among them as a young child and dreamed and giggled and studied among them as a girl. They had witnessed her stormiest outbursts and her highest flights of fancy, her tears and her laughter – and a great many delightfully tranquil days in between.

Thus Lizzy remained near the house, enjoying and treasuring up her memories of each shrub and tree, turning of a pathway, places where she had played or used as a hiding place from her mother's unceasing flutters and foibles… It was a dreamy time and she was in no hurry to return to the practical side of her day.

But return she must. So she thought to make her way from the side of the house toward the front door. Before she came around the corner of the house to the front, she caught sight of her reflection in a window.

Oh dear! Mamá would *not* be best pleased at the sight of her unruly curls sliding out from under her bonnet and her hem six inches deep in mud! Her gown was mussed wrinkled and her gloves were smudged with dirt from her earthbound 'visits'. Lizzy decided she had better bypass the front door and enter through the back where she had come out… heavens, *several hours* earlier at least!

The sun was already high in the sky! It must be, as she judged by the look of it, nearly ten o'clock for certain!

"Pardon me miss," the unfamiliar male voice quite nearby gave her a start, halting her hitherto rapid progress toward the garden entrance at the far side of the house.

"Sir?" Elizabeth blinked in surprise at the handsome young man who came forward to stand before her. She guessed his age at thirty years, give or take. He was blonde and ruggedly handsome, tall but not as tall as Fitzwilliam – a colonel by the insignia on his uniform. His piercing blue eyes crinkled at the corners in a smile that seemed familiar – like someone... she could not quite place it.

"Fitzwilliam miss, Colonel Fitzwilliam to see Miss Elizabeth Bennet. This is Longbourn is it not? Are the family at home?"

"I beg your pardon sir? There must be some mistake, you are not Fitzwilliam! Oh!" Lizzy covered her mouth in embarrassment only to realize that she had just swept her dirty glove across her face, doubtless leaving a brown smear as she did so. "Excuse me, did you say Colonel Fitzwilliam? Then you must be Fitz... Mr Darcy's cousin!"

"I am he," said the man as he tried to cover his guffaw with a cough, "Colonel Richard Fitzwilliam, at your service, miss." With an elegant bow he asked "And *is* Miss Elizabeth Bennet at home then? I assume that this is *indeed* Longbourn!" His eyes twinkled with mirth as he looked her over with obvious approval.

Before she could answer, he went on to say "Tell me your name, pretty miss and I shall admire the dirt on your rosy cheeks!" His rather boyish charm was so engaging that she nearly returned his friendly grin with a forgiving one of her own had she not be-thought herself in time to stop it. But she did not respond in the manner he so confidently expected.

Lizzy *had* thought that her mortification was complete until she realized that he thought she must be a servant or, perhaps a dairymaid or some such!

Having no other recourse but to own the truth she drew herself up to her full five feet and two inches and gave a little huff of frustration as she told him more sternly than was her wont "*I* am Miss Elizabeth Bennet, *sir,* and if you will but apply at the door there, I shall go another way and greet you properly, in the house, directly I have freshened up."

"Oh lord! *You* are Miss Elizabeth Bennet? I must say I was expecting... er, never mind! Have I offended you *already* Miss Bennet? Darcy will *kill* me!" Eyes widened in shock, he pleaded with her. "Please tell me, Miss Bennet, how I may make amends for acting such a brute!" The Colonel was red with embarrassment himself, now; his sincere chagrin plainly writ on his features.

Lizzy's own embarrassment must succumb to her surprise at the depth of his. The irrepressible urge to laugh was not long in following. She tried not, but could not wholly stop a gurgle of mirth from escaping her lips. And then another, and another, until her chuckles brought a hesitant grin to his lips.

Seeing him restored to good humour, Lizzy said "Please do not make yourself uneasy sir, for you have provided me with a morning's worth of one of my favourite things – laughter! Oh, and you must call me Miss Elizabeth. My elder sister Jane is Miss Bennet!" Lizzy had got control of her chuckles, but her eyes were bright with merriment and she could not quite keep the smirk from her struggling countenance.

"Are you laughing at me, Miss Elizabeth?" His smile showed that he was pleased at the thought.

"Yes, at you, and at myself! I confess I did not at all like to be thus observed after a few hours' visiting my friends!" She giggled.

"Friends?" he queried with a look of confusion.

"Yes, my *garden* friends. The lovely walks, special retreats of mine, and the trees and shrubs and grottos of Longbourn. They are the scenes of my life to the present. You see our family is to go away... for many months and I found myself using the time of my customary morning walk to remember and say my adieus. Hence the wild and dirty condition of my clothing and, and everything." At last Lizzy was completely sobered – by the direction her thoughts had taken in explaining herself to Colonel Fitzwilliam.

"Miss Elizabeth, I cannot think of a worthier cause for your... er, disarray." He returned pleasantly "My military service has necessitated my removal from my ancestral home, as well as locales I had learned to think of as home, many times."

Seeing the woeful expression those thoughts had brought to her countenance, he added "Leaving those places for which I have a particular fondness has never been easy for me, I admit. However, I have found that many of my destinations, unfamiliar to me at first, soon earned their own place in my heart – not unlike the ones I had reluctantly left behind."

Lizzy regarded his face earnestly, questioning his sincerity. Was he sharing his true feelings, or was he merely using an easy facility to charm in order to win her good opinion? Wickham's handsome looks and easy manners made a fleeting appearance in her mind. But no, Fitzwilliam trusted him! Indeed she suspected that this colonel had played some part in Colonel Forster's disposition of the cad.

At last she spoke "You are very kind, Colonel Fitzwilliam. I thank you for your thoughtful words." Flashing a brilliant, if a bit smudgy, smile at him she added "And now I really must freshen up before my mother sees me, and you must go in and enjoy my parents' hospitality! Oh! And beware of my younger sisters! They are heart-smitten at the very sight of a man in uniform! And my mother – well you shall have to accept *her* as you find her I am afraid!"

Standing there open mouthed, Colonel Fitzwilliam watched Miss Elizabeth Bennet dash out of sight into the garden at the side of the house. He could plainly see why his obstinate cousin had finally fallen under the spell of love. She was most unusual – even in her dirt she was a bewitching lady indeed! He grinned to himself as he headed up the steps to the front door.

~&~

Just as she had predicted, Colonel Fitzwilliam was quite surrounded by her delighted family when she made her appearance in the breakfast room where all were gathered – including her long-suffering father.

She had been three-quarters of an hour at her toilette; a bath being advisable to remove so much mud and garden debris from her person.

"Good morning everyone; I pray you have all slept well - and Colonel, your travel was easy?"

Amid the morning salutations of the Bennet family, Colonel Fitzwilliam was momentarily speechless at the sight Miss Elizabeth presented, freshly coiffed and scrubbed clean of the remnants of her 'visiting' in the garden and 'round about. She was lovely in a woollen gown of soft buttery yellow with a delicate looping design of russet embroidery setting off its generous neckline and graceful skirt. The colours of her dress perfectly complimented her rich auburn hair and the golden flecks of light in her eyes. Eyes that he suddenly realized were dancing with delight at his stunned expression!

Gulping a little he rose and bowed to greet her. As soon as his addled wits allowed it, he thanked her, explained that he had only come from Netherfield where he had previously been invited to stay. Once Miss Elizabeth had joined him and her family, taking the empty seat to his right at the long breakfast table with her coffee and plate of buttered toast, he expressed his gratitude at the warm welcome he had received at Longbourn.

Their kind welcome, he remarked, was most appreciated on so tenuous an acquaintance as had been possible to accomplish in the short time since his arrival.

"No such thing, Colonel Fitzwilliam!" her mother struck in "You are known to us through your friend Mr Bingley, who is betrothed to my eldest daughter, Jane!"

Ah, so the beautiful Miss Bennet was taken as well!

"Yes Mamá and he is also cousin to Mr Darcy." Turning to Colonel Fitzwilliam she said with her sweet smile "You are most welcome among us on both accounts, sir."

Her father looked up with interest at this intelligence and asked whether he had seen his cousin recently.

"Yes sir, I saw him some weeks ago when I was called upon to do him a small service."

He saw Mr Bennet nod to himself and understood that the gentleman likely surmised that the object of his 'small service' was Wickham's fate.

Thinking it advisable to avoid the same reflections in the minds of the others, he continued "I had *hoped* to see Darcy at Netherfield when I arrived last evening. To my disappointment I was given to understand that he has been in London these past few days. Had I known, had the knocker been on the door, I should have seen him there!" Glancing quickly at Lizzy, he added with a smile meant for all in the room "But then I would have been denied the pleasure of making the acquaintance of your delightful family."

Mr Bennet soon excused himself, after inviting Colonel Fitzwilliam to join him in his library whenever he desired a respite from the attentions of his wife and daughters.

Taken aback by his bluntness, the good Colonel thanked Mr Bennet noncommittally once he saw that none of those same persons seemed surprised or discomfited to hear themselves spoken of thusly.

Mrs Bennet also left the room; she wished to speak to her housekeeper about something.

The young ladies chatted amiably among themselves and with their guest, quite happy to have the unanticipated diversion of improving their acquaintance with the good-looking colonel.

After an hour or so Colonel Fitzwilliam felt he could relinquish their pleasant attentions in favour of fulfilling the errand, as well as he might, which had been the original impetus for his seeking Darcy; first in Town, and failing to find him there, at Netherfield. Indeed, he thought to himself, Miss Elizabeth being the person most immediately affected, *she* was the person who should benefit first by his news.

Taking advantage of a moment when her younger sisters' attention was distracted by some discussion among themselves; he leaned slightly in her direction and spoke to her in a lowered voice "Miss Elizabeth I have... intelligence of some significance to yourself which I would discuss with you - in private if that is acceptable?"

An expression of alarm flickered in her eyes before she responded calmly "Of course, Colonel Fitzwilliam. Perhaps you might join me and my sister Jane in a small sitting room we often use when the two of us seek relief from the energetic bustle of our family."

Noting his hesitation at her mention of Jane, Lizzy continued firmly "I assure you sir that there is nothing you might speak of to me without her already being privy to the subject. We are very close and rely on each other's good sense when our own might be in danger of failure. In any event I certainly shall not meet with you in private without attending to the strictures of propriety. I would never give Fi... Mr Darcy any cause for concern could I avoid it. You are aware that we are courting?"

Colonel Fitzwilliam was pleased to hear her speak of it, and more pleased at her loyalty and care for his cousin's tender feelings. "I am aware to *my* regret that Darcy is here before me! I congratulate him on the excellence of his taste!" he said gallantly. "As to your arrangements for our meeting, I am content to trust your judgment of who shall hear of the matter I have on my mind. Please lead on, fair lady!" He winked.

"I believe, Colonel Fitzwilliam, that you must be an incorrigible flirt!" Pink with faintly embarrassed pleasure at his pleasant foolishness, she rose from her seat and with a subtle signal of her hand to Jane, led him from the room.

FORTY-FOUR
Darcy Storms In

"Do not *tell* me she has been at you *already*!" Utterly horrified to discover that he was too late to prevent or soften his Aunt Catherine de Bourgh's insult to his cousin's ladylove, Colonel Fitzwilliam was red with fury! "How dare she do this; Darcy is sure to cast her off and never look back – or worse!"

Elizabeth was more relieved than she cared to reveal before his cousin that *not all* of Mr Darcy's family shared Lady Catherine's opinions. She could not feel comfortable speaking of the abuse heaped on her by Mr Darcy's Aunt Catherine to anyone but Fitz... she *must* have another name for him! She had reverted to calling him Mr Darcy in her thoughts to reduce the confusion of using his cousin's surname now that the gentleman was a person known to her – and who *flirted* with her - as a moniker of familiarity for her suitor.

"I choose to think of it as a relatively trivial matter, to be glossed over with Mr Darcy, and dismissed from both of our minds as soon as may be. I will not have him distressed by the antics of a bitter old... *harridan!* I apologize, colonel! That shall be the last time you hear me speak disrespectfully of your relation!"

"You are too forgiving Miss Elizabeth! I assure you, Darcy will not be. We both know our Aunt Catherine too well to believe she was anything less than abominable to you in her sentiments no less than in her expression of them!"

"You were at the home of your parents when she spoke of her intention to visit me? I confess I am most interested to know their opinions on the matter!"

"My parents were as appalled as I to learn that Lady Catherine proposed to interfere in Darcy's privacy in such a way. Indeed my brother the Viscount, his new wife, and her parents, were present as well – they having been invited to dine. It was a mortifying scene, enacted perforce before all of them *and* several servants, for her Ladyship would not be hushed, nor would she restrain her vitriol until privacy could be obtained."

"How dreadful for them all!" cried Lizzy in sympathy for their disconcertion, "They must hate me already, without reference to my lack of dowry or connections!" Glancing at Jane, who sat next to her, she added "I could hardly blame Mr Darcy if he should find that so much trouble and strife in his family is too much to bear! Indeed I could not!"

Jane took her hand and leaning forward to look directly into her sister's troubled eyes, she reminded her determinedly "Why do not you tell Colonel Fitzwilliam of the great favour Lady Catherine has done you, my dearest? The banishment you told me of after her visit? I believe that he shall like to hear of it!"

Colonel Fitzwilliam had also leaned forward, eager to reassure Miss Elizabeth of his cousin's constancy. Darcy did not open his heart to many; when he did care deeply for someone, he never let them go. He never stopped caring for them and never stopped feeling the hurt of their loss or their injury to himself. Colonel Fitzwilliam had witnessed how Darcy took the very best care of his friends and family with an intensity of purpose far greater than anyone he had ever known.

Wickham's power to hurt Darcy owed its strength to the bonds formed in their boyhood which Darcy could never entirely dismiss from his heart. Colonel Fitzwilliam suspected that it was Darcy's own attachment as much as the tender feelings of the Bennet ladies which had motivated him to seek transportation for Wickham rather than the hangman's exit.

Jane's reminder brought a wide smile to Lizzy's face, her eyes lit up and she laughingly announced "Yes indeed! I have it in mind to *thank* Lady Catherine for her most helpful interference!"

Scarcely had she spoken those words before her glance caught the figure of Fitzwilliam Darcy halted just inside the sitting room door!

The state of his clothing and hair, and the faint shadow of his beard announced that he had come straight to Longbourn from London, not stopping at Netherfield to freshen up as Lizzy had expected.

Her delight at seeing him so much sooner than expected gave way under the shock and fury of his expression. It was obvious to all three of them that he had heard, and completely misinterpreted her words of determined courage and cheer.

"Fitz... Mr Darcy! I..." She started to exclaim in her relief and joy at his arrival.

"Darcy!" Colonel Fitzwilliam called out at the same time.

FORTY-FIVE
Each Must Trust the Other's Love

Darcy's near shout cut them both off. "What have we here, *Miss* Elizabeth? I am relegated to being Mr Darcy again? And you are grateful, *grateful* for my Aunt Catherine's interference! How *relieved* I am to hear it, having ridden my horse nearly to death in my anxious haste to *protect* you from it!

"And *you* Fitzwilliam! How long have *you* been here?"

"Mr Darcy, you mustn't…" Jane's voice trailed off, under the onslaught of his outburst.

"I *see* what is afoot here, and I, I should *call you out, Fitzwilliam!* I would *kill* any other man for less! I shall never forgive you, *either of you*, for this!"

Lizzy ran after him as he turned and stumbled angrily away. "Fitzwilliam, please! You are making a terrible mistake! Please stop, please do stop and listen to me!"

Darcy paused, supporting his shuddering body against the wall. "I care not to hear lies and pretexts, Elizabeth! Would that I could leave you now and not endure your false attempts to soothe away the truth!"

Lizzy held herself very still, refusing to give in to the agony she felt at his accusations, the terror of his desertion! Wrapping her arms around herself to steady her quaking heart, she considered what to do.

His rejection devastated her! After all of her uncertainties and hesitations, she knew that life without Darcy would be no life at all. The prospect of year after year after year to be endured without him by her side, without the love she had come to rely upon for the happiness of her future life, utterly and completely desolated her! But neither could she bear the idea of his cruelty when he was angry, when he distrusted her and ran from her!

Lizzy knew that she could let him go, let him believe what he would, cherish her pride and disdain his mistaken anger. A man who would think such horrid things of her was not worthy, after all, of her affection! But she loved him – and he was frightened.

He was frightened of losing her, she knew, and his anger arose from that fear. She thought of his constant devotion. Not only to herself, but she knew of the many ways he guided and supported his dear friend Mr Bingley in the management of his leased estate. And later in the heartbreak of his sister Caroline's madness, helping him find a safe haven for her – using his own family connections in her behalf. His own sister had shown in every way that she trusted and almost revered him – her fatherly older brother who had watched over her so tenderly and solicitously as she suffered the loss of her father, and the turmoil of her adolescence.

Moreover his handling of the Wickham disaster had been nothing short of magnificent!

Their courtship had been stormy, but the storms had been within *her* breast far more than his, her doubt must have been difficult for him to bear, yet how patient and kind he had been.

When she was deathly ill from the oil of pennyroyal he had stayed beside her, held her hand, and called her back from the abyss of her dream state. He had shown his love, his constancy, and the excellence of his character so many times and in so many ways!

It was time to make her choice! To own the truth, her choice had long been made; now it was time to make it *known*!

Colonel Fitzwilliam and Jane peered at them from the doorway of the sitting room but she silently waved them away, fearful that Darcy would bolt if he heard them coming.

He had not moved except to brush his hand across his eyes to wipe away the tears he could not bear for anyone to see. He stood, hunched over against the wall as if he could protect his heart from the world, or perhaps to contain his hurt in the prison of his body.

"Fitzwilliam," she said gently "I ask that you hear me out. If you continue, in spite of everything I tell you, to feel that you must leave me, then I shall not stand in your way – though you take my shattered heart with you when you go."

She saw him shift his position slightly at this. "I believe that once you know the truth you will feel a *deal of shame and regret* about your behaviour today. I wish you to know that I forgive you already. For I too, know the dreadful anguish of thinking my love in vain – you have taught it to me this day."

Darcy stiffened, straightening his body but did not look at her. "We must *both* learn to trust each other's *love*, Fitzwilliam. I know that neither of us could long withstand these doubts and tribulations between ourselves; we *cannot* if we are to find happiness together. I would not choose such a life, and I would not wish it for you. But I am convinced that we can overcome this, once and for all, if you are willing to try. Are you willing to hear me, Fitzwilliam?"

When Lizzy spoke of love, Darcy's head shot up and he slowly turned to look at her. He did not trust himself to speak; could not believe his ears, so he looked at her anxious face, her eyes brimming with unshed tears, her arms wrapped around her own body, holding it and protecting it from... him? From the pain *he* caused *her*?

He wanted to rush to her and enfold her in *his* arms, to draw comfort from her closeness and to give her all of the comfort she needed. He wanted to beg her forgiveness and tenderly kiss her tears away.

But he could not. He did not trust his weakness for her. Mayhap he was seeing more than she felt, hearing what she did not mean. She was correct about one thing, the doubt *was* unbearable. He would rather give her up than suffer it for a lifetime.

She was waiting for his answer; he could not keep her waiting any longer. "I do not understand!" he croaked in a voice roughened by emotion.

The corners of her mouth turned up in the faintest suggestion of her lovely smile "I know that you do not, will you walk with me out of doors and hear me, dearest?"

Taking a first step in her direction, he indicated that she should lead the way.

FORTY-SIX
Lizzy's Choice

"You were quite right, Elizabeth." said Darcy when he had learned the reason for Colonel Fitzwilliam's presence at Longbourn. "I *am deeply ashamed* of my behaviour toward my good cousin. I should *never* have entertained the very thought that he might be capable of such dastardly conduct, far less to accuse him of it to his face – *and* before you and Miss Bennet! *God in Heaven, I pray he will forgive me my stupidity!*"

Lizzy did not know the colonel enough to predict his reaction but she felt sufficiently confident to remark "He must love you a great deal to have gone to so much trouble for you! I doubt that he has endeared himself to his aunt, should she hear of it."

Darcy had other questions on his mind "Elizabeth, *why* did you call me '*Mr Darcy*' when I first arrived? I admit that I was *acutely pained* by your use of my formal name! *Why* did you address me as if we were not... we did not..."

"The reason is silly, I suppose, but innocent enough, *Fitzwilliam*. I had been teaching myself not to call you by your given name since I met your cousin, *Colonel Fitzwilliam*!"

Looking away, Lizzy said slowly "I found it... disconcerting to think of you, to use your name as a... as an acknowledgment of the intimacy between us two, while forming a new *platonic* friendship with a man, your own cousin, who must be called by his friends in the same manner."

Turning toward him and laying her hand on his arm, she finished "Indeed, I believe that I have heard *you* speak of him as 'Fitzwilliam' – just today in fact! I hoped that you and I could agree to another name by which I could call you in our private moments – William, perhaps? Or, Darcy would do, I imagine. Would you be willing, could I call you one of those, or another name of your preference?"

Darcy did not dare to move. He was so relieved to feel her touch and to know that hers was a gesture of trust, of reliance on his strength and constancy! He had to ask one more question before he would allow himself to be entirely free of the horrifying spectacle his mind had conjured up upon his seeing the intimate tableau, and hearing the words Elizabeth was speaking as he entered the sitting room where his cousin was…

Shaking his head to clear it of the unwanted memory, and forgetting to answer her question, he asked her. "Why, if my cousin did not… *why* Elizabeth, did you express your *gratitude* for my Aunt Catherine's 'helpful interference'? *That* was *outside* of being the very *worst* thing I could have heard in those circumstances!" Lizzy's hand fell to her side.

"Oh, it is just so… silly, the most *ridiculous* thing of all! You will soon know it is so!" Lizzy swayed a little with the tumult of emotion and the strain of her battle for their future together. To steady herself she reached for Darcy's arm again, this time he covered her hand with his own. It felt like another step toward home.

She adored the feeling of his holding her – even only with his hand, it was a warm, comforting sensation that she wished to experience for the rest of her life!

He gloried in the feel of her soft hand beneath his own, such a delicate hand to hold the whole of his happiness within its grasp – he wanted to hold it there, safe and warm, always!

"Please tell me your ridiculous story so that we may put this behind us forever, Elizabeth. I *need to make sense* of your words."

When Colonel Fitzwilliam told me of Lady Catherine's tirade about me at his parents' home, in front of his brother and new sister, and her family as well, I was *shocked* for them!

"I thought *they must hate* me for being the source of their mortification!

"For a moment I thought I could not blame you if... you were to decide *against* all of the trouble and strife I have caused in your family... This was only moments before you arrived.

"To help me out of my doldrums, Jane reminded me of something I had said after Lady Catherine's 'visit'. She asked me to tell it to your cousin – as a way of reinforcing my resolve I suspect.

"That was when you entered and heard me say 'I have it in mind to *thank* Lady Catherine for her most helpful interference!' That statement was by way of an introduction to the words I actually spoke to Jane after your aunt had gone on her way and Jane and I had been discussing the things she said to me – I confess I was quite... er, *incensed!*

"The words I spoke to Jane at that time were: 'I do believe that I ought to *thank* Lady Catherine for her visit today! Perhaps I shall write her a note of gratitude for *banishing all* of the insecurities and worries that have plagued me in Fitzwilliam's absence. Despite the hurt of her accusations I find myself *quite complacently* awaiting his return with nothing else to worry me but this infernally interminable preparation for our removal!'

"So you see, there was nothing so very bad in it after all!"

"You said that you have forgiven me already, Elizabeth, but I *cannot* believe it! I cannot *allow* it! You should spit in my eye and demand that I leave... but you said that I would take your heart with me if I should go? *How can you say so, when I have been so utterly abominable to you?*"

Darcy had sunk down onto their cedar log, pulling Lizzy into his lap as he went. He was holding her wrapped in his strong arms, so close to him that she could hear his voice rumble in his chest more than from his lips – which were expelling warm puffs of air as they moved tenderly over her hair, her forehead, her nose - everywhere he could reach while holding her crushed against his chest.

She had to struggle to free herself enough to answer him, but Lizzy was determined that he should hear her. His mood was too sombre; *he would* castigate himself too far. "I *do* forgive you, my heart! I said so did I not?"

"So you did dearest one, but *how* can you do it so easily?"

"I did not say it would be easy, sir," she said sternly, but with a tell-tale sparkle in her eyes "indeed I have *two demands* of you. I must have your fullest cooperation immediately before I can be in *perfect* charity with you!"

"I cannot imagine anything that you could ask of me, dearest, loveliest Elizabeth that I would not *leap* to accomplish with the *utmost* alacrity! Please say on, that I might the sooner feel your sweet approbation!" He rose to her playful bait with an effort; he would do anything to please her for he could *never* do enough to make amends for questioning her honour.

"How can I refuse so earnestly enthusiastic a speech; such pleasing sentiments and so prettily spoken? My first demand, sir, is to know by what name I am to call you! I did ask before, but you have given me no answer. I must have it now, before we converse any further!"

"That is too easy! I will answer to anything you choose to call me; anything at all so long as I may hear the melodious tones of *your* sweet voice!"

Seeing that she truly did want an answer from him he told her "Georgiana sometimes calls me 'William'. Perhaps she too, has disliked the confusion of my cousin's surname being the same as my given one. Will you like to call me William, my dearest?"

"I believe I *shall*, my William! And when I am sharing a moment like this one with you, I shall like to call you my *Sweet William!*" Lizzy turned her countenance up to his the better to show him the love shining in her bright eyes.

With a blissful groan, Darcy brought his lips to her upturned mouth in the kiss he had yearned to have, overcome with the feel of her enticing body in his arms and of her full velvety lips responding deliciously to his own.

Until that moment they had each been so caught up in the sharing of information and their emotional ordeal that the tantalizing sensations of holding each other and touching thus intimately had been almost ignored, almost but *not* entirely.

Relief at the increasing certainty of their complete reconciliation swelled their two hearts with the deep love they had for one another.

Lizzy's playfulness lightened their mood and allowed them to awaken to the flood of passion sweeping their bodies as he held her in his lap and kissed her tenderly.

Darcy's breath was short and his breeches uncomfortably snug when he lifted his lips from hers. "*Oh God, Elizabeth; my dearest Elizabeth, how I do love you!*" he whispered hoarsely over the thundering of his heart. "You had best make your *second* demand very soon for I cannot vouch for the continued *coherence* of my brain whilst I hold you close in my arms and kiss your *delectable* lips!"

Lizzy's answer was at first lost in his renewed, and quite emphatic attentions to her mouth, and face, and hair...*His hands stroking down her arms, her back and the bare skin of her neck took her breath and left her body trembling* with thrills and urges she had never imagined possible before!

Gasping from the lack of air and the stunning intensity of her responses to his *enthusiastic* ministrations to her person, Lizzy gently pushed him away enough to allow her to say more than a little breathlessly, "Yes! It *is time*, I think, to insist upon *my second demand*. Circumstances and my future happiness require it!" She appeared to hesitate, considering how best to proceed.

Darcy found himself holding his breath, as badly as he needed to replenish the air in his lungs, watching her face for a sign of her meaning. When she did not speak immediately, he was forced to release it in a burst of warm air sufficient to startle her to speech.

"I believe, sir, that you have a *question* to ask me." At his confused expression she flashed him a brilliant smile and said "Do you not have *a question of great importance* which you have wished to ask me? For if not I have been gravely mistaken, *misled I should say*, and shall be *vastly* disappointed!"

His eyes widened in shock when he finally understood, or hoped he understood, what she wanted him to do!

She confirmed his hopes instantly by adding "But *if so*, I now demand it of you that you *ask* your question this very minute for I *cannot abide* the least uncertainty between us any longer!"

The expression of love and delight in her sparkling eyes sent him precipitately into action. Never mind the delights of their mutual caresses, there would be a lifetime for that! This was the moment he had longed for! The words in his heart, which he had yearned since the day of their encounter on Oakham Mount to declare, were ready on his lips.

He rose from the cedar log with her in his arms and placed her carefully in the seat where they had been so cosy together. Dropping to one knee in front of her, he took her hands and pressed them against his wildly beating heart. His dark eyes turned almost black with the intensity of his gaze into hers.

Darcy's voice shook a little when he began but soon it grew strong and steady, reassured by the evidence glowing in her fine eyes as she returned his heartfelt gaze. "Miss Elizabeth Bennet you must allow me to tell you of the ardent and abiding love I feel for you, *have felt for you almost since first we met!* To my *enduring* shame, I did not, at first, welcome the feelings I soon developed for you; but I have long since learned to be *grateful beyond measure* that my heart knew at once what my head did not. You are *everything* that I ever could have dreamed, and *more than I imagined possible* to have for the companion and great love of my future life. Dearest, *dearest* Elizabeth, will you share my life and my love in holy matrimony? *Will* you *choose me* as your husband, to have and to hold forever? Will you consent to be my wife, Elizabeth?"

"Yes William, I will share your life and love, as I know you shall share mine. *You are my choice*, Sweet William, so yes; *I do consent to be your wife* - with all of my heart, *yes*!"

With tears of joy in his eyes, Darcy brought a small jeweller's box from a pocket in his waistcoat and opened it to reveal a delicate gold filigree ring set with an exquisite multifaceted yellow diamond encircled by dainty rubies. The effect was a dazzling show of brilliance and colour.

Lizzy held her breath, staring at the magnificent ring, afraid to think such a glorious thing should belong to her! "Oh William!" She breathed at last, "this is... beautiful beyond anything I have ever imagined! I dare not... it is too much!"

When she looked up to protest such an extravagant ring, the tenderness in his dark eyes held her. Lizzy forgot everything else in the depth of his devotion.

"I am so glad you like it, my dearest. It was my mother's engagement ring, passed down from my father's mother. Each new bridegroom has made some small alteration to make it uniquely his own gift to his betrothed. My father's was the filigree in the setting. My addition is the ring of rubies; they made me think of the auburn glint in your hair when the sunlight catches it just so. It is my good luck that the glow of the yellow diamond echoes the golden flecks in your fine eyes. Will you wear it for me my love?"

At her speechless nod, he took the ring from the box and slid it onto the third finger of her left hand. "There! Now all of the world shall know that we belong to each other!"

FORTY-SEVEN
Forgiveness and Blessings

The lovers stayed a while longer in their hidden glen, blissfully engaged in the exchange of endearments and assurances in more than one of the languages of romantic love.

Eventually, they recalled the manner in which they had departed the house. Matters of an exceedingly serious nature remained sadly in want of resolution betwixt Darcy and Colonel Fitzwilliam.

"Jane must be feeling *dreadfully* worried and neglected as well!" Elizabeth mused.

"I admit to some trepidation in meeting my cousin again." Darcy replied gravely. "He is reputed to be quite a fierce warrior when he is not charming the smiles out of lovely young ladies! I fear he will not easily overlook the insult I offered him in my outrageous and *highly* regretted burst of spleen!"

Lizzy was surprised to hear it. Colonel Fitzwilliam seemed everything amiable and kind. The thought of his affable flirtation kept her silent, however, as the memory warmed her cheeks with discomfort. William would *not* enjoy hearing intelligence of *that*!

At last she said "Whatever awaits us, I suppose that since we cannot avoid it, we may as well meet it straight-on."

They had been strolling slowly toward Lizzy's preferred entry from the garden, holding hands for encouragement – and because to each, the other's touch felt so very good!

Lizzy, true to her nature, sought to inject a little humour into Darcy's grave looks. "I do hope the colonel allows you to live long enough to apply to my father for my hand!"

"I shall insist on it, my love! He is too gallant to deprive you of an official engagement between us!" Darcy's countenance softened and his eyes warmed at the prospect of claiming her as his own before the world.

They had no difficulty in discovering the whereabouts of Colonel Fitzwilliam, or of *any* of Lizzy's sisters.

The whole party was taking tea in the front sitting room, laughing over one of that gentleman's stories of life in the military!

"Well cousin," he boomed when he spied them hesitating at the door, "has the thunderstorm passed and the sun come out once more?"

Jane looked around at Elizabeth hopefully. The sisters exchanged a private smile of information shared and received with the upturn of their lips.

Chuckling at Darcy's flummoxed expression and his own happy turn of phrase; he rose and excused himself to the ladies. "I suspect a private interview must be had betwixt us ere the ill-weather of the morning can be forgot. Come Darcy," with a wink at Elizabeth "now you may show *me* the garden!"

~&~

The two cousins spent less than an hour in consultation with each other in the garden. They had a close bond of friendship born of shared experience and family.

Although Colonel Fitzwilliam's friendly manners and unflappable temperament differed sharply from Darcy's more solemn and formal mien, the two were well-matched in character and understanding. Thus it took more time to ease his cousin's harsh self-castigation over his unfortunate outburst than it had for Colonel Fitzwilliam to brush it aside as the product of an overworked brain – and heart!

"I suspect, Darcy, that you must be the silliest puppy in the county! Who would *not* be severely distressed, knowing our Aunt's predilection for *rampant* imposition of her selfish and *unthinking* arrogance wherever she goes? I would *dearly* love to know what she *did* say to Miss Elizabeth – and how that young lady bore her undoubtedly *adamant* attempts at coercion!"

'Puppy' indeed! Darcy dismissed his cousin's cheek, he *deserved* it, he supposed. "As would I; and I believe we *must* know all, for Lady Catherine has not done with us, I am sure – although I fear I shall be done with her before this is over! I am surprised that you have not heard it from Elizabeth already."

"No, our discourse had not got that far. Indeed I had the impression that she would not speak of it more than to acknowledge the event. Perhaps she did not wish to repeat whatever vile words Lady Catherine used against her to me, a relative stranger.

"That is possible. She would be mortified to have you, or even me, know the particulars of any accusations our aunt may have made against her, in her determination to frighten Elizabeth away from me."

Smirking at the vision that formed itself in his mind at the thought, Darcy told his cousin, "Little does Aunt Catherine know that Miss Elizabeth Bennet does not intimidate so easily and I thank God for it!"

"Indeed!" Colonel Fitzwilliam answered him. "Then I challenge you to convince your lady to disclose the content of their interview!"

"I certainly shall try; but first I am compelled to seek an audience with Mr Bennet at his earliest convenience!"

"I wish you good luck, cousin!" The colonel clapped Darcy on the back and walked off to re-join the young ladies.

~&~

Darcy peered at Mr Bennet from the door in response to his call to "Come!"

"If I may have a moment of your time, Mr Bennet?"

"Most assuredly! What else am I to do with my time but sit here and brood? Mr Collier returned last evening and I could find no cause to refuse his generous offer to begin managing Longbourn this morning. Mr Collier will lodge with one of my more prosperous tenants until we quit the house. He seems quite prepared to assume the task with all due diligence! Come right in, sir. I shall be pleased to have something useful to do! You do have a request to make of me, have you not?"

"I... Yes sir!"

"Well, it seems you have managed to convince my Lizzy at last!" Mr Bennet remarked with a glint of laughter in his eyes when a by now very dishevelled Darcy presented himself in his library. "She must have led you a very merry chase for you to appear so... unusually uh, unkempt!"

"Indeed sir, I am delighted to tell you that my successful suit required neither the fool nor the saint you mentioned before to win the great gift of Miss Elizabeth's heart; only blind luck it would seem!

"I offer my sincere apologies for my appearance Mr Bennet. I assure you that it means no disrespect to yourself or your family! I had a rather *wild* ride from London earlier because of my aunt, and upon coming directly to Longbourn events unfolded at such a rapid pace and with so much of pathos to them that I have scarcely had a thought to spend on the *most lamentable* condition in which I stand before you. I beg you will excuse it on this one occasion sir. I shall amend the matter at once, after I have spoken with you."

Pausing only for breath, Darcy could not resist the urge to blurt his question. "And now sir, *will* you consent to my marriage to Miss Elizabeth and *shall you grant us your blessing sir?*"

"Young man I have been *prepared* to give my consent and blessing to a union between you and my Lizzy almost since the day your courtship began; it being quite plain to me how things would be in the end. I *do* give my consent and blessing now, son, and welcome you to the family with pleasure!"

Darcy felt all the joy that was to be expected under the highly auspicious circumstances of his formal betrothal to the love of his life, and the particular approbation shown in Mr Bennet's addressing him so quickly as 'son'.

"*Thank you sir*; I promise to do everything in my power to ensure Elizabeth's happiness! It shall always be my fervent wish and heartfelt delight to dedicate my life, everything that I am, and everything that I have, to her happiness and contentment."

"So you have said, sir, and I trust in you to do so." The gentlemen rose for a hearty handshake but before Darcy could excuse himself; his new fiancé's father waved him to re-take his seat.

"Fixing him with a determined eye, the older gentleman queried him "I *am* confused by one thing you mentioned Mr Darcy. What exactly did your aunt have to do with your '*wild* ride from London'?"

FORTY-EIGHT
Bingley, Just In Time

Having the gist of the matter from Darcy, and hearing from him that Elizabeth had not told anyone but Jane of Lady Catherine's vicious attack on her the day before, Mr Bennet considered what must be done.

At length he said "Our family has benefitted from a recent tradition of discussing matters which concern us all in a family meeting. The practice has had some highly salutary effects in some unexpected ways. I believe this matter is such a one as must be treated thus.

"Lizzy must air her grievances against your aunt in order to let them go, or at least the injury she must feel most acutely. She is a loving, compassionate young woman and it cannot but pain her to the quick to discover herself so objectionable to your family."

At Darcy's nod of agreement, he continued "Her sisters may benefit from the opportunity to gain a wider knowledge of the goings-on in the world and to draw closer to Lizzy in understanding. Indeed, I believe that both Kitty and Lydia have shown great promise already as a result of our family meetings – Mary as well.

"My Fanny has made a start, quite recently, on comprehending her own role in the consequences which have already befallen our younger daughters. I have hopes that she will learn to make an effort to curb them and to teach them better conduct than they have shown us in the past.

"You and Colonel Fitzwilliam have your own reason, I am sure to know enough about your aunt's conduct to act accordingly should action be necessary."

Leaning back in his chair, Mr Bennet signalled the end of his arguments in favour of a family meeting; adding only "So if you and your cousin agree, sir, we shall have an *extended family* meeting, thereby allowing my daughter the relief of having to tell her unhappy tale only once and providing you both with the intelligence you require."

"Thank you Mr Bennet, I believe that I may speak for my cousin in saying we shall both be honoured to be included as family in your meeting.

"When do you propose to convene us sir?"

It being quite late in the day, it was decided between them that the meeting would occur after supper. Darcy and his cousin were invited to sup with the Bennets after a short trip to Netherfield to bathe and change their clothes. Before he could leave, Darcy must have a moment to share their good news with his beloved. He found her with Jane, in their small sitting room where they had evidently elected to discuss the events of the day away from the others.

"No dearest, do not disturb yourself to get up for I am off to make myself presentable before I return to you. I wish only to share with you the *agree*able visit I had with your father!"

Elizabeth's elation at his thinly veiled message would not allow her to stay seated. She jumped up and rushed to embrace him, heedless of her sister Jane's presence "Oh William! I am so shockingly happy!" He was not surprised to see tears of joy in her eyes, no more than she was to observe the same phenomenon in his.

After a few moments in which they received Jane's jubilant congratulations, and welcome to her soon-to-be brother, he took his leave of them and went to collect his cousin.

They would return in an hour, more or less.

~&~

While *her* William was in with their father, Lizzy talked with her dear confidante about the reconciliation with her beloved in the garden.

"You know, it was quite cold, there may have been frost on the ground! But I was unaware of it at the time!" She finished.

"I cannot be surprised to hear it, after all you have told me!" Jane's smile, which was as serene as always, was a confirmation to her younger sister of her own trust in the goodness of (most) others and in her belief that things would work out well in the end.

"I do think that you are correct dearest, that Mr Darcy's extreme reaction to what he heard you say was made the worse by his fear of losing you. It does seem that where his heart is concerned, his otherwise healthy self-assurance does not follow. Perhaps it is because he lost his mother so tragically and early in his life – I believe you said he was only ten years of age at the time of his mother's passing?"

Lizzy nodded, listening to Jane's thoughts on the matter of William's singular insecurity regarding her. "And he was only in his early twenties when his father was taken!"

Jane's countenance showed her deep sympathy for her friend. "I believe that you will find that he has strong reactions to *any* threat to those whom he carries in his heart. He dreads the possibility of suffering another loss.

"It may be the cause of his aloof conduct in the company of strangers as well. I have another conjecture Lizzy, you shall judge its accuracy with the passage of time; that if your William feels so vehemently for the safety and well-being of those to whom he is close, one cannot wonder at his need to limit their numbers in some way. Else he would exhaust himself over the vicissitudes of too many lives!"

"I think you may be right Jane. I shall certainly know how to act when we are in company and I see him donning his haughty Darcy-the-Master-of-Pemberley look!"

"I am so happy that he and my Charles are such excellent friends! It is a puzzle, is it not, how such diverse personalities can have found each other in the first instance?"

"On that question, I have ruminated a great deal. I could not comprehend how an amiable man of easy manners and good nature whom I like very much, could be friend to an elegant, haughty *un*easy man whom I had taken in such dislike! My former misjudgements aside the answer, I think, is quite simple. William and your Charles are each attracted to, and strengthened by that in the other which they are less confident of in themselves. Where one is easy in company and has sweetness of temper and engaging manners, the other has the ability and experience to command a large estate with judgment, fairness and firmness of purpose and so on and so forth.

"They are *both men of excellent understanding and character, devoted to their loved ones*; those are the common ingredients that bind the rest together."

"I miss him so terribly Lizzy! If I had it to do over again, I sincerely doubt whether I would insist that he escort Caroline to Scotland!"

"Jane, I am so sorry! How you must be suffering and all I have done is talk about my own situation! You have been so brave, enduring so much with never a complaint. Oh my dear, I do apologize!"

And so they two settled in to a satisfying session of sisterly confidences with the most particular aim of relieving Jane's backlog of distress in the absence of her dearest Charles. Some angst over the impending removal from Longbourn was allowed its due when they could spare the time to think of it.

They only thought to freshen up for an early supper when William emerged from Mr Bennet's library to speak to Lizzy and excuse himself to do the same.

~&~

With Darcy and Colonel Fitzwilliam came an exhausted but exultant Charles Bingley when they returned to join the Bennets at supper. That young man had ridden nearly day and night to return to his dear love before she and her family would have left Longbourn.

Jane was nearly beside herself; she could not imagine that she deserved such happiness! There was a great deal of hubbub, congratulations due and overdue to the two betrothed couples.

Mr Bingley was quite touched at his reception among them all; Lydia and Kitty conducted themselves more demurely and with a degree of sincere courtesy he had never experienced from them before. Mary unbent herself to give her solemn congratulations and welcome to the family as well!

He could not be sure, as he truly did not pay much heed to such things, but Mrs Bennet's effusions might be expressed a tad less raucously than he remembered as well. Most delightful of all was the sight, and feel, of Jane at his side. She could not leave him for a moment it seemed and *that* was exceedingly, exceptionally, wonderfully and perfectly pleasing to him!

The two of them exchanged what they could of news and information about his travels and Caroline's situation, the Bennet's looming removal and her worries over missing his return.

"But dearest, Darcy sent a rider to alert me to the plan as soon as it was certain! That is how I came to hasten back in such a rush! I *practically threw* Caroline from the carriage and turned around the next moment to *hurry back to you!* As it was I left the carriage to follow me and rode horse-back these last three days and part of each night. I shall not be able to walk properly *for a week* at least!" A proud and happy grin belied the severity of his claim.

Mr Bennet had made his family aware of the meeting he planned for after supper; they looked to him for a signal as the meal came to an end.

Bingley had, of course, been brought up to date by Darcy during their carriage ride from Netherfield.

Mr Bennet cleared his throat, if everyone has had their fill; I suggest we adjourn to the sitting room. We shall ask for tea and some stronger refreshments to be provided to us there.

FORTY-NINE
Another, Expanded Family Meeting

"This family may suffer from the odd bit of foolish impropriety; one might even call it something worse, taken in a certain light. But I, for one, have learned that we stand strong when we stand in unity with one another. If we are to be family, and it appears that *we are* indeed, then I *suggest every one of us must feel respected and respectful of the others*. We should act only in a manner that is honest and just, and wherever it is possible to seek to include the good of each one of us along with our own. I feel I need not go on in this vein for I believe that everyone has heard or knows of the agreements we have made, and kept quite admirably I might add, since certain events late last November. Suffice it to say that we guard our family's privacy and reputation by the circumspection of our conduct and the caution of our speech.

"We have had a new development. One which although it affected Lizzy most directly and harshly, is of significance to us all for various reasons – some of which will become apparent, I hope, as she tells us of her visit from Mr Darcy's and Colonel Fitzwilliam's Aunt, Lady Catherine de Bourgh."

Everyone turned expectantly to Lizzy, who had lost an argument earlier with her father not to speak of it. Although she still felt he was wrong to insist upon it, she would *not* be wiser than her father.

Lizzy now sat facing her family, flanked on one side by Jane and the other by Darcy - each of them holding one of her hands.

"You should all know," she began slowly in a voice so low that her sisters seated farther away from her held their breath to hear. "You should all know that I do not want to do this. I begged Papá to allow me to spare you, and spare myself the retelling of it for it is most unpleasant.

"I dearly wished to pass it off as only a matter of little importance, trivial and not to be dwelt upon." She glanced briefly at Darcy, who met her eyes with a tender upturn at the corners of his mouth. "I did not wish to allow the vile things that were said to me to cause a rupture... to unsettle things between me and Mr Darcy. I did not plan for him to hear of it at all! But things have not turned out as I hoped and I suppose there must be good reasons for Papá to insist so I shall do my best, as mortifying as it shall be to repeat some of her words."

Lizzy turned her head to look at her mother, whose expression was unreadable, and then shifted her shoulders and began.

"Lady Catherine arrived unannounced and uninvited when Jane and I were in the sitting room alone. Mamá and our youngest sisters were gone to Meryton. Mary was practicing on the pianoforte, I believe, and Papá was out as well visiting a tenant as I recall." Lizzy did not wish to remind her father that he had been comfortably ensconced in his library with a glass of port while his favourite daughter was enduring the painful and mortifying ordeal of Lady Catherine's scathing rancour.

"Immediately she was admitted, Lady Catherine refused any civility and declared in the harshest manner that she wished to speak privately with me. She *demanded* I bear her company in the little wood to the side of the house, beyond the cedar log.

"I agreed and accompanied Lady Catherine from the house.

"Very abruptly Lady Catherine told me that the purpose for her visit was to' scotch the rumour' which she claimed I had put about that I was to marry her nephew, Mr Fitzwilliam Darcy. I must give up any thought of such a scandalous thing, she said, for she would certainly put a stop to it. She then demanded to know whether I was engaged to him.

"Offended by her presumption and her manner, I answered that she might ask questions of me which I might *choose not* to answer as she was someone wholly unconnected to me. But she said that as almost his nearest relative she had a right to know Mr Darcy's concerns. So when she demanded again to know whether I was engaged to him, I told her that I was not.

"Next she wanted me to promise not to enter into any such connection with him which I refused to do.

"Lady Catherine accused me of trifling with her and announced her... um, her consequence and that she would not be put off. I suppose that if I had appeared to be impressed by her importance in the world things might have gone better. I said nothing but I must have shown the humour and scepticism I felt , for then she brought the main force of her arguments forward without delay or any scruple of civility.

"She claimed that she had not believed the story at first but that seeing my impertinent expression gave her cause *to disabuse my mind of illusion*; t I must cease indulging my fancy with girlish dreams for I was *wholly ineligible* to fill the position of Mistress of Pemberley. She expounded upon the very great disparity of our circumstances, the dictates of polished society, family expectations, and my own conscience to impress me with the impossibility of such a *scandalously imprudent match*."

Lizzy paused, hearing gasps and quiet exclamations of disgust around the room. Looking again at her mother, she sent her a gentle smile which appeared to surprise that lady quite a bit. But Lizzy had been reflecting of late on the much worse sort of mother she might have had the ill-luck to have!

Darcy was holding her hand very tightly. She wriggled her fingers a little and smiled at him to remind him to loosen his grip before she took up her story once more.

"Lady Catherine reminded me that Mr Darcy has every advantage of birth, rank and future. With scorn and disdain she weighed his consequence in the world as the heir to an *ancient and distinguished family* with peers of the realm in their history and close connections, against the daughter of a *country gentleman of no consequence, who married the daughter of a tradesman.*

I am *sorry* to repeat these things to you Mamá and Papá. I pray the hearing of it is worth the mortification included therein.

"I was not at all surprised to hear Lady Catherine claim that I could not expect to wed a man who had been promised since their infancy to *her* daughter for Mr Darcy had told me of his aunt's insistence on a commitment he had neither ever consented to nor looked upon with favour. In any event she had far worse to say to me.

When I did not react as she expected she was still more incensed and approached very close to me - apparently meaning to intimidate me. She told me that she *was not* accustomed to *insolence* and would now dispense with any *pretence* at civility. *I had not been aware that anything of civility had yet been shown!*

I was indeed shocked and disgusted when she *demanded* that I accept an accommodation of ten thousand pounds to renounce any connection between myself and Mr Darcy forever. It was as if in her eyes human beings could be bought and sold for hard currency!

"There was something about her stance; almost as if she held a *whip* in her hand, which brought back a memory, it was of a nightmare I had before... A nightmare I had the night after the Netherfield ball. It was of her and... you all remember how Mr Collins always made her sound so grand and imperious? Well she was dreadful in the dream and she did try to use a whip on me so I suppose it was that nightmare which forced me to speak.

"You may have no such recollection Lady Catherine, I said, but I feel that I have met you before. I confess I am no more desirous of submitting to your will now than I have ever been!"

"She shouted at me then, although she had not been using any *pleasant* tones before! I was an *impertinent, provoking* girl. But that was nothing to her next words! She called me an *incorrigible trollop* driven by *shameless avarice* to use my *arts and allurements to snare susceptible gentlemen!* She had it from *her clergyman, Mr Collins* that I had *maneuvered and insinuated myself* into an infamous attachment with her nephew! Then she tried to burn me up with her glare and called me more ugly names. The worst was that I was *little better than a Corinth, a schemer, and driven by greed.*

"She threatened that if I did not do as she wished that she would 'know how to deal.' I am not sure what she meant but I took it as a threat.

"I hesitated; deeply offended by her ugly demands and by her vile words but I did not wish to make the sharp retort which immediately rose to my lips! I tried to remember my duty to my family and myself and to Mr Darcy to behave with reserve.

I briefly *resolved* to steer a course better calculated to *promote a truce*, in the future, than further enmity in the present. I regret to say that I *was not successful* at modifying my own demeanour much less hers!

"I did try to get Lady Catherine to govern herself. I remarked that her animated language did not alter the fact that we must *both* accord Mr Darcy the dignity of consulting his *own* wishes and that without *knowing his wishes* neither of us had any actual say in the matter.

"I *ought to have been more conciliatory* for Mr Darcy's sake but I confess that I was too incensed to do more than suggest that we converse in language befitting ladies of refinement!

"She *would not* hear me. *She* would not be hushed, but called me *pitiable* because *I could not know* how his family's wealth and consequence would affect Mr Darcy's considerations.

Lady Catherine announced that unless Mr Darcy remembered himself instantly, *she* intended to take the necessary steps to amend the matter herself. I am not sure what she has the power to amend but her manner was imposing and autocratic. Her very self-assurance was both a challenge and a threat to me."

Lizzy's recitation slowed as she concentrated, trying to remember as clearly as possible what she had said to Darcy's Aunt Catherine de Bourgh.

"I could do no more and bear no more so I answered her thus 'In that case Lady Catherine I beg you would excuse me for I have a strong disinclination to hear more of your spleen this afternoon. The accusations you make against me are so far from the truth as to be *too ludicrous* to truly offend *except in your evident desire to injure and discompose me*. You have spoken your vile allegations, I suppose, with the design of leaving me disconsolate and cast down.' I was quite determined that this person who had come seeking to frighten me, should not succeed in intimidating me in the least. I am stubborn that way you know." She glanced at Mr Darcy with a grim smile.

"My desire to make this clear to Lady Catherine won out over my duty to respect my elder and a Lady! I felt compelled to tell her 'I shall only allow myself to bring some small measure of equipoise in closure to our *conversation,* if so civil a word may be applied to it, by telling you *this*:

"'In most cases I do not like to disappoint anyone, Lady Catherine, but I find I cannot gratify your uncordiality in this one. I cannot contrive to suffer a diminution of my confidence or to be borne down by your ill-advised words of censure. I have weathered the experience to this moment and now choose to put an end to our fruitless discourse.' I then excused myself to return to the house.

"As I walked back to the house, I realized that there was a young woman sitting in Lady Catherine's carriage. I believed it to be Miss Anne de Bourgh. I nodded and smiled to her with a curtsey as I passed but did not stop to speak. I thought that Lady Catherine might resent it and I was not wishing to bring any hardship on her daughter. That was the end of it; I went into the house and talked with Jane about what had happened. I truly wished to laugh the entire episode aside; I even joked about thanking Lady Catherine for her visit as it banished all of my... other worries so effectively!"

Darcy and Jane were both gripping her hands so tightly she had to pull them away to restore the circulation to them!

Her first thought was of how William would react to his aunt's extreme disapprobation of their connection. She wished he had not heard of his Aunt's visit at all; she dreaded his being pained by any connection to herself! She turned to him nervously, to see his expression.

To her shock and chagrin he did not look angry so much as crushed! Why should he look defeated? Unless her recital of his aunt's words had had the effect of reminding him of all of the reasons why he should *not* marry her? "I am sorry" she whispered "Has she..."

In the next instant she realized that he was not crushed by his aunt's ugly words, only that *she* had been forced to hear them! "William, all is well!" she reassured him softly "I *love you*, remember? No more doubts!"

She had been correct; his face softened and for a moment she saw the slight quirk at the corners of his mouth that told her he would have smiled if there were not something weighty on his mind! She did not worry; he would speak of it when he was ready, probably when he had whatever it was all neatly resolved and tied up with a pretty ribbon for her to admire!

When she looked up to see the others, her younger sisters and mother were openly wiping the tears from their cheeks, still looking weepy – even Mary! Her father seemed ashamed, and hurt; his eyes red and overly bright.

Jane had gone to Mr Bingley's side as soon as she knew that Lizzy no longer needed her to hold her hand. They were speaking in low tones, no longer aware of their surroundings, by the looks of them.

Lizzy was glad that Jane and Bingley could have a little time together. She had spoken with Jane about Lady Catherine's visit at length; there was no need for *her* to think of it now.

Her glance fell upon Colonel Fitzwilliam, who was staring at her in... well, it looked like... admiration - but she was happier to call it amazement, or better still, shock! Perhaps he had never known of anyone to stand up to his ridiculous aunt before!

Restless and agitated Lizzy stood up; William instantly rose by her side. But this was not yet about him. He was her love and her future; this was... she was going to... This was something she wished him *not* to suffer from her!

Of a sudden she was angry! She was *furious* with Lady Catherine, with her father for making her tell of her mortification, with herself for failing to avoid Lady Catherine *and* for allowing her father to insist on this, this disgusting display – and at all of them for listening and now not saying a word!

Lizzy felt ready to *scream* at them *all*, starting with *her father*.

Impulsively she turned to him, angry words ready on her lips; but when she saw the regret in his eyes she could not hurt him more than he was hurting himself.

Looking around at her sisters, at Jane and Mr Bingley, at her mother who also looked pained, her anger left her as quickly as it had appeared. Her father had been correct. Their family must stand united to be strong and withstand the trials and tribulations that came their way. They were all, even Colonel Fitzwilliam whom she scarcely knew, all here in a bond of family unity *with her!*

She tried to sit down again but her body did not obey her mind; it began to wobble and shake so violently that she doubted she could make it onto her chair! "William!" she cried out!

Directly she felt his arms supporting her to her chair where she began to cry while he held her hand tenderly in his. After her burst of tears began to subside he spoke softly into her ear "I *love you too*, my *Lizzy*, all *is* well and we shall have *no* more doubts."

It was the first time he called her by her family's pet name and the shock of it stopped her crying abruptly, and sent a thrill all the way down to her toes!

He continued to hold her hand, stroking over it with his thumb from time to time, keeping his face neutral and expressionless. But she saw the tiny crinkles at the corners of his eyes and the barest quirk on his lips, and laughed to herself. He was playing with her; he knew the effect his calling her by that name had had on her – mayhap he had done it on purpose!

Captivated by his playfulness, she thought a moment and then gently but determinedly pulled her hand from his and made as if to smooth her skirt, 'accidentally' brushing her hand languidly against his leg as she did so, – then she placed her hand in his once more.

She was gratified to see him stiffen slightly and the heightened colour in his countenance. He slid his eyes in her direction in surprise.

Her answering smirk made Darcy close his eyes in surrender.

Lizzy heard an odd sound from across the room' it sounded like a snort that ended as a choked guffaw! Immediately after, there followed soft chuckles and giggles from all around the sitting room. Instinctively looking up at the party arranged around her, she sensed even before encountering their expressions that *she and William* were the source of their diversion!

They must have been watching her closely, worried because she had been crying, and observed William's whispering and humorous expression when she stopped – *and* her little tease in response!

Flushing dark red with embarrassment, she spoke with some asperity "Papá! I believe that I have provided enough entertainment for everyone this evening, have you another item on your agenda tonight?"

Everyone quieted at her words, taking their cue from Lizzy's mood. She saw her father's face, too late; her sharp address had wiped the amusement from his countenance.

"You are not going to be *missish;* are you my dear? Would you deny your old father, indeed your loving family one *lighthearted* interval in the midst of an uncommonly protracted stretch of onerous perturbations? Come Lizzy, we shall all return to sobriety and travail soon enough! Indeed our situation cannot allow it to be otherwise."

Darcy smiled widely at her, encouraging her to let go of her discomfiture. To her very great surprise, he seemed to be enjoying the general merriment at his own expense!

Everyone waited; several were openly gaping to see Darcy's rare smile, dimples and all!

Lizzy chose to rise to the occasion thus: "No indeed Papá, I shall not deny anyone their fun, albeit at *some cost* to my dignity! I hereby invite *all* of you to enjoy the joke while you may! For you ought to harbour *no illusions* of impunity. I shall be sure to laugh heartily at each of you in your turn when *your* follies and nonsense, whims and inconsistencies divert *me!*[vi]"

The cheerful lilt in her tone gave everyone leave to relax; and the others began to murmur in tones of cordiality among themselves.

Mr Bennet thanked her with relief and pleasure in his visage. Lizzy only smiled at his teasing remark that it seemed at least one *wedding* would *soon* be in order!

William's obvious delight with her was more than sufficient recompense for her exertion to put the room at ease! He appeared to have dispensed with any push to conceal his tender feelings for her from her family – which was as it *should* be!

Mr Bennet had sufficient wisdom to leave well enough alone. A little time spent in agreeable conversation, speaking of those matters which came most readily to mind, would likely do more for the peace of his family than any further discussion he could orchestrate for them.

At last a few yawns could no longer be suppressed. Mr Bennet announced that as the hour was quite late and there were several among them whose fatigue must surely be monstrous, he would close the meeting while the pleasant mood lingered.

They might reconvene, if necessary, at some acceptable time after breakfast on the morrow. *Of course* the party from Netherfield was invited to join the Bennets for the first meal of the day. They were *family*, after all!

FIFTY
Plotting For a Much Pleasanter Theme

The three gentlemen from Netherfield had arisen early to discuss several pressing matters of varying degrees of importance to each of them.

"I must say Darcy; you took Miss Elizabeth's disclosures about our Aunt Catherine quite mildly last evening! I was amazed to see it; I thought you would be livid! Instead you appeared to become quite playful – for the impassive Darcy-of-Pemberley mien. How I would love to know what you whispered in her ear to make her blush and so sweetly take her revenge!"

"I was livid; I am livid! First, you must understand that since the advent of Miss Elizabeth Bennet in my life, nothing, not even her self-important Ladyship, takes precedence in importance over my concern for *her*. Even my terrible *accusations* against you held *much* of frustration and disappointment at the thought of being denied the right to spend my life in her care, in service to *her* happiness!

"Listening to my dear innocent Elizabeth describing how she had been insulted and accused – it was even worse than I had imagined Lady Catherine capable of doing! I could readily have ranted and raged, rushed out the door to... do something, I know not what! I was incensed indeed!

"However I did not wish to add to the distress Elizabeth suffers. She *does* continue to feel it you know, Lady Catherine's rampage against her. I could easily note how delicately she kept her sentiments in balance; her composure was only maintained by the determined effort of her will. Had I selfishly expressed *my own hard feelings* in the matter, she would have first assumed that *she* was the cause of my ill temper. Indeed her thoughts did tend that way but I soon showed her that such was not the case, and focussed her attention another way by merely whispering her name in her ear."

"You astonish me, cousin! I have never known you to be so clear-sighted about the feelings of another. I am delighted to see that you *do* take *prodigiously good* care of her – at least when you are not in the throes of lunatic jealously!"

"I have never been in love before, Richard; it does change one tremendously. As for that outburst of mine, Elizabeth and I have agreed that we shall neither of us entertain any more doubts of each other's constancy. I intend that *all* of my care in future *shall* be prodigiously good – for *her*!

"Hear, hear!" Bingley struck in grinning hugely, "I hope to see nothing but idyllic tranquillity for my future sister! I shall insist on nothing less for myself and my Jane!"

"It is a pleasure to see you back to yourself, Bingley. I take you have had sufficient rest to endure more *serious* discussions this morning?" Darcy slapped him on the back and grinned over his shoulder at his cousin.

"Darcy, I *was* serious!" laughed Bingley.

Colonel Fitzwilliam said "I assume this morning's business includes what is to be done regarding Aunt Catherine, the Bennets' removal tomorrow – it is to be tomorrow is it not?" at Darcy's nod he continued "and how you shall attend to your betrothals from a distance! Anything else?"

"As to that last," Bingley spoke up, "I came to realize while I was away, just how little I appreciate the prospect of having to spend any more time apart from my Angel. I cannot imagine that you are not in a similar state of mind regarding Miss Elizabeth, Darcy. If you do not know it already, I am certain that you will discover the misery of a prolonged separation from her very soon! I came up with an idea to remedy both of our situations when you are ready to listen to it."

"I would hear it now, Bingley, if Fitzwilliam can bear with us. I am relieved that the Bennets shall be less than a half-day's ride from Pemberley, but uncomfortably aware that the distance will not permit of a daily call. Indeed, unless I use one of the cottages round about, a visit from Pemberley could be of no more than a few hours' duration – and involve many hours of travel in the day. Tell me your idea then, my friend!"

"Simply that instead of the family going straight-away to their new home in Nottinghamshire, their servants could be sent ahead to prepare for their arrival. We could accompany them to London for a short visit. Once we arrive, you and I could obtain special licenses and wed our fiancés within a few days. Afterwards all of us could escort the family to their home, which will have been readied by their servants in advance of their need of it."

"And we could take our new brides to Pemberley – an easy distance from their parents and sisters! It would serve to lessen the abruptness of their separation from each other and likely provide the Bennets' consequence the greater protection of two daughters being married to well-connected gentlemen."

"Exactly so! Darcy, do you think Mr Bennet will be amenable to the idea?"

"*I* certainly am so! I believe that it is *possible* that he would agree. He has suffered a great deal of shock of late. I think that either he will be too overwhelmed to object, or he will set aside his own feelings in favour of the good to his family that our expeditious marriages could do. To simplify matters still further, what do you say to a double wedding Bingley? We must consult Elizabeth and Miss Bennet, of course – about all of our fine ideas!"

"There is yet another strong argument in your favour gentlemen." Colonel Fitzwilliam's smirk warned them of his delight with his contribution.

"What is that cousin?"

"Why Lady Catherine can then have nothing more to do to prevent a fait accompli, and any harm she might attempt against Miss Elizabeth's or her family's good name would be disregarded as the disgruntled mutterings of a disappointed mama. All of polished society, London in particular, has heard for ten years at least of your imminent betrothal to our cousin Anne."

"*Great heavens, Richard! Bingley!* I believe we may safely say that Bingley's idea, with amendments duly noted, might well resolve *all three of the problems* we listed this morning!" Darcy was *positively* jovial contemplating how neatly things, well the most pressing things, could be wrapped up!

~&~

Immediately upon arriving at Longbourn the two suitors insisted on having a few moments' discourse in private with their respective ladyloves. Colonel Fitzwilliam was left unceremoniously to the tender mercies of Mrs Bennet and her younger daughters.

Darcy and Bingley were touched and elated to have Lizzy's and Jane's prompt and relieved agreement to Bingley's suggestion. The young ladies had been dreading the prospect of a separation from their lovers as dispiritedly as were the gentlemen.

After their separate conferences, the two couples met together to assure each that it would indeed be a delight and an honour to share their special day. The two devoted sisters' wedding the two best friends would make them all brothers and sisters, husbands and wives, all in the space of one day!

Mr Bennet was at his breakfast by the time the four lovers were assembled, ready to apply to him for approval of the plan.

Lydia and Kitty sat with their mother at the other end of the long table, conferring on some detail of fashion which had caught their interest. They were courteous in their greetings, but more interested in their topic than in the two couples who did not pay them much attention anyway when they were together. Colonel Fitzwilliam was occupied with their father and might just as well not have been present at all in that case.

Mary, who looked up with a prim smile upon their entry into the room, returned to her book once she had greeted her sisters and their beaux.

Colonel Fitzwilliam was seated to Mr Bennet's right; the two had been discussing the current situation on the Continent. Glancing at his cousin's expression, the good colonel gave the newcomers time to fill their plates at the sideboard and seat themselves before he did more than nod and smile at the ladies.

He could not fail to note the resolute look in Darcy's eyes and the air of suppressed excitement among the four. It was good, very good to be present in time to witness Darcy's felicity – and the move he was about to make on his future father-in-law!

"I *am* enjoying my leave very much sir." He said in response to a remark from Mr Bennet. "But I confess it is not easy to be so long away from my comrades when I know that they could be in harm's way at any time! I am so fortunate to be enjoying time with my family and with yours while they sweat it out on foreign soil – far from their homes and loved ones. I do feel it, I assure you."

"I read the other day, Colonel Fitzwilliam, that the Spaniards had old Boney up against it at last. Will not your friends be returning to England soon?"

"I do not put much faith in the reports found in the London papers. They are too far from the source of their intelligence in both time and distance to have my confidence!

"I have heard, though, about the fighters in Spain who call themselves 'guerillas'. The word comes from the Spanish 'guerra', which means war. Those rebels always manage to hold onto some small bit of territory. I hear they have sworn never to be subjugated. The rest of Europe apparently does not fare so well at all!"

"Indeed sir, I am intrigued by the idea of these so-called 'guerillas' you speak of. Are they military men? Surely they are not renegade peasants!"

"I fear there is not much I can add to the bare intelligence of their existence. I know, although I have no reason to connect the two pieces of information, that there are *rumours* that 'The Little Corporal.' plans to lay siege to Tarifa, in addition to the siege already in place at Cádiz."

Seeing that his cousin was waiting for an opportunity to change the subject, Colonel Fitzwilliam turned to include the four who sat nearby with a wink. "I beg your pardon ladies! I'll wager the subject of warfare does not make an appetizing dish when served with breakfast. Indeed for some whose sensibilities are delicate I doubt the discussion is palatable at any time. Perhaps there might be some pleasanter theme one of you would care to introduce?"

"My Lizzy is accustomed to discussing all manner of things with her old father, including the contents of the London papers - which she demands from me almost sooner than I have read them." Her father said with a quizzing glance at his daughters; teasing them for the impatience so plainly writ on their faces.

"Nevertheless I shall be very happy to entertain any topic of general interest to us all if it may provide something of particular importance so much the better!. I am acutely aware that this is to be our last full day at Longbourn for some long while. I shall be exceedingly glad of a diversion from my recollections at present."

FIFTY-ONE
A Most Accommodating Proposal

Darcy cleared his throat uncomfortably and to gain Mr Bennet's attention. "Yes sir, I... the *four* of us *do indeed* have something we hope may not only provide you with some pleasant diversion but also may address several er, *significant* concerns."

Darcy had thought to ask for a semi private interview, with Mr Bennet, Elizabeth, Bingley and Jane. But in the very instant of Mr Bennet's query whether they preferred to meet in his library, the strategist in him shot to the fore and declined that privilege! He had caught sight of his natural ally in the matter of weddings, and understood instantly that Mr Bennet could not deny their application if his wife knew of it.

He sensed the surprise in the four people around him who knew the substance of his forthcoming request. Bingley and his cousin, in particular, seemed ready to intervene. Convinced of the rightness and efficacy of his plan he pushed on, overriding any possible interjections with the firm confidence of his deep voice.

"Mr Bennet, what I have to say will, I believe, surprise you, possibly unsettle you until you have heard all and considered the arguments in favour of our suggestions. I would ask that you wait to respond until I have finished." Taking a deep breath and glancing at his friend and letting his eyes come to rest on Elizabeth he acknowledged Mr Bennet's ultimate right. "Then sir, your decision shall be honoured by all of us no matter whether we find it favourable or not."

"Well Mr Darcy, you have certainly piqued my interest! And you are certain that you do not wish for... a quieter setting for this exposition of yours?"

"Not at all sir, for your decision will surely affect your entire family. I can think of no reason why I should not speak to you here, as we enjoy the last of our coffee and toast." Darcy did not dare look at Elizabeth; he could feel her staring at him, he hoped it was in admiration! She, he knew, would have come to the same conclusion that he had for the reason he wanted her mother in the room for this!

"Then I am at your service young man. I look forward to being entertained at the least, for you have promised me that much!" Leaning back in his chair and rubbing his chin, he regarded Darcy expectantly.

"I must begin by saying that Mr Bingley first came up with the idea and upon further discussion and reflection I, and Colonel Fitzwilliam as a… less interested party, were utterly convinced that our plan has a great deal to recommend it and we could think of little to argue against it. We did consult Elizabeth and Miss Bennet, and I am happy to say that all of us are in happy accord on this."

"Yes, yes, I could not fail to see *that* when you entered the room! Let me hear of the *substance* now, son! Else I shall be ready for my tea by the time we have done!" Mr Bennet was half impatient and half toying with his solemn young friend.

Darcy looked wounded "I thought you were not to interrupt sir." Ducking his head a little like a child who has been chastened, he waited a few seconds and then raised his head as if with strengthened resolve and said "I shall hurry on then."

"Mr Bennet, instead of the family going to Nottinghamshire immediately, why do you not send your servants ahead to prepare for your arrival? That would allow us to escort your family to London for a short visit. I have ample room for all of us in my home there, or perhaps you would wish to visit your relations, Mr and Mrs Gardiner."

Out of the corner of his eye Darcy had an impression of Mrs Bennet's suddenly raised head, and noted a new hush in the room. "Bingley and I would wish to apply for special licenses so we could have a double wedding within a few days. Afterwards we all could travel with you to your home in Nottinghamshire. You would have the advantage of arriving after all has been made ready in advance of your requirements."

"Bingley and I would take our new brides to Pemberley which, as you might recollect, would have them less than half a days' ride from their parents and sisters! The trip might be a bit slower by carriage but the roads are quite good in that region. We hope this would lessen the abruptness of a separation which will occur at some time in any case. We could visit to and fro; I imagine you shall want to make *frequent use* of my library at Pemberley and I shall be *very happy* to share it with you!

"*Oh Mr Bennet!*" came the high-pitched squawk he had been *hoping* to hear. "London! Did you hear? *Special licenses*, a *double wedding in London!* Oh and my brother and sister Gardiner will be so pleased! *Oh Mr Bennet!*"

"I heard Fanny! Please, allow the man to finish!" Mr Bennet did not look pleased, but he waited to hear the rest.

"This is not... I beg your pardon sir but as we learned some time ago, I must speak plainly where a simple truth must out. Your eldest daughters' changed circumstances can, I believe, only help to provide a beneficial degree of consequence which could help protect your younger daughters' condition in life should that become necessary.

"One of the most pressing issues to my cousin and me has been what to do with regard to our aunt's outrageous interference with Elizabeth and myself and her vile threats to do worse. I admit that I could not think of what to do that would sufficiently express my wrath against her and my determination that she would not sway me or my betrothed from our commitment to one another. I could not get past simply being furious, *livid* at her *presumption* to act as she did in a matter that is solely my own affair – in so far as *she* is concerned.

"As Colonel Fitzwilliam succinctly pointed out to me, Lady Catherine can do nothing to stop us when she is presented with a fait accompli!

"Moreover any *harm* Lady Catherine might attempt against Miss Elizabeth's or your family's good name would be disregarded, if we were *already* married; dismissed as the disgruntled mutterings of a disappointed mama.

"*All* of London has heard for years, her bragging of an imminent betrothal between me and my cousin Anne. Neither Anne, who is in poor health and likes nothing better than to be left in peace, nor I have *ever* desired to be wed to each other. It has always been my aunt's ravings made public by her own design, probably to coerce my cooperation through embarrassing me on too many occasions. I admit that I am guilty of deriving a mean sort of pleasure from the vision of Lady Catherine's being *hoist* on her own petard!"

"I dislike very much to part with my daughters so soon, especially in the teeth of so much of folly and flutter as have driven the whole Bennet household precipitously into quite unprecedented improvements in our several ways. Indeed it appears that our collective domesticity has become most heartily cordial – a circumstance I cannot remember occurring at Longbourn for many years!"

It was understood as he went on for some minutes in this fashion that Mr Bennet was talking to give himself time to consider. Preventing his wife from giving voice to her agitated approval before he could make a decision was an equal motive for the length of his speech.

Coming at last to the same conclusions the young men had reached in their discussion at Netherfield, and his daughters had acceded to earlier at Longbourn, Mr Bennet came to a favourable decision.

It had not escaped his quickness of mind, however, that Darcy had intentionally allowed Mrs Bennet to hear his plea for a reason! He would give the rascal a playful *knock* in exchange for pitting his wife against the possibility of a refusal. Darcy had taken the opportunity to secure for the hopeful young couples a *most* unfair advantage!

Narrowing his eyes he fixed the spokesperson of the group with stern scrutiny. "Let me understand the situation fully sir!" he demanded. "Are there any *other* reason why my daughters must be rushed into *hasty* marriages?"

Mrs Bennet's gasp could be heard from the other end of the table. Otherwise the room was again silent except for the slight sound Colonel Fitzwilliam made when he sat bolt upright in his chair.

Darcy's and Bingley's countenances went instantly pale. Lizzy and Jane stared at their father in horror!

His face going from the white of shock to the deep red of angry embarrassment, Darcy strove to keep his tones level and composed when replied "Not at all sir!"

Bingley, who could no longer restrain his urgent craving to have his share of the matter, said "No sir! *No such thing sir!* I simply have no tolerance for further separations from Jane! I missed her dreadfully whilst I was away to Scotland; the prospect of more of the same is... beyond anathema to me sir!"

Glancing apologetically at his two eldest daughters, Mr Bennet smiled at the agitated young men before him. "I never believed anything else! I shall be happy to acquire two such fine young sons, as soon as may be! And now, Fanny, you may enthuse as much as you like. I shall retire to my library, the better to make way for the rapturous ferment of frantic planning and zestful articulations of exhilaration I feel sure are ready to burst forth at any moment! I anticipate a flurry and flutter now to ensue, the likes of which none has ever seen before!"

Lizzy hurried to kiss her father's balding head and thank him most fervently for his consent. Jane at once followed suit, adding "You are the best of fathers, my dear Papá!"

Rising from his place at the head of the table Mr Bennet shook Darcy's and Bingley's hands, they having risen at his cue, and after receiving their heartfelt thanks invited them to join him in his library at their leisure.

To Colonel Fitzwilliam he said "You are quite welcome to join me as well, I doubt I will hear any very erudite conversation from either of those young men this morning! I have enjoyed your company very much, sir, and I do wish to offer you my gratitude for your part in the fulmination of an excellent and efficacious plan! I am much obliged to you indeed!"

To which the colonel warmly answered "I had little to do Mr Bennet but to interject a word here or there. The impulsion of their thoughts, I am convinced, would have brought them to the same point of its own volition. Nevertheless, it shall always be my pleasure to be of any service to you and my favourite cousin, sir!"

The two were soon relishing the halcyon atmosphere of Mr Bennet's haven, Darcy and Bingley being in no such haste to quit the company of their brides-to-be. They sat for a while in silence, each savouring a small glass of port, lost in their thoughts of what the morrow would bring – or, far less turbulent: what the events of the following weeks would bring.

Colonel Fitzwilliam, suspecting that his companion might be suffering something of chagrin at the rapidity of some of those events, remarked "

"I believe I shall be reconciled, in due course, to the defection of my precious daughters, knowing that they are to enjoy such elegances of life as must be theirs at the great estates of Pemberley and Netherfield." was Mr Bennet's rather dry rejoinder. He *meant* it sincerely; but it was far too early for him to *feel* any true comfort in the thought.

He *was* quite pleased when he and the three younger gentlemen agreed that it was time and more that they have leave to adopt the practice of calling each other simply 'Bennet', 'Bingley', 'Darcy' and 'Fitzwilliam', or 'Richard, without the necessity of using more formal appellations.

The alteration in their address to one another conferred upon them all a feeling of manly camaraderie which would ease tensions and encourage bonds of familiarity and regard to last down through the many years to come.

FIFTY-TWO
Done and Undone

"I thank you very much Darcy, for your generous offer to host us all at your town home. As much as I look forward to enjoying your fabled library, I shall regretfully decline *this time*. A future invitation would be most *gratefully accepted!*"

"I believe we must go to the Gardiners for it may be impractical for us to visit them or for them to visit us for quite some time. We have always maintained a closeness with them which shall be missed – by Lizzy and Jane especially as they have spent a month or so every year with them in their home in Cheapside since they were old enough to leave their mother.

"Indeed upon reflection I must add that my wife and I look forward each year to at least one visit with the Gardiners, especially during the Christmas season. Our visit to them shall be perfectly timed; my sister's interesting condition prevented *their coming to us* for Christmas this year."

"I understand sir; your visits shall always be welcome at Darcy House, or at Pemberley – with or without the formality of an invitation!"

Mr Bennet's library was a snug harbour of quiet in the storm of excitement occasioned by the rearrangement of their anticipations. A frenzied sorting through previously packed trunks and parcels, relocation of contents and calling out to each other of various schemes under consideration apropos of the wedding, was underway throughout the house.

A week or more in London visiting the Gardiners, and with a double wedding to produce necessitated an entirely different set of accoutrements than a journey of several days, whiled away in the confines of a carriage, with no end in view but arrival at The Squyres Club – a place they knew very little of and had not yet learned to appreciate.

The four gentlemen had taken no little time refining their final arrangements for travel the next day; still, the day wanted many hours to reach its end. With nothing much to do they simply waited it out.

Darcy and Bingley aspired, at first, to charm their fiancés into spending time with them. It soon became apparent, however, that their hopes would be quashed by the exigencies of Mrs Bennet's highly audible notions of travel and wedding plans.

At present the four men were idling rather languorously after several hours spent sipping Mr Bennet's finest brandy. There was no point in saving it, he reasoned, it would not do for Mr Collins to be rewarded with so superior a bottle as this one, in case that lugubrious lout should inherit in lieu of his own return to claim it.

Bingley appeared asleep; still undone by his arduous trek up and down the country.

Colonel Fitzwilliam was engaged in a languid game of chess with Mr Bennet, neither man entirely committed to winning it.

"I and Darcy House are most sincerely at your service sir." Darcy insisted, "I shall expect you all and your relations, to dine with Georgiana and me frequently during you sojourn in Town!"

"I do look forward to a peek at your library Darcy, and the ladies shall be delighted to see Miss Darcy again."

A long pause ensued, in which both players stared blinking at the chess board for some minutes before Mr Bennet moved his piece and said "I make no doubt that my Brother and Sister Gardiner will wish to return your hospitality with some doings of their own. All in all I imagine we shall have quite a grand send-off before the remaining Bennets sink entirely from the view of our acquaintances."

FIFTY-THREE
Astonishing Disclosures and Amorous Glances

Francine Bennet's countenance reflected an uneasy determination concerning the task before her.

Whilst the gentlemen were sequestered in her husband's library, all of the ladies had rushed about until late in the afternoon, reorganising their trunks and designating which were to accompany them to London and which were to go directly to Nottinghamshire.

At last she could, and must, take the time for *the talk! It was* a prospect she had reviewed many times over the years, with a deal of discomfort! It was her duty, her obligation to her daughters and their future husbands. She would *not* shirk her duty.

It would also be the *greatest gift* she could give to her daughters on the approach of their weddings.

Lizzy and Jane waited with trepidation to hear their mother's instructions on what would and should occur in the marriage bed. They were cognizant of her intention and the general point of view she would express. Mamá had said plainly, when she insisted they join her in the small sitting room away from their younger sisters, that she had something she would speak to them about which had to do with their wifely duties.

Having overheard snippets here and there of Mrs Bennet's voluble 'private' discourse with her married friends, they were quite certain that their instruction would take a most *unappealing and discouraging* direction.

Both young women were deeply in love with their fiancés. *Neither of them* wished to discover that their early passionate responses to their lover's tentative touches and delicious kisses were naught but precursors to pain and disappointment – and ultimately, disinterest!

"My dears," their mother began, "I have something to explain to you and something I would confess!"

Jane cringed a little but did not speak. She could count on Lizzy to be candid enough for both of them!

"Please Mamá, you needn't trouble yourself unduly. We are countrywomen after all; we have observed many times how...er, the *means* of procreation!"

"Ah yes, my girl, your point is taken; and that is as good a place to begin as may be. As your mother it is my responsibility to advise you on the matter in advance of your wedding. I shall speak briefly but frankly of the mechanics of the... of the act itself..." This is precisely what she did.

When Mrs Bennet finished her description of the 'mechanics' of marital congress, she asked her mortified daughters if they now understood what was to occur on their wedding night. "Do either of you have any questions of me?"

Jane, who now sat half-turned away from her mother, shook her head without meeting her eyes. In a voice so meek it was scarcely audible she whispered "No Mamá, I believe that I understand what you have told us."

Lizzy had not enjoyed Mrs Bennet's blunt though mercifully brief intelligence any more than her sister. However, less easily confounded, her lively mind swiftly leaped ahead to something her mother had said at the first. Lizzy was *exceedingly* interested to hear her mother's 'confession'!

Trusting that she might not thus invite further embarrassment to herself and poor Jane, she boldly uttered "No Mamá, I have no questions thus far. Did you not wish to speak of something *more*?"

"Yes indeed I do have something to add to your introduction to the wedded state! *This* is the most important... perception of... *construction* of the event I have just described that I might ever impart to you, for without *this*, your marriages should suffer a sad fate, indeed they should"

Looking straight into the speechless faces of her two eldest daughters, Mrs Bennet asserted: "Where there is tenderness and appreciation, loving kindness and consideration, you shall find what many may name your 'marital duties' to be the source of the greatest pleasure and intimate affection of your lives.

"Do not anticipate the experience with overmuch of trepidation, my daughters; your future husbands are as *heart-smitten as ever a man may be!* I have not the smallest doubt that they each will *'worship'* your bodies with respect and sensitivity to your feelings and *attend to your enjoyment* as thoroughly as their own."

Observing her daughters' stunned expressions, their Mamá announced "Yes my dears, there is a *great deal* of grumbling among many of the married ladies of our acquaintance about their disgust with the physical aspects of their marriages. They go on about the various subterfuges, feigned head aches and the like, they employ to avoid their husbands' attentions.

"For my part, I wish you to understand that your father and I did not produce *five* daughters through disaffection!"

Blushing furiously, she hurried on "Moreover, I confess that I soon learned to *pretend agreement* with my friends' nonsense in order to avoid those ladies' disapprobation – you may have overheard bits of it over the years. I did not concern myself about it then. Gently born young maidens are the more protected if they believe in the stories of disaffected wives, that a man's gratification is the work of misery to a woman.

"So you see," she concluded, "Within the sanctity of marriage, *all forms of love* between man and wife are to be *anticipated with joy and cherished as matchless treasures – the true wealth that sustains a good marriage!*"

"Mother!" Lizzy breathed in awe. "I had no idea... *Thank you Mamá*; you have truly given me a *splendid gift!*"

Jane, her serene smile firmly in place and a new gleam in her eyes, said only *"Yes indeed!"*

~&~

Tea was a confusion of conviviality and astonishment.

The gentlemen arrived in a somewhat slackened condition, though most affably inclined, and bearing the strong aroma of spirits with them.

At a loss to comprehend the cause, three of the gentlemen, two young and one older, were most agreeably bewildered to encounter expressions of a decidedly *amorous* nature in the countenances of their ladyloves; of the which were instantly returned with heavy-lidded looks of ardent longing of their own.

Armed with prior knowledge of his wife's predilections, her husband soon gathered his wits sufficiently to look askance at the situation. He might have found more amusement in the bedazzled expressions on the faces of his erstwhile companions had it not been *his* very daughters who had *initiated* the spate of widened eyes and furious blushing among the two couples.

Mr Bennet's drink-reddened eyes tried to focus on the female activity around him.

Mary was assiduously pouring out the tea; Kitty cheerfully handed out plates of fruit and small cakes. Lydia... what was Lydia doing? She looked a trifle peaked, he thought woozily.

When his attention returned to his Fanny, Mr Bennet forgot whatever it was that had been in his mind to say. Ah well, he was far gone in his cups, though astute enough to lock his lips before he made a cake of himself before his daughters!

Colonel Fitzwilliam, whose life in the military had done much to inure him to the effects of drink, was *not quite* immune to Bennet's excellent brandy though he felt it less than the others. Sitting more slumped in his chair that was his wont, he regarded the looks passing among the couples with heartfelt delight for his cousin tinged with regret for himself. *By God!* He would give much to have a woman like Miss Elizabeth Bennet send a look of such *blatant desire his way!*

FIFTY-FOUR
London

The carriage ride to London was accomplished expeditiously and comfortably in Darcy's and Bingley's luxurious conveyances.

Darcy took Elizabeth, her father, Fitzwilliam and Kitty in his handsome equipage; Bingley had Jane, her mother, Lydia and Mary in his.

Warm bricks at their feet, bundled up in extra blankets, and enjoying the company of their loved ones, they scarcely noticed the deep chill on the countryside as they rumbled past on that first day of the New Year.

Indeed for reasons of overindulgence the evening prior on the part of some, and an unwillingness to part company with their companions on others, several among the travellers were loath to disembark upon arrival at the home of the Gardiners, their first stop before the single gentlemen were to continue on to take up residence at Darcy House.

Lydia Bennet was not amongst those who regretted the end of the journey. That young lady was relieved to exchange the constant bumping and swaying motion of the carriage for the quiet of a darkened room lit only by a cosy fire where she might lie down, and the blessing of a cool damp cloth to place across her brow.

Their youngest daughter's indisposition was not remarked amid the hubbub of arrival, greetings and introductions, except by Mr and Mrs Bennet, who exchanged worried glances as she slipped out of the entry hall.

~&~

The week in London was remarkable only in that everything went just as it ought. There was much visiting and invitations to dine back and forth between Grace Church Street, the Gardiner's home in Cheapside, and Darcy House in Mayfair.

Colonel Fitzwilliam stayed with his cousin at Darcy House until the wedding. His parents and older brother had long since fled London to spend a few weeks in Matlock before the start of the Season.

On January 4th he stopped in at his parents' house opposite Darcy's on Hanover Square to advise the housekeeper that he and Georgiana would come to stay there after the wedding. He was shocked out of his complacency to discover that, although they had left the knocker off of the door to enjoy a few days' peace before bringing their presence to the attention of Society, his parents were at home – had arrived, in fact, that very afternoon! Thinking it best to say nothing to them just yet, or to Darcy who would not be pleased at the prospect of their interference, he kept mum for the present.

The Bennet and Gardiner ladies invited Miss Georgiana Darcy to join them on several hurried shopping excursions in preparation for the wedding. Their large party enjoyed an occasional tea in Bond Street. The place was thin of traffic and shoppers which made their errands go swiftly and smoothly. In an astonishingly short time wedding clothes and rudimentary trousseaus were accomplished.

The gentlemen busied themselves with tailors and marriage settlements while the ladies were otherwise engaged.

Special licenses were procured without complication and the double wedding set to take place in St. George's Church on Tuesday, January 7th, the day after the celebration of the Epiphany.

Afterwards there would be a quiet wedding breakfast at Darcy House which, due to its spacious elegance and numerous servants, was well suited to host the event. There was an added convenience in that it would require little time in the cold and dampness of the out-of-doors for the visitors to make their way to Hanover Square from nearby Georges Street where the church was situated.

When the rest of the party returned to the Gardiner's home in Cheapside, Bingley and Jane would go to his home in Grosvenor Square for the first few days of their married life.

The entire party would depart at last for Nottinghamshire on Thursday January 9, 1812.

FIFTY-FIVE
The Double Wedding

The morning of Tuesday, January 7, 1812 held all of the cold damp fog of any other winters' day in London. In Darcy House and in the Gardiners' home it might have been as bright and warm as a late spring day, so felicitous were the sentiments and cheerful the mood in each.

A wedding promised new beginnings: a new family; new experiences; the anticipation of future children, nieces and nephews, and of grandchildren.

Maidens readied themselves eagerly to become wives to their lovers; gentlemen exulted at their marvellous good fortune, impatient to discard their bachelor's anarchy for a lifetime as husbands to their ladyloves.

Darcy had asked his cousin to stand up with him as his groomsman, a role that gentleman was delighted and sincerely honoured to fill. He had no hesitation in his approbation of Darcy's choice. Miss Elizabeth was perfect for his cousin; she might have been perfect for *him* had he been there first! But he was *not* in love with her; only wistful at the sight of so much happiness. His cousin deserved to be happy after the sorrow and loss attending his mother's death so early; then his father's before he was fully a man; he had been forced to mature too soon, being guardian to his young sister and master of a great estate; and Wickham! As much as Colonel Fitzwilliam despised the scoundrel, he knew that to Darcy his treachery had been devastatingly painful.

Miss Elizabeth, all of her family's trials notwithstanding, was sunshine and fresh air in his cousin's life. Darcy's demeanour since she accepted his hand had been uncommonly genial and easy.

Hearing him laugh at something Bingley said to him just then, Fitzwilliam thought *Good Lord! The man is positively giddy! My parents must soon overcome any objections as to her condition in life.*

Heavens! What was a little ruination compared to *harbouring a criminal* like Wickham and *relations as appallingly unscrupulous and ferocious as Lady Catherine de Bourgh?*

Gilbert and Louisa Hurst had returned to their residence in Town after a few weeks with his parents. Mr Hurst was very pleased to be asked to stand up with Bingley. His fondness for Louisa's family had emerged upon the heels of Caroline's exit from its bosom - and upon the development of the *exceedingly cordial* relations he currently enjoyed with his wife!

It was time! Perkins brought a tray of brandies to the four gentlemen who, impeccably dressed and barbered, would toast each other and the future before taking the brisk walk to the church.

Darcy's and Bingley's carriages would be waiting to bring everyone back *after* the ceremony; but they all agreed that a bracing walk would relieve some of their tension *before* the ceremony.

Mr Hurst surprised the others when he approved the plan; he had quite recently rediscovered the *pleasures* of using his person for activities other than lolling about.

"Are you nervous Darcy?" Bingley asked in a shaky voice.

"Fit to be tied!" His friend answered in tones that betrayed his humour was not entirely free of anxiety.

"I am quaking in my boots; what if she changes her mind?"

"Precisely"

"Do you really think she might?"

"Bingley; If you must persist in frightening yourself, I beg you would do so out of my hearing! I am quite proficient at worrying on my own!"

Mr Hurst smirked and Colonel Fitzwilliam grinned. Then they looked at each other and guffawed!

"Do not dare laugh at me, cousin; I shall pay you back in kind when your day comes!"

"And Hurst, if you do not desist I shall tell your wife about the time you got so drunk at Boodles that you fell over into your soup and had to be rescued from drowning!"

"I do not fear your laughter cousin, as I have no lady in my eye to tempt me into adopting *your* role!"

Mr Hurst merely looked thoughtful "Did I do that?"

~&~

The sigh of relief form the gentlemen waiting at the altar carried all the way to the end of the centre aisle when they each espied their own visions of loveliness, one upon each of Mr Bennet's arms.

Instinctively Colonel Fitzwilliam and Mr Hurst both touched their charge's sleeve to stop the movement of their bodies as they swayed forward at the sight of their brides coming down the aisle toward them.

Lizzy's smile lit up Darcy's heart; how was it possible for her to be *more* beautiful every time he saw her? Coming toward him on her father's arm, gifting him with her most dazzling smile, *she took his breath away!* For once he could comprehend Charles Bingley's references to Jane as his *Angel.* There could *be* no more angelic vision than *his* Elizabeth strolling toward him with *all of the love and tenderness of paradise captured in the glow of her fine eyes!*

Lizzy saw his face light up with joy as she walked with her father, closer and closer to her *Sweet William!* How noble and dignified he was; his handsome features alive with his smile for her! His *precious love was in his smile; his constant and wholehearted love and devotion!*

She was ready to be his wife; ready to have him as her husband. All of her uncertainties and fears had dissolved since their engagement; she had a clear sighted view of her future.

Theirs was of the deepest kind of love. They would laugh and play together; quarrel and misunderstand each other; debate and discuss; and enjoy times of peace and contentment throughout all of the years of their lives. They would go through it all together, united in marriage as one to mourn their inevitable losses and rejoice in the bliss of their union and the blessings to come from and within it.

Jane's serenity deserted her in favour of a rush of tender solicitousness at the sight of her *dearest Charles, nervously twisting his gloves and looking decidedly pale!* Instantly surmising what he needed, she raised her eyebrows in silent query and smiled her widest smile, *sending him all of her love and her unfaltering faith in him* from her deep blue eyes fixed constantly on his.

Charles could hardly restrain himself; he wanted to *leap down the aisle to her side!* Beautiful beyond his *wildest* imaginings, Jane was everything he could ever have wished for and more. He adored the way she gave him her heart so unreservedly and how she always seemed to know what he needed before he did. *His future with his Angel at his side would be filled with the tenderest love and deepest, most joyful contentment!*

~&~

The vicar cleared his throat and, after welcoming their family and guests, he began their wedding ceremony.

When it was time, the couples, Darcy and Elizabeth, Bingley and Jane, were bid to turn to each other, take each other's right hand and make their vows.

Calmly, confidently, with unfaltering conviction they each offered their pledge. The two pairs uttered the words signifying the commitment born of the love in their hearts; promising that in wedding each other they would hold to each other from that day forward, for better for worse, for richer, for poorer, in sickness and in health, they would each love and cherish the other until death did part them.

Lizzy's promise of obedience to William was accompanied by an impertinent flash of amusement in her sparkling eyes before she solemnly intoned "According to God's holy ordinance, and thereto I plight thee my troth."

As he slid the delicate band of gold onto Elizabeth's finger, William offered fervently "With this Ring I thee wed, with my body I thee *worship,* and with all my worldly goods I thee endow: In the name of the Father, and of the Son, and of the Holy Ghost. Amen."

FIFTY-SIX
My Lord and Lady Matlock

Darcy did not notice his Uncle, the Earl of Matlock and Lady Marianne where they had joined the Bennets and the Gardiners to witness the marriage of their nephew to Miss Elizabeth Bennet.

Colonel Fitzwilliam had not dared to disrespect his parents so much as to participate in his cousin's wedding with never a word to them! With dread in his heart of instigating a scene at Darcy's wedding, he advised the Earl and his Lady that the wedding was to take place. Darcy was implacably resolved to it, and their best course would be to attend with good will and an open mind, or stay away and avoid a complete rupture with Darcy.

They attended, unwilling to disrespect their beloved nephew's nuptials in the eyes of the *ton* by keeping away.

A sumptuous wedding breakfast awaited the whole party when they arrived at Darcy House. The celebratory repast was replete with a wealth of rich dishes and delicacies to delight every palate.

Mr and Mrs Darcy were pleased to welcome their assorted family members to their home. Standing together in the entry hall for the first time as husband and wife, Darcy refused to release Elizabeth's hand as they greeted and received congratulations and good wishes from the arrivals as they entered the house.

Charles Bingley and his bride stood near the door to the smaller dining room which was to be used for this intimate gathering of close family. She held securely to his arm as they too enjoyed the felicitous attentions from the guests as they made their way thither.

Bingley's normally ebullient nature was sobered somewhat by his wonderment at having secured an Angel for his wife. He had placed his hand over hers where she held his arm, with a feeling akin to reverence – so in awe was he of his beautiful and sweet natured... Jane Bingley! But Jane would *not* be revered! She tightened her hand on his arm and stole a sidewise glance at him from under her lashes that quite jolted him out of his innocent reverie - so amorous was the gleam in her eyes!

Gulping in surprise, he did not fail to return her ardent look with a sudden blush of passionate fervour.

When the Earl of Matlock and his Countess entered, Darcy introduced them to his bride with such pride and delight that the Earl, who was most displeased at his nephews effrontery in marrying so far below himself and without seeking his approval, was moved to express his reservations about their union thus: "I cannot do otherwise than wish you well Darcy, Mrs Darcy, as we are met with your union as a fait accompli. Family unity before the eyes of the *ton* demands that we support your marriage and I shall make every effort to do so.

"However I wonder, Mrs Darcy, whether you might find the strictures of the ton on the condition and... er, *eccentricities* of your relations too burdensome for your youthful shoulders to bear!

"Certainly those of his sphere shall regard it as a scandalous piece of impertinence on your part to contract a marriage between Darcy, who is a man of noble birth, rank and fortune and yourself, the dowerless daughter of a country squire."

Sensing Darcy's ire and wishing to prevent an angry retort, Lizzy touched his sleeve to be permitted to answer. As soon as she knew that Darcy looked her way, she flashed a brilliant smile at Lord Matlock and simply agreed. "I do *comprehend* the opinions I must expect from those who value their superiority of position, my Lord."

With a sparkle of amusement in her eyes she turned to her new husband so as to include him in the conversation and added "However as Mr Darcy *would* have it no other way, I believe it shall be best to preserve the *amiable fiction* that *neither* of our families includes those who might be considered eccentric! I should tell you that I did have the honour of a most instructive visit from Lady Catherine de Bourgh, little more than a week past. I believe she is *one* of Mr Darcy's relations, is she not?"

My Lord Matlock gaped at her in surprise! Taking in the loving gaze between a foolishly grinning Darcy and his astonishing bride, he allowed "Touché Mrs Darcy. I truly hope your perceptive wit does not fail you in the teeth of less friendly censure!"

Lady Matlock, who had been standing silently by her husband's side assessing the young woman who had won her elusive nephew's affections, came to a decision. "I shall make certain that it does not, Kedrick. With my backing I believe she shall carry the Darcy name with all of the aplomb and dignity it deserves."

Speaking to Darcy and Elizabeth she stated rather than asked "I assume that you shall be away on your wedding tour for some weeks. When you return to Town the Season will be in its midstride if not approaching its end. I shall invite you, Mrs Darcy, for tea immediately upon hearing of your arrival back in London. We shall have much to do to prepare you for your introduction to the *ton and* plan for the ball I intend to give in honour of the marriage of my beloved nephew and his bride."

"Aunt I do not think..." Darcy slipped into his habitual pose of aloof indifference. He would not be bullied into dancing attendance on the *ton*!

"Indeed we *must* Fitzwilliam, and Elizabeth shall be presented along with Georgiana next year when your sister comes out."

Apprehending from the obstinate expression on his face, Darcy's dislike of the scheme, she reminded him with asperity "Surely you comprehend that your sister's prospects must be affected in the near term, and ultimately those of your future children by your wife's acceptance in polished society!"

Squeezing her dear husband's hand, Lizzy looked up at him with an expectant smile, encouraging him to answer graciously "Thank you my Lady, you are quite correct. Although my *inclination* is to ignore the insincerity and constant fawning amongst many members of the *ton*, I shall appreciate your support in scotching any adverse murmurings against our family which may arise upon their learning of my marriage."

Darcy, as always, found his stiff countenance softening under the radiance of his beloved Elizabeth's fond smile and the glow in her fine eyes.

Knowing himself too happy to care about propriety, he relinquished his dignity to accommodate the joyful smile that *would* overtake his features!

To his Aunt he offered, in tones too warm to reflect real regret at the digestive disorder his loss from its list of eligibles would undoubtedly produce in Society's marriage mart, "I do recognise that, while to *me* it is cause for the *greatest imaginable happiness*, to a number of disappointed mamas and gossiping sycophants my choice could be fodder for much chewing and dyspepsia."

"Indeed, Fitzwilliam. Now, Mrs Darcy, I shall call you Elizabeth as I have already done so once already! I shall be pleased to have you address me as Lady Marianne. I find it flows more smoothly over the tongue than Lady Matlock."

"I thank you Lady Marianne; it shall be my great honour and privilege to address you thus, and I am thankful for your acceptance and support as well. I am fully cognizant of the reservations my husband's family have about our union. I wish you to know that I shall always endeavour to bring only honour, respect and dignity to the name he has chosen to bestow upon me; and to our marriage. My unqualified devotion shall always be to his lifelong happiness and contentment."

"Lady Catherine does not represent all of the Fitzwilliams, my dear. You will certainly be under scrutiny from all sides it is true. Lord Matlock is a severe stickler for adherence to propriety and rather fixed in his consciousness of the demands and dignities due to rank and connection. I cannot fault him in general for his pride or his high expectations of his relations. However he is a just man and he dotes on Fitzwilliam. I am fully confident that he will at least treat you with respect until he recognizes as do I that our nephew's future happiness is secured by your union and that you love each other very much."

Lord Matlock and Darcy had been speaking quietly nearby, but others were waiting for their opportunity to speak to the Darcys.

"Please allow me to express my gratitude yet again, Lady Marianne, for your generous words this morning!" With this Elizabeth curtsied deeply and waited for her Ladyship to end their encounter.

Nodding her approval and excusing herself, Lady Matlock joined her husband who had begun to move away.

After properly congratulating the newlywed Bingleys and speaking briefly to Richard and Georgiana, my Lord and Lady Matlock spent a few minutes in cool but polite conversation with the Bennets, the Hursts and the Gardiners.

To the general relief of the rest of the party, who felt keenly the formality under which their jovial spirits must be suppressed while in company with a Peer of the Realm, the Earl and his Lady then made their excuses and departed for a previous engagement.

FIFTY-SEVEN
You Are My Hearts' Desire

Darcy and Elizabeth gratefully bade farewell to the Bennets and Gardiners – the last of their guests to depart. The tears of joy and the pathos of bidding goodbye to their beloved Jane and Lizzy had been copious and heart wrenching. With this parting, gone were the two lovely maidens from the bosom of their family. When next they met it would be as families – related but separate.

Bingley and Jane had not lingered long after the grand meal was finished. They pled fatigue from all of the excitement of their wedding and the stresses and strains of the past weeks. They would see everyone again in two days when their trek to The Squyres Club would begin in earnest.

By way of a wedding gift Colonel Fitzwilliam had drawn Darcy aside to relate that Wickham was to sail at last. He would be on the Platonia, leaving in two days' time from Portsmouth. Relieved to know that his nemesis would be out of his life forever, Darcy thanked his cousin and bade him visit at Pemberley once he and Elizabeth and Georgiana were settled there.

Gilbert and Louisa Hurst had set off soon after their brother and his wife. Louisa was suffering a mild indisposition and wished to rest in her boudoir – a most delightfully tranquil situation of late!

Georgiana had bid her brother and new sister a fondly tearful adieu knowing she would not see them for several weeks at least. She embraced them both twice over and wished them Godspeed on their travels. She was eager for the lively wit and loving kindness Elizabeth's presence would surely bring to the Darcy's ancestral homes. Her new sister and her brother's newfound easiness of manner and jovial repartee promised well for the future!

Happily anticipating the new family they would form together, Georgiana went off with Colonel Fitzwilliam to Matlock House, content to stay with her Aunt and Uncle Matlock until the newlyweds returned to collect her for the trip to Pemberley.

~&~

Elizabeth!

Darcy was mesmerized by the enchanting arch of his wife's pretty mouth, the curves of her body so enticingly draped in the flowing lace and shimmering folds of her lovely wedding gown; he wished they might dispense with every consideration of propriety and retire instantly to the privacy of his bedchamber! The strength of his reaction at the thought befuddled him; nearly rendered him incoherent! He could think of nothing but that she was his wife *at last*, and she was an exceedingly beautiful, *passionate* woman who loved *him*; who *wanted him!*

Alone with *her* at last; he wondered how he would endure the hours remaining before it would be proper to retire!

Could they simply ignore the servants and go to the master's suite immediately? Wondering how his beloved would react to his impetuous ideas, he belatedly brought his attention to the *expression* on her face.

Darcy was chagrined to realize that whilst he was entertaining lustful thoughts of her body, his darling wife, his precious Elizabeth had been surreptitious watching him and had uncharacteristically relapsed into a blushful silence!

"My *dear love*; Mrs Darcy! *Please* forgive me for being such a beast! I have thoughtlessly... well not entirely *thought*lessly... I have allowed my mind to run ahead... *Oh God! Please* tell me what I may do to set myself up in your good esteem once more!"

She gave him a wondering look "Have I suffered some injury from you which requires my forgiveness? I assure you that if that is the case I am sublimely unaware of it, my love!" After a meditative pause his Lizzy squared her shoulders and turned to stand directly in front of him and asked "I would however enlist your aid in understanding what is next to transpire."

Darcy's ardency wilted under the daunting task, one he had assumed would not be his, of *explaining* things to her!

"Er, perhaps we might relax together in the sitting room for this conversation dearest." He wished to do everything in his power to be reassuring and considerate of his bride's endearing innocence. He reminded himself that he must draw her into their marital relations slowly and carefully so as not to frighten her.

She was young and innocent; her innate passion could easily be turned to abhorrence if he did not take his time to ensure her comfort and her pleasure. He would treat her with the tenderest consideration. He would exercise the utmost restraint while he and his sweet bride discovered together the magic of physical love between a man and a woman who loved each other deeply and passionately.

"*That* is *not what I meant!*" his sweet Elizabeth announced repressively!

"Then pray what *did* you mean?" Darcy's mood underwent another shift as confusion emanated from his expression and his tone!

Elizabeth chose to employ a surprisingly whimsical approach declaring "My *every feeling* is so entirely consumed with *being your wife in every way* that I have been pondering whether we might... whether it might be within our discretion to retire early... *very* early to our bedchambers?"

Darcy stuttered the only response to be made under the circumstances "M, my d, darling wife! It surely is *fitting that I deny my bride nothing her heart desires!*"

Emboldened by the warmth in her admiring look, he took her hand, and drawing her closer to his side, leaned in to kiss her smiling lips before he led her toward the wide staircase leading to their chambers. "Come my own dearest loveliest Elizabeth, allow me to adore you!"

She rewarded him with a rapturous smile as they climbed the elegant staircase together toward the beginning of the rest of their lives.

"I love you my Sweet William – my dear husband!"

"As I love you my darling Lizzy – my beloved wife!"

[i] From Pride and Prejudice, by Miss Jane Austen
[ii] Sir Aubrey Vere Hunt was a real person who did own the Island of Lundy at about the time our story takes place. According to an internet site called 'Slieveardagh, Ireland's Hidden Corner', he did show a much greater generosity and foresight toward the less fortunate than his peers. Any reference to him or claim of acquaintance with any character in this story is purely fictional.
[iii] The comments about Lundy in this paragraph are paraphrased or inferences from the 'Slieveardagh, Ireland's Hidden Corner' website.
[iv] Information about this area of Scotland was obtained from Wikipedia one the subject of the Isle of Skye. The hunting lodge, as is its owner, is purely fictional.
[v] According to Wikipedia, Nottingham County was administratively united with Derbyshire, under a single Sheriff until 1568.
[vi] The language in this sentence, although rearranged and used in a different context, owes most of its content to the incomparable Miss Jane Austen's original Pride and Prejudice. Although I do not like to use direct or lengthy quotes, believing such to be a form of disrespect, or sloth, there are those expressions of hers that (in my mind at least) simply BELONG where I have placed them in this work. Miss Jane Austen's words simply cannot be improved upon – and every now and then I must use them!

About the Author

A Native of Southern California, Clytie Koehler is a semi-retired attorney. She currently lives in San Diego County with three teenagers and a cat. She is delighted to be able to pursue her lifelong dream of writing – at last.

Clytie has been an avid reader from the first moment she discovered her fascination with words, their meanings, and the wonderful illumination a well put-together collection of them can evoke. In other words, ever since she learned to read.

Clytie first discovered Jane Austen's brilliance during her early teens. There were a great many wonderful authors whose contributions brightened her life, but of them all she has loved the works of Jane Austen longest and best.

Clytie was born with embryonic toxoplasmosis and is consequently legally blind.

Lizzy's Choice is Clytie's first 'Austenesque' novel.

Look for clytiek on Twitter

Coming soon: clytiesamiablefictions.com

Or email ClytiesChoice@yahoo.com

Made in the USA
Lexington, KY
10 May 2012